Ruby Jackson and her husband live in a small village in Surrey. Ruby, who worked for an international charity, now writes full time, with a particular interest in how women cope under pressure. When she's not writing she is probably in their large garden coping with weeds.

RUBY JACKSON

Churchill's Angels

HARPER

Harper
An imprint of HarperCollins*Publishers*
77–85 Fulham Palace Road,
Hammersmith, London W6 8JB

www.harpercollins.co.uk

ISBN: 978-0-00-750623-1

Set in Sabon Lt Std by Palimpsest Book Production Limited,
Falkirk, Stirlingshire

Printed and bound in Great Britain by

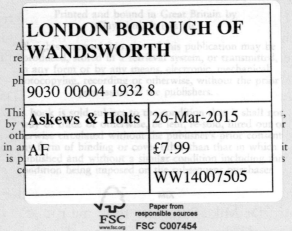

FSC
www.fsc.org
Paper from
responsible sources
FSC C007454

FSC™ is a non-profit international organisation established to promote
the responsible management of the world's forests. Products carrying the
FSC label are independently certified to assure consumers that they come
from forests that are managed to meet the social, economic and
ecological needs of present and future generations,
and other controlled sources.

Find out more about HarperCollins and the environment at
www.harpercollins.co.uk/green

Acknowledgements

This book could not have been written without the help and support of many people.

Firstly my agent, Teresa Chris, who not only has always had faith in me but also has the ability to make me believe in myself.

All I knew about Dartford when I started my research was that it was on the flight path of the German bombers during WWII. I went to Dartford to find out for myself.

Thank you to all the lovely helpful people of Dartford who answered all my questions. I would like to thank all the librarians and historians in the central library who found books, maps, memoirs, letters, newspaper articles, films and who patiently explained all the things I did not understand. Very special thanks are due to the archivist, Dr Mike Still, who took me round the town and patiently showed me interesting places, nooks and crannies that I would never have found without him and who has since continued to send me snippets when he finds something that might be (and always is) of interest to a writer.

*   *   *

Personnel at Leuchar's Air Force base were friendly and helpful and set me on the right path! – Thank you.

Enormous thanks and admiration are due too to the staff of the National Flight Museum on the East Fortune airfield near Edinburgh. The staff in the bookshop made browsing – and buying – an absolute delight, but most of all I would like to thank Duncan Johnston, Peter Moulin and Alistair Noble who patiently answered all my questions about aircraft, flying, and learning to fly. Like all knowledgeable enthusiasts, they told me so many things that I didn't know I needed to know but which have proved invaluable.

Michael Hilton generously shared his knowledge of Wilmslow – and I would ask him to thank 'Alec' whose maps made it so easy for me to design my own airfields. Thank you both.

I am so grateful to Dr Andrea Tanner, archivist at Fortnum and Mason, who kindly shared her knowledge concerning the availability of supplies of honey, both home and imported during WW11 and even gave me accurate prices.

And, of course, without Ian and his scrambled eggs, this book would never have been finished.

This book is dedicated to Sarah and Colin Ramsay

ONE

August 1939

'Cheerio, Mrs Richardson.'

Daisy Petrie held the door open as her last customer, still grumbling under her breath, left the shop.

'Give me strength,' Daisy muttered. 'I have got to get out of here.'

She stood for a moment watching the old lady's progress along the crowded High Street. Two large trams passed each other as they flew noisily along their tracks and the indistinguishable words of a carter and a van driver drifted over to her on the warm air.

The day promised to grow even warmer, and she caught the smell of fresh fish from the open window of a neighbouring shop.

Hope somebody buys them before they go off, she thought ruefully as she stepped back into Petrie's Groceries and Fine Teas.

She looked around the family's small shop, the place where she had worked almost every Saturday while growing up, and full time since she had left school. It

1

was, as small, family-run grocery shops go, a pleasant place. Behind the counter was a wall that, to the child Daisy, had seemed a magical place, lined as it was with large black tins, each one exotically painted with brightly coloured Chinese dragons. Inside each tin, sweet-smelling tea leaves waited to be weighed out for knowledgeable customers.

The large window, into which her dad, Fred Petrie, put out the bargains of the day, looked out over the busy High Street, and there in the middle of the street now stood Mrs Richardson, chatting enthusiastically to young Mrs Davis, who was obviously trying to be polite while keeping an eye on two active toddlers.

'Not too tired to stand now,' said Daisy.

Mrs Richardson had grumbled loud and long about having to wait while Daisy had dealt with the three customers before her.

'Should be two assistants working every day, Daisy, not just when it suits you, and so I shall tell your dad or your mam when I see them. Kills me, all this standing about, absolutely kills me.'

Daisy had apologised, explaining that her father was at the market, since it was market day, and her mother . . . she had not given the actual explanation, but had taken refuge in 'busy in the back', a euphemism that covered a multitude of explanations. Her mother was actually upstairs in the family flat baking for the party Daisy and her twin sister, Rose, were giving for their friend Sally Brewer. Sally, to Daisy's delight and more than a little envy, had actually been accepted at a drama college.

What would it be like to go to college, to learn new

2

things every day, to earn a certificate with your name and special letters after it, which would show the world that you were very good at something?

I want to do more with my life than weighing tea leaves and lentils, but what?

Daisy looked at herself in the spotless mirrored art deco panel on the locked cupboard that held patent medicines. She frowned at her image. Oh, to look like Sally, tall, slender, with glorious eyes and blue-black hair, or even her own twin sister, Rose, who was as tall and slim as Sally but had the Petrie family's corn-coloured hair, which reached almost down to her waist and which she usually fashioned into a long pigtail. Daisy could see nothing exciting in her own short dark hair, her beautifully shaped eyes or her compact athletic body. She did not see the kindness in those green eyes or the willingness to see the best in people that shone from them.

I'm stuck here because Mum needs someone to help out in the shop when she's busy upstairs. Simple as that.

Four years. Four years, five and a half days every week. Rose had worked in the shop on odd Saturdays and sometimes during school holidays, but none of the three boys had ever been behind the counter. Sam, the eldest, had driven the van on deliveries and maintained the engine, a skill he had passed on to his sisters. They had learned how to drive while still in primary school and both girls could strip an engine almost as well as Sam by the time they were fifteen.

Neighbours and friends had often said to Sam, 'You'll be taking over from your dad, a big lad like you,' but Sam had made it clear that he had no wish to continue in his father's footsteps. He had joined the army as soon as he could. Ron, Phil and Rose had followed one another into local factories as soon as each left school, but Daisy had been given no choice.

'You're finer made than Rose, Daisy, pet. Working here in the shop you won't never get wet or cold in the winter. Shut the door at six o'clock and you're home.'

And bored stiff. Daisy could think it but could never say it.

Years before, her mother had got it into her head that Daisy was delicate – possibly because Daisy was not as tall as her sister and brothers, though certainly not because she had suffered more than her share of childhood illnesses. The Petrie children, well-fed, well-clothed and well loved, had sailed through childhood with the minimum of trouble. But nothing that anyone, including the local district nurse, said could make the over-anxious Mrs Petrie change her mind. And so 'delicate' Daisy stayed at home and dreamed of a different life. What it might be, she had not yet discovered.

She stepped behind the counter where her father's pride and joy, the beautiful old till from the National Cash Register Company from far-away Ohio, had stood for as long as she could remember, and looked along its length. She spotted a tiny pool of oil on the usually spotless surface. She sniffed it. Sardines? How had oil from a tin of sardines got on the counter? She took a clean cloth from a bucket hidden under the counter and mopped up the oil, noting that the fishy smell still hung in the air. Opening the door to let in fresh air would take care of that.

'Well, I timed that perfect.' Her father had arrived on the doorstep just as she opened the door. He looked questioningly at the cloth still in her hand.

'Sardine oil on the counter.'

'Sorry, love, I opened a tin for next door's cat. Like to encourage him to visit, very discouraging to any little mouse who happened to pass by. Anything happen while I was gone?'

'Just the usual. Steady stream first thing and then three of the usual complainers complaining one after the other. Mrs Richardson made a fuss because she was last in line and had to wait, Miss Shoesmith complained about the price of bacon. Miss Partridge asked why we never had the width of knicker elastic she needed, and I bit my tongue and didn't remind her that this isn't a haberdashers. Even the vicar said with sugar already as scarce as it is what shall we do if there's a war and rationing. A usual Friday morning.' She looked at him more closely. 'You look a bit tired, Dad. Why don't you sit down and I'll run upstairs and make us a cuppa?'

'Good girl, Daisy. I am a bit worn. Afraid I don't handle heavy sacks the way I used to, so I've left supplies in the van till the lads get home. And next time Mr Tiverton comes in tell 'im there isn't going to be a war. I fought in the war to end all wars.'

'Yes, Dad, and that's why they're reopening the old fever hospitals, like the Joyce Green – and not for plague victims.'

'They've all got it wrong, pet. Besides, the King, God bless him, is family.'

'That'll make a difference, I don't think,' whispered Daisy as she hurried up the narrow carpeted stairs to the crowded flat in which the family lived. Her mother was in the comfortable, cosy kitchen and the smell of baking apples filled the air.

'Time for a cuppa, Daisy, love? Did I hear yer dad? He's early back from the wholesaler.' She moved the always-filled kettle over on the stove to an already hot plate.

'Apple turnovers for the party, Mum?'

Flora Petrie, as round as her apple turnovers, smiled. 'I might be able to spare one for a hard-working shop assistant.'

Less than ten minutes later Daisy was sitting on the bottom stair drinking her tea and reading the newspaper. Her father drank his propped up behind the counter ready to deal with any customer.

Daisy read the papers cover to cover as often as she could in order to keep up with everything that was happening, not only in their home town of Dartford but in the wider world. Newspapers and the wireless kept the family abreast of all the rumours that were flying around.

'Grand baker, your mum,' commented Fred when Daisy joined him.

'Is that a *Times* you've got there, Dad? Don't get apple on it. Mr Fischer hasn't been in for his yet.'

Before Fred could answer, the door pinged its warning. 'Lovely smell of baked apple in here this morning.' The local postman, Bernie Jones, was framed in the doorway, and bright sunshine poured in behind him.

Bernie held out a slim envelope. 'Got a fellow in the army, Daisy, or do I recognise Sam's handwriting?'

'Very funny.' She turned to her father, who had stopped reading to pass the time of day with the postman. 'You all right here, Dad, while I run up and read this to Mum? See you tomorrow, Bernie.'

Upstairs Flora was busily preparing sandwich fillings.

She was excited that there was a letter from her eldest son, but a little disappointed that it was not addressed to her. 'What's he saying?'

Daisy sat down, opened the flimsy envelope, and read it quickly.

Hello, Daze,

Tell Mum sorry I haven't written, been busy. Rose says as you're arranging a party for Sally on the 18th. Wish I could be there. Drama college, imagine. Little Sally Brewer. She'll be too posh for the likes of us when she's finished. Remember there was an order for men my age to sign up for six months last April? Lads even younger did too, and you bet my words our Phil and Ron'll be joining them afore long. I like the life, Daisy, and it's treating me right. Got room to breathe. Don't listen to them politicians, Daze. Either they don't know or they don't want to tell us but there's going to be a war and women'll be needed, so think careful about what you're going to do. Best to choose than wait to be ordered. Rose is fine in Vickers. Shouldn't think they'll shift her, but the shop has three employees and happen they'll say two is enough.

If this gets to you before the party, tell Sally, well, wish her all the best.

Sam

'It's nothing really, Mum. He likes the army and he says hello to Sally.'

'That's it?'

Daisy nodded. 'At least he writes to us.'

Flora almost grunted. 'Daft lad is sweet on Sally, always has been, and she'll not look at him.'

Daisy was startled. Sam, sweet on her friend Sally? No, Sam was kind to everyone. 'Don't be daft, Mum. He's just as kind to Grace, or to me.'

'He sees Grace as a wounded bird. Too soft, by half, my Sam. And not a word about where he is or what he's doing.'

Daisy took some troublesome thoughts down to the shop. If there was a war, and surely Sam was in a good place to know, would the Government decide that a local shop with three employees – even if one was mainly for delivering – was overstaffed? Might an opportunity for her to spread her wings be just round the corner? Scary. And then there was Mum's remark about Sam and Sally. Sam sweet on Sally? No. Never. If Sam was sweet on anything it was a machine, not a girl. Her big brother had always looked after his twin sisters and their friends.

'Bernie says enjoy the party. Seems the whole street's talking about it.'

'Talking about it is all that has happened, Dad, except for Mum's baking.' She frowned. 'What do you think about moving the tinned beans up to the shelf below the Spam, and the tinned pears below them? Could give a customer an idea for a whole meal.'

'Good idea. We haven't shifted many of those pears. I'll deal with customers.'

What a brain you have, Daisy Petrie. World-shattering idea there. Daisy started work on the shelves beside the door that led to the stairs. War, according to Sam, would bring opportunity. *But do I want opportunity at such a price?* Thoughts went spinning around in her head as she worked, completely ignoring the musical ping of the doorbell as customers came in. Mr Fischer, an elderly resident and a particular favourite of Daisy, came in to buy his paper. He also bought some tea and, as tin after tin of various teas was opened, the scents of the east obliterated the mundane smell of sardines.

Daisy thought of her sister, Rose, busy at the Vickers munitions factory until seven and so unable to help with party preparations. The boss there obviously had no faith in the 'there will be no war' newspaper articles and had, in fact, stepped up production.

Baked beans, Spam, pears followed one another onto her dusted shelves and at last she was finished and free to return to the flat to prepare for the party.

'I've given the front room a bit of a dust, and brought in some extra chairs. Any more turns up and they'll have to sit on the floor.' Flora was now arranging her sandwiches on her best plates.

'Thanks, Mum, but we can't dance if the floor's cluttered up with chairs. I'll have a look once I've washed.'

'You should have a rest, pet.'

The words, 'I'm as healthy as one of Alf's horses' formed on the tip of her tongue but she managed to swallow them. If there was going to be all-out conflict, she would not spend many more days weighing porridge oats and rice and reading the newspapers. 'Don't be scared, Daisy. Start thinking about what you can do that's useful,' she muttered under her breath as she effortlessly carried two bedside chairs – complete with pink ruffles – back to her parents' bedroom.

* * *

9

The party went with a swing. Flora Petrie had made new full skirts for the twins: Rose's was a multi-coloured floral, perfect on her tall, slim body, but for the daintier Daisy she had chosen a dark green cotton that went perfectly with a puff-sleeved sea-green blouse that she had found on a stall at a local market. Even Grace Paterson, Daisy and Rose's other close friend, had dressed in party mood and confided to her friends that she had found her sleeveless, full-skirted black and white dress on sale in the charity shop managed by her sister.

Somehow it seemed as if no one had told Sally about her 'surprise' party. The postman knew all about it – and therefore everyone on his route knew – but Sally swore she did not. She exclaimed over the large poster, drawn by Daisy and Rose, which said in large letters, 'Good Luck, Sally', and, 'Sally Brewer, Dartford's Star', and asked if she could have it to hang in her own bedroom in her parents' flat next door to the picture house, where her father worked as the projectionist. Of the nineteen former school friends who had been invited, four had had to refuse the invitation or have it refused for them. Two lads had already joined a branch of the growing military and two others were working overtime in the Powder Lane munitions factory.

The fifteen remaining ate the sandwiches and apple turnovers, and drank the fruit punch to which a carefully measured amount of alcohol had been added, and proceeded to dance the night away. Most of the young people had left school aged fifteen. Only Sally, Dartford's star, had gone on to a grammar school. Now that she was to begin a three-year course in speech and drama, her friends dreamed of seeing her on screen in the local cinema.

10

Daisy, Rose and Grace intended to keep the friendship strong.

The twins had known Sally since primary school. Grace, however, had arrived in Dartford at the age of seven when, for reasons that no one seemed to know, she had been sent from her foster home in Scotland to live with her adult half-sister, Megan Paterson. Sally and the twins, children from loving homes, had unquestioningly accepted the newcomer into their solid friendship.

The party was finally over and when all the others had taken their leave, the twins and Grace made Sally sit down in the best chair.

'We have a present for you, Sal. Close your eyes,' ordered Rose.

There was the sound of paper rustling and then, 'Open your eyes. Tada!'

The three girls had saved part of their wages all summer and Sally saw herself looking at a most elegant two-piece costume. It was navy blue, perfect with her blue-black hair. The jacket had the new squared shoulders and a close-fitting waist, and the fashionable-length skirt had a small pleat that would make movement easy.

Sally was speechless. 'I don't know what to say,' she managed after a while. 'It's fabulous.' She thought for a moment and gave it the ultimate accolade. 'It's exactly what Margaret Lockwood would wear, and perfect for interviews. But you're all very wicked. Now I know why no one's had an ice cream at the pictures all summer. Next Friday the ice creams are on me.'

'Oh, and I forgot,' said Rose later as they stood chatting in the middle of the brightly coloured rag rug, 'Mum tells me big brother Sam wrote today.' She made a pose

11

perfect for a swooning heroine in one of the desert sheik films so loved by all four girls. 'He's sweet on you, Sally; can you believe it? Our big Sam and Sally.' She began to laugh and the others laughed, Sally, Daisy, Rose . . . but not Grace. Quiet Grace, in appearance more like Daisy than Daisy's own twin sister, was not laughing. Little orphaned Grace, who had been protected by the tall, blond, sports hero Sam Petrie since her arrival in Dartford all those years ago, and who had loved him devotedly ever since, stood on the edge of the rug looking as if her world had just fallen apart. Grace, who had been taught by her sister that she was both worthless and useless, had never expected the shining light that was Sam to love her but she had dreamed of a miracle.

'He sent her a special message, Rose, didn't he?' teased Daisy. 'Couldn't quite bring himself to say, "Tell her *to come with me to the Kasbah*," but you could see where he'd scraped something out.'

Sally turned to her. 'Daisy, you are wicked. Poor Sam; he wouldn't say anything of the kind. Don't you think that's funny, Grace, me and Sam? Sam Petrie. I've known him my whole life.'

Grace had half turned so that she was not looking directly at her friends but had not really turned her back on them. Her eyes were suspiciously bright but possibly the others did not notice. 'I don't think that feelings should be laughed at. Whatever Sam said, it was a private message to Sally and not a joke.'

'How about a nice cuppa before we all trot off?' Daisy, aware that the frivolous atmosphere was now heavy – and she would worry about the reason later – broke in. 'Rose, Mum and Dad'll want something hot before bed, and Dad did say he wanted to walk Grace home. He'll pass your door too, Sally, and help you carry your loot.'

'And didn't I do well considering it isn't a birthday or anything?' Several of their friends had brought 'good luck' gifts.

'Try it on, Sally,' begged Daisy. 'We've had it hanging on the back of the bedroom door for two weeks now and we just have to see if it fits.'

Sally looked towards the kitchen door beyond which the Petrie parents were listening to the wireless. She held out her arms. 'Come here, all three of you. You are the best friends I will ever have and I want nothing to come between us.'

'If you squeeze us much more, Sally Brewer,' laughed Daisy, as the girls hugged one another, 'a flea couldn't come between us.'

The moment of tension passed but was not forgotten.

A few days later Daisy was reading the local paper, the *Dartford Chronicle*, when the shop door opened. She looked up to see her favourite customer, Mr Fischer. He was carrying a newspaper.

Daisy grimaced, guessing what the problem was, but managed to greet him politely.

'There was a sticky bit on the sports page of this one, Daisy, and so I'll have one you're not reading today, if you don't mind,' the old man said with an understanding smile.

Daisy hurried to get a pristine copy from the pile behind the counter and handed it over. 'Sorry, Mr Fischer, no charge today.'

'But of course I will pay, my dear. It is a privilege to

walk calmly into a shop, be greeted by a pretty girl, and be allowed to buy what I can afford.' He put the coins down on the counter. 'Anything of interest I shouldn't miss today?'

Over the years, while she had worked in the family shop part time and then full time, Daisy and the elderly man had developed a friendship. Daisy knew that he was German and that he had left Germany almost ten years before for reasons he did not divulge. The family had decided that he was Jewish and gradually they had learned that he was also very well educated, for he had talked to Daisy about things that her parents could not begin to understand. She was in the habit of reading the newspapers while she waited for customers, and when there was a picture or a headline that she did not understand she would talk to gentle Mr Fischer about it. In this way she had learned about stars and galaxies, early civilisations, the development of language and of mathematics, and of countless other fascinating things. He discussed with her the life cycle of a frog, the birth of a butterfly, and he tried to explain how a bird or a plane could fly and even why a huge ship did not sink under its own weight. These days, however, all their discussions were of the prospect of war.

Daisy looked at the old man, wondering for the first time if he was as old as he appeared to be. What horrors had he encountered that had forced him to leave his own country to live in another where he could worship in his own way? Every day that he came in for his paper or a few groceries, he was always perfectly dressed: collar, tie, hat and, in cold weather, gloves. He had his standards and dignity. She smiled at him with affection. 'I don't suppose you're interested in wedding pictures and lists of the guests, but . . .' she looked at him shrewdly and decided cricket rather than football might interest him, '. . . there's some cricket coverage and a very good recipe for cabbage soup.'

'Today no war and rumours of war, Daisy?'

'Not really, but my brother Sam – the one in the army – well, you do know that he has been saying since last year that there will be a war with Germany. He says I should think hard about what I want to do for the war effort.'

'And what have you decided, young Daisy?'

Daisy shook her head ruefully. 'It'll be factory work, I suppose, same as Rose. Clever girls with an education will get the exciting jobs.'

'Someone will still have to sell the newspapers, with or without jam on them.'

'Actually, it was stewed apple. Mum baked turnovers for the party. Sorry, Mr Fischer, I like you, and most of the customers, but measuring out bits of cheese and weighing tea leaves isn't very exciting, is it?'

The old man folded the newspaper. 'One day, Daisy, you may thank God for the comforting ordinariness of it. As always I like our little chats. I may try the cabbage soup; I have a liking for cabbage. Good morning.' He left the shop, lifting his hat to Daisy as he went and she stood looking after him. Such an odd Dartford resident . . .

Someday I might be glad to be doing something ordinary – I don't think so, Mr Fischer. What happened to you? Daisy wondered. She recalled some of their serious discussions and many of the wonderful things he had explained so that she could understand. He should

15

have been a teacher, she decided, and went back to reading the paper until several housewives arrived, almost every one accompanied by children of various ages.

It was a very tired Daisy who closed the shop at the end of the day and climbed the stairs to the flat. Customers accompanied by children were always the most difficult to serve. Sometimes children whined or opened the doors of cupboards they had been specifically told not to touch, and tried to pull out the contents. Some mothers were good at keeping their children in line, others paid no attention to them; it all made extra work.

In the kitchen a pot of carrot, not cabbage, soup was keeping warm on the back hotplate.

'Thanks, Mum,' Daisy said aloud to the empty room as she helped herself to a large serving and cut herself a slice of bread.

Daisy had been on duty in the shop all day because Flora and Fred had gone to an afternoon meeting in the Market Street Clinic. Mr Chamberlain might still be telling the nation that there was not going to be any conflict but Dartford had taken the threat of war very seriously and had been preparing for some time. The town had been designated a vulnerable area. To find out the exact meaning of that word, the family had consulted the heavy dictionary in the front room.

Early in May Fred and Flora had gone to the State Cinema in Spital Street to see a film called *The Warning*, which dealt with the possible effects of an air raid, and Fred had been so affected that he had immediately volunteered to become an air-raid warden.

'Dartford's not the safest place to be if war comes,'

16

Fred had told his children. 'The enemy'll have to fly over us before they reach London.' He tried to smile. 'Could get quite noisy here.'

Already there were thousands of sandbags, stacked like secondary walls, protecting important buildings, and since it was believed that, if war came, there would be gas attacks, gas masks had been issued. Air-raid shelters and first-aid stations had been set up in the St Alban's Hall and at the County Hospital. Trenches that reminded Fred and others of the 'war to end all wars' had been dug in Central Park and on Dartford Heath. As one of the first wardens to volunteer to help in assuring that Air Raid Precautions were carried out, Fred was learning how to deal with incendiary bombs at the clinic. Flora went along to all the meetings. After all, Fred would often be away from the flat and the shop, and she was determined to find out how to deal with anything that might fall on her home and her children.

'Nothing learned is ever wasted,' she was fond of telling her children, 'but what on earth we're going to do with all the sand when them that's in charge decides we've been wasting our time, I do not know.'

Daisy decided to make toasted cheese to go with the soup and was busily slicing cheese when she heard the flat door open and her parents and sister come in. They had met on the way home.

'The boys show up yet, love?' Flora asked as she hung up her lightweight summer coat and looked for her apron.

'Sorry, Mum,' Rose interrupted. 'I'm that tired I forgot to tell you. They're doing overtime and said not to worry about their tea, they'll get some chips on the way home.' She took herself off to the small family bathroom to

17

change and to wash off the grime from a long day's work in the oily munitions factory.

'They'll have a proper tea when they get home; chips isn't nourishment for such big lads.'

'Don't worry about them, Flo. I bet they take some liquid nourishment with their chips.' Fred was already sitting in his chair by the empty fireplace, a glass of his favourite Reffells' ale in his hand while they waited for Rose's return.

When she reappeared, he teased her, 'I think it's our Rose needs nourishing.'

Rose, her long fair hair released from its firm elastic bands, and washed and combed, sat down at the kitchen table. 'It'd be easier if the people in power would make up their blinking minds. Down the factory we're past caring, we're that tired, but we do want to know. There's been more than enough muttering. I can deal with the truth but all the shillyshallying is getting on my nerves.'

An outburst like that was so unlike Rose that even her father took notice. 'Pour your sister a cuppa, our Daisy,' he said as he reached across and patted Rose's knee. 'Don't fret, love; they don't know neither.' He turned back to Daisy, who was filling the big breakfast cups. 'Anything I need to know about the shop, Daisy?'

'No, except, thank heaven, it's Sunday tomorrow and I don't have to go near the place.'

Two Sundays later, after church, the family put their gas masks in the hall cupboard with their Sunday coats and settled down in the front room to listen to the wireless while their dinner was being prepared. Fred was reaching

18

for the switch when, with a groan of exasperation, Flora turned to Daisy.

'Be an angel and run down the shop for peas. Go nice with that lovely bit of beef, and I forgot them yesterday.' She gestured to the table by the door. 'My purse is in my shopping bag.'

Daisy took the purse and hurried downstairs. The Petrie family were meticulous about never taking anything from the shop without paying for it. According to Daisy, reading the newspapers from cover to cover was 'not exactly stealing'. She stood for a moment enjoying the unusual quiet of the empty shop. The blackout blinds were still on the windows and she pulled one aside for a moment to light her way. Sunlight streamed into the little shop, burnishing the polished oak counter and the brass scales and making a tiny rainbow as it shone on a glass jar of multi-coloured boiled sweets. No customer ever saw it like this. Daisy smiled in satisfaction as she found a tin of peas. She toyed with the idea of opening the old till to pay for her purchase – she loved the musical ping that the machine sang out each time the lever was depressed – but decided against it. After all, it was hardly worth opening the till only to close it immediately. She left a shilling on top of the till, closed the blinds again and hurried back upstairs. Mum wouldn't mind waiting for her change and, first thing Monday morning, she would finish the transaction.

She found her family standing in a stunned group in the kitchen. Flora was sobbing loudly as tears ran down her cheeks and Fred and Rose were patting her back in an attempt to comfort her. Her older brothers, Phil and Ron, standing close together, watched helplessly.

19

'What's happened?'

Everyone except Flora turned to look at her. 'We're at war with Germany, Daze,' her father said as he continued to hold his almost hysterical wife. 'Prime Minister's just announced it on the wireless.'

Everyone began to talk at once but eventually Fred's voice rose over those of his children. 'Do the dinner for your mum, girls, and that'll give her a chance to take it all in.' He turned back to Flora. 'That'll make you feel better, love.'

Poor Flora had no time to feel anything for, just at that moment, the air was full of the piercing wailing of an air-raid siren.

Flora screamed and the twins clutched each other in terror.

'In the kitchen, under the table,' ordered Ron. 'Come on, Mum, kitchen's safest. You know we decided that earlier. Good girls, keep calm; it's a drill, let's show we know what to do if . . .' He could not finish his sentence.

The family struggled to get under the large table, wincing both at their crushed uncomfortable positions and the fiendish sound that went round and round the room. They held their hands over their ears, willing the shrieking to stop. Ron held his mother, who had closed her eyes as if, somehow, that action might make the noise go away.

'Ron's right, Mum, it's a drill.' Phil was always ready to look for the brighter side. 'I'll put the wireless on. There'll be news or music or something.'

'Spilled a half of best golden ale,' complained Fred as he peered under the table at his wife and daughters. 'I got to go, love. Our Ron's right, it's only a practice, but I have to be out there. The boys'll take care of you. We forgot the gas masks. I'll toss 'em under before I leave.'

'I don't want to be gassed right here in my kitchen.' Flora felt silly sitting under the kitchen table being held by her son as if she were a five-year-old, but she tried to smile. Feeling silly was better than feeling a bomb land on her head. She grabbed hold of the twins' hands. 'We'll have such a tasty dinner, a nice bit of good beef, perfect for roasting with potatoes; glad I were a bit late with it. Awful to have it too well done, right, lads?'

At last the alert was over and the family, each one with tingling limbs, crawled out from under the table.

Ron stretched. 'All I can say is thank heaven our Daisy isn't as tall as the rest of us. Would've had to push you out from under, Daisy. No offence?'

Daisy said nothing but playfully slapped her long, lanky brother. 'Come on, Rose, we'll get the dinner on before we die of hunger.'

Even though the mouth-watering smell of roast beef permeated the small room, no one had much of an appetite. Once Fred had come home, however, and Flora had pulled herself together, they were able to sit down and talk.

Phil was full of bravado. 'Don't fret, Mum, we'll sort 'em out in no time. With Sam, Ron and me in the Forces, you'll see. Just watch them run.'

The younger Petrie boys had decided to enlist immediately. 'We'll get the top jobs, Mum. Our Sam was right,' Phil said.

That night, unable to sleep, Daisy and Rose sat up in bed and talked. Rose brushed her hair until it shone.

Daisy envied her. 'You really ought to leave it hanging down, Rose. You look like a princess in a fairy story.'

'Princesses don't work in munitions factories. Even with my horrible turban on, dust seeps in somehow.'

Daisy yawned. 'You should let it down at the dancing. Being tall, you can get away with such long hair.'

Rose laughed and began, as usual, to braid her hair for the night. Then she stopped. 'Blinkety blink, I completely forgot. Paul Robeson was on at the pictures, Daisy; we should have gone.'

'Too upset. What was the film?'

'*King Solomon's Mines.*'

Daisy, who loved going to the cinema, thought about that. 'Can't really see much great singing going on down a mine, Rose. C'mon, better get to sleep.'

'You scared?'

'Dunno. Haven't had time to think. I mean, what could happen to me? The Germans are hardly likely to be interested in a grocery shop on Dartford High Street.'

'Suppose not.' Rose was quiet for a moment. 'But there's the docks, Daisy, the Vickers factory, chemical works, Hall's engineering . . .'

'They're not on our street.' Then Daisy threw back her blanket and jumped out of bed in alarm. 'God, did you hear me, Rose? I was working out that no one will drop a bomb on me, and you and the boys work in a munitions factory.'

'Don't fret. Get back into bed and go to sleep. You're the one what's going to have to handle all the worried old ladies in the morning. Lads'll be off enlisting.'

But no old lady rushed into the shop next morning. Daisy was measuring out tea leaves when Sally almost burst through the door. 'It's closed, Daisy.' She looked round the little room to make sure that no customers were lurking among the shelves. 'What am I going to do? There was a notice on the college door.' She drew the shape of a large notice in the air. 'Closed for the duration. What will I do? Look, I even put on my new costume.'

'You look lovely,' said Daisy automatically. 'What did your mum say?'

'They don't know. They're already at the picture house.' She could say no more. Huge tears began to spill over and run down her beautiful face.

Daisy was at a loss. She put her arms around her sobbing friend. 'The duration, Sally. It's not going to be long, really it's not. Everybody says so. It'll be over by Christmas and you can start college next year. New year, new career.'

Sally pulled herself away. 'Christmas. That's a lifetime away,' she said dramatically. 'And what if it's not over? What will I do – work in a factory? I can't go to a university now because I turned them down.' Her voice rose hysterically. 'First one in the family ever to qualify for a university and I said no because I wanted to be in pictures.'

'Stop it, Sally.' Daisy's voice was kind but firm. 'So one college closed. That's not your fault. Ring up another one somewhere else.'

Sally straightened up and was suddenly very mature. 'How can a working-class girl like me afford to go somewhere else?'

Heavy footsteps on the stairs heralded Flora's arrival with a tray. She smiled when she saw Sally. 'Hello, love, I thought you was starting in the acting college today.'

Sally stared at her for a moment, burst into tears, turned and ran from the shop.

'What on earth . . .?' began Flora, and Daisy filled her in, finishing drily, 'She'll be a great actress once she gets started. First the local rep, then London, then Pinewood Studios, I bet. Something exciting is bound to happen to Sally.'

'But such a shame the school closed. Poor Sally. That shows it's really beginning, Daisy.' Flora broke off to greet a customer cheerfully. 'Morning, Mrs Richardson. Your usual Monday shop? We've got some nice tinned peaches just in.'

The declaration that Britain was at war with Germany had, on the surface at least, made very little difference to daily routine. Life went on more or less as it had been before the Prime Minister addressed the nation. Phil Petrie was excited because he had been accepted for training in the Royal Navy and younger brother, Ron, discovered that his mechanical skills were much prized by the army. 'I told 'em I could drive anything, Mum, and strip and fix it too. The recruiting sergeant was thrilled. "We gotta keep our army moving," he said, and told me I would be invaluable – that's the exact word he used – invaluable. We've got to take medicals first and learn basic drill and stuff, but then we're off.'

'We'll come home before we join our units, Mum.'

Daisy listened to their excited boasting and found herself wishing heartily that she too was joining a unit, any unit, anywhere. But for the next few months she continued working in the family shop and, with Grace, took a first-aid course.

'Some use I'll be Mum,' she moaned. 'Even working on a doll makes me ill. Remember how useless I was when the engine fell on Ron?'

'Without knowing what to do, Daisy Petrie, you did the right thing and you helped your brother. You'll be fine if and when something happens.' Flora laughed. 'Then you can be as sick as you like.'

'Thanks a lot,' said Daisy, but she was laughing too. She was determined that, in whatever way she could, she would contribute to the war effort. Therefore she forced herself to attend all the first-aid classes and also to work a few hours a week in Grace's garden. With the help of her friends, Grace, who was the only one of the four friends to have a garden, attached to the tiny rented cottage halfway up West Hill, had started growing vegetables as part of her war effort. Almost every week there were fresh vegetables for the three families and everyone was delighted when the tiny patch Grace had been able to dig over yielded enough crunchy Brussels sprouts for the Paterson, Brewer and the Petrie Christmas dinners.

Flora had ordered a capon from the usual farm near Bexley and, on the Saturday before Christmas, Daisy drove out to pick it up.

Nancy Humble, the farmer's wife, was in her kitchen. 'Alf's down the old stables, Daisy, love. Walk round there and you won't believe your eyes when you see what we're housing where the shires used to be.'

'What is it? You've not put pigs in there?'

Mrs Humble looked as if she was seriously considering the proposition. 'What a good idea; I'll suggest that to Alf. Now off you go, you have to see it with your own eyes. Go on, it won't bite you, and I'll have a pat of fresh farm butter for your mum when you get back.'

Encouraged by 'it won't bite', and being naturally curious, Daisy left the van in the yard and made her way past the big hay barn and a pen of hens busily pecking at some discarded cabbage leaves. Hmm, wonder if there's room at Grace's for a hen. We've got plenty of cabbage it could nibble, she thought.

Hens, cabbage leaves and even the Christmas capon went out of her head when she reached the stables that had once housed seven magnificent shires on which Daisy and Rose had used to sit.

'It can't be real,' she said aloud.

'It jolly well is,' said a cultured voice reprovingly. 'I'll have you know, madame, that this beautiful aeroplane is an extremely fine specimen of the Aeronca C-3, manufactured in Ohio in the United States of America in 1935. It's one of an amazing number of aircraft – one hundred and twenty-eight, to be exact – to be built that year.'

At the word 'Ohio', Daisy had almost laughed. Dad's till and this aeroplane. Was there anything that was not made in Ohio, USA?

A young man in an oil-spattered overall had finally manoeuvred himself up out of the cockpit, not an easy task as the wings were in the way, and so he towered above her. Daisy had no idea whether to laugh or to run away. His face was streaked with oil and grease, which had managed to get itself into his almost flaxen hair. In one hand he brandished a spanner and the other held an extremely dirty rag with which – as he addressed Daisy – he was having no luck at all in cleaning his face.

Daisy gave up and started to laugh. The man's feet

and legs were inside the plane and so she had no real impression of how tall he was. Having grown up with three tall brothers, she decided that the odds were that he was not as tall as they were.

'Does it really fly?'

'Of course it does,' he said as he jumped to the ground. 'At least it will when I've got a few minor problems ironed out.'

'Shame my brothers aren't here. There is nothing they don't know about engines,' Daisy informed him. It was then that she realised that she was every bit as good as any one of the boys, having been taught by her brothers not only to drive but also to look after the engine. 'I could have a look at it for you, if you like,' she offered diffidently.

He looked at her as if he could not believe what he was seeing – or hearing. 'You? A girl?'

'Don't mess with a Petrie, lad,' broke in Alf Humble, the farmer. 'They were born with wrenches and spanners in their hands.'

'Beautiful picture that, Alf. Not sure what my mum would think of it.'

'No woman is capable . . .' the young man began, and then blushed to the roots of his hair. 'I do beg your pardon, that was fearfully rude, but I mean, I'm sure you have some ability and that's to be applauded, but this beautiful little yellow bird is going to help defeat the German might.'

His embarrassment made him more like one of her brothers, and Daisy smiled. 'You plan on throwing things at them, then?' She could scarcely believe that she was bandying words with a toff. Usually such a voice alone

27

would have had her hiding herself away. Perhaps it was because, with oil all over his face and a wrench in his hand, he could have been Sam.

'Don't be facetious. She's not going to be fitted with guns, although chaps are doing that to planes all over England. But she's roomy, can reach speeds of eighty miles an hour; she'll carry equipment, even personnel, between aerodromes. We'll beat the blighters, just see if we don't.' He hauled himself athletically back under the wing and lowered himself into the cockpit.

'Come on, Daisy. I've got a good, fat capon for your mum.'

Daisy and Alf walked together back to the farmhouse.

'What's facetious mean, Alf?'

'No idea, love, but it can't be good! Don't think badly of the lad, even though he's out of a top drawer. He's in the air force – just got a few days' Christmas leave – and he's giving the plane to the country.'

'Nice – if you've got the money.'

'He hasn't, Daisy. Third cousin, God knows how many times removed from the money.' He stopped and turned back to face the plane. 'Want a cuppa, Adair?' he called.

A muffled answer came from the depths of the aeroplane.

'I take it that's a no then,' said Daisy, who continued her walk back to the house to collect the star of the family's Christmas dinner. 'Adair? Never heard the name before.'

'Me neither, but the lad doesn't get all uppity when we use it. Known him since he were living here during his school holidays. He were Adair then and he's still Adair.'

Daisy tried to match her stride to Alf's longer steps.

'But this is Lord Granger's place, isn't it? We used to be chased away if we came here on our bicycles.'

'Young Adair's mother was a relative of 'is lordship. Died very young; the father went back to America. Adair came 'ere in his holidays and now the house is closed he stays in the attic above the old stables.'

A picture of her three brothers came into Daisy's head. 'Is there a kitchen up there, Alf? My brothers would starve to death if they had to look after themselves.'

'He does sometimes come for a meal in our kitchen. Nancy'd have him move in but the lad's proud, has a little Primus stove, and now he's in the air force he's hardly ever here.'

'What does he do in the air force, Alf? There's a war on but nothing happens, if you know what I mean.'

'I suppose they practise, and he teaches them as wants to fly.'

'But he's only a lad, same age as our Ron, by the look of him.'

'Seems he's been flying for years. Lads are joining up, he tells us, wanting to fly, and some of 'em han't never seen a plane outside a picture house.'

'Just as well nothing's happening then,' said Daisy as she refused the offer of some tea and, picking up the capon, and Nancy's creamy-gold pat of newly churned butter, got back into the van to finish her deliveries.

Only the Petrie twins were at home for Christmas, but still the family tried to behave as normal and all preparations went ahead as they had done for as many years as Daisy could remember. Because Christmas Day was on Monday they were delighted to have two days' holiday, as the shop was never open on a Sunday. The family members who were not on active service relaxed in their front room, the little Christmas tree twinkling in the window. Flora insisted that the tree be placed there every year.

'Lots of folk who don't have a home, never mind a tree, pass our place,' she said. 'This way we can share a bit of Christmas spirit, and isn't that needed more than ever in these awful times?'

Presents had been opened and exclaimed over, and Flora was summoning up the energy to get up out of her nice comfortable chair to put the capon in the oven. With roast potatoes and fresh Brussels sprouts from Grace's garden, followed by Christmas pudding and custard, Christmas dinner would be a feast fit for a king.

'Come on, Mum, I'll give you a hand,' said Daisy, just as they heard the front doorbell. She was nearest and so she pulled herself up and went to answer it.

'Have you seen Grace? Sorry, everyone. Merry Christmas,' said Sally as she spilled into the room. She was wearing the costume bought for her by her friends, but it was obvious that she had not come to have them admire it or the smart red hat, perched on the back of her curls, which her parents had given her for Christmas. 'Sorry again, but she's never this late and there's no one at their house.'

Sally looked as if she was about to burst into tears. Grace had spent Christmas Day with Sally's family almost every year since she had arrived in Dartford as a timid seven-year-old. Megan Paterson had very unwillingly taken in the little girl but, apart from providing a bed for Grace to sleep in, had done little to make

Grace feel welcome. Megan, manageress of a charity shop on the High Street, lived her own life. The presence of her half-sister was obviously an inconvenience and not a pleasure.

'Where else could she be, Sally? Can't think of any other close chums.'

Sally shook her head. 'You know Grace; she's not a talker. I don't think I've even heard the names of anyone she works with. Dad and I went to the shop in case Megan had got a delivery she wanted unpacked and sorted, but it's definitely closed and empty.'

She waited but no one spoke and so Sally carried on. 'She's been funny since my party but I thought she'd forgotten all about that silly teasing. Mum took her to the pictures one night last week and they spoke about Christmas dinner as usual. Today we can't find her anywhere.'

'Maybe her sister—' began Flora.

'Oh, please, Mrs Petrie. We're all old enough to know exactly what her sister is. Grace won't be with her. Dad went round the house; it's empty. We hoped she'd be here. Maybe she's gone to somebody at her work but why didn't she tell Mum?'

'No idea. I don't think Grace'd do a thing like that. We'll just have to go looking,' said Daisy decisively. 'Probably she went for a walk, and lost track of time – and distance.' She looked at her mother.

'Dinner'll keep, pet. Go and find your friend. After all, we're planning to eat her Brussels sprouts.'

Rose followed Daisy into the hallway where they picked up their woollen coats, and rammed the new berets that Flora had knitted for Christmas onto their

31

heads. 'Sorry, Mum, you and Dad start without us.'

When the door had closed behind them, Flora and Fred sat down by the fire. They had no option but to celebrate Christmas without their sons. 'I'll be damned if I touch a mouthful without my girls,' said Fred.

Flora nodded and picked up her knitting.

The scarf she was making for Daisy was well under way by the time the girls returned.

'Sorry,' the twins said together. 'We found her, would you believe, in that awful Anderson shelter; passed it twice, never thought to look in. She's all right, Mum. As usual says nothing, but maybe she had a row with Megan. We talked her round and Mrs Brewer had the dinner keeping nice and hot.' She looked suggestively towards the kitchen.

'You had five more minutes, girls. Your dad wouldn't start without you. Come on, it'll be grand, and wait till you see what your dad 'as brought up from the shop.'

Neither girl had much experience of alcohol and each was thrilled to be given a glass of sherry.

'Spanish,' said Fred. 'Best kind there is. Don't neither of you let anyone give you sherry from anyplace else.'

Was the meal perfect or did the excitement of drinking sherry help cast a golden glow over it? No one appeared to notice that the capon was a little dry or that the sprouts had been cooked a little too long.

Daisy looked at the firelight shining in the liquid in her glass and found herself thinking of the pilot. Was he drinking real Spanish sherry with his Christmas meal? He had to be. Surely sherry was the height of sophistication.

TWO

8 January 1940

The alarm clock woke Daisy. She groaned, as usual, burrowed even further under the counterpane, as usual, and then, remembering her promise, threw back her covers and jumped out of bed. It was cold, so cold that, completely forgetting her sleeping sister, she did a little war dance right there on the strip of carpet between the beds. A quick look proved once again that Rose Petrie could sleep through anything.

Daisy slipped past her bed to the window and pulled the curtain back sufficiently to let her see out. 'Crikey.' She could see nothing but beautiful paintings by one Mr Jack Frost on the window-pane. Daisy breathed on the glass and rubbed it with the sleeve of her nightgown until she had a peephole.

Outside lay a frozen world. The year had blasted in accompanied by snow storms that seemed determined to maintain their icy grip. The snow that had fallen over the weekend and been churned into muddy heaps by the traffic was now frozen solid. Daisy grabbed her clothes, washed her face and such parts of her neck as she thought might be seen, dressed and slipped out. She looked towards the kitchen door. No time to boil the kettle for some scalding tea. She crept down the stairs, pulled on her heavy outdoor coat and the cheery hat and now-finished scarf that her mother had knitted for Christmas, grabbed her hated gas mask – there weren't going to be gas attacks; there was no sign of *any* attacks – and hurried out.

Her breath seemed to freeze in her throat and, for a second or two, she panicked. It was cold, colder than she had ever known. Then she pulled herself together and began to stumble over the frozen sculptures to a stretch of fairly clear road.

Slithering and sliding, Daisy battled on to the little cottage where Grace lived with her half-sister. Grace opened the door and ushered her in. It was obvious that she had been crying.

'What's up, Grace? Ever so sorry I'm late; road's treacherous.'

Grace shook her head. 'Doesn't matter. They're all ruined. Come on through.'

In her hurry, Daisy put her gas mask haphazardly on a chair. It landed on the wooden floorboards with a loud thump. Daisy winced and looked towards the ceiling.

'She didn't come home last night and, anyway, takes more than a noise like that to wake our Megan.'

Daisy followed her friend through the cold little house. Grace was almost fanatically tidy but Daisy had time to see at least three pairs of fully fashioned pure silk stockings hanging from a wire across the fireplace in the kitchen. She looked down at her lisle-covered legs. 'Bet they feel ever so wonderful on, Grace.'

'Much, much too expensive for me, Daisy, and you an' all, I should think, if you get my meaning. I saw some in Kerr's Stores. Three shillings a pair.'

'Nine shillings spent on stockings. Who's got that kind of money, Grace?'

Grace said nothing but opened the door to the back garden, and she and Daisy stood for a moment looking at the disaster that had been their pride and joy, their garden. Even Sally had risked her precious long scarlet-painted fingernails to work there.

'It's froze solid, Daisy. Not so much as a sprout fit to eat.'

The previous evening Grace had gathered two cabbages, one for the Brewers, one for the Petries. She had admired the amazing number of plump firm Brussels sprouts that were still on the stocks. Now, less than twelve hours later, she saw disaster. 'Damn it, Daisy, it weren't that great to start with but look at it now.'

'We've had lovely fresh veggies for weeks, Grace, and I'm sure Mum will make soup with this lot. It'll be delicious.' She looked at Grace, wondering how to read the expression on her face. 'What is it, Grace? It's not just a few frozen sprouts.'

'No, I suppose. It's just . . . I was really happy working here, Daisy. It were special somehow, a good feeling, being in touch with the soil, putting in a little seed and weeks later frying up my own cabbage. I planned to be really serious this year: better beds, deeper digging and not just doing the safe old stuff like cabbage, but peas – can you imagine fresh peas, Daisy. And why not rhubarb and strawberries?'

'And lovely fresh lettuce, maybe even tomatoes.'

35

'You are going a bit far,' smiled Grace, and Daisy was pleased to see her looking happier, but she was serious.

'I think I saw tomatoes growing down The Old Manor once,' she said. 'You'll do it, Grace, and I'll help you. We're stronger than we look, you and me. Come on, let's put these ruined sprouts in the bag with any of the kale worth keeping.'

'Glad we finished the spuds at Christmas,' interrupted Grace. 'Frozen spuds are the worst. They fall apart and they smell something awful.'

'Where did you learn that?'

'Dunno, musta read it somewhere.' Grace sliced a stock bearing several sprouts off at the base and popped it into Daisy's bag.

Since Grace was due at the munitions factory where she worked in the office, Daisy left her to close up and she walked home with the bag.

Flora was in the shop. She ignored the bag. 'Who was it said something about rationing, Daisy, love?'

'The vicar, I think, Mum. Why?'

'Why's sugar so scarce? Between that and the shortage of butter and bacon, some customers is saying they'll take their custom elsewhere.'

'One thing at a time, Mum. Sugar's scarce because it's shipped into this country – we don't grow it. Ships are needed now for other things – munitions, soldiers, I don't know – but there's no space for sugar. Same with bacon and butter.'

'We know Nancy Humble makes lovely butter up at the farm and there's two farms near her as keeps pigs.'

'Not enough to feed the whole country. I don't know where these things come from, but could be as far away as New Zealand; the Commonwealth, you see. But, Mum, more important right now, can you do something with poor Grace's veggies?'

''Course, waste not, want not, and are we not going to be singing that song a lot more? If that freeze was all over the country last night and not just in poor old Kent, then there'll be greengrocers closing faster than you can run upstairs with those vegetables.'

Daisy picked up her shopping bag of unpleasantly defrosting vegetables and, two stairs at a time, soon reached the kitchen where she dumped them unceremoniously in the sink.

'Porridge on the back of the fire,' her mother's voice floated up to her, and so Daisy helped herself to a bowl of porridge. She put a scraping of Nancy's Christmas butter on top to melt and pulled her father's comfortable chair up to the fire. What a lovely smell a fire had; simply smelling wood smoke made Daisy feel warm.

A few well-fed minutes later, Daisy, washed properly in hot water, dressed in a warm woollen skirt and a fair-isle jersey, descended to take her turn in the shop. In the short time that she had been upstairs, the store had filled with people all talking and gesticulating. At first Daisy thought there must have been an accident.

'You all right, Mum?'

''Course I am, love. Vicar's just brought some unwelcome news.'

Daisy looked around until she could see the kindly, wrinkled face of the local Church of England vicar. 'Good morning, Mr Tiverton, bad news, is it?'

He smiled, a particularly sweet smile, and Daisy smiled back. She couldn't help it; there was something about that smile – the smile reserved, according to Sam, for saintly Church of England vicars.

'Well, my dear,' said Mr Tiverton, 'that will really depend on how we deal with it. Rationing came into force this morning: sugar, butter and bacon. From today we are officially allowed four ounces each of butter and bacon or ham, and twelve ounces of sugar, per adult per week. We will each be given a jolly little ration book that must be registered with local shops. I'm quite sure that soon everything but the air we breathe will be rationed.'

'If there are indeed to be gas attacks, Vicar, we won't want our air.'

Daisy and Flora stared at each other in disbelief. Miss Partridge had a sense of humour. Who'd have thought it?

Fred, who had been stocking up at the strangely empty wholesalers, came in the back door just as the last customer went out the front. As wife and daughter began to speak Fred held up his hands. 'I saw 'em leaving as I slithered down the street. Telling you they was looking for the best deal, was they? Well, if they don't trust us enough to know our prices are the best we can do, Flora, love, then they can take their custom elsewhere. The 'alt, the lame and the lazy will stay with us, and we'll deliver to our 'ousebound any time they needs something delivering.'

'I don't fit in any of those categories, Fred.' Mr Fischer had come quietly into the shop while Fred was talking.

'I don't worry about a gent like you, Mr Fischer. You're always welcome in this shop.'

'I hope that will always be the case.'

'And why wouldn't it be?' Fred asked somewhat belligerently.

The old man looked at him sadly. 'You really do not know, my friend? I am not only a hated German, Fred, but a hated Jewish German.'

The family stared at him in consternation. Flora recovered first. 'What's that got to do with the price of tea, Mr Fischer? Why, you was one of our first customers. You came in here two days after me and Fred got married.'

'And, my God, wasn't that a lifetime ago?' said Fred, attempting to lighten the mood.

'And you will take my ration book?'

Fred and Flora reassured him while Daisy stood in the background and thought of all the implications hidden in the simple conversation she had just heard. Poor Mr Fischer. To be hated in his own country because of his religion and hated everywhere else because he was German. People could be horrid. They were not at war with Mr Fischer; surely just the Germans that lived in Germany. But she didn't much like that idea either, and decided to think instead of what she should now be doing.

There was the first-aid course, and God help anybody who needed aid from Daisy Petrie. 'I can't even get the blasted bandages right,' she said aloud, earning a reproving look from her mother who was still talking to Mr Fischer. As well as the first aid, her dad thought she might sign up for a bit of fire-watching. Fine, she would do that. But compared to what others were doing, was it enough?

Her racing thoughts focused on the young man with

the plane. Alf had said that he was already in the air force. Where was he now, back with his unit, or in Alf's old stable working on the plane? It could not possibly be fit for active service in its present condition.

I'm good with engines, Daisy reminded herself fiercely. I could work on it if he's had to go.

Doubts flooded in, undermining her resolution. He's a toff and he owns a plane. He'd laugh me out of the yard. Bet he'd say, 'No woman's capable of working on my beautiful aeroplane.' But he talked to me like we were both human beings. And if he's more interested in planes than in girls, he might, just might, not care that I'm a girl. Woman, she corrected herself quickly. Maybe he'll just see another good mechanic.

'Daisy, love, fetch some porridge oats from the store-room, please.' Mr Fischer had gone and her parents were alone.

Daisy took a deep breath and a life-changing decision. 'Sorry, Dad, I promised Nancy Humble I'd deliver some tinned peaches when they came in. I'm off to get the van.'

She was whipping off her apron as she spoke and, without giving her parents a chance to speak, she took the keys to the van from their hook and hurried out into the back lane. The van was in the garage directly across the lane. With some difficulty because of the sheet of ice that *was* the back lane, Daisy backed it up to the shop's rear door. 'Come on, Dad; give me a hand with the boxes.'

Flora returned to the flat. Monday was her usual washing day and as Christmas Day and New Year's Day had been the last two Mondays, she was behind with her household chores and could see no way to spend any time in the shop. The weekly wash took hours. First water had to be boiled in kettles and pots. The clothes were sorted and washed, much use being made of Flora's scrubbing board. Next the clothes had to be rinsed, put through the mangle that Fred had set up on the iron tub in which the family took baths, and then hung up to dry, either on the pulley on the kitchen ceiling or, if the weather was good, on the clothes line on the small square of concrete beside the garage. On washing day it was virtually impossible for Flora to help out in the shop.

Downstairs, Fred propped open the door so that he could hear the front doorbell, and began to load.

'Starting at Old Manor Farm, Dad. I promised Nancy I'd deliver there first. One of the family's there, on leave, I think.'

'He'll have gone, love. Lucky to get twenty-four hours, never mind a week.'

'Just in case.'

Fred grumbled but loaded the van in the order that Daisy wanted and soon she was on her way. A cloud of butterflies cavorted in the pit of her stomach. It was a pleasant excitement.

Think positively, Daisy. After all, what can he say? No or yes. When she drove through the ancient iron gates she felt her heart beating rapidly. And by the time she reached the old stables her hands were sweating. Why? Surely it had nothing to do with the toff, even though he has a nice voice and nice eyes and he's a real, live pilot. No, Daisy assured herself, I am excited by the machine, the plane.

Anti-climax. The stables were deserted and all the doors

and gates closed. There were windows high up on the main stable doors, but they were inaccessible. Daisy looked round but all that remained to show that an aeroplane had once stood on these cobblestones was a patch of engine oil. She bent down, touched it with her fingertips and lifted them to her nose. Now that was a lovely smell, better even than logs. If only . . .

Thoroughly cast down, she went to the farmhouse.

'Well, this is a nice surprise. Wasn't expecting anything today, Daisy, since you was here on Saturday.'

Daisy pulled out a small box. 'I thought you might like some tinned peaches.'

Nancy looked at her in some surprise and, blushing, Daisy explained, 'I know you put up berries and apples but thought maybe a peach would make a nice change.'

Nancy nodded in agreement. 'Well, if that isn't right thoughtful of you, Daisy, love, and has nothing to do with a handsome young flyer that was here. My Alf says if he sees another jar of stewed rhubarb he won't be responsible. Me, I never tire of it.'

Daisy looked at her, blushed even more furiously and decided that she had to ask about the plane before she lost her courage. 'Sorry, Nancy. Dad knows I'm up to something; peaches wasn't a great idea for someone with an orchard.'

'We don't grow peaches, love. 'Course I'll take them.'

Daisy sighed and relaxed. 'Where's the plane gone then?' she asked bluntly.

'Plane or pilot, Daisy Petrie? Which one are you really looking for?'

'The plane, of course. I wouldn't recognise Adair whatsit if I was to fall over him. But rationing coming in makes the war real somehow, and I've got to do something . . . meaningful.'

'Your mum needs you, Daisy.'

'No, sorry, Nancy, but that's just not true. I'm in the shop because I worked in there Saturdays and Mum's got it into her head I'm delicate, kidding herself really, probably because I'm smaller than Rose. Everybody's smaller than her. You know I'm good with engines, Nancy, as good as my brothers. I thought I could help with the plane. Can't be all that different from a lorry engine or the van, and I can take them apart and put them together again. I'd be doing something important, more valuable than sitting in a cosy little shop weighing dried peas.'

'Folks've got to be fed, love.'

'Mum and Dad can do that, and if things get tough they can hire someone.' She was surprised by the idea that jumped fully formed into her head. 'For instance, I just bet old Mr Fischer would jump at the chance of earning a few extra bob a week.'

'Happen he would. Now, I'll take these into the larder and make us a cuppa.'

'Wait,' said Daisy, grabbing Nancy's arm. 'I mean, Dad's alone in the shop so I can't stay, but what about the plane?'

'Lad's a pilot, Daisy. He comes here whenever he has a spare weekend to work on it, but he just turns up. He looks after himself, has the odd cuppa with me and Alf in the kitchen, no more. I've no idea where he's based – happen Alf does. But if Adair does come back I'll tell him what you said. Best I can do.'

Daisy had to be content with that. She finished

43

the deliveries with ideas and plans spilling around as the butterflies had done earlier. He had to come back some weekend to see his beloved plane and Nancy would tell him what Daisy had said. He would be delighted by the offer of help and very soon Daisy Petrie – shop assistant – would be doing something that was vital to the war effort.

But weeks passed and he did not return.

Grace was absent from the first-aid classes at the beginning of February. Daisy did not concern herself too much. Everyone seemed to work longer and longer hours these days and all the extra hours did seem to be affecting Grace. Without much expectation of discovering anything, Daisy went to Megan Paterson's shop.

'Grace missed the classes this week, Megan. She's not sick, is she?'

Grace's sister looked nothing like Grace. She was tall and very thin, and her extravagantly styled hair was, to Daisy, the most peculiar unnatural shade of red. Her frock was certainly very modern and Daisy supposed she could possibly be described as sophisticated. To Daisy, however, there was something not quite right in the picture presented. Megan's antagonism to Grace's friends did nothing to help.

'How would I know?' Megan answered Daisy's question. 'I got more to do than look in her room every five minutes, haven't I?'

A picture of the cold, cheerless kitchen and the three pairs of expensive stockings flashed across Daisy's mind. She bristled. 'I'm quite sure you have more to do than look after your sister. You certainly never have before, so why break the habit of a lifetime?'

'Get out, you cheeky little bitch,' snarled Megan, lifting her hand as if to strike.

'You do that, Megan Paterson, and my dad'll be round here in two minutes. If you see Grace, tell her we're worried about her.'

Heart beating unnaturally quickly, Daisy hurried home. She could hear her voice shouting at Megan but could scarcely believe that she had lost control of her emotions so completely. She discussed her concern for Grace with her mother. She left out the bit about being rude to Megan and almost being slapped for it.

'I think it started the day rationing started, the morning all the sprouts were frozen. Haven't seen her much since then but we're all busy and it's been too cold to do much except stay in and listen to the wireless. But now she's missed two classes and she loves them. She's so good at first aid, much quicker at it than me. Why hasn't she popped in for a cuppa in weeks, Mum? You don't think she could have died, do you?'

'Lawks a' mercy, Daisy Petrie. 'Course she hasn't gone and died. Megan's a . . . well, she's not the best sister in the world but even she would know. Now, my girl, you need to take yourself off dancing with Rose and her friends. She meets lots of nice lads in the factory and at the Palais. Doesn't mean you've promised to marry a chap if you dance with him, love, and you used to enjoy the dancing. Why don't you go with them next Saturday, take Grace along too? Be good for her.'

Daisy stood up. 'Can't seem to think about anything but the war, Mum, and I can't take Grace if I can't find her. I'm going to pop round to the theatre, see if I can have a word with Sally. Maybe she's heard something. Seems I've seen hardly anything of her since the theatre company took her in to train and it'd be ever so exciting to see backstage.'

Mother and daughter looked towards the door as they heard the bell and breathed a collective breath of relief as Bernie Jones entered.

'Morning, ladies, you got a bumper crop today: one each, and some nasty ones I'll put over here for Fred.'

They both laughed at this old joke, offered Bernie tea, which he declined, and turned to their letters.

For a few moments the only sound in the room was the tearing open of envelopes.

'It's from Phil, first from 'is ship. Imagine, Daisy, a letter from a ship.'

Daisy said nothing but continued to stare at the page torn from a jotter, on which her letter was written. She read it again and again, turned it over and looked at the blank back as if somehow, somewhere on that empty space, there was a message that would explain it. Nothing. She turned it over and read it again.

Dear Daisy,

I've gone and joined the Women's Land Army. I don't know where I'll be sent but right now I'm here in Kent, but that's just for learning and when I get sent to a permanent farm I'll let you know and Sally, and maybe you'll write to me. We'll have proper tools for digging and such and I'll learn lots and growing our own food is really important. I got a uniform, Daze, and everything from the skin out brand new.

Tell your mum and Sally's mum thank you and sorry to have left like this but I just had to.

Grace

P.S. Tell your mum and Sally's I'll write when I get nice paper and if you write to me and please, please do, will you tell me if Sally's an actress yet?

'Are you all right, Daisy? You've gone all funny.' Flora was looking at her daughter, her eyes full of concern. 'It's not bad news, is it?'

'Some friend I am.' Daisy handed her mother the letter.

'Poor Grace. Now, did that trollop of a sister know she was gone when you went over there? Well, just in case she didn't, we won't tell her either, Daze. Let her stew a little – do 'er the world of good.'

'Why didn't she put an address on it? She asked me to write and she hasn't put an address. Did she never have anything in her life that was new, Mum? And she paid her share of Sally's costume. Why didn't I help her?'

Flora pulled Daisy into the alcove and sat her down on one of the rickety chairs. 'Pull yourself together, our Daisy, and think. Of course you helped her. She wrote to you, didn't she, not to anybody else? And she had new things; me and your dad and Sally's mum and dad, we gave her something new every Christmas, even if I made it myself. I want you to put on your outside clothes and go over to the picture house and tell the Brewers because they're worried too. Grace will write when she's ready, when she's got used to her new life.'

'She was happy in her little garden, Mum.'

'Then think of the fun she'll have in a blooming great

47

field. In the meantime, there's work needs doing here so you can pop round the Brewers when the shop closes. Days are getting longer and so you can run down to the theatre if Sally's not at home.'

Daisy gave in gracefully. 'All right. What needs doing?'

'Be a good girl and fetch in a carton of the Bonn's digestive biscuits. They're a good seller and there's only one or two packets left. And I think there's a roll of nice, yellow Lancaster cloth somewhere in there. Your dad was just after saying the shelves need a bit of brightening along of our spirits.'

Those two jobs, plus attending to customers who always came into the shop late in the afternoon in the hope that something perishable had been marked down, kept Daisy busy. Two boys in particular worried her. The older one tried always to seem tough but Daisy felt it was all a pose. When she could, she slipped something extra into their bag, earning a look of scorn from the older boy and a dazzling smile from the younger one.

As soon as her father had locked the shop door she hung up her apron, rushed upstairs to wash, and changed her shop overall for a smart lightly fitted blue wool skirt and a round-necked striped blue and white short-sleeved woollen jumper.

'I won't be late back,' she called to her parents, and hurried out.

She was prepared to find the house in darkness as Sally's parents were usually in the picture house. She was therefore delighted to see a light on in the Brewers' front room.

Sally herself, looking as if she was dressed for a special meeting, opened the door and was equally thrilled to see her friend. 'How terrif, Daisy. Mum and Dad are at work but I have lines to learn. We'll have a cuppa and you can hear them for me. It'll be like old times. Remember doing our homework together in primary school?'

Daisy nodded. 'Yes, Sally, and I'll be thrilled to listen to your lines, but I've got a letter here I need to show you.'

'Sounds scary, Daisy. Who's it from?' She was leading the way into the kitchen. 'Sit down and tell me.'

Daisy handed the letter to Sally.

Sally stood quietly beside the table and read the letter. Daisy was not surprised when Sally, the great dramatic star of stage and screen, started to cry. 'Oh, Daisy, poor, poor Grace. She must have been so miserable and we didn't notice.'

Sally, a much loved and, to be honest, somewhat indulged only child, was not given much to introspection. She had accepted some responsibility for Grace because the twins had accepted her, and they always did things together, but she had not really thought about what it must be like to live, an unwelcome guest, in a home without love.

Daisy, a member of a large loving family whose creed could have been 'we are responsible for those less well off than ourselves' knew what Sally was feeling and gave her a quick hug.

'You're right, we didn't realise how miserable she was, but we did know her life wasn't happy. How could it be – living with that horrible, selfish sister? And, look, she loves our mums – and dads too, probably. So, cheer up, we can't have been too bad. Next time we hear from her we'll write back to tell her she's always welcome with us.'

49

'We can't,' said Sally, pointing dramatically at the letter, 'unless she tells us her address.'

'Don't go looking for trouble,' Daisy quoted her father. 'It finds us easy enough.'

'I have to go,' she said some time later, after the girls had gone over and over the problem. 'She'll write again and she'll write her address, but we have to be patient and wait till she's ready. Now you go and learn your lines and we'll all come and see the play. We're all looking forward to it.'

A few days later, the *Dartford Chronicle* spread out in front of her, Daisy was totally involved in a report of German aggression all over Europe when she heard the melodic ping of the shop bell. She looked up. A tall fair-haired young man in air force uniform was standing looking at her with a puzzled expression on his face.

Cigarettes, Daisy decided, and stood up with a friendly smile. 'Can I help you?'

'Yes, if you really know how to take an engine apart, clean it, and put it together again.'

'Well, if you don't scrub up well.' The words came tumbling out of her mouth before she could stop them, and Daisy wanted to bite her tongue at this evidence of her lack of sophistication. She just knew that no one had ever spoken to him like that before. Girls from his class weren't rude.

To her surprise he laughed. 'So my grandmother used to say.' He held out his hand. 'Adair Maxwell.'

Daisy took his hand and the most pleasurable jolt went through her whole body. Why, why, why had she not put on the dark blue real linen dress with the pale blue Peter Pan collar that Mum had found in the market? She blushed furiously but obviously the jolt, or whatever it was, had not been felt by the young man in front of her, and so she managed to stutter, 'Daisy Petrie.'

'Who was born with a hammer in her hand, or was it a spanner?'

Had it been one of her brothers or one of the hordes of boys and young men who had been in and out of her home all her life, Daisy would have known how to answer. She would not have been left standing, as she thought, like a raving idiot while a real live pilot stood before her.

He put her out of her misery. 'I have a twelve-hour pass, drove to the farm, and Alf passed on your extremely generous offer.'

She looked at him. Was this some kind of joke? How was she supposed to respond? 'You're welcome, I'm sure' or, 'Think nothing of it'? Again she said nothing.

'Miss Petrie,' he began, and then he laughed. 'Your eyes shot open like one of those toys – what do they call them – automatons. I'll start again. Miss Petrie, Daisy, I am extremely grateful for your offer of assistance with . . . my plane. Thank you very much.'

Daisy, who was now staring at the floor, said, 'You're welcome.'

Adair looked at his watch. 'Nine hours and twenty-three minutes left, twenty-two, twenty-one.'

'Stop laughing at me.'

'Oh, my dear Miss Petrie, I'm not laughing at you, but it's very difficult to talk to someone who finds the floor so fascinating. Did you mean it? Will you come out with me and have a look at her? Damn, you've done your automaton again – and lovely eyes they are too.'

51

A strange feeling travelled right down Daisy's spine. She should have worn her new frock. He said she had lovely eyes. Sally had lovely eyes; everyone said so. She gained control of herself. 'Right now? You want me to come and see the plane right this minute?'

'Yes, please, my car's outside.' He looked again at his watch.

'I'll have to find my dad.'

He was startled. 'You're perfectly safe with me, Miss Petrie.'

'Maybe, Mr Adair Maxwell,' said Daisy, and this time she was laughing, 'but somebody's got to mind the shop.'

THREE

I'm helping a pilot friend maintain his aircraft . . .

I am doing war work, as it happens. I'm working on an Aeronca. You don't know the Aeronca? American, of course, and practically the aircraft that started the entire craze for owning a plane.

Adair had to drop Daisy at the end of the back-street as he was already in grave danger of returning late to base, an unpardonable offence in the military. She walked slowly down the dark length of the street, feeling the euphoria of the afternoon seeping away, desperately trying to recapture some of it; trying out ways in which she might astound friends and family, and especially her brothers, by telling them about the experience. None of her carefully prepared little remarks would work with her brothers, of course. They would just laugh at her.

She got the fright of her life when she collided with a rather solid form.

'Look where you're going, young Daisy. You almost had me on my backside. What are you doing out by yourself at this time of night in the freezing cold?'

'Sorry, Mr Griffiths. I was . . .' She stopped. 'I was working

53

on an aircraft' would not be believed, and besides, might it not be possible that Adair would prefer that the fewer people who knew of the aeroplane's existence, the better? 'I've been out with a friend. I'm on my way home. Dad'll be looking out for me.'

Mr Griffiths, their local ARP warden, turned and looked up at the black shape that was the Petrie flat. 'They better not be showing any lights, my girl. You get on home and tell your young man to see you to your door in future.'

'Yes, Mr Griffiths,' said Daisy again.

'Your young man.' Heavens. Mr Griffiths actually thought Daisy Petrie had a young man. She laughed. Adair Maxwell was not a 'young man'. He was much more important than that. He was a pilot.

She carried on to the shop, feeling her way carefully. Not only was it impossible to see any distance at all because of the blackout and the starless sky, but the ground under her feet was very treacherous. She was relieved to put her key into the keyhole and happier still when she slipped inside. Immediately there was the glow of a muffled light from the top of the stairs. Her sister stood there with a candle.

'Mum and Dad are in bed, too cold to stay up,' she explained quietly as Daisy climbed the stairs. 'We're out of coal. Was it fun? Have you had a fantastic time? Did you get to sit in it, the plane? Come on in the kitchen and we'll have some cocoa, and there's a sausage and some mashed potatoes left if you didn't have your tea. Crikey, look at your nails,' she went on as they sat down in the kitchen. 'No one's going to want to buy butter from you tomorrow, Daisy Petrie.'

Daisy was tired and somehow too deflated to talk. She sat quietly, watching Rose prepare the cocoa.

'Want the sausage, Daze?'

'No, thanks. Nancy made us coffee and we had a big slice of what she called a game pie, whatever that is. It were . . .' she began and then corrected herself, '. . . it was delicious.' Daisy smiled quietly. She was learning more than just how to maintain a plane.

'Come on, tell us all.'

'We drove out to The Old Manor and—'

'Tell me about the car and about him, this pilot person.'

'I won't be able to tell you anything if you don't stop interrupting.'

Rose carefully undid a curl, rearranged it and pinned it down securely with a kirby grip before picking up the cold sausage. She began to eat it and so Daisy talked. She remembered little about the motorcar, having been too aware of Adair Maxwell to concentrate, but she described the little aircraft in detail, enumerating all its parts and telling Rose just what its owner thought needed to be done in order for it to be offered to the Royal Air Force.

'Doesn't seem to be too much, Daisy. Not too different from a lorry.'

'Adair says he learned to fly in just a few hours, simple controls.'

'A few hours? Don't believe it. Two hours and you could maybe get it to go along the ground but how does it get up in the air?'

'No idea, but I'm going to find out. He talked about something called . . .' she thought for a moment, '. . . aerodynamics, whatever that is. Didn't tell him I hadn't a clue but I'll find out.' She clenched her fists. 'Somehow. Anyway, he says when we get it ready, he'll take me up. It's got two seats, one behind the other. Remember Sam's big go-kart?'

Rose nodded.

'It's like being in that but with higher sides.'

'Time you two was sound.' Their father, wearing his pyjamas, his disreputable old dressing gown, his hat and a scarf, was standing at the door. 'You're at the factory early tomorrow, Rose, and you need to clean your hands, Daisy. Picture the poor vicar's face if you was to cut his cheese with hands like that.'

Daisy, laughed, said, 'Aircraft oil,' as nonchalantly as she could and blew out Rose's candle.

Rose had the last word. 'Sally'll be ever so excited, Daisy. Mrs B told Mum she thinks Sal will get a real theatre job soon with real actors an' all, not just training, and here's you meeting a toff and being friends. You two are for the high life.'

'Don't be daft, our Rose. Adair and me . . . and I . . . are working together is all.'

'I know, Daisy, and I sing as good as Vera Lynn.'

Daisy became accustomed to such phrases as dual ignition, interchangeable ailerons, magneto generators, which soon became as easily recognisable and understandable as spark plugs, brakes and crankshafts. By May of 1940 she was as at home in the cockpit of Adair's beloved little yellow plane as she was in the driving seat of the family's old van. Adair managed to get away only twice in those months but he wrote long letters in which he answered Daisy's many questions and each time reinforced his feelings of gratitude towards her. Never, however, did he repeat his promise to take her for a flight. She had not expected it, and so was not overly hurt. After all, he was one of those brave young men who, every day and night, flew on what they called missions. Some never returned, having sacrificed everything so that others might live in peace.

She did keep the letters and read each one several times – for the information, she told herself, not because they were from a rather handsome young man.

Adair managed a pass early in May and, for once, had been able to bring Daisy to the farm. Usually she cycled, as petrol was now very scarce and the Petries' allowance was needed for deliveries. Daisy had watched for him, one ear on her customer, the other desperately listening for the sound of his motorcar on the street outside.

'I'll pick you up about eleven,' he had written, and Daisy knew that meant that Adair Maxwell, pilot, would come into the shop and happily introduce himself to whichever parent was there. For a reason she could not quite understand, Daisy did not want that to happen.

Was it because her parents, solid hard-working people, did not quite trust young men like Adair, who had been born, not in a crowded flat above a shop, but in a magnificent manor house surrounded by thousands of acres of family-owned land? She pushed the disturbing thought away.

The trees around Old Manor Farm were in glorious pink, white or purple bloom. The scent of lilacs floated gently around them as, after working hard for a few hours, Daisy and Adair sat on the ground under a great beech tree to enjoy the sandwiches Flora had prepared for them.

'This is too good of Mrs Petrie,' Adair said as he bit happily into a fish paste sandwich. 'I never think of sensible things like food, and I ought to bring your mum something.'

'She's used to feeding boys.'

He looked straight at her and Daisy felt her face warming, and not from the May sunshine.

'I'm not a boy, Daisy,' he said as he reached for a second sandwich.

Daisy was speechless. No, he was not a boy, he was a man, a very exciting man. A thought entered her head and she tried to stifle it. Could he possibly be reminding her that she was no longer a girl? At eighteen, she was a woman. A woman who could . . . who could what? Love a man? Be loved by him in return? That thought was just too much. She was someone who could help him repair his engine and that was all.

After a few minutes of slightly uncomfortable silence Adair spoke again. 'You ought to go into the WAAF, you know; you're wasted in a shop.'

Daisy knew what the WAAF was: the Women's Auxiliary Air Force. She had read about it in the *Chronicle*, and even the London papers, which a few of their customers ordered. She thought she could learn how to pack a parachute and probably she would be qualified for a catering job – after all, she had washed dishes and peeled potatoes all her life – but how could she be a meteorological officer or work with ciphers and such? She almost wept as she realised she scarcely knew what the words meant, let alone how to do the jobs.

'Thanks a lot, and which job do you think the air force might be anxious to give me?'

'You're a good mechanic; we need mechanics.'

'You need bits of paper, Adair. I left school at fourteen. I walk in there and say I'd like to be a mechanic in the WAAF and, after they've all had a good laugh, I'll be dishing out plates of egg and chips to people like you.'

'Vision, Daisy. You could train to be a pilot. Damn it, woman, you're smart. Sometimes education is what goes on after you leave school, you know.'

Woman. Her heart began to beat more quickly. What was happening to her? She felt wonderful but strange. She tried to joke. 'You're mad, Adair Maxwell, nice but mad. Come on, finish the apple pie and let's get back to work.'

He stood up and, reaching down, pulled her up to stand beside him. 'I'll teach you. Every day I teach men who're not half as smart as you are.'

Now her pulse was racing. She tried to remain calm and focused. Never once had she thought seriously that she might learn to fly. Her vision, as Adair called it, had allowed her to think, hope, pray that perhaps she might be accepted to help out with aircraft engines, but flying . . .

'You don't mean that.'

He held her by her shoulders. 'Dash it; I didn't when I said it. The words popped out . . . but, Daisy, why not? You know my little plane every bit as well as I do myself. Besides, she's basically a glorified powered glider; she always lands gently, very different from some of the planes I'm flying as an air force pilot. Next time I can get away I'll take her up; I wasn't going to tell you, but she's ready, thanks to you. If I bring her down again safely, then we're in business.'

They cleared up their picnic and returned to the stable yard where the plane sat waiting.

'Don't tell me you haven't handled the controls and thought, I bet I could get this crate off the ground.'

Daisy smiled but said nothing. Of course she had enjoyed wonderful daydreams in which she soared above Kent in the Aeronca, but they were just dreams. Planes did get off the ground and into the air but how they got up there was still a mystery.

'Come on, you can steer the old girl into the stable. All she needs now is a name. Can't take her up without a name.'

'What was her name before?' Daisy asked as she lowered herself into the cockpit, the excitement in her stomach threatening to spoil the experience.

'Don't remember, something trite like *Messenger of the Gods*.' He looked at her sitting there in the pilot's seat. 'You've never asked why she was in such a poor condition.'

'Not my business.'

'She was my father's but he died in a silly accident before he could fly her.'

'I'm sorry.'

'Long time ago, Daisy. Park her right in the back, please.' He was himself again, professional, businesslike.

When they had closed up the stables, they walked up to the farmhouse to let the Humbles know that Adair was leaving.

'Take care, lad. Any idea when we'll see you?'

Adair shook his head.

'We'll see you, Daisy?'

'Only with grocery orders, I think, Alf.'

'The best mechanic in England has brought the plane up to scratch, Alf. Our Daisy is going to be the RAF's secret weapon, but right now I've got to get her back home.'

They said nothing during the drive into Dartford. Adair easily found a parking place on the High Street and moved as if to get out of the car. Daisy jumped out before he could.

'You need all the time you've got, Adair. Thanks for letting me work with you.'

She turned to hurry towards the shop door but he caught up with her, his firm grip on her arm making her pulse race again. 'This isn't thanks for working your socks off and goodbye, Daisy. I meant what I said. As soon as I can I'll be back and I'll teach you to fly.'

For a moment he looked as if he wanted to say more. After a long moment he said, 'Scout's honour,' before hurrying back to his car.

Daisy stifled the urge to turn and watch him drive away. She did not look after him but walked on into the shop. *Scout's honour.* She smiled. She just bet Adair Maxwell had been a patrol leader.

'Good time, Daisy, love?' Flora was sitting knitting behind the counter in the empty shop.

'Work's finished, Mum, and Adair thanks you for the sandwiches.'

'He's welcome. You should have brought him in for a nice cuppa.'

Adair and her mum sitting chatting in the front room?

Never. Her mother found it difficult to chat to the vicar. How would she cope with Adair's even more polished tones? 'He's not that kind of friend, Mum, and besides, it'll take him all the time he has left to get back to his base. If you don't need me in the shop I'll go up and have a bath.'

Flora waved her knitting. 'Really quiet day. Don't know why but customers aren't fighting to get in. I only started this sock for your dad this morning; two more rows and I'll be turning the heel.'

Daisy went to the flat, turned on the wireless and almost immediately ran back downstairs. 'Put the wireless on, Mum. No wonder the shop's quiet. The whole of Dartford must be listening to the wireless; Mr Chamberlain has resigned.'

Daisy and Flora stood in the unusually quiet shop and listened to the news with bated breath.

The Prime Minister, Neville Chamberlain, had lost the confidence of the Government and had resigned.

It appeared that what had been dubbed a phoney war was very, very real indeed. There had been questions in the papers and on the wireless about the German invasion of Norway and, more important still, about Britain's ill-fated part in the defence of that country. Now it appeared that German troops were swarming across both the Belgian and Dutch borders. In the House of Commons, Leo Amery had made a vitriolic speech against the Prime Minister and ended it by quoting Oliver Cromwell: 'In the name of God, go.'

Mr Chamberlain had gone.

Now, in almost the middle of the beautiful month of May, after countless debates and questions, King George

VI had asked Mr Winston Churchill to head a truly national government.

'I have all three of my lads in the forces,' Flora said quietly.

'You just wait, Mum, Churchill will get it all sorted. The boys will be home in no time, full of stories about their deeds of derring-do.'

'I don't give a toss about deeds, Daisy Petrie. I want my boys home in their own beds. I don't even know where two of them are.'

Daisy put her arms around her mother, who suddenly looked frail and tired. 'They're fine, Mum, but if you're on a ship, you can't pop a letter in the post. Who's going to pick it up and deliver it – a seagull?'

As she had hoped, Flora laughed. 'Oh, I'm sorry, Daisy, pet. Don't let on to your dad. You're right, o'course. Mr Churchill's the right one for the job. And don't tell your dad I were a watering pot.'

'He'll be here in a minute. Let's have a nice tea all ready for him.'

Fred had heard the news but was more positive than his wife. 'Now we can really get in and teach mighty Germany a final lesson. We thought we'd done it in the Great War but sometimes lessons needs relearning. And we're the ones to do it.'

As if there wasn't enough for the Petries to worry about, more foodstuffs were rationed. Many of the customers were stoical but a few complained bitterly and seemed to believe that Daisy could provide more if she really wanted to do so. It was hard sometimes to remain friendly and calm.

'Meat, eggs, cheese, jam, tea, milk. Wot's left for God's

sake? Rabbits and fish. If you can catch them you can eat them.'

'It's a sensible measure.' Fred was not so easy to intimidate as Flora and Daisy. 'This way everyone's looked after, and anyways, eggs and milk isn't rationed, they're allocated.'

'And wot does that mean when it's at home, Fred Petrie?'

'You can't tell a hen how many eggs she has to lay, or a cow how many pints she has to give. It all depends on supply. If there's a lot, we gets more, if the animals slows down a bit then we gets less. Whatever comes in gets divided equal. Allocated. Simple.

'Don't take no nonsense, Daisy,' Fred told her later. 'I got to queue up everywhere to get supplies, and customers is going to have to queue up to get theirs. Tell 'em there's a war on, if there's any more grumbling.'

Almost everyone accepted the growing lines outside every shop. Housewives like Flora, and Nancy Humble at the farm, had preserved fruits in their larders and jars of jam on their pantry shelves, and both shared generously. Flora looked at her diminishing stocks and decided that toast, scones, and oatcakes would be served with either butter *or* jam, never with both.

'Wish Grace were 'ere, pet. We could have encouraged her to grow strawberries. Next year Alf's putting potatoes where most of his strawberries are.'

'Maybe the war will be over by then, Mum.'

Mother and daughter smiled sadly. Each knew that it would not be over.

For weeks there was no word from any of Daisy's brothers. They were gone and no one could or would tell the Petries where they were. Rumours abounded. The war had begun badly and was taking an even more downward course. Thousands of British troops, who had gone so bravely to free Europe, were themselves now marooned on a French beach, the sea in front of them, the enemy behind them.

'No war, no fighting,' Daisy whispered one night to Rose. 'All the time we thought that nothing was happening, a bloody war was going on in Belgium, France and Holland, and our boys, and Sam maybe, were fighting there.' And where's Adair, her heart continued quietly. Not so much as a postcard had been received from him since the day they had finished the work on the plane.

A few days later the newspapers were full of the story of the rescue of British and French troops from Dunkirk.

'Our Phil's a sailor,' Flora tried to tell her customers bravely. 'Maybe he was on one of them boats as saved men, and our Sam hinted in a letter that he might be going abroad. Very keen to see a foreign country, our Sam.'

'They'll be home in no time, Flora,' said Mrs Roberts, one of the most faithful of the regulars. 'Just you wait and see if I'm right.'

She was wrong. Weeks went past and no news was received from any one of the boys.

Daisy was worried about Adair, but she reminded herself that she was only the handy mechanic who had worked on the plane with him. Had he time, he would be reassuring his family. His parents were dead but he had said nothing about other family members.

'He's a third cousin, God knows how many times removed' – she thought that was what Alf Humble had said all those long months ago. Someone had to know something about him. She would be told, all in good time.

In the meantime his suggestion that she join the WAAF went round and round in her head. According to the newspapers, girls like Daisy would be conscripted soon. Better to go, as Sam had said, without waiting to be ordered. But every time she tried to talk about war work with her parents, they changed the subject, telling her how important it was that Daisy was able to drive the van, continue with her first-aid course and dig even half-heartedly in the missing Grace's little garden. She had never once seen Megan Paterson when she had been working, and Grace had not written again. Sally, who was going from strength to strength and had even had a small part in a propaganda film, managed an occasional visit, thrilling all the Petries with her talk of plays and musicals and exciting things like film sets and real live professional actors.

'It's important war work,' Sally told her friends. 'We're going to be entertaining the troops, in hospitals and at their camps; boosting morale, it's called. Who knows, maybe even go overseas. Won't that be amazing?'

Daisy smiled and congratulated her friend. She did not say, 'I've boosted morale and helped the war effort,' but reconditioning a plane that would one day be used in the air battles that must soon take place, surely that was war work?

Like so many people in Britain, the Petries loved listening to the wireless. Fred and Daisy had been captivated by the new Prime Minister, Winston Churchill. Not only did he write superb speeches but, according to Daisy, 'He speaks them as good as an actor.' When his speeches were not broadcast they were covered in the local press and Daisy would read the paper, trying to hear the Prime Minister's voice in her head. In June, Churchill warned the nation of the battle that was about to happen and Daisy read the report of the stirring speech so often that, had she wanted to, she could have quoted it.

Greatly moved by Churchill's eloquence, Daisy was persuaded that counting rations was *not* anyone's finest hour. There must be something better.

She broached the subject with her father when they were together in the shop at closing time one day.

'Dad, I want to join the Women's Auxiliary Air Force. You have to make Mum listen to me. Ensuring that everyone in the area gets their proper rations is not enough for me. I'm a good mechanic. Adair even said he could teach me to fly.' She stopped; she had not expected that most precious secret to spill out.

Fred looked at her, both love and concern in his eyes. 'Fly, pet, fly, like a pilot in a plane?'

'Of course, Dad. Adair says I'm just as clever as some of the men he teaches. He says I'm a great mechanic.'

'Well, me and the lads taught you that, love, but a pilot in the WAAF, a lass from a shop in Dartford? He's having you on, Daisy, and so I'll tell him to his face.'

'He meant I could be a pilot, Dad; no one's saying anything about being a pilot in the WAAF. It's the RAF has pilots.'

'Happen he did mean it, you being a pilot, but he hasn't been here in weeks, and you've not heard from him, else your mum would've told me. Forget him, Daisy. His kind aren't for the likes of you. Not that you're not as good as he is, every bit, but putting water and wine together spoils both.' He looked at his daughter compassionately. 'Don't you go getting in over your head with this lad, Daisy. I know it's exciting; it's like what happens in pictures when the rich hero takes the poor girl off on his white horse to live happy. Pictures and stories isn't real, Daisy. Don't . . . no, you wouldn't run after a lad, would you?'

Daisy looked at her father, kind, caring, conscientious Fred Petrie, and knew that in many ways she was very lucky. 'Dad, me and Adair, it's not like that. We're friends is all. We worked together on the engine. Smooth as honey, it'll fly.'

His look now was shrewd. 'Then why do you want to try for the WAAF now, pet? You've no idea where he is or even if he's alive.'

The words struck Daisy like a slap and she almost reeled back. 'What a dreadful thing to say. 'Course he's alive but . . . but he's busy and . . .' Daisy stopped. In a moment she would be crying and if she started she felt that she might never stop. No word from Adair, but there had been no word from Sam or Ron or Phil either.

'We have to face facts, pet. We're all worried. Your friend is a pilot. They flew over Dunkirk helping to keep the stranded lads safe. Planes ditched, Daisy, and some got shot down.'

'You have to tell Mum. I'm going to try. None of them's dead and when Adair – *if* Adair – needs me or wants to teach me, he'll find me easy enough.'

Fred shook his head sadly but turned and left the shop. Daisy sat down and listened to his steps on the stairs.

That night Rose persuaded Daisy to go dancing with

her and some friends from the munitions factory. It was a chance for Daisy to wear an emerald-green rayon dress that Flora had altered for summer wear but which would not be out of place on the dance floor Apart from its attractive heart-shaped neckline with the yellow edging, it was spangled with white flowers, which Flora had crocheted on winter evenings. Daisy did try to enter into the spirit of the evening but she was aware that, apart from herself, everyone on the floor was actively involved in war work. She dismissed her time spent fire-watching and the hours she spent in the first-aid classes – it was not real work. Her father could talk as much as he liked about the necessity for honest shopkeepers in this time of trouble.

It's too easy, she said to herself. Apart from the few deliveries you make – and those will come to a halt if the rumours about petrol rationing are true – you don't even have to go out in the rain. Time to come to a decision.

Seeing her sister and her friends a happy part of the throng on the dance floor, Daisy slipped out. No doubt Rose would think she had found a partner in another part of the hall. The lads from Vickers were good lads and would see all the girls home safely and so she need not worry about her sister. Stan, who often partnered Rose at dances, was a favourite with all the Petries.

Daisy hurried home through streets strangely unfamiliar, the lights dimmed or non-existent. Here and there, people scurried about their business as unobtrusively as possible, and no cheery greetings rang out on the still summer air. She was relieved to see the front of the shop loom up before her and slowed her pace in case her parents were still awake. They would be sure to ask why she had had to hurry and why she was alone. She stopped at the shop window to make sure she had her key to the side door. Her little change purse with the key inside was deep down in her coat pocket and, as she stood fishing it out, she heard a strange sound coming from the alley that ran along the side of the shop.

Daisy, suddenly reminded of her father's constant warnings to her and to her sister about 'wandering home alone late at night', froze to the spot and listened more intensely.

Scuffling and rustling and occasional hushed voices.

Someone, obviously up to no good, was at the side door to the family flat. What was she to do? Her parents, if they were awake, were on the other side of the building. Even if she were to break the shop window – and how she could manage that she had no idea – it was probable that Fred would not hear it. And what if she smashed an expensive window only to discover that a courting couple were sheltering in a doorway?

Come on, Daisy Petrie, there's a war on, and you keep moaning about wanting to do something meaningful and the first chance you get – you do nothing. Holding her breath, she listened again. Was that a crackling noise? What made crackling noises? Fire.

Daisy raced round the corner.

A tea crate was on fire. Two shapes – boys, she thought – were manoeuvring the crate against the wooden door, not of the flat but of the lockup across the alleyway.

'Hey, stop!' she shouted.

The boys stopped – for a split second.

'Give 'er one, Jake,' yelled the bigger one. 'The door's catching perfect.'

Jake was obviously afraid to hit Daisy, who shook her head in mixed sorrow and anger. She knew these lads. Were they not always in the group who needed anything that was being sold at a discount? A quick glance told her that they had tried and failed to force the door open. Silly boys. Inside the lockup stood the shop van. Did they want to steal it?

She tried to scare them off. 'ARP warden'll be round here in a jiff, you two – with a policeman, I shouldn't wonder – and you two'll be in Borstal afore you—'

She had no time to tell them what they would have no time to do as the older and larger of the boys, furious both with Daisy for interfering and Jake for not 'giving her one' threw himself at Daisy, knocking her to the ground. The last thing she heard was, 'Oh Gawd, our George, you've killed her.'

Daisy woke several hours later with a splitting headache and an immediate irresistible urge to be very, very sick. The next fifteen minutes were too hideously uncomfortable for her to worry about modesty, which was just as well as she found urgent unknown hands stripping her of her nightgown and the same hands, surprisingly competent, washing her.

'Well, and won't you be after feeling a lot better now,' a soft Irish voice said. 'And such a pretty frock you were wearing too, Irish green; must say, I'm surprised to see a frock like that in a brawl.'

A brawl. Daisy tried to sit up but fell back again as the pain exploded once more in her head.

'Am I dead?' she heard her voice say.

71

'Sure, you are not, but with a bump the size of the egg on the back of your skull, I don't doubt you wish you were. There now, that's the second time I've cleaned you up in less than an hour so will you be a good girl and keep your head and your stomach quiet while I take care of someone else.'

Daisy stayed quite still; she could not have moved had she wanted to, for the nurse, if the Irish woman was a nurse, had tucked starched white sheets tightly around her.

'Good, *macushla*, now I'll be letting your mammy in for five minutes and then I want you asleep.'

Daisy lay, aware of nothing but enveloping pain, and then a voice she knew and a touch she welcomed.

'Daisy, Daisy, my dearest girl, you could have been killed by those boys. Lucky for you that Rose and Stan was there.'

Rose and Stan; boys, what boys? Daisy closed her eyes and, her hand tightly clasped by her mother, drifted off to sleep.

She woke much later in a narrow hospital bed in what she later discovered was a women's ward in the County Hospital. 'You sustained a nasty crack on your skull, Miss Petrie.' A doctor was taking her pulse and looking down at her with clear, sympathetic eyes. 'Seemingly you're quite a little heroine, preventing those young vandals from setting fire to a garage door. Could have been quite nasty. A policeman was here earlier to speak to you but we'll let you get over your unpleasant experience before we allow that.'

'My parents?'

'Will be here at the regular visiting time. Now, tell the

72

nurse if you feel like eating. The porridge isn't bad.' And he was off.

Daisy lay there remembering what had happened. The police had been informed. Who had done that? Surely not her dad? The last thing he would want would be more trouble for that particular family, who always seemed down on their luck, and Jake and George forever dodging the law.

'And if I don't really remember what happened . . .' Daisy was shocked by the way her mind, usually so aware of the difference between wrong and right, was working.

FOUR

Daisy had expected no family visits in the afternoon as the shop was always open – and busy – between four o'clock and closing time, and so she was very pleased to see Miss Partridge, complete with gloves and Sunday hat, walking smartly down the ward between the long rows of identical iron bedsteads.

She won't be coming to see me, though, Daisy thought, and closed her eyes so that Miss Partridge might not feel obliged to speak to her.

'Daisy, dear, if you're tired I'll drop this off . . .'

Daisy tried to sit up, a bad move as pain shot through her head. She did open her eyes, though.

'Oh, you poor girl, I do hope there is no serious injury.'

'No, they want to keep me until tomorrow, just to be sure, but apart from a lump and a headache, I'm fine.'

Miss Partridge pulled a chair up to the bedside. 'I was in hospital once, a long time ago, Daisy dear, and my papa brought me a magnificent basket of fruit. I'm afraid there was no fresh fruit today.'

'There's a war on,' they said together and laughed.

Daisy had been mulling over her problem all morning. Was Miss Partridge an ideal confidante?

'I did bring a box of embroidered handkerchiefs, Daisy, dear, unused, of course, and so useful in a situation like this – and Mr Fischer sent you this.' Miss Partridge opened her large, much-used leather handbag and took out a book with a beautiful Moroccan cover. 'Rather fine, isn't it. It's a copy of *Palgrave's Golden Treasury*. He says it was his first poetry book in English and so he hopes you will enjoy it. He has inscribed it to you.'

Daisy opened the book and saw thin spidery writing on the very fine inside page.

For Daisy, my very first English friend, in the hope that within its pages she will find some words to make her feel better.
   Siegfried Fischer

Her stomach churning with happiness and excitement at the amazing kindness. Daisy said, 'I don't know how to thank you both.'

'By enjoying our little gifts, my dear. Now I must be off.'

Daisy held out a hand to keep Miss Partridge near. 'You haven't asked what happened?'

'Flora told me who Rose saw. You could have been seriously injured, Daisy. George and Jake Preston are becoming quite wild and, I'm sorry, my dear, but if something isn't done about them, they'll both end up in prison.'

Daisy said nothing. She had known the boys and their mother since their arrival in Dartford six years before.

There was a rumour that, somewhere, there was a Mr Preston, but no one knew with any certainty. A second rumour had it that Mr Preston was in prison. All that the Petries knew for sure was the boys were badly cared for, and that the bigger fourteen-year-old George grew, the more impossible he was to control.

'Jake will be as wild as George if something isn't done, Daisy. He follows George like a puppy and does everything his brother tells him.'

'No, Miss Partridge. He wouldn't hit me when George told him to.'

To Daisy's surprise, Miss Partridge laughed. 'You're more than a match for Jake.'

'Not with the crowbar he was holding.'

Miss Partridge almost fell back into the chair. 'That settles it. You must report them to the police; breaking and entering, fire raising, causing serious injury – or worse.'

Daisy moved her head as if to shake it and winced as pain shot through her skull. 'No, please, Miss Partridge, those boys have nothing, and I could have handled George easily if he hadn't taken me by surprise. What would the police do with him?'

'Send him to a correctional institution, which will do him a power of good, my dear. You are much too soft-hearted.'

'And if his father is in prison? What might the police say: like father like son? Please, Miss Partridge.'

'It's you they're going to question, dear. I will say nothing to anyone. If you are absolutely sure . . .'

'Yes.' The kindness she was receiving strengthened Daisy in her purpose even more. The boy must be given a chance.

When the policeman spoke to her much later that

afternoon, perfectly aware of what she was doing, Daisy Petrie did not lie but she seemed confused.

'Medication,' said the Irish nurse, 'plus quite a knock on the head. Give her a few days.'

The might of the law withdrew.

The next day, when Daisy was allowed to return home, she found that her father did not agree with her. 'Daisy, that lad almost set fire to the lockup. There is petrol in the van – it would have gone up like a firework, and what about the houses either side?'

'He only wanted to burn the door down to get inside.'

'"Only wanted"? Are you out of your mind?'

'Dad, maybe he wanted to steal the van, maybe he thought you kept food in the lockup. They're always looking for marked-down scraps, and they're skinny as . . .' she could think of nothing thin enough, '. . . too thin,' she finished.

'Daisy, love, you're always ready for the halt, the lame and the lazy. What that lad did was criminal. He coulda killed you.'

'Never. He took me by surprise is all. I should have handled it better, Dad, chased them away. That policeman wants to put him in an approved school. There was a lad in Sam's class came out worse.'

Realising that they would never agree, Daisy was glad to go to her room for an afternoon's rest.

She was surprised to be disturbed by her mother.

'Daisy, a policeman was here. Did you tell him you couldn't remember what happened?'

'I told him that it was pitch-black out there and that I saw two shapes, possibly boy size.'

'They'll be watching them close.'

'That's good, Mum. I'll warn George and he'll stay out of trouble.'

Flora shook her head and returned to the shop.

When she could no longer hear footsteps on the stairs, Daisy carefully sat up. No explosion of pain, not even a dull ache. She manoeuvred herself out of bed.

I am, she decided, perfectly well and able to return to work. She dressed and followed her mother down to the shop. Flora was anxious but Daisy's mind was made up. Every day after that, she added another hour to her workload until she was full time again. George and Jake were nowhere to be seen. A neighbour did their mother's shopping.

'A bit busy,' she excused Mrs Preston.

'I think I'd like some fresh air, Mum. Can you manage for half an hour?'

'I managed for eight when you was in the hospital, Daisy, but don't you go tiring yourself.'

Assuring her mother that she would not strain herself, Daisy hurried out of the shop to a poorer part of the town where the Prestons lived.

George was leaning against the wall of the building, a pack of Capstan cigarettes ostentatiously visible in his hands. Slowly, so as to show her that he was not afraid – although Daisy saw the pack tremble a little – George eased his thin body off the rough brick wall and stared at her.

'Your mum home?'

He said nothing but gestured with his lit cigarette to the door.

'Gives you horrible breath for kissing,' said Daisy, and walked past him.

Mrs Preston started with fear when she saw who was standing on her doorstep, but she moved aside to admit Daisy. 'Are you going to tell the polis?'

'I'm hoping George didn't intend to put me in the hospital, Mrs Preston.'

George's mother burst into loud sobs and between sobs she told Daisy a long, heart-breaking story of how she was trying to bring up the boys on very little money and little or no support from her husband, who was, she said, in and out of prison like a yoyo. 'And when he's 'ere he's too 'ard on Georgie, brutal really. Lad's never 'ad a chance.'

'Mrs Preston, if that door had burned, the whole lockup, van and all, would have been destroyed. The van would probably have exploded and the houses on either side could have been damaged or destroyed. Have you explained that to him?'

More heart-broken sobbing. 'He never listens to me.'

'Then he'd better listen to me or I'm going straight from here to the police station.'

'I'm sorry I hit you. What d'you want to say?' George, the cigarette gone, had entered so quietly that neither had heard him.

Trying to remember that he was only fourteen years old, Daisy repeated everything that she had said to his mother. 'My sister told the police she saw a boy run off but she was too concerned about me to be sure who it was. You have a really bad reputation, George, and the policeman I talked to wants to have you sent to Borstal. What do you think of that?'

'Get three meals regular,' he said with bravado.

His mother began to wail again. They shouted at each

other for some time with neither actually paying any attention to what the other was saying.

'Be quiet, both of you,' said Daisy. 'Maybe you would be better off in gaol, George, because the way you're going, looks like you'll get there anyway. If you don't want that you have to get a Saturday job till you leave school.'

'I tried. No one wants me.'

His reputation was known all over Dartford. Was there no chance for him or his younger brother?

'Have you asked my dad?'

'You're crazy. I near set fire to his van.'

'Keep out of trouble till I sort something out or I'll be down the police station with a list of complaints. All right?'

He looked at her and she could not read his expression.

'Are you willing to try?'

She decided to be content with his nod and hurried out of the dirty, damp little house. It was worse than Grace's old home. At least Grace had tried to keep it reasonably clean and tidy.

Now to tackle her father.

Fred Petrie was not at all keen to hire a boy who was constantly in a great deal of trouble.

'Plus I don't need a lad, Daisy. What is he supposed to do?'

'I'll be called up soon, Dad. What then?'

'Then I might think of taking on someone to help out, someone dependable who doesn't half kill my daughter or set fire to my lockup.'

'If you was to bring him in an hour or so after school, Dad, then I could help him a bit.'

Eventually, much against his wishes, Fred found himself agreeing to 'try to keep that holy terror out of jail.'

'But I'm not paying him, Daisy. He can have his tea here, him and Jake, and maybe I'll pay their way into the pictures of a Saturday and we'll see how it goes. And no cigarettes smoked anywhere near my shop.'

George grumbled, but with the threat of a stint in an approved school hanging over his head, he reluctantly agreed.

So, every afternoon the Preston boys made their way from school – on the days that George bothered to attend – to the Petrie shop and were set to work tidying shelves, unloading boxes and even cleaning the van until the shop closed. Then they were taken upstairs where they scrubbed their hands in the sink before sitting down at the table where Flora took delight in putting plates of hot, nourishing food before them. George said nothing, refused all offers of second helpings and sat quietly while his younger brother tucked into an extra plate of whatever was offered.

Daisy said nothing either, but she and her mother were delighted to see the boys fill out a little.

'See, Fred, told you,' teased Flora, forgetting that she had not wanted the boys in her immaculately clean home.

'Leopards don't change their spots,' said Fred firmly.

Daisy watched quietly while she made plans and then at last her mind was made up. If she stayed at home any longer a letter would come telling her that she had been conscripted into a potato-peeling unit at some godforsaken army base somewhere or – possibly even worse – storekeeping. All of the service units she had read about were very keen on that, but Daisy Petrie had already spent more than enough time in a shop. Today, instead of eating her sandwiches behind the little curtain in the shop, she would cycle over to the Recruitment Office and attempt to make her case. She tried to feel positive. If only she had bought that stunning costume she had seen in the windows of Horrell and Goff in the High Street last week. It was so elegant, just exactly what a well-brought-up young WAAF would wear, and it was in her favourite colours. The white linen jacket was collarless and was link-buttoned, like the cuffs on Dad's best shirt. Under it was a blue and white backless, sleeveless dress in the new diagonal stripes, finished with a collar and tie. So gorgeous. With it, the model in the window wore a dashing man-type little hat pulled down over one eye. It had to be the latest word in fashion. The hat was extra, of course, but she could just have managed to scrape together two pounds, two shillings for the costume.

At the thought of spending her entire holiday savings on clothes, Daisy went hot and cold, and regretfully put the flattering picture of herself in the beautiful outfit to the back of her mind. But oh, it would have made the recruitment officer sit up and take notice.

Besides, Daze, she consoled herself, a frock like that needs the hat, good shoes and a bag, not to mention silk stockings at three shillings the pair.

Then: I bet Adair Maxwell knows lots of girls who wouldn't have to think twice about buying it.

She did not want to think about Adair and was delighted to be disturbed for the next hour by the constant ping of the shop bell.

Bernie Jones and Mr Fischer arrived together. For once Bernie was not smiling.

'Your dad around, Daisy?'

A cold hand seemed to clutch Daisy's heart. There was something about the tone of Bernie's voice. 'He's off getting his petrol ration, Bernie, but Mum's up in the flat.'

'There's a telegram from the army, lass, and maybe your mum shouldn't be alone when she reads it.' He handed her the thin buff-coloured envelope, and Daisy was surprised to notice that both his hand and hers were shaking as the envelope was handed over.

'I'll leave it here till Dad comes back. He'll only be a minute and it could be anything, couldn't it?' She turned as she saw her kind and generous friend Mr Fischer heading towards the door. 'Your paper and your . . . sausages, wasn't it, Mr Fischer? Don't go, I've got them right here.' She tried to smile cheerfully. 'Thanks, Bernie; see you tomorrow.'

The postman left quietly and Daisy went into the back shop to find Mr Fischer's sausages.

'I am so sorry, Daisy. It might be bad news, but we trust in God, not the worst news. And here is your father.' He put a half-crown on the counter. 'I can receive the change tomorrow.'

Daisy and her father, who had come in with his usual cheerful smile, which had changed immediately to a half-fearful look, were alone in the shop, the envelope on the counter between them.

Fred looked at it for some minutes without touching it.

'Put the "Closed" notice on the door, pet, and we'll take this up to Mum.'

Her heart pounding, Daisy did as she was asked. She considered adding a note to George, but decided that they would be open by the time school was out.

Priority Mr F. Petrie, 21 High St., Dartford, Kent.

Regret to inform you that your son, Sgt Samuel Petrie, is reported missing from operations on the night of 2 June.

Letter follows.

Fred had no need to read the date. What difference would that make?

'Make your mum a nice cuppa, Daisy, there's a good girl.'

Daisy went into the kitchen and tried to think of nothing but the simplest things, like making a pot of tea. Her mind was refusing to work and she closed her eyes, hoping that might clear her head. Missing, no; make tea. How? Boil water, warm the teapot, find Mum's favourite cup in case she's able to notice. Daisy found herself reacting automatically. What was that posh word Adair had used about her eyes opening and closing like those of a china doll? She could not remember, but trying to remember stopped her thinking about the pitifully thin sheet of paper with the few lines of typing on it.

'My Sam's a sergeant, Daisy.' Her parents were sitting side by side on the sofa and Fred was holding Flora's hand tightly. 'Can't drink my tea if you don't let go, Fred. Oh, this is nice, Daisy, you've put sugar in. I never take sugar, gave it up for Lent once and never went back to it.'

'The first-aid manual says to put sugar in,' said Daisy, gulping her own tea.

'Told you you'd know what to do, our Daisy.' Flora sobbed a little but drank more tea. 'A sergeant. They only made him a corporal a few months ago.'

'Sam's a good soldier, Mum.'

Flora put down her cup so fiercely that some tea slopped out into the saucer. 'He's only missing, my Sam, only missing, and there's nothing about Ron and Phil so they must be all right.'

Fred stood up. 'Maybe you should have a wee lie-down, Flora, love. Daisy, I'll mind the shop if you stay with your mum.'

Daisy stayed sitting by her mother's bed long after Flora had fallen into a fitful sleep. She forced herself to be positive. Buying the costume would have been a ridiculous waste of money. How glad she was that she had not done that. She would not be joining the WAAF, not for the present. How could she leave her parents while Sam was missing? When they heard that he had been found then she might try again, but for the moment her place, whether she liked it or not, was by her mother's side.

Was there anyone in the entire nation who was happy? Daisy found the next few months almost unbearable. Flora seemed unable to cope without news of her sons, and her care and most of the work in the shop fell on Daisy's narrow shoulders. She and Mr Fischer became even closer friends as he came into the shop almost every day and stayed to discuss news items with Daisy, and even to laugh over a programme they had both heard on the wireless. Both found Tommy Handley very funny, but they loved Mona Lott and her catchphrase, 'It's being so cheerful as keeps me going.' It was even funnier spoken in Mr Fischer's light German accent.

Each day they started up in hope when the cheerful ping of the door handle alerted them to the arrival of the postman and, at last, just as Daisy thought she would go out of her mind, there was a letter for her parents, not from the War Office, as promised, but from their middle son, Phil.

'If you trust me, Daisy, I will mind the shop while you run upstairs.'

'Can't think of anyone I trust more, Mr Fischer. I'll only be a minute.'

Daisy took the stairs to the flat two at a time. 'Mum, look, it's from Phil, from his ship.'

Flora held the letter to her heart for a moment before opening it. 'Read it to me, our Daisy. My eyes is watering.'

Daisy thought quickly. Who usually popped in at this time? The vicar? He'd be all right with Mr Fischer. 'It'll have to be quick, Mum; I've left poor Mr Fischer minding the shop.'

'He's a clever man, Daisy, very educated, your dad says, with letters an' all after his name. He'll yell up the stairs if he needs you.'

'Sorry I haven't written as I've been busy and was sick a lot on the boats at first. That's all gone now and I even walks jaunty like a real sailor. We've been in action is all I can say and you never heard the likes of the noise and I hopes you don't never hear it, but we did well. Our captain who's a really posh guy but very decent with it says we all ought to get a medal and maybe we will.

Learning to be on a ship was fun but a bit scary, like when we used to play Tarzan up the woods. Remember how you used to yell at us for jumping from tree to tree but some of the blokes I sail with has never seen a blooming tree, never mind climbed one. It's easier than the way we did it. We got this thing called a breeches buoy – looks a bit like one of your apple fritters but on a rope. It's better than Tarzan except when there's

'Next bit's scraped out, Mum, and then he talks about learning all the aeroplanes. I must go.' She handed her much happier mother the thin water-damaged sheet of paper and started down the stairs just as the siren went again.

The Petries, having no garden in which to put an Anderson shelter, had been forced to prepare a refuge room to which they could run if there was an air raid. The kitchen had only one window and only two outside walls and so they had thought that would be the best choice. But they were told that, on no account should the refuge room be on the top floor.

'Incendiary bombs will probably burn through your roof and then through to the ground floor,' they were told. 'Have you got a basement? Best place, but if not, on the ground floor.'

There was no basement but there was a storeroom between the shop and the back door, which they were told would be perfect. It had a small window, which was there only to allow a little natural light to enter from the back door and only one outside wall. The Petries put as many of the stored goods as possible into the small corridor and carried everything else, especially the tins, upstairs. Daisy did not look forward to having to carry tins downstairs each time they needed to restock but, as her father reminded her, 'There's a war on.'

Into the rather claustrophobic refuge room they put candles, matches, an ancient oil lamp and a tin of oil, several air-tight tins in which food could be stored, and bottles of water. Every night before bedtime, Flora or one of the twins filled a Thermos flask with tea and put it inside the door of the room. It had been suggested that a wireless set might be a good idea as it was likely that the family would spend several hours at a time cooped up, but there was no electrical outlet for their precious Bakelite wireless and so it remained on Grandma Petrie's old dresser in the kitchen. Instead they took playing cards and some old board games: Snakes and Ladders, and their favourite, The Farmyard Game with the awful Freddie the Fox. All of them were heartily sick of rushing into the room at the first wail of the siren, only to find that it was one more false alarm. One day soon, it would be real, if this was not the day.

But now Flora and Daisy sped down to the shop. Flora hurried to the refuge room but Daisy saw that Mr Fischer was still standing behind the counter and wearing Fred's apron. 'Oh, Mr Fischer, you should have gone to your shelter.'

'It's a street away, Daisy. I'm safer here under the counter.'

Daisy thought quickly. She locked the shop door. 'Quick, into the refuge room with me and Mum. Dad'll have gone to a shelter and there's plenty of room.'

If Flora was surprised to have one of her customers in the room with them, she showed only pleasure at seeing the old man. 'So much better than the Anderson shelter you'll have, I think, Mr Fischer.'

'Indeed, this is most luxurious, Mrs Petrie. There is an entire family of cockroaches in my shelter and various other species of entomological life.' He looked at his companions' puzzled faces and laughed. 'Sorry, ladies, old habits die hard. Creepy-crawlies, Daisy.'

'Ugh,' mother and daughter said together.

'Were you a teacher, Mr Fischer, in Germany, I mean?' Daisy asked.

Flora mumbled something about nosiness but Mr Fischer didn't seem to mind the question. 'In a way, I suppose,' was all he said.

'Let's see if that tea's kept warm, Daisy, and there's a biscuit in the tin, Mr Fischer.'

The tea was barely warm but they pretended to enjoy it and Flora asked Daisy to read their guest Phil's letter.

'Can you believe that I too played in the trees like Tarzan? I know, I look too old and stooped, but I was once a boy like Phil.'

Just then the ghastly high-pitched droning stopped and silence fell sweetly. They looked at one another, smiled, but waited for the all clear to sound before getting up and returning to the shop.

'You'll take a hot cuppa, Mr Fischer?'

'Thank you, no, Mrs Petrie. I have promised to show the vicar how to use his stirrup pump. He is determined to be the best fire-watcher in Dartford. It's not a popular job, as you know – hours and hours alone in a church tower or some such place – but he says if the vicar won't take his turn to protect the church, how can he expect anyone else to do it?'

They said goodbye and Daisy promised to see him in the morning.

She worked in the shop all the next day but he did not come. He did not come the day after or the day after that, and so, without telling her parents, Daisy went round to The Rectory to speak to the vicar. She worried that the old man might have become ill.

'Come in and sit down, Daisy.'

'He's not dead?'

'No, my dear. A large motorcar came the night before last, very late. I was on the church roof but it was still quite light, you know, and I saw it. Two men went into the building and later they came out with poor Mr Fischer.'

Daisy's world was turning upside down. 'But why? Who took him away? Were they policemen?'

Mr Tiverton patted her hand. 'I don't know, my dear. They were plainly dressed and Mr Fischer did not seem frightened or concerned. You must know that all aliens have been rounded up, especially Germans. Frankly, I'm surprised that he was here so long.'

'Where have they sent him?'

'I have no idea where he is, Daisy. Many aliens have been put into camps, some have been sent away, even as far as Australia. But many have been questioned and allowed to return home – to their home here, that is, not the country from which they originally came.'

'Or fled.'

'Indeed. Or fled.'

'When will we know?'

'Oh, Daisy, I know so little. Perhaps someone will inform his landlady; perhaps she has already been told.'

But a very angry Mrs Porter had heard nothing and was extremely annoyed. 'Best lodger I ever had. Near fifteen years he's been with me, causes no trouble, reads 'is books, ever such fat ones, listens to 'is music, bit 'ighbrow for me but nice, and pays his rent on time. They just knocked on the door, came in and went up to 'is room – I 'eard them talking, quiet, like, and then they came down, without a by-your-leave and was gone.'

'He wasn't . . . they weren't holding him, Mrs Porter?'

'No, pet. He 'ad his old leather suitcase – ever such good quality – and 'is spare clothes is gone, some photographs, I think, but none of 'is books, but then I wouldn't really know, would I?'

'If you hear anything, Mrs Porter, would you let us know? We have his ration book and he's bound to need that.'

In tears Daisy returned home.

'Alien is not a nice word,' she added after she had told her parents the news. There had to be a nicer word that meant someone from a different country.

'He'll be fine, Daisy, love. He'll write to us to ask for his ration book and then we'll be able to keep in touch.'

But he did not write and for a while the little book remained in the drawer of Fred's splendid till. Eventually Fred took it round to Mrs Porter, to keep with the rest of Mr Fischer's things, and the Petries stopped talking about Mr Fischer's disappearance; it was just one more tragedy of this ghastly war.

Daisy, however, thought of him often.

The family had grown so accustomed to false alarms that they were taken completely by surprise when the first attack actually came.

The siren sounded.

'C'mon, Daisy, run,' Fred shouted, but she went on counting cash and nodded to him, which was her way of saying, 'I'll be there in a jiff.'

But then the coppers fell from her hands and rolled in every direction across the floor as they heard an ominous droning sound, a sound that they had never heard before.

'God Almighty, Daisy Petrie, leave that bloody money and move, girl.'

Possibly more stunned by her father's language than by the sound of the planes overhead, Daisy seemed rooted until they heard another sound, a splattering sound as if the biggest hailstones the world had ever seen were being thrown ferociously at the taped windows.

'Guns, Daddy,' screamed Daisy as she vaulted over a barrel of barley, which she had been repackaging, and fled after him through the shop door. She stopped dead in the hallway, turned and ran to the stairs. 'Mum,' she screamed. 'Come down quickly.' She was leaping upstairs as she called.

Flora was on her hands and knees crawling under the kitchen table. 'I were just peeling potatoes, Daisy, and the table was right here.'

Daisy got down and held out her hand. 'We've got to go to the refuge room, Mum; it's safer. C'mon, before Dad comes to fetch us.'

Still clutching her potato peeler, Flora allowed herself to be led downstairs. They waited for a breathless moment just inside the shop, listening to the planes, and there was Fred, obviously about to look for them. Unceremoniously, Fred grabbed them both, pulled them through the back door and shoved them into the old storeroom. They slumped to the floor and then Fred, red in the face from exertion and sweating with fear for his family, said very quietly. 'I panicked there, us not being in the same place.' He turned on Flora, in anger. 'What was you doing, not running down? You know the drill. First sound, wherever you are you head for this place.'

'I were under the table.'

'Gimme the knife, Mum,' said Daisy, but her speaking brought her father's wrath down on her.

'And you, Daisy. You move when that damned thing goes. My God, I haven't smacked you since you was about five but you do that again, my girl . . .' He could not continue but reached over and awkwardly patted her foot, the only part of her he could reach.

Daisy stayed where she was on the floor waiting for her heart to stop beating so quickly. She could not believe how terrified she had been. Was it fear for herself or for her mother? As if she could read her daughter's mind Flora reached out and took one of her hands. 'Is this the real war then, Fred?'

She was answered by the sound of an explosion, and she burst into tears. Fred stopped glaring at his daughter and turned to comforting his wife. 'There, love, don't hear no more planes. Blighters have gone over. Be battering London by now.'

'But it's broad daylight, Dad. There's people out shopping, children playing in the parks. It's inhuman, that's what it is.'

'It's war, Daisy.' He was quiet for a moment and then voiced all their thoughts. 'Rose'll be all right; they have a big shelter at Vickers.'

No one spoke until the all clear sounded. They sat, each alone with his or her worries, but their hopes and prayers were for the same family members.

'I never locked the door, Dad, but I don't think it would have made much difference.'

They discovered that the front door of the shop had been blown off its hinges and several windows were smashed. The barrel of barley lay on its side and what was left of the barley was scattered, with everything that had been on the shelves, all over the floor.

'Hope you got a lot of that barley packaged, our Daisy,' said Fred with an attempt at a smile. 'No, never mind the brush now, pet, George'll do it. He likes things tidy. How about making a pot of tea? In fact, if the Christmas sherry bottle is whole, we'll all have a snifter. Your mum's shaking like a blancmange.'

He handed her an unopened bottle of brandy that he unearthed from under the counter.

'First-aid manual, Daisy, love. Brandy for emergencies and this is one stinker of an emergency. You go on up with your mum. Make her sip some of that, even if it makes her cough, and just talk to her while I have a look outside. The joiner'll be busy so I'd best get to him quick as.'

Daisy was only too happy to return to the family flat. The last thing in the world she wanted to do was look outside. Bullets had rained down on the street. What if someone had been walking there?

But Dartford was not too badly damaged on that first raid. Chimney pots, doors windows, garden walls, bicycles had all suffered, but there were no major casualties.

Fred, for the moment unsure whether or not he should have sought shelter or gone out into the fray – after all, he was an ARP warden – left his daughter to begin the clean-up once he was sure that Flora was fine. He picked up his respirator, although for the life of him he could not smell gas. The unpleasant smell of burning accompanied him as he headed off through the smoke-filled streets to the ARP station. What could he say? He had acted on instinct and he hoped that his instincts were right.

'You're only expected to patrol when you're on duty, Fred, and this afternoon wasn't your hours. We got off light but this shows the way it's going. We're right between Herr blooming Hitler in Germany and Mr Churchill in London, and the German Air Force'll fly over us every time they want to take a poke at him.'

'Then likely we'll be 'it on their way back too.'

'Afraid so, Fred. Lots to look forward to, I don't think. How's the missus? Any word on your lads?'

'There's a war on, Harold. They got more to do than write letters. Flora's fine, a real brick, and Daisy and Rose is a great support.'

'Daisy not left the nest yet?'

'No, she knows what she wants; biding her time, I'd say. I'd best get off home. Got next week's pulses all over the place. Where I'm going to get more at such short notice, I do not know. At least the weather's fine and the ladies isn't making thick soups.'

The men said goodbye and Fred, his uneasiness at rest, hurried off home, via the home of the nearest joiner, and was delighted to meet Rose on the way. She looked rather shaken but made no complaint.

'Going in for an extra shift, Dad. We are really increasing production.' She stopped suddenly right in the middle of the High Street, and drew his attention to a large sign on the King's Head Inn. 'Look there, the very thing. You should take Mum out for lunch one day soon. That'll cheer her up. You two's done nothing for months.'

Fred's gaze followed her pointing finger. They had just experienced the first raid of the war but a sign showed that life had to try to go on.

'Luncheons for one shilling and sixpence, and they're advertising Loman Ales. We could all go on Sunday after church. Do us good. Six shillings for four and then a few shillings for drinks and a tip. Your mum couldn't do that at home. I'd have walked right past that, Rose. May I take you to luncheon on Sunday, madame?'

'You're ever so kind, sir,' she teased, fluttering her eyes at him, 'but I can't. I'm going to teach physical jerks at the factory. Big posters all over the walls. "Fitness in Defence", they're calling it, and besides, we're probably doing an extra shift, Sunday. You should do some classes with the wardens; some of them look like they need exercise. It's direct from the Government, Dad, and I bet you can still shin up a tree faster than any of us.'

'I think I've enough to do, Rose Petrie. I'm needed in the shop and will be even more when Daisy goes, and now that the raids have started I'll spend hours patrolling my area and helping when I can, and assessing damages and reporting it when I can't.'

They had reached the back door of the shop. Just inside was the staircase to the flat. Fred moved to put his key in the lock.

'What do you mean, Dad, Daisy going? She hasn't said nothing to me. Has she had a letter?'

'Not yet. She was excused with the boys away and me needing another driver, but your mum can manage the shop and, I hates to say it, but them Preston lads is good workers. We've even had a couple of Mum's

96

beetle drive ladies saying they could use a few hours' work. Daisy wants to join the WAAF and we can't hold her back.'

FIVE

The film was everything they had hoped it would be. It was called *Storm in a Teacup* and was touted as being very amusing. It was. Daisy thought it hilariously funny and Vivien Leigh the most beautiful woman she had ever seen. Sally, though, was still very faithful to her first favourite, Margaret Lockwood.

Daisy would not be so juvenile as to tell Sally, but it had also been really lovely to spend an entire evening with her. Their old school friend, Sally, a rising actress, was more glamorous and elegant than ever. She might be well on her way to becoming a real star, but inside, Sally seemed little changed since the days when they had played together in the playground or on the floor of the projectionist's room at the cinema.

'I don't think we've had an evening – all four of us – since that party you gave for me, Daisy, just before war was declared.'

'Feels as if that was a long time ago. Do you think we all seem much older because of the war? Don't know about you, Sally, but I feel a hundred years old sometimes.'

'You don't look it. I miss us all getting together. Don't

know what's happening to Grace. I don't think she's forgiven me for laughing at Sam, and now he's gone too.'

'Missing, not gone, Sal. We'll soon find out where he is. I think Grace has what our lovely vicar calls issues, things, probably from her early childhood, which she has to come to terms with. Maybe she'll tell us, maybe she won't. She knows we're here.'

'Hope you're right. Gosh, I forgot to tell you. Dad says he's getting *Wings of the Morning* back for reshowing. Did you see it? It was the very first colour film made in England. You'll love it, lots of horses and – Henry Fonda.' Sally said his name as if it were written in huge lights before her. 'His eyes are incredible, look right into you. He is just so . . . so . . .'

Such intensity made Daisy slightly uncomfortable. She decided to tease Sally. 'Sally Brewer, you haven't, you know . . .?'

'Wash your mouth out with soap, Miss Petrie. I'm saving myself for Clark Gable.'

'Now you're talking,' said Daisy, who had sat, motionless and almost breathless, through *Gone with the Wind* three times, and would probably have seen it more often but for the fact that it had to be sent to the next cinema on a long list of waiting customers.

They were laughing the way they had laughed together as schoolgirls. It felt good.

'Damn.' Sally had tripped over a rough part of the pavement.

Daisy grabbed her. 'Are you all right?'

'Fine, frightened the life out of me, that's all. I really hate being in the dark. Feeling your way around, not knowing who is near you, is one of the worst parts of blackouts. Creepy.'

Daisy could think of nothing to say.

They had reached the Brewers' little house. 'Come in and have some hot chocolate.'

'Can't, Sally. Dad's in the markets tomorrow and customers'll be at the door before eight.'

They hugged, promised to see each other before too long, and Sally let herself into her house. Daisy hurried on towards home, being as careful as she could, still moving with the many other people who had been at the cinema. In less than five minutes she would be climbing the stairs to her comfy bed.

The air-raid sirens seemed to blare from every factory in Dartford. The frightening noise filled the air and sent people stumbling and running towards the nearest shelters. Dartford had prepared well, and there were excellent shelters on the streets and in the basements of department stores.

Daisy found a seat beside a rather large but very pleasant woman, who smelled, unfortunately, of disinfectant, and prepared to wait it out with as much fortitude as possible. There was a light, limited but still a light, and seats. So many people had packed into the shelter that it was warm. Even inside this concrete box, however, they could hear the droning of enemy planes and the ack-ack and rat-tat, rat-a-tat of guns, both friend and enemy. Low booming sounds were heard and then the floor of the shelter seemed to shake as something heavy thudded down near to it.

'That's a bomb,' came a frightened man's voice. 'Right beside us. God 'elp us. It goes off and we're all done for. I'm getting out.'

He tried to force his way to the entrance but was stopped by several men. 'You're safer in here, lad. Sit yourself down and think of something else. Anyone know a good song?'

Immediately a rousing chorus of 'Pack Up Your Troubles in Your Old Kit Bag' began. The air was soon full of singing voices, the smells of unwashed bodies and of too much cheap perfume. Not a nice mix, thought Daisy, as she tried to think calm thoughts. She was beginning to relax when there was a piercing scream.

'Help her, help her, my sister's having a baby.'

The singing grew quieter and quieter and above it rose the distressed sounds of someone young trying hard not to scream.

'Quiet, everyone,' came a voice of obvious authority. 'Anyone here with any medical knowledge?'

The woman beside Daisy sighed, said, 'No rest for the wicked,' and stood up. 'I'm a hospital nurse,' she said. 'Anyone else know anything, even how to hold someone's hand?'

Feeling as cold as ice, Daisy forced herself to follow the nurse. Holding hands I can do, holding hands I can do, she repeated to herself as she found herself, the nurse, and a thin woman kneeling on the cold cement floor beside two very frightened young girls, one of whom was possibly about to have a baby.

The thin woman looked at the girl and then at the nurse and whispered, 'I've 'ad three as lived; should remember something.'

'Very encouraging,' said the nurse. 'How far on?' she asked the young woman and when she said nothing she asked, 'Come on, pet, seven months, eight?'

'She doesn't know.' The sister was stroking the whimpering girl's forehead.

'Is her husband here?'

'Missing since Dunkirk.'

Daisy was holding the pregnant girl's cold and very small hand. *She's younger than I am; she has a missing husband and she's worried sick and terrified of having a baby.* 'There, there,' she soothed. 'It's going to be all right. This lady is the best nurse in the whole of Kent, you know, and she'll take super care of you.'

'Good girl,' whispered the nurse. 'Carry on talking to her while I have a look. Shine that light here, please, Warden, and would you hold your coat up to give us some privacy.'

The girl had stopped sobbing and although she moved in embarrassment and discomfort, she seemed to be calmer. Her sister kneeled on the floor beside her, holding her other hand, and Daisy chattered about the film she had just seen.

'We was there,' said the sister. 'Rex Harrison's ever so 'andsome, isn't he?'

There was no time for Daisy to reply as the nurse had straightened up with a smile. 'Baby's in no hurry, love. False alarm. You had a bit of a fright but everything's fine.'

Daisy's first emergency was over and she hoped she had been of some use.

'Thanks, pet.' The tired nurse, who had arranged with the ARP warden that the girl would be taken home by car, turned to Daisy as they stood together outside the shelter watching them leave. The all clear must have sounded but neither was aware of actually hearing it. 'Our "three as lived" wasn't much of a bargain; God knows what she'd have done if that child had been in labour, but you kept your cool. Well done. If my bike hasn't been pinched, I'll be in bed and sound asleep in five minutes. Far to go?'

'Just down the High Street. Can't say as I really enjoyed that, Nurse, but I did like working with you and helping a bit. Good night.'

'Go careful, lass.'

'You too.'

Daisy managed to straighten her cramped limbs. Somehow she felt a bit flat, though she was sure that she should have been exhilarated. After all, had she not actually helped a young pregnant woman? She had stayed calm. She prayed with all her might that the baby would grow up to be a happy person, surrounded by love, if not by wealth, and that the father would return safely from some prison camp. She followed the crowds along the pavement. How quickly the days had grown shorter. Surely at this time only a few weeks ago she had cycled across Dartford Heath in lovely summer twilight.

She was so busy thinking that she had bumped into a bulky figure without noticing. 'I'm so sorry,' she began just as the man, for it was a man, started to say exactly the same thing. They laughed and began again but then stopped, again in tandem. She would know that lovely voice anywhere. She had not looked up into his face and could scarcely bring herself to do so now. Adair . . . It was Adair Maxwell and he was very solidly and healthily alive.

'Well, if it isn't my favourite aircraft mechanic. Daisy, how absolutely splendid to bump into you. I was on my way to your shop, hoping someone would still be awake, when the raid started. We ran and literally fell into a trench in the park. I can still smell it so I apologise. Now I have to get some chums back to base.' He gave her no time to talk. 'Are you alone? Are you on your way home? We'll drop you off, if you don't mind perching in a military vehicle – if it hasn't been totalled, that is. Not good to be out alone in a blackout.'

'No, yes,' she began but he had taken her arm by the elbow. Sally would be impressed. They had seen Trevor Howard hold a woman's arm like that in a film.

Two other men in air force uniforms were with Adair, 'Toby and Simon,' he introduced them, 'but ignore them; they're not fit for you to know, especially after they've been face down in a ditch.'

Toby and Simon laughed. 'We didn't believe there was an angel in Dartford who made sick planes better,' one of them said. 'But, wicked Adair, why did you fail to tell us that the angel had soft brown hair and lovely, lovely eyes?'

'Because I didn't want you two to know, and as for the angel bit, I told you I never lie. Upbringing.'

'Me, I always lie,' said either Simon or Toby, and the other immediately said, 'Upbringing,' and all three laughed.

Their vehicle was still in one piece although they had been very lucky as there was a large hole in the road almost beside it.

The airmen looked, without speaking, at the hole.

'Right, boys,' said Adair after a few moments of deep thought, 'best to lift it.'

To Daisy's amazement, they picked up the small truck

or Jeep or whatever it was and carried it over the hole to an undamaged stretch of road.

Adair then lifted Daisy into the back of the vehicle and turned to the others. 'I need to talk to Daisy, lads. One of you two drive, and I suggest that means the one who's drunk the least.'

He then gave them directions to Daisy's home and with something of a screech and a squeal of tyres, they set off.

'How are you, Daisy?'

'I was . . . we were all worried . . . Alf and Nancy, I mean.'

'It's been hell,' he said, and then went quiet.

Daisy, so aware of him that she was scarcely able to breathe, plucked up courage to speak. 'You were at Dunkirk. We read Mr Churchill's speech in June. It was wonderful.'

He grabbed her hands and, aware that he did not know that he was hurting her, Daisy did not struggle.

'Dunkirk was a nightmare, not just the hours but the scenes we saw, the knowledge of how little we were able to do, watching men drowning or being strafed as we tried to fight off the Luftwaffe. I don't want to talk about it . . .' He gulped. 'But I want you to believe that in the past two months, if I had been able to get back to The Old Manor, I would have been there.'

She said nothing because she did not have the words but she continued to hold his hands. She was in the cockpit with him, looking down at the water tinged with blood, seeing heads bobbing up and down, hearing cries for help. Was Sam there? Was Phil?

'Do you believe me, Daisy?' he broke the silence.

She was startled, so far into his scenario had she gone. 'Of course, and I'm pleased that you are safe.'

'Watch out, you idiot.' The voice came from the front.

'Sorry, but damn it, I can't see a bloody thing. Grandfather said that someone used to run in front of him with a lamp. Where's the bugger when I need him?'

'Language, language, lady present. I apologise for my . . . associates,' said Adair, and Daisy laughed. Never before had she been called a lady. It sounded rather nice.

The laughter had lightened the atmosphere. 'I have a forty-eight-hour pass, Daisy. I rang Alf to let him know that I was coming. We need to get her up tomorrow. Will you come?'

'To see her fly?'

'Well, yes, but to fly with me. There's nothing like a first flight, Daisy. I can't explain what it feels like to be up there looking down and looking up too. It can't be explained, only experienced. Are you free, Daisy, for the afternoon at least?'

'Yes,' she said, 'of course.' She would worry about Saturday being the shop's busiest day later.

Flora still spent a great deal of time looking out of the windows and listening for the postman, but she determined to try to be brave and not to allow her rising despair to blight the lives of the already suffering members of her family she had around her. Usually a whirlwind of activity, she sat quietly in her front room or in her kitchen and allowed the rooms to fill up with the remembered happy voices of a large family. Two adults and five children had lived and laughed and, yes, sometimes cried in this tired-looking flat. 'I'll make new curtains,' she told the echoes with a sniff. 'New curtains'll brighten us all up and my Sam'll notice, although I'll have to hold 'em up under Phil's nose. Daisy'll help me; good with her fingers, our Daisy, comes of being small built, I suppose.'

She stood up, determined to pull herself together and stop moping. Women all over England were waiting and hoping, and here was Flora Petrie behaving as if she was the only one entitled to twiddle her fingers. First step was to give Daisy the afternoon off.

Flora sat down abruptly. 'I'm going to lose her too, my baby. That pilot lad'll fill 'er head with dreams an' we won't be able to hold her down. She'll fly like his damn plane.'

'Time for a cuppa, Mum?' Daisy had come up from the shop.

With an incredible force of will, Flora stood up and smiled. 'I was just thinking, pet, that we need new curtains in the front room – cheer it up a bit for the boys coming home.'

'Great idea, Mum. I'll give you a hand.'

'Not this afternoon, you won't. You'd best tidy yourself up if you're going flying.' She lifted a folded newspaper and held it out. 'Look, there's an ad in the *Chronicle*. Heddles on Lowfield Street's got flannel slacks at five shillings the pair; lovely turn-ups on the legs, very smart. Perfect for flying. Be a bit windy up there, I should think.'

'Oh, Mum, thank you.' Daisy held out her arms and her mother moved quickly to hug her.

'Dad and me'll pay. Go on down and tell him you're running over to Heddles and I'll take him down a cuppa in two ticks.' Before Daisy had a chance to reply, she carried on. 'Grey or dark blue would be ever so smart and useful, and you could wear them with your pale blue blouse and my dark blue cardigan.'

'But, Mum, that was your Christmas—' began Daisy.

'It's a bit tight on me, love, and you'll be a right smasher in it. When I finish these socks I'll knit you a new one. I found some ever so pretty buttons in my button tin, never used.'

Daisy hugged her again. 'Thanks, Mum,' she whispered, and turned and hurried back to the shop. She could be forgiven for wondering if the airmen and her mother were right about her appearance. The lads hadn't called her a smasher exactly but they had sort of said she was pretty, hadn't they?

A few moments later, Flora heard the friendly ping of the doorbell. She stood for a moment with her arms tightly wrapped around as much of her body as she could reach before taking a deep breath and going into the kitchen. Life had to go on.

Daisy cycled out to Old Manor Farm. Her dad, as the van owner, was only allowed two hundred miles a week, and deliveries on two days could easily take care of that. Daisy used a rather elderly bike that had a large basket on the front for local deliveries these days, but she rode her own lighter one for the trip out to the farm.

As she cycled along leafy country lanes, hearing only the occasional sound of growing lambs plaintively reminding their mothers that lunch time had arrived, and smelling the clean, warm smell of ripening crops, she hoped fervently that the air would not be filled with the shrieking of the sirens. Hardly likely, she decided, that a Messerschmitt would come speeding towards her

108

across buttercup-filled, rolling meadows. Her very flattering new flannels would be absolutely ruined if she were forced to dive into the ditch.

She scanned the blue sky above her, wondering if she might see Adair and his beautiful plane, but only an occasional inquisitive bee circled her head before zooming off in disappointment.

The plane was not in the stable yard but on the long driveway that led to the moth-balled manor house.

'Runway,' explained Adair as Daisy got off her bicycle and put it down on the grass under a brilliantly flowering rhododendron bush.

She had not expected him to compliment her on her new outfit but still felt a tiny awareness that he did not.

'How did it go?'

He smiled. 'How do you know it went?'

'You look . . . pleased.'

'Put this on and climb aboard.' To her surprise and intense pleasure he handed her a real flying helmet. Daisy felt that she might choke with pleasure and excitement.

'Is that cardigan all you've got? It's cold up there.'

Daisy was crushed. All she had thought of was her appearance and now she had shown how stupid she was. She should have thought, should have known. How many pictures of pilots had she seen, and every one wrapped up warmly against penetrating cold?

He was shrugging off his jacket. 'Here, put this on. I'm sorry, I should have brought you something. We cover ourselves from head to toe when we're up: one-piece suit, no draughts.'

She looked at his elegant slacks, and the sweater, obviously fine cashmere, that he was wearing with it.

'This isn't serious flying, Daisy, and I have another jumper in the cockpit. We won't be up long enough to freeze.' He was laughing and she tried to join in, all the while hoping that he was right.

She began to pull herself up but was so surprised by what she saw that she almost fell into the cockpit and, for a moment, lay awkwardly on the wing unable to move.

'Like it? Perfect name, considering everything. Shall I give you a push?'

She wanted to say yes, but to push her he would have to touch what she considered to be a very personal part of her anatomy and she knew she would die if he were to do that. 'No, it was just such a surprise. Thank you.'

Adair stepped back as she hauled herself up and into the co-pilot seat. He had a blue and white handkerchief in his hand and he leaned over and very carefully dusted the little painting on the nose. 'Simon painted the flower; good, isn't it? He was at the Slade when war broke out. But I managed the name. *Daisy*. We christened her properly, but you'll have to wait for your bubbly till I get more leave.'

He seemed not to expect an answer and so Daisy stayed silent. He had named his plane Daisy, after her. Could life get any better?

It could, because just a few minutes later Alf was there at the nose. He rotated the propeller and skipped onto the grass. While telling Daisy what he was doing with every move, Adair pressed a button and the engine fired into life. The plane began to move straight as an arrow along the grass verge of the driveway and then, before it reached the gates and the road that ran past the estate,

110

it appeared to lurch or hiccup, and Daisy's stomach – in fact everything in the lower half of her body – seemed to move around and . . . they were in the air.

'Dear old Alf's run back towards the house, Daisy,' shouted Adair through the speaking tube. 'Give him a wave.'

Daisy looked out over the side. The farmhouse was a child's toy below them. On the road in front of it stood a doll-like man waving a red handkerchief. Daisy waved back enthusiastically now that her organs seemed to have found their proper places again. She put out a hand in an attempt to touch a puffy cloud that floated beside them and drew it back in quickly. How cold it was.

'There's the Darent, Daisy, and over there, that really wide one is the Thames.'

'I'm a bird, I'm a bird,' she called, and the air stole the words out of her mouth as Adair laughed.

'Me too,' he shouted, and Daisy felt somehow warm and very happy. How could the sound of a voice warm her?

It was time to descend and the ground seemed to rush up to meet them instead of waiting patiently for them to land.

How could she thank him for the experience? How could she possibly explain the feeling, the exhilaration, to her family? Never, never would she forget that patch-work stretched out below them, or the feeling that only she and the birds knew what it was like to fly.

'Do you think birds think about the beauty of the earth as they fly over it, Adair?'

'Too busy worm-spotting, I should think,' he answered practically, and she laughed a little shame-facedly.

'You're a natural, Daisy. Next leave, I'll give you a

lesson, but the war's hotting up, and it will be worse than Dunkirk; who knows when I'll be able to get away?'

'I understand. But I've made up my mind about what I want to do, not just because of today, but my mum's beginning to be more her old self, able to cope a bit more, though she can't fool me that she's not worrying about the boys.'

'Lucky lads,' he said, and his voice was sad.

'I'll worry about you, Adair Maxwell.' Oh God, she hadn't meant to say that, all serious. 'And so will Alf and Nancy,' she added quickly.

She shrugged herself out of his fine leather jacket, aware that she had really enjoyed the feel of it around her, the warmth from his body still in the fur lining. 'I'd best go. Wait and see, there'll be an air-raid warning before I get home and everything'll be spoiled if I have to sit for hours in a ditch.'

'Be safe, Daisy Petrie,' he said as she mounted her bicycle.

'Be safe, Adair Maxwell,' she replied as she cycled off down the driveway, wanting desperately to turn round for one final look – at the *Daisy*, of course, she reminded herself – but determined not to.

Her parents and Rose were obviously thrilled to hear of her first flight and the uniqueness of the event certainly took Flora's mind off her worries, at least for a time. Fred had to leave for ARP duty but Daisy assured him that she could tell him all about it when he got home and meanwhile she enjoyed answering all her mother's questions.

'Is it cold up in the air, love? Did you feel sick like when you were on that whirly thing at the funfair?'

Daisy, who had to keep pinching herself to make herself

believe that it had actually happened, smiled and said, 'Yes to question one, and no to question two. I can't begin to imagine what it's like in the winter but Adair let me wear his jacket, lovely soft leather and with real fur inside. Ever so cosy. Oh, and I had this leather helmet, bit like our gas masks but with bigger goggly eyepieces. Wind makes your eyes water and you can't fly if you can't see where you're going. Guess what I saw from up there. The River Thames and the Darent, and even the salt marshes, and Alf's farm and him waving a big red hankie at us. It was the prettiest picture I ever saw in my life. Adair flew over the church and if it was night we would have seen Mr Tiverton up there fire-watching on the tower. What a surprise if he'd seen Daisy Petrie flying over him. I'll never forget today, not if I live to be a hundred years old.'

Rose finished plaiting her long fair hair, which she had to tie up for safety at the factory, and leaned forward. 'Will he take you up again?' She was as thrilled as her parents at Daisy's adventure.

'Better.' Daisy leaned forward on the sofa. 'He says he'll teach me to fly. Easier than the van, he says, and I've had a good look at the controls. Only thing really that I don't have in the van is a compass because you have to know which direction you're flying in or you'd get lost. When in doubt, look for a river, is what Adair said.'

'Oh, you are brave.' Rose began to speak just as ear-splitting blasts on what Fred had told them was a 'fixed-pitch' hooter sounded, followed by sharp blasts from police and wardens' whistles. Flora covered her ears and seemed to shrink inside herself but the family were better prepared by now, and had become more accustomed to reacting promptly.

'C'mon, Mum, it'll be over in a jiff,' whispered Rose, who had been told at the factory that hearing the hooter at the Burroughs Wellcome works meant that the enemy were dropping deadly flying bombs. These bombs were huge cylinders, which descended quickly but silently.

Rose kept her worries to herself, and quickly and quietly they got into their shelter. It now held magazines and playing cards, air-tight tins and jars filled with Flora's scones and whatever fruit she had been able to get, on this occasion apples. Flora's knitting was there, and the three women sat quietly and chatted while Flora tried to concentrate on the cardigan she was knitting.

'What pretty lilac wool, Mum,' said Rose. 'Who's it for? Refugees?'

'Oh Lord, I never thought of them, poor souls. Next time, love. This one's for Daisy. I thought as how you'll be wearing blue all the time when you go off, you might be glad of another colour and it will look nice with your new slacks.'

'Oh, Mum, you are lovely,' said Daisy, and she leaned across her sister's long legs to hug her mother. 'But who says I'm leaving? I haven't applied for anything and the Government doesn't seem in any hurry to use me. But never mind that, I thought any time you had, you was going to make curtains.'

'First things first and I haven't got any material yet. I've been checking a new source but there's a lot of work involved preparing and I'll do the cardy first.'

The twins looked at each other and it was obvious that their thoughts were identical. 'Mum, you haven't found a market that sells the silk that's used for lining coffins? That would be so awful.'

"Course, I haven't.' She looked slightly guilty. 'It's not actually muslin, which, by the way, my dears, would make ever such lovely undies, but it's as good as, and it's used . . .'

Two pairs of wide eyes, one pair blue, one brown, were gazing at her, forcing her to tell the truth.

'. . . butcher's wrap . . .' Daisy and Rose covered their ears but they still heard, '. . . carcasses in it. It's lovely quality but needs a lot of soaking and, girls, I wouldn't make you new undies, unless you need them, just new curtains. Soon we'll be grateful for anything we can get. I'm sure you've grown again, Rose, and a new coat will cost at least twelve pounds and heaven knows how many coupons. I'll let down your winter coat and I'll try to find a nice piece of contrasting material for a new hem, collar and cuffs. Fake fur would be classy, don't you think, or a nice bit of black velvet. Black's ever so smart with grey.'

'I'll be fine, Mum, and I have enough coupons saved for a new coat. Please alter that one for Daisy.'

'She's talking too much, too quickly, Rose,' said Daisy when they were finally able to get off to bed. 'Anything to avoid thinking about what's really bothering her. What are we going to do?'

'Not a problem for you, Daisy, if you go off with the WAAFs. I don't blame you, not for a second. If Vickers would release me, I'd be off like a shot. They need drivers in the army, did you hear? And I know I'm a good one, and I can fix the engine too.'

'Adair says it's hotting up; worse than Dunkirk, he says, and that was bad. The country'll want both of us, Rose. Me first, probably, since you're actually churning

115

out munitions and being really useful. I can't leave Mum, not unless I get conscripted. She depends on me.'

'Too much, Daisy. She's always expected you to be there, doing the shop, delivering orders, fixing the blooming van. We're all going to leave her; it's the natural way of things, so join up while I'm still here.'

Daisy was quiet for a while. Was Rose right? Should she enlist and hope that Flora would cope without any of her brood? Adair and Sam thought she should. Flying. That surely was an impossible dream. Even if she joined the WAAF, women did not fly planes; they worked on them, keeping them and their male pilots in the air.

She lay down, covering herself with her quilt. 'Rose, can you imagine anything more wonderful than being able to fly?'

Rose smiled. 'No, I can't,' she said with a giggle, 'especially if the teacher's someone you fancy like mad.'

Daisy shot up in the bed. 'Rose Petrie, no I don't. Is that all you factory girls talk about all day, fellas? Me and Adair, it's different. He sees me as a mechanic what could help with his engine, and me, I see him as a toff as owns a plane.'

And as she lay down again she felt rather ashamed of herself. She knew perfectly well that her feelings for the 'toff' were changing and softening.

SIX

There was no time to think of flying lessons in the next few weeks. The phoney war was well and truly over. Night after night, and even day after sunny day from late June onwards, the RAF battled it out against the German Luftwaffe in the skies above southern England. There were rumours that the enemy forces wanted to destroy as many British fighter planes as they could in as short a time as possible so as to make an armed invasion a definite plan of action.

The air-raid sirens sounded in deadly earnest almost every day or night, and Daisy had long since given up all dreams of being taught to fly. She felt as if she were the most incredibly selfish person in the whole world. Every day Adair, and men like him, challenged the enemy and risked their lives in a superhuman effort to keep Britain safe; all Daisy Petrie could think of was that he had not returned to give her a flying lesson. Surely she would forget the little she had learned. Was there nothing she could do?

She scoured the newspapers in an attempt to find a reasonably close flying school. People who were not in the air force had learned to fly, therefore there must be schools, or – horrible thought – were all flyers rich men who taught one another?

One evening she did find a small newspaper advertisement at the very bottom of a page. 'Flying lessons, experienced trainers, three guineas per hour.'

Daisy groaned. That was a fortune, more than a whole week's wage. Where would anyone find money like that? She could not possibly ask her father. Then another fabulous thought came: what if she were to work at the school in return for lessons? But when she looked closely at the advertisement she saw that it would take her most of a day merely to get to and from the location of the aerodrome.

'You'll just have to hope he comes back soon,' she told herself, and sat down with a thump on her bed.

She laughed, remembering how she, Rose and their brothers used to play as children. They could be anything, do anything. One day they were knights in shining armour jousting with the enemy, who always lost, and next day they were cowboys galloping across the plains, always on white horses. The bad guys stood no chance against the white-hatted cowboys.

Her bed became a plane. She sat there, going through all the motions she had seen Adair perform, hearing his melodic voice in her mind; what speed had he said? If she could not have a plane, she would do the next best thing.

Her trusty old bicycle became an Aeronca, which she named *Adair*, but naturally told no one. Up and down the roads she went, imagining herself gaining speed and lifting off. She played the same game with the van, keeping the windows wide open on even the windiest, rainiest day and all the time, from switch on to switch off, she practised flying a plane. Until Adair came back, that was the best she could do.

Every time planes were heard or seen in deadly combat in the sky above Dartford, Daisy prayed that, if he were up there and surely he must be, he would be safe.

It became known that Britain had a brilliant weapon at its disposal, a priceless asset called radar. Radar constantly scanned the skies over the sea between Britain and mainland Europe for approaching planes. When planes were spotted a highly skilled ground control system sent details of the exact position of enemy aircraft to the RAF pilots.

Dartford came in for more than its share of air raids as the enemy planes passed over its streets both on their way to London and on the survivors' way home.

On the morning after a particularly intense raid, Fred took over the shop while Daisy went to the post office to buy stamps.

'Have a gander round, Daisy, love, see wot's wot, afore your mum goes to her bingo. Don't want 'er seeing anything that'll worry 'er.'

To be out of doors felt wonderful. Daisy walked along Spital Street and onto the High Street. Her heart sang with joy when she saw that the fifteenth-century Holy Trinity Church was unscathed. Five hundred years, give or take a year or two, it had stood there. Daisy felt that she would be content to live in Dartford always. She loved its mixture of ancient and modern buildings, its unappealing built-up areas, and its wide green spaces. But she knew that she would be compelled to leave when she was called up for war work, and she would go willingly. This summer she had learned so much, not only about planes, but about herself. Would she be afraid to join the war? She hoped not, but if she was, she would do her best to hide it. The raids of the next few weeks tried everyone's patience. 'I've had it,' moaned Daisy. 'I'm tired of being stuck in the shop or in that airless, windowless refuge room. Almost every time I've been out for the past three weeks I've ended up diving into a shelter.' She remembered her splendid feelings as she had contemplated leaving home to do something special and wished she could reignite them. How she wished it were all over or, even better, that it had never started. She continually asked herself, why do people fight with one another? She could not give herself an answer.

'Me an' all, Daisy,' complained Rose, who was relaxing at home, for once. 'Goodness knows, I like a lot of the folk I work with but I sometimes feel I'm spending more time in the factory than at home. I'm sure some feels the same way about me. All right to work with, but eating and sleeping with is getting just a bit much. Plus, if I don't straighten these long legs of mine, they'll set in a bent position. I'll soon be the same height as our Daisy.'

That nonsense made her parents laugh and earned her an affectionate swipe from her sister, who realised that Rose's working life was so much worse than her own. Sometimes Rose got home after hours spent in the factory shelter, with little time before she had to leave to start her next shift.

'Come on, girls,' coaxed Fred, who was also very tired

and over-worked, 'it can't go on for ever. Our lads are downing those Messerschmitts like nobody's business.'

And we're losing Spitfires. Daisy thought it but said nothing.

'They was over yesterday and the day before, Daisy. Bet they don't come today. We could have a nice run on the Heath.' Rose turned to her mother. 'And be home before you miss us in time for tea.'

'"And is there honey still for tea?"' Daisy had absolutely no idea where the words had come from.

'Honey? I don't remember when I last saw honey. Do you remember, Fred?'

'Nancy must have given us some, I suppose,' said Fred doubtfully.

'Sorry, Mum, the words just popped out; some old poem, I think.'

Flora looked at her daughters. She knew how difficult it was for them to be cooped up. Since early childhood they had cycled for miles in the countryside, played exhausting games with their brothers or just run for the sheer exuberance of it. They wanted her to agree with Rose's suggestion but she could not. She felt her legs trembling and tried to still them so that her girls would not see how afraid she was.

'Happen Rose's right, Flora, love. Even Germans needs a rest, and it's Sunday. Besides, why would anyone want to drop a bomb on Dartford Heath? No munitions dumps or engineering works wot I know of. Mind you, there's one really big gun they might want to take out, if they know it's there, that is. Trust me, love, it's our factories they're after. Go on, girls. Have a nice run.'

121

Flora said nothing and the twins looked at each other, hope in their eyes.

'They're sensible girls, love. They'll dive in a trench or ditch first sign of a Jerry plane; won't you, girls?'

'Right, Dad.'

Flora could only try to smile as she watched them leave. 'I'll have the tea on, but no honey, Daisy Petrie.'

The twins could not hold back a swift glance at the blue summer sky. One or two puffy white clouds drifted along on the breath of a slight breeze.

'Perfect,' said Daisy, and then grimaced as the smell of burning reached them on that same breeze. It was not a welcome smell, like that of wood smoke from a family picnic fire. This smoke carried the stench of wanton destruction.

'Forget what Mum says about being hoydens, Daisy. Let's run,' suggested Rose, and side by side the girls began to lope easily along the High Street, then on to Lowfield Street and further, to Heath Lane. Rose had longer legs but Daisy was faster over shorter distances, and they arrived together, exhilarated but exhausted, on the Heath.

'I'd forgotten how good exercise is.'

'You should come into Vickers and take my physical jerks class.'

Daisy smiled at her sister. 'No, thanks, but I am enjoying myself. It's ages since we had any fun together and I really miss Grace and Sally. Suppose that comes with growing up.' She pointed to a grassy hillock. 'Look, other people have had the same idea, a lovely walk in the fresh air. Oh, look, Rose. That little boy and his mum are trying to fly a kite.'

The girls wandered for a while, keeping the boy and

his mother in sight, willing and able to give assistance if necessary.

'Oh, does little Rose want to play?' teased Daisy. 'I'm sure the mum will let you try flying it.'

Rose did not reply. She stood, every muscle in her body tensed as she listened to a low ominous sound. At that instant, out of the bluest of summer skies, shrieked a Messerschmitt.

Daisy saw the mother freeze. 'Dive, dive!' she screamed, but it was all over before the second word had left her lips.

They heard the hail of deadly bullets and the scream of the plane as it flew low across the Heath and then up into the blue summer sky, and then there was the deadliest of silences.

'Are we dead, Daisy?' whispered Rose.

'Nothing hurts, 'cept my legs where you're lying on them.'

Rose picked herself up from the rough grass and for a second, unable to function, looked at what lay horribly mangled just a few yards away. She began to scream, a high-pitched wail of unutterable anguish.

Daisy crawled across the rough grass and, at the sight of the two bodies, she bent over retching. Nothing she had learned in her first-aid course was of any use to either of these pitiful bodies. Above them, released by death from the child's hand, his kite swooped and spiralled in the air currents.

She forced her unwilling body to stand up. 'Rose, Rose,' she said calmly, squeezing her sister's upper arms tightly. 'You need to go and get help. We passed a report centre and a first-aid post on the way. They'll know what to do. I'll stay with . . . with . . .'

Rose wiped her eyes. 'Oh God, Daisy . . .'

'I know, but hurry, just go.'

Rose ran. To Daisy, it seemed that her athletic sister had never moved more quickly. Soon she had disappeared over the brow of a slope. Daisy took a deep breath and kneeled down in the grass beside the mother and child. Tears of which she was completely unaware ran down her cheeks and great sobs shook her entire body. Thoughts and questions chased one another around in her head. Was a young father somewhere down there in the town waiting for his family to come home? Perhaps he was on active service somewhere, unaware that the worst thing that could possibly happen had happened.

Pure innocence on one side, and on the other . . .

'It was murder.'

Daisy was startled to realise that the loud condemning voice was her own. But it was murder. The pilot had to have seen the young child playing there with his home-made paper kite. He had seen them and deliberately strafed them. What kind of sub-human species could wantonly murder a small child?

She looked now at the disfigured bodies and this time her stomach remained calm. 'We'll get them,' she told the pathetic bodies. 'I promise you.'

She was still kneeling in prayer when the rescue services arrived.

Bernie delivered two letters on Monday morning. One, on a good-quality paper, was for Daisy and the other, in a thin buff-coloured envelope, was for her parents.

'Can't stop, Daisy, too many of these,' he held up a

fistful of buff-coloured envelopes, 'but I heard about you and Rose. Well done, pet, you was marvellous.'

Daisy shook her head as the tears threatened to flow again. 'We did nothing, Bernie, absolutely nothing.'

She sniffed her envelope as she walked slowly, unwillingly, upstairs to the flat where her mother was up to her elbows in soapsuds. The letter had to be from Adair. It smelled of nothing. She stopped on the second stair from the top, her heart thudding. Was she being fanciful? Surely a letter could not smell of death? The newly learned smell of death was still with her from the day before. She wondered if she would ever be rid of it. It had accompanied her as she thought out her plan for the future. She had promised the kite flyer. 'I promise you,' she had said.

She felt numb. Otherwise she would be reacting to the buff envelope.

Flora saw her and smiled. She raised her arms from the water and dried them on a rough kitchen towel. She went white as she saw what was in Daisy's hand. 'Is it my Sam?'

Daisy held out the letter. 'I don't know, Mum. Do you want me to run and find Dad?'

Flora said nothing but held out her hand for the envelope. She closed her eyes as if in prayer, then calmly opened them and then the letter. She read it slowly, closed her eyes and, holding the sheet of paper to her heart, said quite calmly. 'Your dad's in the lockup.'

'Mum . . .'

'Go, Daisy.'

Daisy ran and when she returned a few minutes later with her oil-covered father, Flora was still standing silently in the middle of the kitchen, tears streaming down her face. She held out her arms to Fred. 'It's our baby boy, Fred, our Ron. A sniper. It were quick, Fred, love. He felt nothing. This is from a major. That's a proper top one, isn't it? "Ron Petrie was one of the ablest young soldiers I have ever commanded and he will be greatly missed by everyone."'

Her control snapped and she fell wailing into her husband's arms.

It was several hours later before Daisy even remembered her letter. Her parents were finally in bed and she and Rose had cried themselves hoarse. No one had eaten. The vicar, alerted by Bernie, the postman, had sat with them for some time and had eventually encouraged the twins to make their parents hot drinks, which he had laced heavily with brandy. He had not prayed with them.

'I'll pray, girls, and they'll pray when they're ready. Prayers are so much more than words, you know. *Laborare est orare*. Do you know what that means?' He did not wait for an answer but answered himself. 'To work is to pray, and you are both exceptionally good at hard work. I will come at any time. Don't hesitate to send for me.'

'Let's have some cocoa,' suggested Rose when they had seen Reverend Tiverton out into the night where a bright moon, a bomber's moon, shone in the starry sky.

Daisy nodded. She didn't really care whether she had cocoa or not. She put her hand into her pocket to find her sodden handkerchief and found the letter. She read it quickly and stuffed it back into her pocket. It was words, merely words. She could feel nothing.

Tomorrow she would look at it again.

Dear Daisy,

Dartford's having a beastly time.

I see your street is undamaged – no, I'm not spying from the cockpit but we receive detailed reports.

The *Daisy* is terribly lonely but I rarely have more than a few hours free and all I do then is sleep. What a lot of time I've wasted. Had I swallowed my stupid male pride and asked for your help last year, I'd have had you flying solo by now.

Daisy, please try to get into the WAAF. There are tests you have to take but be brave and make sure they know that you have actually worked on an aircraft engine. They won't ask you because no one expects women to do such work. Feel free to use my name, if it's of any use.

Do let me know how things are going. I wish your people had a telephone. I'll ring Alf when I have any time and, if you're still in Dartford, I WILL TEACH YOU TO FLY. Now that I think of it, there's a Czech pilot here, Tomas Sapenak, who's a real ace. He's sharing the teaching hours with me. First time we're free I'll bring him home with me.

Take care, Daisy Petrie,

Adair

A Czech pilot? Her somewhat limited geography lessons had not, so far as she remembered, involved Czechoslovakia. Where was it located? Not that it made the slightest difference, not today. Ron, not even twenty-one years old and he was dead. Her sweet, funny brother, who had gone into the army because he idolised his big brother, was gone. All his short life he had wanted to be just like

Sam – and now he was dead and Sam was missing. After all this time that had to mean that Sam, too, was dead. Why didn't the army just write and say so and put them all out of their misery?

She crumpled up Adair's letter. Join the WAAF, learn to fly? Dreams were not for shop girls. How could she leave her mother now?

Daisy looked at herself in the mirror of the little dressing table she shared with Rose, the dressing table Dad and the boys had made for their sixteenth birthdays. She saw an ordinary girl with a very pale face, swollen, red-rimmed eyes and soft brown hair that had just reached the length where it needed cutting to avoid the dreaded unfashionable curls growing.

Dreams are for rich girls, Daisy Petrie. She tossed the crumpled sheet of writing paper into the wastebasket and walked out of the room.

But before she had reached the head of the stairs she ran back, picked up the letter, smoothed out the wrinkles and, after folding it carefully, slipped it into her drawer.

The next black day was when Ron's effects arrived. 'Effects', that's what the army called his belongings, and how pitifully sparse they were.

'They're sending his wages. I don't want his wages,' sobbed Flora, who, all her life, had had to budget in order to buy a new pair of shoes. 'I don't want their money. I want my son.'

No, Daisy could not leave.

'If we could just get some good news about our Sam . . .' Fred was suffering too. 'Good or bad. It's the not knowing that we can't handle.'

Daisy said nothing. Reminding them that parents up and down the land were suffering just as they were would not help. She remembered the curtain project.

'Mum, why don't you and me go down the market and get some of that material you was talking about? Just think what a nice surprise Sam and Phil'll get when they walk in. Lovely sunny days for bleaching it.'

Flora frowned. 'Don't feel much like sewing in this hot weather.'

She went off into the kitchen.

'Don't push her, love. She's working it out.'

'Will she go to a matinée with me? She hasn't been out, not even to church, and there's cowboys and Indians on at the pictures.'

'Remind her of Ron, love. Give her time. I'm going off down the shop to start the accounts before there's another blooming raid.' Half-way down the stairs he stopped. 'You don't want to tell me what that boy said?'

'Weren't nothing important.'

'If you say so,' he said sadly, and continued down to the shop.

This time Daisy answered Adair's letter; only polite, she told herself. She made sure that the layout of her letter was just like his. She had learned how to set out a letter at school, but that seemed like such a long time ago. Address on the right and the date under that. Then you wrote the letter and signed it. When was she supposed to write 'Yours faithfully' and when 'Yours sincerely'? She could not remember, but Adair used neither and so she would be just as casual.

Dear Adair,

Thank you for your letter.

I can't join anything at the moment as we have had a death

No, she could not tell him about Ron. She took another sheet of Basildon Bond notepaper, blue, and started again.

Dear Adair,

Thank you for your letter and the advice. This is not a good time for me to enlist but I will as soon as I can. Maybe I will be gone the next time you get to the farm.

Thank you for letting me help you with the plane. I will never forget it.

Be safe, Adair Maxwell,

Daisy

There, that was it done and she was glad that she had not needed to ask where Tomas Sapenak's country was. Just lately there had been an article in the *Chronicle* about the pilots from different countries who were joining the RAF and fighting with the British for their own countries, most of which had been overrun by the advancing German armies. Pilots from a country called Czechoslovakia had featured strongly in the article. Perhaps one day she would meet the Czech pilot. If she was accepted by the WAAF, she would probably meet pilots from all the countries mentioned.

She sighed. How exciting life could be.

SEVEN

Life, at least life as the country had known it, seemed to have changed. The summer sun still shone out of a clear blue sky but few, if any, summer games were played. The green playing fields of England no longer echoed to the sounds of cricket or tennis balls, and few picnic baskets were unpacked and enjoyed in soft flower-filled meadows. Children playing in the streets were watched by frightened mothers, who looked too often towards the sky. The children complained that, day after sunny day, they were rounded up and ushered indoors before the game was completed. Heavy rain fell, not gentle healing water but bombs, bombs of every shape and description that the mind of man could create: incendiary bombs that could light as many as three hundred fires in a few minutes. Houses were destroyed and others were so badly damaged that they had to be razed to the ground. The toll of dead and injured grew at an alarming rate, and parents who had found it unbearable to send their children away as evacuees now begged the authorities to send them somewhere, anywhere, that offered the slightest hope of safety.

Fred's hours of voluntary service had to be increased

as needs became greater and casualties grew among ARP wardens themselves. His family saw less and less of him as the raids continued. He would stagger home, exhausted, hungry – but too tired to eat – and smelling always of smoke and destruction. He would not have wished it to happen this way, but it seemed that the harder he worked, the more Flora found strength within herself to take his place in the shop.

In early September, Rose was slightly injured during a daylight raid in which her factory was hit. She was taken to the County Hospital – and to the same bed that Daisy had occupied just a few months before. There she was treated for fairly minor injuries. A few days later two wards of the hospital were destroyed and many patients and two nurses were killed. Rose made light of her injuries, preferring instead to tell her family of the incredible courage of one of the nursing staff.

'Can you believe, there was this sister and she filled a bowl with syringes – they all had morphine in them, which is ever so strong – and she crawled in the dark and smoke, Mum, over broken furniture, under beds, looking for injured patients. Twice she was lowered headfirst into wreckage to get to the patients. She followed the screams and moans until she found someone, treated her, and then moved on looking for the next one. I think she's the bravest person ever.' She was quiet, remembering the dead bodies on the Heath. I wasn't no use, she thought to herself. Daisy was the one told me what to do.

Rose was only too pleased to be sent home to recuperate. Seeing that most of the women in the beds around her were seriously ill, she felt slightly ashamed of her comparatively minor head and hand injuries. Her parents, however, insisted that she be treated as a recovering casualty and her plea to be allowed to dress and return to work was brushed aside. Flora and Daisy were determined to nurse her devotedly.

Each evening, after the shop closed, Flora and Fred sat down, one on either side of Rose's bed and looked at each other. One son dead, one missing, and a daughter injured. Where would it all end?

'At least we've got our lasses here with us, Fred. They're safer with us than out there.'

Fred tried to cheer her. 'Lightning doesn't strike twice, Flora, love. Soon as our lass's hand is out of the bandages, she'll be back turning out munitions.' He smiled at Rose. 'Won't you, pet?'

'Right, Dad.' She stuck out her injured hand, copying the First World War poster of Lord Kitchener. 'He wanted us to pull our weight, Mum; Mr Churchill wants the same this war.'

Flora was not convinced.

Before the war, Daisy, like her sister and their friends, had enjoyed a full social life. She went to the cinema, to dances in local social clubs and church halls. She played tennis with Rose, and was much in demand as a doubles partner – but with the advent of conflict, life changed. Friends changed. Some joined the services immediately; after all, it would be over soon and in the meantime it was steady paid employment and a chance to try new experiences. Some became very serious, others almost desperately frivolous. War marked each one.

Since the bombing had started in earnest, Daisy, who still felt that she could and should be able to do more, had added fire-watching to her duties. She continued attending the first-aid classes but her skills were not in steady demand. She actually enjoyed being on duty at night, a little nervous and tense but determined. Together with employees from several other shops, she was ready to spot any fire on the High Street and to attempt to extinguish it with the brand-new stirrup pump before it could flash out of control. She also had to learn to judge when she would be unable to deal with the fire and when to alert the regular fire brigade. Fires were started during daylight hours too. It was after a particularly intense bombing raid, when hundreds of the small but devastating incendiary bombs had been dropped, and as quickly as possible dealt with, that she remembered Mr Fischer. She was exhausted but it was a much more satisfying exhaustion than that which came from dealing with disgruntled customers.

I'm not going home until I find out what's happened to him, she decided, and so, instead of heading home for a meal and a hot bath, she made her way, dusty and reeking of smoke, to the house where Mr Fischer had lodged for so many years.

Mrs Porter, the landlady, did not want to open the door. September evenings were drawing in but it was still quite light, only the pall of smoke from extinguished fires making the early evening darker than normal.

Daisy called through the letterbox. 'It's me, Mrs Porter, Daisy Petrie. Could I have a quick word?'

The door opened a crack, just enough for an elderly face to peer out. 'Oh, it is you, Daisy. I don't like opening the door after five, not since Mr Fischer's been gone.' Reluctantly she opened the door wide enough for Daisy to be admitted.

'Have you heard anything from Mr Fischer, Mrs Porter? I worry about him.'

Mrs Porter led her down a hallway where exotic climbing plants and even more exotic birds rioted happily across the wallpaper. This jungle stopped at the door to a small, scrupulously clean kitchen. 'Was there anyone else out there?'

'Why are you so nervous, Mrs Porter? Really, there's no one there. People stuck in shelters are making their way home but no one came down this road.'

'Good. A policeman, in uniform would you believe, came to my house in the middle of the day so that all my neighbours would see him. A policeman. There has never been a policeman on my doorstep, never. What must my neighbours think?'

Daisy looked at the old lady. 'Oh, Mrs Porter, no one would think anything. He could have been looking for a cat or a dog.'

'He wanted Mr Fischer's ration book.'

She sat down at her kitchen table and ushered Daisy towards it, and there was an expression on her face that said, quite clearly, 'And what do you think of that?'

'I wonder why. They couldn't be sending him back to Germany with his ration book.'

This time Mrs Porter's expression said, 'Why not?' and Daisy answered it.

'A British ration book wouldn't do him any good in Germany.'

'That's true, Daisy. Oh, ever such a nice man, Mr Fischer, and that awful Megan Paterson in the charity shop on the High Street saying as how he was a spy. "No smoke without fire," she said.'

Daisy now had two pieces of unwelcome news. Mr Fischer's ration book had been taken and Mrs Porter, of the fastidiously clean home and the one refined gentleman lodger, was now patronising the local charity shop.

'I'd best be off; Mum'll be wondering.' Her mind worked busily as they walked towards the front door, but Daisy said nothing until the elderly woman had turned off the hall light.

'I was just thinking, Mrs Porter, seeing as how you was always such a popular landlady, if you had considered taking in a displaced person? There was a bit in the paper about Belgian refugees. Be a bit of company for you. You could take a nice family with kiddies an' all.'

She had gone too far.

'Kiddies? Sticky fingers on my surfaces. No, thank you, Daisy.'

Out again in the darkening evening, Daisy turned, not towards home but towards the police station. Her heart was in her mouth. What would her parents say if anyone should see Daisy Petrie walking into a police station? She thought for a moment, straightened her shoulders and walked in.

Less than twenty minutes later she walked out again, but now she was smiling.

Her father was out on his rounds checking that blackouts were secure, but she found her mother and sister in the kitchen listening to the wireless. They were laughing and that sounded so good.

'Who is it tonight, Mum, Colonel Chinstrap?'

'Where've you been, our Daisy? And no, we was laughing at Hattie Jacques. I can just picture 'er when I hear 'er voice, a large lady, they say, but with a lovely face.'

She fussed over Daisy, getting up to make sure that there was hot water for her to wash in and 'a nice one-and-a-half-egg omelette when you're in your pyjamas, Daisy. Alf Humble brought some stuff.'

'Alf. What stuff?'

'Oh, nothing,' teased Flora casually, 'just some tins of ham, and a joint of mutton.'

'You're forgetting the French wine, Mum,' said Rose.

Daisy looked at them. Were they serious? French wine. 'You sound like you've been drinking French wine, Rose Petrie.'

'Go and get cleaned up, love. You're exhausted. Your young flyer sent Alf a parcel for us because – seemingly – he'd put your letter away so careful, he couldn't find it. He said thank you for the delicious sandwiches. Wasn't that ever so nice, Daisy?'

But Daisy had hurried to wash. She had been exhausted. She had been hungry. But now she felt young and exhilarated. Fish paste sandwiches, delicious? Indeed.

'Was there a note, Mum, with the parcel?' she asked as she returned, clean and tidy in her cotton pyjamas and favourite pink dressing gown, to the kitchen.

She did not look at her mother as she asked but sat down as nonchalantly as she could beside her identically dressed sister.

'There's an envelope addressed to you, pet. The parcel was to me and your dad and the nicest note.'

'And there *was* French wine, Daze, but Mum's saving it for Christmas.'

But Daisy paid no attention as she read her note.

Dear Daisy,

We have been rather busy, you too, I suppose, but Tomas and I have been given twenty-four-hour passes. Since he seems to have no objection to sleeping in a stable he's coming with me. *Ergo*, two qualified flying instructors at your service.

It has to be Tuesday morning, as early as possible. Nine o'clock? That would give us a clear three-hour stretch.

Do hope to see you.

Be safe,

Adair

She looked up into two pairs of interested eyes.

'Rose, are you well enough to help out in the shop on Tuesday morning? I've got a flying lesson.'

Apart from saying that she was, at long last, to be given a flying lesson, Daisy said nothing else until her father got home. Then she was able to tell them about her visit to the police station.

'The police station? Daisy Petrie, what did you want to do that for? What will people say?'

'Mum, people were too busy rushing home after the raid to bother about who was going anywhere. Besides, we was told at school that if you needed help, ask a policeman.'

'What help did you need, pet?'

Daisy smiled at her father. 'I'd been to see Mrs Porter, just to ask if she's heard from Mr Fischer. Sorry, Mum, but he's ever such a nice man and I was worried.'

'Had she heard?' Rose was interested.

'Not exactly, but she said a policeman from our station

138

had come for Mr Fischer's ration book. She was like you, Mum, so worried about what her neighbours would think.'

There was silence for a moment. Fred frowned. 'So, obviously he's somewhere where he'll need his ration book.' He looked at Daisy. 'Go on, love, tell us exactly what they said.'

'I asked to see the policeman in charge and the young policeman said that depended on who wanted him. I said Daisy Petrie. He didn't say anything and we sort of looked at each other. I think we knew him, Rose, three years above us at school, hopeless footballer but good in long distance. Can't think of his name.'

'I don't care what his name is, you two, what happened?' Fred reached for the teacup Flora had filled and drank thirstily.

'Nothing, really. He looked and I looked and then he said, "Wait here," and went off. I waited and when he came back he said I was to come in and go to the second door down. I were a bit nervous but I thought, what can go wrong in a police station?' She heard Flora's intake of breath and rushed on. 'And I was right, for an older man opened the door and said, "Come in, Miss Petrie, I've almost been expecting you."'

'No, never, expecting you?' three voices echoed.

'Yes. He didn't tell me where Mr Fischer is but said he was vital, yes, vital, and he would come back to Dartford in due course. Those were his word, "in due course".' She blushed and went on. 'He had told them that a Miss Petrie might just ask about him. Isn't that nice, Mum? He knew we cared about him. What do you think he's doing, Dad?'

Fred cut himself a thick slice of Flora's home-baked wheat bread and spread it with a thin scraping of raspberry jelly. 'Well, we always knew he was clever, educated, like. But if the police's got him, then he's working on our side, stands to reason.'

Daisy smiled. 'Imagine, Mum, he knew I'd ask about him; that makes me feel ever so good, almost as good as Adair coming.'

Fred, who had been about to bite, put down his bread, 'Adair coming? What's all this, Daisy Petrie?'

And the exciting story had to be told all over again.

On Tuesday morning, wearing her new slacks and carrying Rose's last year's winter coat, Daisy cycled out to Old Manor Farm. The Aeronca was already at the top of the sweep, and Adair and another airman were standing beside it, looking not unlike a recruitment poster. Daisy dismounted and Adair introduced her. The Czech pilot shook hands with a small bow. A year before, she would have been keen to rush home to share that romantic gesture with her friends but she knew she would keep it to herself.

Wing Commander Tomas Sapenak was older than Adair. Daisy was surprised, having expected a younger man. Were not all the Bomber Command pilots frighteningly young?

He was tall and rather too thin, not the thinness that comes from healthy regular exercise. He hasn't had enough good food growing up, thought Daisy, thinking of her three tall healthy brothers. Two brothers. The appalling realisation hit her again but she schooled her face to hide her thoughts as she smiled at the pilot.

She judged him to be at least thirty, or even older, but still worth smiling at. His hair, once black, was now speckled with silver and there were lines of sorrow or worry around his eyes, rather lovely eyes, in a most unusual shade of grey. He was, she decided judiciously, rather good-looking in a Jimmy Stewart sort of way.

'We'd best get busy, Daisy.' Adair was keen to get on. 'Glad to see you have some warm togs with you, but Tomas found you a flying jacket. First flight – and we have to be really sparing with fuel – will be you and me. Watch everything I do, memorise it – I'll tell you exactly what I'm doing – and then, Miss Daisy Petrie, you will take her up with Tomas, the best in the business, sitting behind you. You won't let her fall out when you teach her how to dip the wings, will you, Tomas?'

'I try not to, Adair, but she is very small. Maybe she slip right past me.'

Surely they had to be joking, but their faces were so serious. Pretend they're Sam and Phil, Daisy thought. Boys, just overgrown boys.

'I'm ready. What do I do first?'

'Usually we have ground crew to pull the chocks away – that's what we call the blocks that stop the plane moving of her own volition. Here it's usually Alf or, today, Tomas. He's multi-talented and, besides, since he became a wing commander, he has got rather a bit above himself. *Ergo* manual labour; he'll spin the propellers too.'

Ergo? It was that word again. What did it mean? She could not ask. A picture of Mr Fischer reading the newspaper in the shop flashed before her. She could have asked him. She would, one day, ask him.

She pulled a second polo-necked jumper over her head, put on the genuine flying jacket and goggles, and climbed aboard and into the seat behind Adair so that she could watch his every move.

Adair was impatient, aware of the passage of time. 'This button starts her up – after the ground crew have turned the propeller,' he said. 'Then it's really not much different from driving your father's van.'

They were moving slowly along the sweep.

I'm in a Spitfire, fantasised Daisy, and am about to intercept a Messerschmitt.

It was as if Adair could read her mind. 'Remember when you asked me if I was going to drop things on the enemy?'

'That was a joke.'

He was smiling. 'I know, Daisy Petrie, and it made me laugh. It's useful having something funny to remember.'

She could think of nothing to say and sat quietly as the plane picked up speed. Faster and faster they ran until . . . they were in the air. One moment they had been on the ground, the next climbing towards the blue sweep of cloudless sky. She saw The Old Manor, with its boarded-up windows, far below them, the farmhouse, the stables.

'Pay attention.'

Looking down on the world, Daisy had felt sophisticated, mature. Now she felt like a naughty child. 'I'm sorry; it's all . . . I was listening . . . '

'Then go through the sequence for me. I do understand how amazing it all is and I wish we had time—'

He stopped and she wondered what he had been going to say.

'Tomas is already decorated by two governments,

142

Daisy. Men stand in line to have a chance to fly with him, work for him, even talk to him. You're a very lucky girl.'

She bowed her head.

'Cheer up, little Daisy. Already he thinks you're absolutely splendid. Now, from the beginning . . .'

She was surprised and relieved to discover that she remembered everything and was able to enjoy the remainder of the short flight.

They landed, with Adair once again explaining his every move. When they came to a stop, she began to clamber out.

'Into the pilot's seat, Daisy.' Adair was climbing out. 'Be nice to her, Tomas,' she heard him say, 'I forgot she was a girl.'

'Now, that I could never forget, my friend.' Tomas folded his long frame into the seat behind Daisy. 'Ready, Daisy. Off we go.'

With his attractively accented voice encouraging her, Daisy found herself calm and in control. The hordes of butterflies that had been cavorting around her stomach since she arrived at the farm had flown away and she was aware of nothing but the sky above her, Tomas's quiet voice, and the controls in her hands.

'We land now and this little *Daisy* is the sweetest plane, so easy, so comfortable. The American flyers call her a flying bath tub, not polite, but it's because the pilot sits so close to the ground; fly by, you will excuse me, the seat of the pants.'

It was all over. Dreamed of for so long, and the realisation had taken less than an hour.

It's not enough. I want more, thought Daisy as she

climbed out, removed her jacket and returned it to Tomas. I have got to learn how to do this by myself.

'Thank you both very much,' she said, all the time feeling as if there was a lump of ice where her heart should be. Why did this wonderful day have to end?

Adair was looking at his watch. 'How stupid. I forgot. Daisy, Nancy has some eggs for you to take home. She asked me to send you back to the kitchen.'

Fresh farm eggs. That would make a lovely addition to her mother's larder.

'Super, I'll just run.'

The pilots stood on the driveway beside her bicycle and watched her run back to the farmhouse.

'She's a natural, Adair, great balance, hand-eye co-ordination, name it, this girl has it. Why don't we let her take the *Daisy* up?'

Adair looked at his friend in amazement. 'Fly solo? Are you completely out of your mind, Tomas? She needs more time.'

'But of course, my friend, but time is among the many things we do not have. Take her up again; we'll find fuel somewhere. Let Daisy handle the controls, tell her to listen and remember every word you say, bring her down, get out, and tell her to repeat the flight. Make it short, just enough to gain some altitude, turn around and come back. We're at war, my dear friend. You and I, who knows the odds? Maybe there won't be another chance. As I get older, I realise that I regret in life things I did not do, but not a thing I did do.' He was still for a moment. 'Except maybe to steal apples from the priest's garden when I was not even hungry.'

'How old were you?'

144

'Eight, nine perhaps.'

'What a wicked child you were, and from the garden of a priest? I'm stunned. So glad I had no idea when I invited you to share my stable.' Adair smiled. 'But I trust you with my life and hers. I'll do it, if you really think she's ready.'

'Do you not think so, Adair?'

'I find I am not thinking these days of Daisy as a rather useful mechanic or as a pupil, Tomas. How did that happen?'

'Life happens, my friend. Accept with joy. Here she comes. Daisy,' he called, 'flying lessons won't wait while ladies gossip.'

'Sorry, but Nancy made us tea.' She held up a battered Thermos flask.

'Later, when you have flown solo, we will celebrate with British tea.'

'I certainly hope not,' laughed Adair, but neither Daisy nor Tomas understood his joke.

Daisy was standing, Thermos clasped tightly, and looking slightly dazzled. 'How long do we wait for tea?'

'Climb aboard, Daisy.' Tomas relieved her of the Thermos. 'After your solo.'

Somewhat stunned, excited and terrified in turn, Daisy looked at these two men who meant so much but whom she had known for a very little time. She nodded her head as if in silent agreement and managed to get into the plane.

Adair climbed up effortlessly and levered himself into the pilot's seat. 'You're capable, Daisy Petrie. Watch what I do. Listen to every word I say and memorise them. Ready?'

Unable to speak, she nodded.

'Daisy?'

'Yes.' The word came out clearly.

Adair flew the *Daisy* around in a small circle, his beautifully modulated voice seeming to make poetry out of the instructions, and Daisy, thinking she would die of happiness, stored every word in a special corner of her brain.

He brought the plane down and taxied her to a halt beside Tomas. 'Right, Flying Officer Petrie, into the pilot's seat. Take her up, Daisy, take her up.'

'You're joking and that's not nice.'

'Miss Petrie, Tomas has spent over four thousand hours teaching idiots to fly. You're not an idiot and he says you're ready. *Ergo*, take her up.'

Daisy did.

Her heart was back to normal, if beating a little more rapidly than usual. She felt that her excitement, her exhilaration would lift the *Daisy*, but calmly she went through the routine, ticking off each instruction in her brain.

And then – she was airborne. She was an eagle. The beautiful world was laid out below her for her to admire, and clouds danced past her.

Below her, the two men, experienced pilots, watched, willing her to succeed, feeling their muscles tense as they tried somehow to put all their strength behind the small plane and its young pilot.

'It's good, it's good,' muttered Adair.

'Did I not tell you this?' asked his friend with a smile.

Five minutes or so later, Adair and Tomas watched Daisy change course, gradually losing height and speed. She landed with the gentlest of bumps and taxied along the grass verge. 'She's a baby house martin returning to the nest,' said Adair with a smile. 'Look at her; even the plane looks joyful.'

The plane came to a halt and a very relieved pilot lay back in the seat and whispered, 'I've done it.'

'Look at her,' Adair said again, 'she's muttering her instructions, mutter, mutter, mutter, switch off fuel, mutter, mutter.'

He laughed with a mixture of happiness and relief, as Daisy, whose muscles had turned to water, tried to climb out of the cockpit, lost her balance and fell into his arms. He hugged her tightly. 'You feel the plane, don't you? You'll make an excellent pilot.' He swung her around, yelling, 'She did it, Tomas, Daisy flew.'

'So she did,' said Tomas calmly, 'with the help of a perfect little plane and two of the world's best pilots.' Having worked out Adair's funny remark, he added, 'Now we will celebrate with Nancy's "I hope not British" tea.'

They drank their tea and Daisy wondered if she was the only one who knew how much of her precious tea leaves Nancy had put in the pot for them.

But it was time to go. Daisy stood up and thanked them.

'You are most welcome, Miss Daisy Petrie.' Tomas smiled and shook her hand. 'I hope to fly with you again.'

'Yes, sir,' agreed Adair. 'You are a natural. I'll try, Daisy. We'll try to get back if it's at all possible. I'll have to, actually, if I intend to hand her over.'

'Thank you.' She stopped, knowing that it was time for them to leave. She did not want them to go. It seemed . . . final. 'Well, goodbye, both of you, and thanks again.' She turned and walked towards her bicycle.

'Wait.'

She stopped and looked back. Adair was running towards her. 'Here, Daisy Petrie. Take my good luck scarf.

It will keep you warm on this bicycle of yours.' He held out the long, pale-lemon cashmere scarf.

Daisy had never received a present from any man but her father or her brothers. She wanted to take the scarf; it was beautiful and it was his. She told herself that she really wanted to accept because it would be very useful in the winter. But still she hesitated.

He smiled at her. 'Take it, Daisy Petrie. There isn't any social etiquette about accepting an old scarf.'

'Thank you.' She took the scarf and mounted her bicycle.

'Be safe, Daisy Petrie.'

She smiled. 'Be safe, Adair Maxwell.'

She looked back as she approached the gate but the plane and the men had gone.

Half an hour later Daisy arrived home, her mind still ablaze with sensations: the thrill of flying solo, the heady mix of fear and excitement when she had been in sole control of the plane, and the wonderful feeling of trust when Adair had held her tightly against his chest. 'If I died now, I would be happy,' Daisy called out to a bird sitting on a windowsill, and then realisation hit. Were she to die today, happy or not, she would never see Adair again, nor Tomas, she added quickly. Euphoria vanished as mist vanishes in the warm rays of the sun.

I'll tell Rose, she decided, but I don't think Mum's ready for solo flights.

EIGHT

'I'll be back at work in no time, Mum,' Rose said quietly one afternoon as they sat together in the kitchen, listening to the lifeline that was the wireless. 'Don't you think it's time to let Daisy go?'

Flora said nothing but next day, without a word to either of her daughters, she went out with her shopping basket, returning an hour later with a heavy parcel.

'Our Rose will be back at work soon, Daisy, and I can easily manage the shop on my own.'

The twins looked at her. Was this their mother back with them again? But was it too sudden? If they blithely accepted the transformation, would they be disappointed when the endless grief and continual worrying attacked again?

'There's a piece in the paper today, girls, about getting your winter wardrobe fit for the shelters. Warm pullovers, it says, and best with a polo neck, and rubber boots or snow boots. I can do nothing about the boots but I plan to knit pullovers and I'm going to make those curtains.' She prodded the parcel to indicate the butcher's wrap before continuing, 'And Miss Partridge, can you believe,

149

prim little Miss Partridge, who never worked a day in her life except to do flowers and such in the church, is going to help me out in the shop. A few hours here and there. Poor dear wants a bit of company in the bad times, I think. Well, she'll get it here, and a nice cup of tea with a biscuit when we have it. We also think she might be good for the Preston lads; well, she's better educated than your dad and me.'

It was a long speech from Flora and she looked a little embarrassed by it herself but she was not finished. 'You've been my rocks, girls, mine and Dad's, but it's time for me to join the fight. First thing tomorrow morning, Daisy, before they start their raids again, I want you to go and volunteer for the WAAF. No, don't say anything or I'll cry and I want to get this steeped before . . . well, I want to get it steeped.'

The curtain material had to wait, as once again the strident noise of the air-raid warning sounded.

Exhausted from yet another night in the refuge room, listening in terror to the destruction going on around, Daisy scarcely felt able to drag herself into the recruiting office next day. When she did, she was asked a few simple questions, including her age.

'We're not taking babies, you know, love.'

'I'm nearly nineteen and I want to do my bit. I'd like to serve in the Women's Auxiliary Air Force, please.'

'Very commendable. I dunno about the WAAF. They're really looking for women with a bit of . . . experience.'

Daisy was sure that she had been going to say 'class'.

'Never mind,' the woman continued, 'fill in a form and then go home and wait.'

'Will it be long?'

'Dunno. Depends on who reads your form and who needs what. When did you leave school?'

Blast. She should have kept quiet. 'In 1936.'

'What have you been doing since? Working, I hope.'

'Yes, in my dad's shop.'

'Well, who knows? Off you go.'

'I can drive, and strip an engine and I've worked on an aeroplane.'

'An' me and Princess Elizabeth went riding our 'orses at the weekend. Frightfully lovely it was, an' all. Go home. You'll hear one way or the other.'

Her hopes in tatters, Daisy went home. She was furious with herself. Adair had said to tell the WAAF recruiting officer about the plane, not the local recruiting sergeant. She had been so anxious to make a good impression that she had made an absolute fool of herself. Would the woman who had laughed at her write something unpleasant on the form? 'Shop girl with ambition and no qualifications'?

For the next few weeks it seemed that she had, for Daisy heard absolutely nothing.

There was great excitement when a second letter arrived from Phil. It told his parents no more than that he was alive and liked the navy. Those few words, however, were more than enough for the little family.

'One of our boys is safe, Fred,' said Flora, who went to sleep that night with the letter under her pillow. 'Now I'm going to tell our Daisy, no half measures, I want her to go away. They always learns the quickest way home, don't they, Fred, when you've let them go,' she finished bravely, tears threatening to spill down her pale cheeks.

As the days rolled around towards the second Christmas of the war Daisy tried to think positively.

Surely thousands of young women were now trying to join the services before there was forced enlistment. It would take time.

Her heart broke, though, as she walked through her town. Everywhere there was destruction: roads were pock-marked by great holes, buildings by empty windows, broken chimney pots and smoke was hanging thickly over everything. She hated the stench of it. People scrambled over the ruins of their homes or gardens trying to find some part of their former lives.

Daisy looked down as she made to cross a street and almost stepped on a child's winter boot. It reminded her of the blood-soaked little body on the Heath. His shoes had not been blasted from his frail body and she hoped fervently that this little boot had been lost in a childhood game. She stood looking at it, wondering if she should pick it up and put it on what remained of a garden wall.

'There it is, Henry. And 'aven't I told you before not to take yer shoes off without unfastening 'em?'

A small boy, a year or so older than the child on the Heath, darted out, almost bumping into her, picked up his boot, and ran back towards the damaged house.

His cheeky grin cheered her and she carried on home.

The family flat was dark and quiet, strangely so, since Freddy Grisewood was usually presenting his programme, *The Kitchen Front*, at this time, and Flora never missed it.

'Hello, the house.'

The light went on, startling her, and there in the kitchen doorway stood her mum, waving a letter. Fred, grinning from ear to ear, stood behind her.

Sam? Oh, what a Christmas present that would be.

'It's for you, love.'

It was a buff envelope and so she knew it was not from Adair. Grace might write but surely her envelope would be white.

'Come on, love. Open it up.'

Trembling, Daisy took the envelope and with shaking fingers, tore it open, took out the two pieces of paper it contained and began to read.

'What's it say, Daisy?'

'Sorry, Dad, they want me to go to London next Tuesday. This is a railway warrant, which means I don't have to pay a fare. I can't believe it, I really can't believe it. I was so sure I'd made a mess of it.'

'Where in London, pet?'

'The actual headquarters of the Royal Air Force. The RAF. Me, Daisy Petrie, in their offices. I've got the address here.' She looked at the letter again as if she could not believe it. 'It's for a medical, not the questions Adair told me about. And, look, I have to take my night things, my washing things and my ration book, in case they keep me.'

'Well, they do move fast once they start moving, our Daisy, and here's you waited near a year for it and it's come. We're damned,' he stopped and started again, 'dashed proud of you, aren't we, Flora, love?'

With tears in her eyes, Flora hugged her daughter. ''Course we are. An' I'm sorry I made it hard for you, love.'

'I understand, Mum.'

'They're bound to keep you and so we'd best check things, undies especially, and your stockings. We should get new, shouldn't we, Fred? Don't know who's going to be seeing them.'

'Nobody better be seeing them,' said Fred fiercely.

'It's a medical, Daddy.'

'Wonder how much that'll cost. Never mind, my Daisy will have the best. Don't worry about it. My, but we'll miss you, pet. Miss Partridge's pleasant enough and her counting's good, but she's not one of us, is she?'

The prospect of losing Daisy to the WAAF was the family's sole topic of conversation for the rest of the week and everyone who came into the shop was told all about her prospects in ever more glowing detail. George and Jake said nothing, but on her last day in the shop George gave her a bar of chocolate.

'An' he never nicked it neither,' explained Jake.

'I know, boys. Thank you. I'll send you a postcard every now and again.'

'Dad'll have me "Head of the Air Force Petrie" come Tuesday, Mum,' complained Daisy, but on Tuesday morning she found it difficult to pull herself out of his arms and climb aboard the train that, barring an air raid, would have her in London in plenty of time for her appointment. She took comfort from the feel of the soft scarf wrapped around her neck.

Flora had admired the scarf and, unlike Fred, accepted the expensive gift at face value. 'He's out of her life, Fred, and so he's given her an old scarf.'

The train heaved and puffed as it sat waiting to set off, all the time filling up with men and women in uniform of one colour or another, but predominantly khaki. Daisy knew that, with the increased movements of troops, her chances of finding a seat were slim, but she stayed at the door waving to her parents until long after the train had pulled out of Dartford Station.

If Dartford was a nightmare of destruction, London was ten times worse. A pall of smoke had settled over the city and, because of road closures and diversions, it took all the time she had at her disposal for her to arrive, winded and slightly dishevelled, at her destination.

A uniformed official directed her to a ladies' room. 'Tidy yourself up a bit,' she suggested curtly.

'Wonder what she'd look like if she'd just run from the station,' Daisy muttered as she peered at her face in the pock-marked lavatory mirror.

'Even worse than the poor old thing does now,' said a cultured voice from behind her. A slim and beautifully dressed young woman emerged from a cubicle. Her lemon dress with toning pale grey coat made the 'dream' outfit in the shop in Dartford High Street look like something from a market stall. 'But, bless,' she said, 'both her face and her disposition were set at birth.' She held out her hand. 'Charlotte Featherstone.'

'Daisy Petric,' said Daisy as she shook the slim hand, which she could not but notice was as beautifully mani-cured as the blue-black hair was styled.

'Here to be interrogated?'

What a frightening word. Daisy's surprise must have registered on her face, for Charlotte smiled. 'Interviewed, Daisy. I'm afraid I tend to levity when the old butterflies swarm.'

'I'm a bit nervous myself.'

'Good, that's two of us. Let's find the interview room. They're running late and so we have a few minutes.'

There were several young women in the room assigned to those waiting for the medical. Daisy and Charlotte joined them. Obviously they were not alone in battling with nervousness for no one spoke at all. Some stared at the photographs on the walls while others seemed to study their fingernails or even their shoes.

One by one the room emptied.

'Featherstone.'

Charlotte stood up, turned and smiled at Daisy. 'I'll wait for you. I know a Lyons Corner House nearby; let's have lunch, frightfully inexpensive and awfully good.'

'Featherstone.' The voice was louder, more demanding.

'Coming,' said Charlotte, and smiled at Daisy as she left the room.

Forty minutes or so later, after a far-from-comprehensive medical examination, Daisy walked out carrying her little suitcase, a warrant for the underground to Uxbridge, and a postage-paid card to send her parents to say that she would not be returning home. It seemed that, on the basis of what she had written on the original form and the satisfactory medical examination, she was now Aircraftswoman Petrie D. She had been too nervous to take it all in, but the words 'four years' had been uttered. She hoped that was not how long it was going to be before she returned home.

'You look as if you could do with a nice hot cup of tea.'

Charlotte had waited and stood there at the foot of the steps, smiling. She too carried a little suitcase and, no doubt, a ticket for the underground. Daisy was slightly uneasy, feeling that perhaps they ought to go straight to their next interview.

Her hesitation was not lost on Charlotte. 'They were hours late doing the medicals,' she exaggerated, 'and so I'm perfectly sure time is relative at this moment. I need to eat and so do you. The WAAF seems to have us, body and soul, for years, which was a teeny-weeny shock, but *"Courage, mon ami, le diable est mort."*' She laughed at the expression on Daisy's face. 'Sorry, this does seem to be my day for alienating the rest of the world. That's just a sentence from a book my grandfather read me when I was about eleven. It means, "Courage, my friend, the devil is dead." They were the first words I learned in French and the family use them as a sort of mantra. In other words, Daisy, dear, everything's going to be all right. Come along, a bowl of soup, not nearly so good as Mother used to make, and a cup of tea, and then we shall deliver ourselves to the war effort.'

They did just that, and when they got to their next destination the reception was the same as before. The girls were late. 'Don't look so worried, love,' a uniformed WAAF encouraged Daisy. 'We do know there's a war on. Get off your feet for a few minutes – Gawd knows when you'll get the next chance to sit – and do go to the little girls' room.'

'Before or after we get off our feet?' Charlotte wickedly asked Daisy.

But eventually the time came for Daisy to be interviewed by a careers officer.

'What would you like to do in the service? Any other experience apart from shop work?'

This was it. Remember what Adair had said. 'I'd like to work on aircraft, miss. I have been driving since I were . . . was . . . fifteen, and I can maintain the engine.'

The careers officer eyed her carefully. 'You're a shop girl.'

'Yes, miss, but my dad has his own shop and a delivery van for . . . deliveries,' she finished weakly. 'Most days I did the deliveries. The van's past it really, but I can get her going again.'

'Interesting. We'll have you take a test,' began the woman.

'I spent a lot of time this year stripping an aircraft engine and putting it back together again.'

'Really, Miss Petrie . . .'

'An Aeronca C-3.'

'Which is?'

'A plane, miss, an American one. And the pilot took me up in her and I had a few lessons.' She would not mention the Czech wing commander. That really would sound as if she were boasting. 'Once he even let me fly solo.'

'How wonderfully useful you would have been to us had your American followed through with a recommendation. Sit at that desk and answer as many questions as you can.'

She doesn't believe me. She thinks I'm a storyteller and she hates me. And the cow thinks I can't answer her questions. Well, maybe I can and maybe I can't.

Daisy walked over to the desk, sat down and picked up the pencil.

Her parents would be thrilled.

With all her might, Daisy hoped that was so. Mum had been so down and clinging one minute and the next saying how much she wanted Daisy to go. Which was truer? Sometimes Daisy had heard her mother weeping from her parents' bedroom – difficult to hide anything in a building like theirs. 'My boys is gone . . . my Rose near lost her hand . . . I can't let Daisy out of my sight . . .'

Hard to bear her mother's tears. But now a pleasant RAF officer had told her that the tests showed that she was much too intelligent to work in the stores, which was where the female interviewer had suggested that she work.

'You show aptitude for engineering, and I think it was said that you have worked on an aircraft engine. Had it been car engines only, I might have suggested you transfer to the ATS, but we desperately need aircraft mechanics. You won't let me down, Petrie, if I put you there?'

Stunned, Daisy could only shake her head.

'Good, it's a Grade Two occupation, well paid, two shillings per day.'

Two shillings. How could she live on that?

Her terror must have shown on her face for he said very gently, 'And of course that's your pocket money, as it were. We take care of everything else.'

She smiled with relief.

'Good luck, Aircraftswoman Petrie. Welcome aboard.'

She tried to walk smartly out of his office. Aircraftswoman Grade 2. She would not snivel because she could not tell her parents face to face.

She met Charlotte crossing the frighteningly vast parade ground. She was grinning too.

'Well?' they chorused.

'Grade Two, and, Charlotte, he believed me about planes and he's given me a job working on them. I've got to do

159

a course but he says as how I probably know it all. What about you?'

'An office job somewhere.' She laughed at Daisy's disappointed expression. 'Call me Charlie, by the way, and don't worry about me, I won't be typing the boss's letters, Daisy. Trust me, it's exactly what I wanted.'

Everything, apart from her black lace-up shoes and her grey lisle stockings, was blue: blue skirt, blue tunic, blue overcoat, blue cap and blue underwear.

'Hope to God it doesn't come out in the first wash, or worse still, on me. I'll be blue apart from white hands, white legs and feet, and a white face.'

Daisy looked down at the complete uniform she had been given when she and Charlie had finally arrived at RAF Wilmslow, after an uncomfortable twenty-minute walk from the station. Daisy had often walked for far longer than twenty minutes, but not wearing heels or carrying suitcases. Wilmslow, also known as No. 4 School of Recruit Training, was where, for the next eight weeks, they were to learn the basics of becoming WAAFs. The walk, however, was not over at the gate, for it seemed that the building housing WAAF intake was as far from the main entrance as it was possible for it to be.

'Whose little joke was this?' asked Charlie as she rubbed her right heel where she could feel a blister forming.

But they had got there, been processed, assigned a hut, and issued with uniforms in double-quick time. RAF or WAAF efficiency?

'Are you all right, Daisy?' asked Charlie now as they tried to find places both for the clothes they had brought with them and also for the issued uniform. 'You had such a strange look on your face, as if you'd remembered something nasty.'

'Not exactly nasty, Charlie. I had a friend who went into the Women's Land Army; a dear girl; we were great friends growing up. She didn't have much of a home life and she wrote a letter when she reached her first posting. They'd given her a uniform and she was so pleased because everything was new. I'd never thought of real poverty before. My mum and dad have a little shop. There are – no, were – five children and we didn't live in luxury but we always had enough and a little over for people like Grace.'

'Where is Grace?'

'No idea. She wrote once, said she'd write again, but she hasn't.'

'Christmas in a week. Maybe she'll write then. Oh, my God, Daisy, did you hear what I said? Christmas in a week and we're here in what has to be the most miserable place in the entire country. My mother will not be pleased.'

'Don't suppose mine will be singing "Joy to the World" either.'

'Oh, clever, Daisy. I love that hymn. We'll sing it together in our . . .' she stopped and looked around at the ten other beds, most of which had suitcases on top of them, '. . . charming little holiday let. Maybe they'll send us all home for Christmas.'

But when she asked the question next morning at their first briefing, she was reminded in no uncertain terms that there was a war on. 'I'm sure if your parents really try, Featherstone, they'll come to terms with your absence.'

161

'If my father really tries,' confided Charlie later. 'He'll be asking a question in the House. It's almost worth telephoning him just to burst her little bubble.'

Once again Daisy had no idea what her new friend was talking about but she merely smiled. She liked Charlie and it seemed that Charlie liked her. It would have been terrifying to have faced this experience alone.

To someone who had spent eighteen years in an over-crowded flat, the vastness of the airbase was frightening. Ugly squat concrete buildings, which included chapels or churches of various denominations, a cinema just for new recruits, a sick room and an RAF hospital – definitely ghastly; would sick or injured WAAFs be abandoned to their fate? – were dotted here and there on what seemed endless acres of concrete. Charlie, an only child who had probably grown up surrounded by servants, had no terrors of the enormous mess where hundreds of blue figures of both sexes queued for food. Daisy's healthy appetite shrivelled up completely and she would have turned and escaped had it not been for Charlie.

'English boarding schools prepare their pupils for everything, and let me tell you, the food that is passing our little noses is much better than what my poor parents paid a fortune for.'

They spent much of the first day learning how to march on the parade ground where one day soon they would hope to march in what was termed a passing out parade – 'Define passing out,' said naughty Charlie – and by the end of the day almost every girl in their hut was exhausted.

'Josephine and Emily have two left feet, poor darlings,' said Charlie as they waited in a line for the showers.

'There must be some way to help them.'

'Don't think so. There was a girl at school like that, hopeless, but she fell over the dreamiest boy at her come-out and married him this summer. So life will go on.'

'That nasty drill sergeant is terrifying them,' went on Daisy, who was sure that life for debutantes who fell over their own feet was quite different from that of the Josephines and Emilys of this world.

It was, at last, her turn for the shower. For a girl who had been scrubbed in a basin of hot water in the kitchen before graduating to the local public baths, this part of military life was luxury.

'Petrie, there's twenty more after you,' yelled a voice, and Daisy hurried to finish rinsing her hair before the cubicle door was wrenched open.

Drilling, or square bashing, as the more experienced called it, was easy for Daisy, an athletic girl, and for Charlie who was also very fit. But why, they wondered, were they being taught to march when what they really wanted was to get down to real work?

'I can't see me doing much marching about if I'm half inside an engine, Charlie. You may be a girl that talks right—'

'*Who* talks properly, Daisy, dear,' interrupted Charlie who had been quite prepared to correct Daisy's speech after Daisy had tentatively asked her.

'A girl *who* talks proper . . . properly,' repeated Daisy. 'Maybe girls who talk properly and have nice, clean office jobs in London, maybe they could march around while the rest of us is—'

'Are,' said Charlie automatically. 'While the rest of us are doing a proper job. Very funny, Aircraftswoman

163

Second Class Petrie, but I assure you I will be too busy "doing a proper job" to march anywhere.'

Daisy sat down on her bed and looked seriously at her new friend. 'Can't you tell me? Hush-hush, is it?'

'So bloody hush-hush, they haven't even told me, Daisy. But, silver lining, we're getting to know each other and that, my dear girl, is a bonus.'

Daisy had no idea what to say. Charlotte, however, had no compunction in saying what she felt. 'Daisy, friendship is very precious. If we survive this war, let's promise to remain chums.'

'Chums?'

'Friends. It's an old, old word, even older than Frau Führer.'

Frau Führer was the nickname that Charlie had given their immediate commanding officer, a middle-aged WAAF who wanted everything to be perfect at all times. Captain Jenner scared Daisy and almost everyone else on the base except Charlie. 'Poor old dear reminds me of every head girl who ever blighted my innocent youth,' she explained, 'and so I'm inured.'

Daisy could only nod. Just talking or, more often, listening to Charlie was an education in itself.

Day followed endless day with classes of various types, marching, climbing, often over anything that would remain still enough to be climbed; aircraft recognition, cloud formations . . . By the end of the first week Daisy could unerringly recognise at least eight different aircraft. Cries rang out, 'Don't want you shooting down the wrong ones, Petrie,' or 'Featherstone' or whichever poor recruit happened to be nearest to the instructor. Weather

164

conditions meant nothing to the military and the recruits were outside regardless of rain or cold. Shouts of, 'Pick your feet up, Petrie,' regularly echoed around the base, but those cries were mild compared to the ones addressed to Aircraftswoman Featherstone.

Night after night Daisy fell into her bed and was asleep in minutes. She was happy with her new life.

Flora forwarded a letter from Adair.

Dear Daisy,

After all your brilliant work the *Daisy* isn't suitable for combat; as I feared, guns would be too heavy. Machine guns are mounted on the wings, and poor old *Daisy* would crumble under the weight. At first I was fearfully disappointed but then a chap in the mess told me about this new endeavour – the Air Transport Auxiliary – make note of that name. It's basically a civilian organisation BUT, Daisy – words ten feet high here – they train women to be pilots, not to fight, naturally, but to ferry new aircraft practically from the factory floor to wherever a chap needs one. Totally outstandingly brilliant idea. A former commercial pilot came up with it and he's recruited experienced pilots who're too old for the air force or who have glasses – yes, the Government does know there's a war on – and women. The *Daisy* has been accepted and will be used by them to move pilots from base to base or supplies or whatever.

But you know how very much I want you to have more flying experience. I've been given four days next week – someone thinks I need a rest – and I'll be at the farm, to pick up *Daisy*, I'm afraid, and hand her over. If you're at home, then we could go up at least.

He finished by giving her Alf's telephone number at the farm. A note had been added after his signature.

'At least let me know how you are. Safe and well, I hope.'

She wanted to burst into tears. Why could he not have been given leave before? Then she remembered the non-stop air raids and knew why. She smoothed down her blue uniform skirt and admired the shine of her sturdy shoes. The *Daisy* was gone and Adair was gone. What did that matter to her? Why did she suddenly feel so bereft? They hadn't even been real friends, for pity's sake. She remembered her delight on seeing the lovely flower painted on the fuselage and the name, *Daisy*. She remembered his teasing words, 'Will I give you a push?' when she had been so overwhelmed by joy that she had half-fallen across the wing.

She stood up and straightened her tie. Oh, but she looked smart. Better this way, she told herself. If he'd been there, flying with her, she might have grown quite fond of him. She wondered, now that she was a WAAF, if she should write to tell him. This dilemma was too personal to discuss even with Charlie.

Less than a week later she received a letter from her mother but there were no enclosures. The wonderful words, 'We've had news about Sam through the Red Cross,' seemed to jump out of the page. After all these months, the family now knew that he was alive, that he had been shot while wading out to a ship off Dunkirk, and had been assumed dead as he floated there in the bloody water. No accurate knowledge of how he had ended up in a hospital staffed by Roman Catholic nuns was available, but once he was well enough to walk he had joined many other soldiers of different nationalities on a forced march to a prisoner-of-war camp – somewhere.

'You're much happier with that letter than with the last one, Daisy.' Charlotte was sitting on her bed painting her toenails.

Where did she find nail varnish these days?

Daisy smiled. 'Oh, it's fabulous news, Charlie. My brother Sam, he's alive. Taken prisoner at Dunkirk and in a prison camp, but he's alive. My mother will have to be held down or she'll start to bake ready for him coming home.'

'She sounds wonderful, and it is wonderful news; we must celebrate.' She looked out of the window at the rather grey and forbidding concrete structures. 'Sadly, as yet I have no idea where.'

She finished admiring her scarlet toenails. 'I am pleased for all of you. The Red Cross are such troopers, aren't they? The Geneva Convention makes it a rule that names of all prisoners must be sent to their own government as quickly as humanly possible. I'm almost sure that families can write a little letter back, only a few words, about two dozen or so. Not much, and only about family, but better than nothing. Things like, "Daisy is in the WAAF and has a terribly attractive friend called Charlie. Mum won Best in Show at the WI bake-off." But these are the things he'd want to know anyway. Perhaps he wouldn't want to know about Charlie and he might wonder at the name, I suppose.'

'You are funny, Charlie. Sam would like you, even though you are unbelievably vain.'

Charlie smiled. 'My mother's the local Red Cross president and thinks that the organisation is quite wonderful. Tell Mrs Petrie to send a letter, short remember, to her local branch and they'll make sure it gets to him. I think Mummy said something about all mail being sent to Switzerland. I don't know whether to say, write loads of notes in the hope that at least one will get there or to write one every few weeks.'

'I'll let her know straight away.'

'Good, now if you're feeling very friendly, will you come to the gym and help me with the dreaded climbing? I'm determined to get over that bloody wall with a smile on my face. Won't that be one in the eye for Frau Führer?'

For some reason Charlie seemed to find it impossible to get to the top of the climbing frames. Daisy would shin up and down like a monkey, passing Charlie both on the way up and on the way back down.

The gym instructor had had no sympathy. 'Pull yourself together, Featherstone. Afraid Nanny won't be able to help you with this one.'

'Cow,' whispered Daisy, but Charlie still clung to the bar with hands so tight that her knuckles showed through her skin.

'Why am I doing this?' she asked Daisy – and herself – as they walked towards the huge gym.

'Because you can,' said Daisy.

'Wish I had your faith.'

They had hoped to have the facility to themselves but several other women and men were using the apparatus.

'Look, chaps,' an airman who was hanging upside down

168

on a bar called. 'God is good. Two perfectly lovely little WAAFs. What can we do for you, ladies?'

Charlie did not reply, but Daisy had three older brothers. 'Growing up a bit would be a good start.'

The other men laughed at their friend and Charlie looked at Daisy admiringly. 'Some men I can handle, but I never know what to say to chaps like that.'

'But he's one of your lot,' said Daisy.

'Not really. Oh, Daisy, I don't want all these people to see me make an idiot of myself. Let's come back tomorrow.'

'I won't let you fall, Charlie. I'm small but I'm ever so strong and you're only a half-pint yourself. You can do it. It's only a fancy ladder really, and if you keep looking up you'll be at the top in no time.'

Charlie thought for a moment. 'Very well, I'll try, but I feel sick already.'

'Problem, ladies?' A man, older than the others but every bit as fit, was on the wall frame. His fair hair had faded almost to silver, his lean face was heavily lined, the weather-beaten skin pulled tightly over high cheekbones. Not bad for an old man, as Rose would have said.

'We're just having a go at climbing,' said Daisy since Charlie seemed to have lost her tongue. Daisy glanced at her quickly to make sure that she was all right. 'We're going to climb it together.'

'Jolly good idea, and why don't I take this side, no racing, just one spar after the other.' He looked directly at Daisy and suddenly she understood that he knew that Charlie was terrified and that he did not think badly of her.

'Yes, sir,' she said, for his voice was that of someone used to giving orders.

'Sometimes I find it easier just to look straight ahead,'

169

he said as tentatively Charlie set one small foot on a rung. 'Never down, of course, and rarely up because the top always seems so very far away.'

'You're doing it, Charlie,' Daisy whispered.

They progressed steadily and then Charlie stopped. She was leaning forward against the wall and her fingers held the bars in a vice-like grip.

'Do you know,' said the quiet soothing voice, 'I have a brother who was always so much better than me at everything: riding, swimming, running, climbing, diving. Diving? Either of you young ladies like diving?'

There was no answer and he seemed not to expect one. 'I still can't dive but I no longer apologise. My big brother sat me down one day and told me that he hadn't always been good at everything. He said that he had decided very early that he would do only what he was sure he could do and wouldn't be bullied into trying things until he was satisfied that he was ready. So I started saying, I'm not ready for this yet. If a big strong boy like my wonderful brother could back off then so could I. Sometimes I said, I'm not ready yet, and then sometimes I said, I'm ready.'

A small quiet voice whispered, 'I'm ready.'

'If you're quite sure we'll do it together. Ready, one, two, three . . .'

They were quiet as they walked back to their hut. A soft drizzle was falling and drops caught on Charlie's hair and shone like diamonds in the lamplight.

Mine must be shining too, thought Daisy.

Suddenly Charlie stopped. 'Daisy, did I make a bloody fool of myself?'

'No. I must say there really is something about the

ruling classes. I'm lucky to be able to say I've never been scared of anything physical or heights or stuff like that. I'm quite sure if I had I'd have lost control, if you know what I mean.'

'I nearly did. But wetting one's knickers in front of a wing commander is not one of the war stories I want to tell my grandchildren.'

Daisy gulped. 'A wing commander?' She knew one wing commander; now she had had, as Charlie would say, a jolly time with a second one.

'Yes, Wing Commander Crawford Anstruther, DSO, et cetera. Daddy pointed him out at a garden party one summer before the war. Decorated by every country on our side. Quite a storyteller, though.'

'Storyteller?'

'According to Daddy, he has a married sister and two nephews at Eton, no other relatives.'

'Makes me like him even more. I'll have to try that. Can't you just hear me? Sorry, Frau Führer, I'm not ready for this yet.'

The happy sound of a splutter of natural laughter from Charlie was a perfect ending to the evening.

NINE

The Petries were more than sad at the idea of Daisy being, as they saw it, all alone on Christmas Day. They sent a large parcel, which they hoped would arrive on time, and forwarded a Christmas card, and a letter that they were sure came from the pilot. Fred had actually fought with his conscience over the sending on of that letter. He had considered tossing it on the fire. After all, Daisy hadn't mentioned the man in her letters, never told them what the lad had said in the first one. 'Not that it's any of your business, Fred Petrie,' he told himself.

Rose was still stepping out with Stan, the lad from the Vickers factory. Nice enough lad, who had been two years ahead of her in school. Too early to think about marrying, but it was nice to see them so easy with each other. Daisy wasn't easy with her posh pilot, forever changing her words; 'was' instead of 'were' and sometimes the other way round, until Fred and Flora had no idea of which one was right. As if it mattered – 'cept it did for posh lads like Adair Maxwell.

'I don't want nothin' to happen to you, lad,' he

addressed the absent Adair, 'but I don't want my little Daisy 'urt, and 'urt her you will, sure as eggs is eggs.'

Daisy was delighted to receive the letter and the parcel, which she decided to leave until Christmas Day.

Charlie had received several packages, one or two of them sent from rather splendid London department stores.

'The cookhouse is promising us a delicious Christmas lunch,' she informed Daisy, 'but I have a lovely feeling that there's a heavenly party for our little home-from-home in that box.'

'Mum's probably sent something too; she's a good baker, best in the local WI.'

'It will be the battle of the Titans then; Mummy's President of our local branch. Mind you, everyone's terri-fied of her, which is so silly, but perhaps she doesn't deserve to win all the time. She's actually stopped entering her sweet peas in the show.' She looked at the envelopes in Daisy's hand. 'Aren't you going to open them? We need to decorate our palatial quarters.'

Obligingly Daisy opened the first envelope and with-drew the card.

'Lovely,' said Charlie as she looked at the snow scene, complete with shepherds. '"As Shepherds Watched". We shall sing that too. Read it and tell me it's from a divinely handsome man who has an equally divinely handsome brother.'

'Better than that, it's from Grace.' She read the few lines inside the card. 'I'm so happy. Seems she's written to everyone and given the latest address. She's in Scotland.'

'Fishing? Sorry, being facetious again.'

'Great, hold that thought.' Daisy was very happy as she

hung the card over the string they had fixed to the wall behind their beds.

She broke off to say hello to three of their roommates who had just come in, soaked to the skin and freezing cold. The girls pulled off their wet uniforms, threw on their dressing gowns, and trooped out again to the showers.

'Poor lambs. I do hate rain dripping down the back of my neck, don't you? Now what thought was I supposed to hold?'

'Facetious.' With Adair's letter seeming to burn in her hand, Daisy asked the meaning. She did not mind asking Charlie for help. Charlie was a toff and had a wonderful education – even spoke French as easily as she spoke English – but she was . . . nice. That was it. There was bound to be a word that explained it better but Daisy hadn't learned it yet. 'What's it mean, Charlie?'

'Difficult to explain, Daisy. It's saying that a person is not being serious, trying to be funny.'

'But if a person was to say you was facetious, it wouldn't be . . . nasty or anything like that.'

'No. For instance, when I suggested that your friend was fishing in Scotland, I wasn't serious. I know perfectly well that she's working on the land, doing an absolutely tip-top job. I was being facetious.'

'So if you knew someone with a plane and he was giving it to the Government for the war and you asked him if he would throw things at the enemy out of it since it didn't have guns, that would be facetious?'

'Absolutely.'

'But he would know you was joking.'

'Yes, Daisy, your pilot knew you were joking.'

'He's not my pilot,' said Daisy with a happy smile, and sat down to open Adair's letter.

Dear Daisy,

Nancy tells me you have joined the WAAF. Very well done.

I'll spend Christmas Day with Nancy and Alf. Can't thank them enough. They have been absolutely splendid since the house was closed. By the way, I believe it's going to be reopened as a convalescent hospital, War Office management, of course.

My lovely *Daisy* has been very busy over the last few weeks. The ATA pilots find her both roomy and dependable.

I'm not sure where I'll be stationed after Christmas but, one never knows, we may be close enough so that we can take to the skies again. I do like to pay my debts.

Have a happy, happy Christmas.

Adair

P.S. The address at the top of this letter will always find me.

Adair. A pleasant quiver ran through her entire body. 'He doesn't owe me anything,' she said aloud.

At least five pairs of interested eyes were looking at her and she blushed furiously.

The shops, hotels, and churches of all denominations tried to encourage their members or patrons to plan for a happy Christmas. The Salvation Army played on the streets. Christmas music floated on the cold December air. Small bands of carol singers collected money for war wounded and for the elderly.

Rose's "keep-fit" group in the munitions factory collected spare change from their workmates for the many refugees who were flooding into Dartford from Belgium and Holland. Although the town was still dealing with almost daily air raids, one or two groups took their courage in both hands and sang or played in the open air, their senses attuned not only to their music but to warning sounds from the sky.

On a quick outing for her mother, Rose stopped to listen to some carol singers.

'Joy to the World,' they sang.

How, Rose thought, could there be joy to a world enduring such appalling conditions? She stopped walking to find some loose change for the collection box that was coming her way and then she saw an air force officer. Tall, too thin, grey eyes, black hair that was already a little bit grey. Could it be Daisy's foreigner pilot?

'Merry Christmas,' she said boldly. 'You look a bit lost. Can I help you?'

He smiled at her. 'How very kind. I am looking for the home of a young friend. It is, I think, a little shop for the groceries.'

It's lovely to have to look up into a man's eyes, thought Rose as she smiled at him. 'I thought so,' she said. 'You're Daisy's foreigner friend.'

'Daisy? Miss Petrie? I am indeed her foreign friend. Tomas Sapenak. And you, madame?'

Rose held out her hand. 'I am, believe it or not, her twin sister.'

He laughed, and what a pleasant laugh he had. 'The twin? How very nice to meet you, Miss Petrie.'

'Rose.'

Again he laughed. 'Daisies and roses; such pretty flowers, and so different. It is a pleasure to meet you.'

'Can I help you?' Rose saw some of her workmates passing and smiled blindingly up at Tomas. Being seen with a senior officer, and such a good-looking one, would certainly cause some talk.

'I had some business at . . . a factory and thought I might call. Is it possible that Daisy has leave?'

'I'm sorry, Tomas, not till March. She's hoping to get a twenty-four-hour pass sometime soon.' She shrugged. 'But who knows?'

'Ah, well, that is war. I am pleased to have met you, Rose, and I wish you a happy Christmas.'

'You too.'

He touched his hand to his cap. 'You will tell Daisy, no, you know where she is stationed. I did not ask Adair and it was only that I was here . . .' His voice trailed off.

'Course I'll tell her, and she's at a place called Wilmslow. You know it?'

'It is famous. I will find it.' He touched his cap again and was gone.

Well, well, Daisy Petrie, two of 'em stuck on you. Lucky Daisy.

When she reached home Rose told her mother all about the foreign airman. 'He's sweet on our Daisy, Mum. Wonder what Adair wotsit will think of that?'

'Don't be daft, pet; Daisy said as he were old. She wouldn't be interested in an old man although, mind

177

you, she was very fond of Mr Fischer.' She thought for a moment. 'He's foreign too.'

'I'm teasing. Tomas isn't old, and besides, our Daisy's in love with engines, not men.'

'Thank goodness for that.' Flora went back to trying to prepare mincemeat that might resemble, even in a small way, the mincemeat she had made before the war.

That night a plane limping back to Germany from a raid on London, jettisoned a bomb as it passed over Dartford. The bomb destroyed a charity shop on the High Street. The remains of two people were found inside, the manageress, and a Canadian airman.

'What was Megan doing in the shop after closing hours?'

That question was asked in several homes. When the Canadian airman's body was found people drew their own conclusions. Some people were charitable and decided not to speak ill of the dead, but in many other homes gossip was rife.

'She always were a flighty piece. And where's that sister of 'er's? No better, I'll be bound, and no sister neither.'

'Daughter, I always thought. I mean, who's twenty years older than her sister? And would you believe, my ma said she never even went to meet the kid at the station. A nun brought her, didn't she, Gladys? Scrawny little thing, still is, even though them 'igh and mighty Petries and Brewers took her in.'

'An' where is she now, and her sister lying dead in all her shame? Just up and left, without a by-your-leave. In the family way, probable.'

Apart from the limited circle of small-minded people, the

people of Dartford were kind, and no one kinder than 'the high and mighty Petries and Brewers'.

They could think only of one person. Grace. Megan had been a poor sister but, as far as anyone knew, she was Grace's sole relative.

'And the house was rented,' said Flora. 'What on earth will happen to Grace? Her sister's dead and now she has no home.'

'Who'll tell her?'

'The police, I think,' said Fred, 'but maybe it'll be someone in the army since the poor child's a land girl.'

'What a Christmas. There'll be a funeral and I expect Grace will get compassionate leave. With Daisy gone and my boys, we have plenty of room; she can come to us and welcome.'

'She's always spent Christmas with us,' Elsie Brewer, Sally's mother, reminded her.

'Of course, and now I have to let Daisy know. Maybe she'll get leave.'

'Not for a friend's sister, love,' Fred broke the bad news.

Daisy was devastated when she heard of the tragedy. She and Charlotte, together with the other residents of their billet, had been on a forced march and were exhausted, soaked to the skin, and hungry. Frau Führer met them on their return.

'A moment, Petrie.'

All the girls stopped in distress. What could Daisy have done to be summoned?

Daisy was astounded to find herself seated beside a small electric fire and handed a very large cup of hot, sweet tea. 'Oh God, what is it? Who is it? It's Sam, isn't it, my brother, Sam?'

'Drink the tea, Petrie. It's none of your family. I'm afraid your vicar telephoned and asked me to tell you that a Megan Paterson was killed in an air raid and her sister, Grace, has been given compassionate leave to arrange the funeral.' She saw hope lighten Daisy's eyes. 'I'm sorry, Daisy. We can't give you leave. War doesn't stop, no matter how sad we are. Finish your tea, and then you had better go, have a good hot shower and then supper and bed.'

Daisy gulped down the tea and stood up. Poor Grace. Megan was hopeless as a sister but she was all Grace had. How she wished that there were some way to contact her. Where was she staying? Surely not in that ghastly damp little house. Mum would take her in, or Sally's mum. Thoughts raced around as she made her way back to the warmth of her billet.

'I'm sure all your lovely family and friends will rally round, Daisy.' Charlie had insisted that Daisy go straight to bed after her shower and she had then talked the cookhouse staff into allowing her to take a plate of nourishing stew into the billet. Charlie had supplemented this with a shot of brandy from the mess. 'Medicinal,' she had assured the barman.

Probably because she celebrated in ways that she had never done before, Daisy thoroughly enjoyed Christmas Day. There were services conducted by military chaplains and then a Christmas lunch that released usually untapped depths of culinary skill from the cooks. Wine was served and, for just a moment, there was a lump in Daisy's throat

180

as she pictured her family, in the little kitchen in Dartford, drinking Adair's French wine. She thought about him, glad that he was with Alf and Nancy, who loved him, and she remembered, too, Sam, Phil, and Sally, Mr Fischer, and, of course, Grace.

'Penny for them, Daisy. You look so sad.'

'I were . . . was thinking about all the people I miss.'

'Good. You have people to miss,' said Charlie. 'I would say that more than one of this riotous lot has no one. Now finish your pudding because I have a small surprise for you.'

Daisy looked around the room hung with gaudy paper garlands. Men and women wearing, in most cases, extremely unflattering paper hats were talking, laughing, singing. Was Charlie right? Were some of them hiding sorrows?

'They've found family here then, haven't they, Charlie?'

'Yes, they have. Now, let's go. I've told the girls in our billet to be back by five. We'll make our own tea on our wonderful stove. In fact, it's so hot, I swear we could have cooked the Christmas dinner on it.'

Both agreed that the huge black stove that stood on the concrete floor of the billet was an incredible source of heat. In fact Daisy had complained in a letter home that, since joining the WAAF, she was either too hot or too cold. But to come indoors after hours of hard work in pouring rain, wet through, cold and hungry, and to stand around the stove drinking hot sweet tea was an unqualified delight.

Now she hurried back to the billet with Charlie, apprehensive about the 'small surprise'. She prayed that it was not a Christmas present. She had been so involved saving up for family and her old friends Grace and Sally that to buy a present for Charlie had never occurred to her. There had been no money left over anyway.

'Right, let's get the food out. It's in the Fortnum parcel. You open that, but do open your mother's first and we'll just pile everything together, on a tablecloth, if we can find one.'

'A tablecloth?'

'Forget I said that. A blanket will have to do. We'll pin some holly to it to cheer it up.'

By the time the other residents had arrived, a delicious picnic was set out on the spare bed that had been hauled into the middle of the room. Flora's jam roly-poly sat side by side with smoked salmon and lobster pâté. Daisy hoped she would not be the only WAAF never to have tasted such luxuries.

'Here, Daisy, this is for you, and I hope you won't be offended.'

Charlie, not looking her usual serene self, handed Daisy a small packet wrapped in silver paper and with a silver bow.

'Too pretty to open,' said Daisy.

'Quick, the others will be here in a sec and . . . oh, Daisy, maybe I shouldn't have . . .'

Charlie was as nervous as she was, thought Daisy, and she very carefully eased the silver ribbon off the silver parcel. She could practically hear Charlie's teeth grinding in frustration as she tried to open the parcel without tearing the paper. At last it was open. Inside was something wrapped in the softest of tissue papers.

'Tear it, for goodness' sake, Daisy; it's only paper.'

Daisy managed to unwrap the package without tearing

182

the paper and gasped. Inside was a knickers and camisole set in pale blue silk embellished with delicate lace. Daisy looked at the gift for some time. She had never seen anything so beautiful, and of course had never dreamed of owning such underthings.

'Oh God, you hate it. Mummy said you'd be insulted. It's not new, you see, Daisy. They've never been worn. My godmother gave the set to me for my last birthday and, poor darling, hasn't had my size right in years.'

Her eyes wet with tears, Daisy tried to smile at the other girl, who was so obviously concerned about her. 'I don't hate it, Charlie. I've never owned anything so lovely in my life, and when you think about it, we're doing something for the war effort – waste not want not.'

'Exactly what I thought.' The words almost exploded from Charlie. 'Waste not, want not.' She waited a moment as Daisy still sat touching the silk with one finger. 'You're not angry?'

Daisy shook her head. 'No. You're a very nice human being, Charlotte Featherstone.'

The girls, so alike and so different, stood for a moment looking at each other and then hugged spontaneously.

'Time to put the kettle on,' said Daisy, gathering up the underwear and the wrappings. 'You do that while I hide the prettiest knickers ever to be seen in this billet. Thank you, Charlie.'

They could hear the rather noisy arrival of their roommates as they hurried to complete the party celebrations.

'Oh, how lovely. Are we all welcome? I have a bar of chocolate I could contribute,' said one of the girls eagerly. 'Sorry it's not very much.'

'All donations welcome,' sang out Charlie. 'Especially if it's chocolate.'

Other donations were found in lockers and someone remembered seeing a gramophone in the gym and went off to see if it had already been taken. But they were in luck, and although dancing all the new dances, together with the old-fashioned ones, with another girl was not nearly so much fun as dancing with a man, no one dared defy Frau Führer by trying to smuggle in one or two airmen.

Daisy managed to dismiss thoughts of Ron, who had given his young life for his country, Sam in his POW camp, Phil, somewhere on his ship, Grace, homeless and now without her sister, and even Mr Fischer, until much later that night as, too tired and too full of unusual rich food, she lay staring at the soft glow from the coke-fired stove. Around her she could hear light snoring and a few muffled sobs and suddenly, as if a tap had been turned on, all the sadness came rushing in. *I don't want to be miserable on Christmas night. What can I think about?*

'Charlie? Are you awake?'

'Who could sleep with all this noise?'

'It's not bad. You should share a room with my sister, Rose.'

'No thank you, if she's louder than Baker over there. I've had thoughts of silencing her with a pillow.'

'Oh, you don't mean that,' gasped Daisy, sitting up.

'Ssh. Of course not, naïve little Daisy. Now lie down and think nice thoughts until you fall asleep.'

'All my thoughts are unhappy.'

'I'm thinking of my absolute joy at getting over the

obstacle course; that makes me feel like dancing. You must have at least one happy thought like that.'

Daisy could feel her heart swelling as if to make room for her joy. Of course she had a happy thought – the most incredible wonderful happy thought – and the words spilled out, 'I had a flying lesson.'

'Liar.' The ugly word shot across the room from one of the other beds. 'Working-class girls like you don't have flying lessons. Half of us wonder how on earth you got into the WAAF in the first place, but then I suppose we do need drones to peel the potatoes.'

The verbal attack was so unexpected and vicious that the over-tired Daisy began to cry. In a moment the room that had been settling down for the night was buzzing again as the girls who were awake took sides. It was only much later that Daisy realised that most of them were firmly on her side.

'Tell us about your flying lesson, then, Wing Commander. In a Spitfire, was it?'

Daisy said nothing but, feeling humiliated and embarrassed, crawled even further into her blankets.

'That's quite enough.' The voice was Charlie's, and so full of authority was it that the clamouring girls quietened immediately. 'We are, each and every one of us, in the WAAF; there is a war on and we need to work together for the greater good. Now let's try not to spoil our lovely Christmas any more than it has already been spoiled by stupid jealousy.'

There were murmurs of 'Hear, hear.'

Later, when all the muttering and sniffling had died down, Charlie slipped out of bed and crossed to Daisy. She kneeled down beside the bed. 'Awake, Daisy?'

'Yes.'

'Carmyllie's a jealous old cow. Some day, when you're ready, please tell me all about the lesson.'

'I did have a lesson.'

'I know. You're the most truthful person I've ever known, Daisy Petrie.'

'Why don't you join the ATA, Charlie? It's women like you they want.'

'Maybe, but my mother just couldn't handle it. I'm delighted to have come this far. I'll live my dreams through you. You will tell me, won't you?'

'Nothing much to tell, but I could tell *you*.'

Charlie crept back to her own bed and in a few moments everyone in the warm quiet dormitory was sound asleep.

TEN

Great excitement. There was to be a dance on New Year's Eve, and more exciting still, the band was to be real; no records, no trying to find good music on the wireless, but real live musicians. Charlie was discovered to be a clarinettist and another girl in the billet had a saxophone with which – she was forced to admit – she had more than a nodding acquaintanceship.

'Only slightly more,' she said nervously.

Other band members, both male and female, were found and brought together for a rehearsal.

'We are superb,' Charlie told Daisy. 'Benny Goodman, jazz . . . name it, we've got it. I hope, incidentally, that the bar can come up with cocktails, not flat military beer and cheap whisky, but real cocktails. We need to believe we're at the Ritz.'

Everyone was excited except Daisy. Not only had her mind been full of thoughts of Grace and how she was coping since her sister's death but also she had been ordered to report to Captain Jenner's office at eleven thirty on the morning of New Year's Eve. She had told no one except Charlie but was terribly worried.

Something's happened to Phil. No, they would have told me right away. Sam. No. She went through her entire list of family and friends and decided that it was obvious that each and every one was perfectly all right or she would have been told immediately. *So stop worrying.*

But then I must have done something. What could I have done?

Daisy was modestly pleased that all the instructors appeared to be quite happy with her progress.

She scrubbed her face with her washcloth, brushed her hair until her scalp almost squealed in protest, stood in her underwear and ironed her uniform until Charlie teased her that she was in danger of wearing a hole in it, and still worried.

'You've done so well you're getting a forty-eight-hour pass.'

'Right.'

'It's time. I'll walk over with you.'

Charlie left Daisy at the door of the Führer's office. Daisy knocked and a deep, vaguely familiar voice told her to enter.

Adair Maxwell, in full flying gear, was standing beside the desk.

The strangest feelings swamped Daisy. It was like nothing she had ever experienced. Her stomach was churning but in the nicest possible way, the way she had felt when at fourteen she had been waiting to run in the finals of the one-hundred-yard race. She was aware that her face had turned pink, and the awareness only caused her to blush more furiously. She was incredibly pleased to see him.

'Adair,' she said, and immediately wondered if she

should have saluted him. He was an officer and he was in uniform.

'You look very smart, Daisy Petrie.'

'Captain Jenner?'

'Thinks this is a romantic liaison. She has tactfully withdrawn but will be heard coughing in the corridor – about now,' he finished as there was a discreet cough from outside.

Daisy saluted as Frau Führer entered.

'Thank you, Captain Jenner,' said Adair. 'I'll take Aircraftswoman Petrie off for a flying lesson now, but I'm delighted to accept your very kind invitation to the dance.'

'You're more than welcome, Squadron Leader. Wing Commander Anstruther did tell us you might be visiting.'

Daisy was looking in fascination at the rather worn beige carpet. She had no idea what to make of what she was hearing. She had seen the wing commander several times in the distance and now it appeared that Adair knew him. With the first pang of real jealousy she had ever experienced she found herself wondering if he also knew Charlie.

'Ready for your lesson?'

That was Adair, the young man she had worked beside for hours, the same young man who had taken her up for her first ever flight.

'Yes, sir,' she said, and saluted Captain Jenner.

They were quiet until they had left the office block.

'Sorry, I wasn't able to warn you, Daisy. We've been really busy and I wasn't told until yesterday.' He stopped. 'It's lovely to see you.'

She said nothing as she could think of nothing to say.

'You too' didn't sound right and might give the wrong impression.

'You are free to come up with me? There isn't something else you'd rather be doing?'

'You really mean you're here to give me a flying lesson?'

'Of course, Daisy Petrie. I told you I'd teach you to fly. I was asked to fly a VIP down and now that he's safely delivered and I'm here, I asked if you could be allowed to take a lesson with me. You're my reward for good behaviour. I need to fly my passenger back tomorrow and so I'm free to escort you to the dance.'

'Escort? It's not the kind of dance with posh frocks.'

'Good. I don't have a posh frock. There, Daisy, how would you like a little spin in her?'

Daisy looked at the little yellow bi-plane. 'A Tiger Moth.' She knew that it was constructed of wood and Irish linen and not much more, and yet it was a powerful little plane. 'I've read about it but never seen a real one. You're really going to take me up in her?'

'No. You're going to fly me. To be honest she's even easier than the Aeronca.' He leaned over into the cockpit and brought out a flying suit. 'Do your best to pull this on over your uniform; my passenger's a bit bigger than you. I'll stroll over towards the hangar. Cough loudly when you're dressed.'

He walked off, his back to Daisy and the bubbles of pleasure that had been building up exploded in her stomach. What a wonderful New Year's Eve.

As quickly as she could, she pulled on the flying suit. Should she cough or call him?

'Ready or not, here I come,' called Adair.

'You are very funny, Adair Maxwell.'

'I know, and you look adorable in that suit, Daisy Petrie. Climb aboard.'

Why was it that the controls seemed made to fit her hands, that the plane responded to her commands, that the quiet voice behind her was definitely the most beautiful voice she had ever heard? Soon they were in the air, and below them she saw, not the fertile land of Kent, but the vast concrete mass of the airbase. Why did it suddenly look so beautiful? She smiled and listened to the disembodied voice.

'Time to descend, Daisy. You won't see the ground exactly as you were able to see it in the *Daisy*, but trust yourself and the plane, and put her down.'

There were several airmen and WAAFs standing watching as gently and surely Daisy set the little plane down and taxied her towards the hangar.

'Well done. Now, out you get and greet your admiring public.'

'Adair?'

'Every person out there thinks you're a man. What a lovely little surprise we have for them.'

The last thing Daisy sought was notoriety. 'I can't,' she said. 'What will they think?'

'What do you want them to think? You're a girl and you're learning to fly. That's it. If you treat it as the norm, so will they.'

Muttering, 'I hope you're right,' under her breath, Daisy clambered out and dropped to the ground, followed by Adair.

'Well done,' he said loudly, and held out his hand so that she had no option but to shake it. 'I'll take the helmet.'

Daisy would have preferred to keep her identity hidden

but had no choice. She took off the helmet, handed it to him, and said, 'Thank you, sir,' in as steady a voice as she could muster.

There was nothing but the sound of their shoes on the tarmac as they walked away from the plane and then someone clapped. By the time they reached the hangar everyone who was standing around was clapping or stamping feet, not only the women but many of the RAF personnel too.

'Well done, sir,' shouted one. 'Always choose the stunners.'

Daisy blushed furiously.

'Enjoy, little stunner,' came Adair's voice beside her. 'I'm afraid it won't last.'

What did he mean? She could not possibly speak to him with so many WAAFs and aircrew standing around, and then she saw Felicity Carmyllie from her own billet and the dislike in her eyes was palpable.

'Wonder what the working-class tart had to do to get a flying lesson, or do we really need to wonder?'

Daisy had never been subjected to such animosity and she felt the tears well up in her eyes.

'Cry and I'll hit you, Daisy Petrie.' It was Charlie, who went on talking cheerily as the base personnel let them through, many still clapping and congratulating her.

Adair had disappeared into the office block. Had she thanked him? Did he really mean that he was taking her to the dance? It was an all-ranks party to celebrate the start of the New Year, but he was a senior officer, and a decorated one at that.

Once Daisy and Rose had been reading about military decorations and both girls had thought decorations meant streamers and balloons and had tried hard to visualise brave soldiers 'decorated by the King'. Now Daisy knew that a decoration was a medal. How many decorations did Adair have and would he wear them to the dance?

'Why have you been hiding your tame squadron leader, Daisy Petrie?'

Daisy had missed lunch and so Charlie was taking her back to the billet to drink tea, eat up all the Christmas leftovers and, she hoped, tell all about the dashing pilot.

'He's not my squadron leader. I didn't know he were a squadron leader when I met him. He were only a lad in an old plane.' Her newly learned grammar had deserted her in her stress.

'I'm so glad.'

'About what?'

'That he's not your squadron leader, for he is totally divine and now fair game. You did hear him say he would call for you at eight?'

Daisy looked around at the slim and not quite so slim figures relaxing on their beds. 'You're having me on, Charlotte Featherstone.'

Charlie crossed her heart. 'Scout's honour. Now, come on, tell us about the flying lessons. The very idea makes me feel faint. Where, when, why, how much, the whole lovely story.'

After Daisy had told the audience that she thought them all rather silly, she told them, in as few words as possible, how she had met Adair, worked with him on the engine, and had eventually been given a flying lesson. She did not mention the Czechoslovakian ace.

The girls were wide-eyed with excitement.

'Are you stepping out, Daisy?'

'Much more important: have you met his family, Petrie? I thought not.' The clipped tones came from Felicity Carmyllie. 'I hear he's heir to an earldom. They don't marry plebeians; sleep with them, yes.'

'Ignore her, Daisy,' Charlie hissed. 'If you react, the bitch will never leave you alone. Now tell me,' she said in a much louder voice, 'what is it like to actually look down on the earth?' Charlotte, who must have flown to holiday destinations several times, led the questions.

'Even more, what's it like when you're flying the cardboard box, because that's all they are, isn't it, some plywood, and a few bits of wire? You'll never get me going up in one of them.'

'Did your stomach flip, Daisy, like on a funfair?'

The questions went on and on, especially when Felicity tried to say anything.

'Anyone on duty?'

For much of the past week, even after a long busy day, the entire hut had been on duty after seven as a defence precaution and so that they could familiarise themselves with the routine in case of an attack.

One WAAF raised her hand. 'Don't worry about me, girls. I volunteered. I can't dance and I loathe New Year's Eve. I shall be perfectly happy.'

'What do you feel about New Year's Eve, Daisy?'

'I love it. My parents invite the world in. It's great fun, singing, dancing, listening to the wireless. What about you, Charlie?'

'Oh, it's all right, but sometimes seems like a poor excuse for bad behaviour. What do you plan to wear?'

'Not much choice; must have missed the bit that said

194

party frock on the list they sent. I've got a nice blouse but it'll have to be my uniform skirt, though I do have my best shoes – with a heel – and stockings my sister sent me for Christmas. What about you?'

'My family packs for every emergency. I did bring a pretty frock.'

As well as the stunning outfit she had worn when they met, Charlie had two day dresses with her, both simple but beautifully tailored. Charlie was always just right.

Several of the girls went together to the mess for their evening meal, called tea, and had a tasty stew of a meat that no one quite recognised, and vegetables, followed by a piece of cake, an apple for those who wanted one, and mugs of hot sweet tea. It was judged a fine meal by military standards, if not particularly festive.

They hurried back to their billet to change. Almost everyone was excited and cries of, 'Anyone got a pink lipstick?' or, 'Who's got a steady hand? I need a line drawn up my legs?' rang out.

Daisy felt those pleasurable feelings in the pit of her stomach. Would he really come? Did she want him to? Adair as a workmate, even as an instructor, was very different from Adair as . . . as what? An escort? A date? Daisy Petrie who lived above a shop in Dartford and Adair Maxwell who . . . Daisy laughed. Adair seemed to live above an old stable on a Kentish farm.

They had had several days without air-raid warnings. How awful it would be if the Germans decided to unleash a real offensive. Surely no one would want to fight on New Year's Eve. Stupid Daisy. No normal person wants to fight.

Charlie was rummaging in her bag. 'Honestly, it's worse than school,' she said. 'There's always someone who just can't be seen without nail varnish.'

'Remind her there's a war on,' teased Daisy, who was loving every minute.

Charlie's dark green velvet dress was voted the prettiest frock ever, although Daisy was slightly disappointed. For a dance she had expected some glitter or other embellishment but Charlie's dress was surprisingly simple.

'It's a dress up or leave alone, according to the occasion, Daisy,' she explained. 'I shall dress it up with this wrap. What do you think?'

'Stunning.' The wrap was an unusual mix of pale green, dark green and gold, and was of fine wool.

Charlie was digging in her drawer. 'Now what do you think of this?' She held up a long chain of silver links.

Daisy felt that the chain, although lovely, was quite wrong for the dress but was too unsure of herself to say so.

'Don't you think it's pretty?'

'It's lovely, Charlie, but . . .'

'Good. Would you like to borrow it to dress up your skirt? If you use it as a belt and let all the extra links hang down to your knees, I think it will look quite partyish.' She had threaded the links through Daisy belt loops as she spoke. '*Fait accompli*, Daisy. You look lovely.'

'Silver doesn't disguise class, Charlotte.' Felicity Carmyllie was looking on, displeasure written all over her face.

'I know. So sad. But then, Felicity dear, neither do elocution lessons. Come on, Daisy, our escorts are waiting and I must get over early – toe-tapping music should be heard as the merry-makers arrive.'

Charlie swept Daisy past the startled Felicity and outside, grabbing Daisy's coat on the way.

'Why does she dislike me so much, Charlie?'

'She dislikes everyone. Poor old Carmyllie is doomed to go through life disappointed. Don't allow her to hurt you, Daisy. She can't, you know, unless you allow her.'

Two tall men in casual clothes were walking along the path towards them but Daisy paid no attention until, instead of stepping aside to let them pass, the men stopped in front of them.

'Hello, Daisy, and you must be Charlie. Adair Maxwell,' he finished with the slightest bow. 'And I believe you know Wing Commander Anstruther.'

'Ladies.' The senior officer shook hands with each girl in turn. 'Shall we walk over with you?'

They turned and headed towards the recreation hall where the party was being held. Automatically, Adair stepped behind to walk with Daisy while the senior officer escorted Charlie.

'The wing commander won't be able to stay as he's involved in meetings with my passenger but he does want to talk to you at some point about flying.'

'Is he angry?'

'Gosh, no.' Adair grabbed her hand and squeezed it and then, as if suddenly aware of the intimacy of the gesture, released it. 'He's fascinated and very forward-thinking. There's a tremendous amount of resistance to women pilots, you know, and believe me, I can't think of anyone who would condone women pilots in combat situations, but why shouldn't women fly? They drive. They sail. Only thing left is flight.'

'Maybe men want to keep it to themselves.'

He laughed. '*Touché.*'

She was quiet – another of those words she didn't understand – but she smiled; why, she didn't quite know. Her hand seemed still afire with his touch and Daisy felt that she would be happy just to walk on and on, listening to him speak or laugh. Even if he never said a word, it would be lovely, she thought.

'Are you happy here, Daisy? Are the courses going well?'

'All marching, climbing and book learning at the mo. Never even set eyes on an actual engine.'

'That will come at your next posting.'

They had reached the hut and both Charlie and the wing commander had disappeared. Loud jazz music was pouring out of the hut, together with the happy sounds of revelry.

'Why did he walk over with you, Adair?'

'He knows her family. Doing the polite, nothing more. He certainly doesn't want to make her an object of gossip. Come on, let me take your coat and I'll fetch us drinks. Don't worry. No one's in uniform, no stripes visible.'

'You look very nice, Daisy Petrie,' he said when she removed her coat, 'but you look good in anything.'

Two girls from her billet were sitting at a table where there were a few empty spaces and they called out to Daisy to join them. 'Listen to Charlie,' they shouted above the noise, 'and Edith. Aren't they fantastic?'

Daisy smiled her agreement. She knew nothing about music but loved the sound she was hearing from the several men and women on a dais at the far end of the hut.

One of the men stood up and pulled Daisy to her feet. 'Let's dance, beautiful.'

'Sorry, chum, Beautiful is dancing this one with me.' Adair had set down the drinks and was offering Daisy his hand.

'I'm not a good . . .' began Daisy but she was already in Adair's arms and almost galloping around the room.

'What was that?' she gasped as they came to an exhausted halt.

'Something called bebop or was it the Turkey Trot? Haven't the slightest idea, Daisy, but I knew you could do it. You're fit and have superb balance.'

The evening flew on. They danced and they sang and they cheered the band and one another. By the time the band leader announced that it would soon be 1941, Daisy had met and talked or danced with more people on the airfield than she had met in her weeks of training. She really felt like a WAAF and was immensely proud.

Charlie had joined them for a drink during a band break.

'Well, well, Aircraftswoman Second Class Petrie. I don't blame you one bit for hiding him. If he were teaching me to fly – or anything else for that matter – I am quite sure I'd need hours of instruction.'

'I wasn't hiding him,' said Daisy, and then looked at her friend Charlie and laughed. 'He's rather hard to hide.'

'The band sees all, Daisy, and the green eyes of envy were standing out on stalks all over the room. When are you seeing him again?'

'I'm not, Charlie. He's a fighter pilot. He's never here. Besides, we don't have that kind of relationship. I just happen to live near the farm where he kept his plane and I helped him strip the engine. He's grateful for my help.'

'Trust Aunt Charlotte, gratitude is not uppermost on his mind. And here he is with our – wow, Adair, bubbly for the New Year.'

'Bubbly for Daisy; I promised her some, seems like a lifetime ago.'

'Then off you go, my children. I'll take mine to the bandstand.'

Bubbly? Champagne. The Christmas sherry seemed so long ago. Adair had the bottle and two glasses in one hand and he took Daisy's with the other and followed Charlie to the dais where he set down the champagne. It was all so normal for them and so exciting for her.

'Let's stand here for the countdown. We don't want to miss it.'

He poured the champagne into the glasses and handed one to Daisy. She looked down into the liquid where little bubbles jumped and tumbled, exactly like the ones in her stomach.

'Happy New Year.' The call rang out.

'Happy New Year, dearest Daisy,' said Adair as he touched his glass to hers and then, before she had had a chance even to sip, he had leaned over and kissed her very gently on the lips. They stepped back for a second and then Adair leaned forward and kissed Daisy again. It was not a gentle kiss this time but one full of both passion and longing, and Daisy surprised herself by responding fully.

There was no time to say anything for the huge room erupted with excited cries. Complete strangers hugged and kissed, and in less than ten minutes Daisy felt as if she had been kissed more often in this one night than in her entire life. Adair was there at her side to intervene gently when things got rowdy.

'How's your champagne? Some blighter's pinched our bottle.'

'It was perfect.'

'Next time, a lovely restaurant, great food . . .'

She put her hand to his lips, a gesture that surprised her more than it did him, but just then a uniformed airman interrupted them. 'Sorry to disturb, sir, but the group captain wonders if you could join them in his office.'

'Daisy—' he began.

'I know. There's a war on.'

'Have I time to take the lady . . .?'

'Rather urgent, sir.'

'I'm fine.'

'I'll walk back with her, Adair.' Charlie had jumped down from the bandstand, her clarinet in her hand. 'Me and Clarence here.'

The airman had already started to walk away. Adair looked at Daisy and Charlie for a moment, and then turned and walked away smartly.

'That was exceedingly good champagne, Daisy.'

Daisy smiled. 'I wouldn't know. The bubbles went up my nose. Happy New Year, Charlie.'

'And you, my dear. Come on, let's walk back to the billet, but I, for one, am far too squiffy to sleep. Guess who nicked the bottle.'

'Charlie!'

'Noble cause – I shared it with the band.'

'Especially me,' said a slightly inebriated voice. Edith clambered down with her saxophone. 'Thank you, Daisy.

I have never had champagne before and I think it went straight to my head.'

They found their coats and left the slowly emptying hall. Daisy noticed that they turned right instead of left. 'Will we be able to find our way back if we go round the wrong way?'

'They'll throw us out of the WAAF if we can't, Aircraftswoman Petrie. Find the North Star.'

'I can't find my hand, never mind a star, Charlie. All the lights have gone out.'

'Oh, all right, let's just follow the road. It does go all the way round.'

They walked in complete darkness, stumbling as they came to the edges of pavements, past buildings they recognised and others they did not.

'Good Lord, how did we get to the office block?'

Before anyone could hazard a guess, Charlie grabbed each girl and pulled them towards her. 'Ssh,' she whispered as a door in the office block opened and light, together with four men, came out. One man was in civilian clothes. 'Don't breathe,' whispered Charlie.

'Good night, Doctor. Wing Commander Anstruther will escort you to the mess. Sleep well. Young Maxwell here will fly you out first thing.'

They did not hear the reply but as two men peeled away from the others, the light shone on the civilian and Daisy gasped.

The civilian Very Important Person, addressed as 'Doctor', was the man she had known all her life as Mr Fischer.

202

ELEVEN

Adair and his passenger had taken off long before Daisy rose on New Year's morning. She had pulled on gym clothes and run over to the aircraft hangar, with the excuse that she needed to clear her head, but the very bleary-eyed technician on duty had denied that there had ever been a Tiger Moth on the airfield. Obviously then, he had not been on duty on New Year's Eve.

'Mind you, I did hear that some pilot took a girl up yesterday and they might have said it was a Tiger Moth – don't really remember too much about yesterday.' He looked carefully at Daisy. 'Was it you? Did a female actually fly a plane? God, what is the world coming to?'

'Me? I only came over to see the plane. They must have left early.'

'Wouldn't know.'

'Thanks,' said Daisy, and started to run.

His voice followed her. 'They? Who's they?'

But Daisy was soon out of earshot.

Back at the billet she made a pot of tea. Many of her roommates, including Charlie and the unpleasant Felicity, were asleep, and Daisy had no real wish to go over for

203

breakfast by herself. Edith, the saxophonist, had been violently ill during the night – 'intolerance to alcohol', Charlie had decided – but she was now awake and very thirsty.

Daisy held a large mug of hot sweet tea to her lips.

'Don't fret, Edith. It's not the end of the world.'

But, with a groan of abject misery, Edith slid down under her blankets.

'Just as well she's not on duty.' Charlie, looking remarkably bright, had just emerged. 'Good grief, Daisy, did you go to bed at all?'

'Of course, and been out for a run.'

'Adair gone?'

Daisy hesitated. She certainly did not want to lie but neither did she want to talk, even to Charlie.

'Don't worry, not another word. Give me five minutes and we can have breakfast, unless you've been over.'

'Not hungry.'

'Love does that, or so they tell me. I'm ravenous and will even try that revolting-looking porridge.'

The dining hall was almost empty. Those on duty had eaten early and left, and it looked as if those not on duty had elected to spend the morning in bed. Daisy had been pleased to assure her parents that food in the services was not only plentiful but also tasty. She made a pretence of eating toast while Charlie demolished a tray of hot food, including the rather lumpy porridge.

'Delish. You should try it, Daisy, so good for you.'

'I believe you. I think I'll write letters today. Goodness knows when we'll have another chance.' She wondered whether she should say anything to Charlie about seeing

Mr Fischer – if it was he. Surely she could not really judge, having caught only the merest glimpse in poor light. If Adair's passenger had been her old friend then he was not only safe but also rather important. 'Another cuppa, Charlie?'

Charlie, with her mouth full, nodded and handed over her cup. Daisy walked over to get refills.

'Did you actually fly that plane yesterday?' A uniformed sergeant was standing beside her.

'With an experienced pilot, yes, Sergeant.'

'Can't you join me for a moment? It's just so amazing. Flying is something I've dreamed of for years. My brother's a pilot; Bomber Command.'

Daisy looked round to where Charlie was sitting. 'I have—' she began.

'Sorry, I shouldn't have interrupted your free time. Please rejoin your friend but first tell me – does one really feel like a bird?'

Daisy smiled. 'I did the first time I was taken up, but yesterday I was just so anxious to get it right that I don't remember thinking anything.'

The sergeant stood up and held out her hand. 'Claire Johnstone,' she said. 'Thank you, and carry on for all of us, my dear. I wish you a very happy year.'

'You too,' said Daisy.

'She wished me a very happy year, Charlie, and I said, "You too." Is that wrong?'

'Not in this particular situation. Usually one merely repeats the greeting. Don't worry about small things so much. The sergeant seems nice.'

'I think she is. Her brother's a pilot, bombers, but I think she'd love to fly too.'

'Bombers? Perhaps you'll run into him, Daisy. You'll probably be posted soon to a field with bombers.'

Of course. The induction course would soon be over. They would all be sent home on leave and Daisy would have to say goodbye to Charlie. Perhaps they would keep in touch. That would be nice, but Daisy remembered very well swearing undying friendship with her old school friends and was aware that none of them had replied to the Christmas letters she had put in the envelope with the Christmas cards. She had not expected a letter from Grace but decided that she would write to her first, even before she wrote home.

Dear Grace,

    I hope this reaches you as in the letter you wrote you said you might be going to another farm. Since that letter there has been Megan's death and I am sorry since she was your sister. I have a friend here whose name is Charlotte but we call her Charlie and her people have a telephone. She talks to them when she can as there is a public box here. The only people I know with a telephone are the Humbles at the farm. It must be nice to be able to talk to people on a telephone. That's all rubbish but it would be special to talk to you on the telephone and say I hope and pray that you are fine and that you had a nice Christmas. I know the Brewers would want you to be with them, and my mum and dad would too. If you get this please reply and don't forget me as I will never forget you.

    Your old friend,
Daisy

Her letter to her parents was, if anything more difficult. The events that were burning in her brain, her flying lesson with Adair, possibly catching a glimpse of Mr Fischer, and Adair's New Year's Eve kiss could not be mentioned.

She avoided contentious issues by telling them as much as she felt she could about the New Year's Eve dance. She wrote about Charlie and Edith and their musical abilities. She told them she had danced almost every dance – omitting the fact that her partner had almost always been the same man. She even admitted to having enjoyed a glass of real champagne and told them that experiencing bubbles going up her nose had been interesting. She described how Charlie's silver chain had brightened up her party outfit.

It was real silver, would you believe? Charlie's dad brought it from Mexico. I think we saw a cowboy film about Mexico, once, maybe with Roy Rogers. A fine scarf would do just as well, Mum. Would you keep an eye out in the market?

Please write as soon as you get this and tell me about Grace and what's happening to her. I did get a Christmas card but it was sent before the bombing and I'm worried. We're being posted soon. Any letter that comes here will get sent on.

She finished by assuring them that the food was still plentiful and very good, but not up to Mum's standards, which she actually thought was not really true but she could not hurt her mother's feelings. She told them that her marks and reports so far had been good and asked if there had been Christmas messages from her brothers.

She did not tell them that by working hard she felt she was continuing to keep her promise to the small boy who had died on Dartford Heath.

A week later Daisy wrote announcing her arrival home on Saturday 15 March for fourteen days' leave.

'Two whole weeks, Charlie, of not having to worry about doing something stupid.'

'What are you planning?'

'Not a thing, apart from buying a few new clothes and going to bed on the same day as when I got up.'

'Good grief, Daisy. The WAAF is giving you fourteen days to devote to riotous living. That means that if one wakes up on a Tuesday one has to be sure not to tumble into one's little bed until well into Wednesday morning. Anything else is terribly elderly.'

'Not in my house. What have you planned?'

'Oh, this and that. Stay with Mummy in the country for a few days and then I'll escape to London with my father. He's a big Agatha Christie fan and will be sure to get tickets for one of her plays. There always seems to be at least one on somewhere in town.' She stopped talking for a moment and a broad smile crossed her pretty face. 'In fact, Daisy, Dartford's no distance from London. You must come with us. I know Daddy would love to meet you.'

Daisy blushed furiously with embarrassment. She would love to go to a London theatre but how could she possibly go with someone like Charlotte, or her father, who asked 'questions in the House'?

Charlie smiled at her. 'You don't have to say anything now. I'll talk to Daddy and see what he can get. Oh, it

208

would be lovely. We do deserve a treat after all we've been through. The theatre, supper at the Savoy and then you could bunk in with me at the flat and tootle back to Dartford next morning. See, you wouldn't be deserting your family.'

'You're very kind, Charlie, but—' began Daisy.

'No buts, and I'm not being kind. I'm being very selfish. But just in case it doesn't work out – there is a war on, you know – let's exchange addresses. Remember, you did promise to be a chum.'

Charlie's address was easily recognisable as a rather grand one and Daisy wondered what she would make of Petrie's Groceries and Fine Teas, High Street, Dartford, but Charlie said nothing and merely put the slip of paper in her purse. Two days later they parted at the station. Daisy was taking the train to London and Charlie was being picked up.

'They're sending a car for me, Daisy. I'd take you but we're going in the opposite direction.'

Truth to tell, Daisy was quite happy to be alone, away from all the noise and bustle of the camp. She would have liked to walk around on her own to say a fond farewell. After all, it would always remain a special memory. There she had tasted her first champagne, she had flown a Tiger Moth . . . and she had been kissed.

Why, she wondered as she sat in the station waiting room, had the kiss been so memorable? It was not her first kiss; several of her brothers' friends had kissed her, but almost as if they felt they were expected to, when they had brought her home from the pictures or a social or dance in the church hall. None had been memorable, except perhaps the first one, which had disgusted her more than anything, as she had been aware first of noses bumping and then – oh gross – a tongue trying to force itself into her mouth.

But the kiss from Adair . . . at first so gentle, a mere brushing of her lips with his. Had she closed her eyes? She could not remember but she did remember looking into his eyes and reading something there. With the second kiss, she blushed now remembering, she had been filled with an most overwhelming feeling of desire, but desire for what?

He had gone and the man who might or might not be Mr Fischer had gone with him. A new life was starting. She was going to an airbase in Wiltshire where, at long last, she would be working on aircraft engines, actually doing something to help Britain win this war.

What was it that Mr Churchill said? Something about everyone working together? That's it, decided Daisy as the already heavily overcrowded train pulled in to pick up more passengers. *We will win the war if we work together*.

It was wonderful to be home. Daisy had been pressed to the window of the carriage since leaving London, so anxious had she been to see Dartford Station. She wondered who would be there to meet her. It never occurred to her that no one would be there. And so it proved. She looked, face as close to the glass as she could get. Dad? Mum? Rose?

She squealed with pleasure as she almost fell out of the train into the arms of her brother Phil. For a long moment neither said a word as they hugged and Daisy fought back tears.

'Just in time, our Daze,' he said. 'I'm off to Portsmouth first thing. Dad's in the shop since Mum's killed at least three fatted calves and is cooking enough to feed the entire British fleet. Give us your bags. The van's in the car park.'

How many months was it since she had seen or heard from her brother? Daisy took refuge in anger. 'I haven't heard a word from you, Philip Petrie, not even when Ron . . .'

'I'm not good at the writing, Daisy.'

He looked and sounded so disconsolate that she laughed. 'I had our mum convinced that a seagull had to fly over and pick up letters, Phil.'

'You look . . . different, Daisy. Beautiful. That's a word I never thought I'd use about my own sister.'

'You're daft, you are. How's our Rose? She never answers my letters either.'

'Too tired, love, and maybe too fed up. She wants to join up, the ATS, but Mum's . . . I don't know the words, Daisy . . . but Sam in a POW camp, Ron dead, you and me away . . . Forget all that. Are you doing well?'

'I think I'm doing all right, Phil, met some nice people—'

He interrupted her. 'Heard you had a flying lesson. Did you really? Did you really go up in one of them little crates?'

'I did. More than once. It's freedom and space you can't imagine, Phil. I love it.'

'Not so much space when the bloody sky's full of damned Messerschmitts. They're better planes than ours. They can't manoeuvre like our pilots, real circus performers they are, but Jerry's got the shooting A1.'

'You shouldn't say things like that.'

'The truth's the truth and I'm only talking to you. Now you're a WAAF you'll find out things for yourself.'

They had reached the van and Phil threw her kitbag in the back while she settled herself in the passenger seat. It was difficult driving in the blackout but for once a pale moon gave some light, and in no time they were home.

Daisy, who had never before been away from home, found her parents very changed, and they, like Phil, said that she too was different. Flora, who had lost a great deal of weight, had tried to prepare family favourites, among them apple fritters.

'We still seem able to get apples, Daisy; and Nancy Humble has some lovely Bramleys in one of the attics.'

The celebration went on for some time. Would they ever enjoy an evening as a family without the fear that in a moment a siren would blast the peace of the night? They tried to be as normal as possible as they caught up with everyone's news. Grace was back on her Scottish farm but had promised to return to Dartford whenever she had leave. Elsie and Ernie Brewer, as well as Flora and Fred, had assured Grace that she would always have a home with them. Daisy was brought up to date with news of as many of her old friends as possible but no one mentioned Mr Fischer. The old man who had been almost a fixture in the shop seemed to be quite forgotten.

Again she wondered – was he dead or was he alive? Had he indeed been the tall, slender figure she had glimpsed so briefly?

'Any news of Mr Fischer?'

'Funny you should ask, love. Mrs Porter, all excited, brought over a Christmas card. Lovely picture of a manger scene on the front and a ten-shilling note inside. From the National Gallery in London, no less, and it was signed, we think, Fischer. Terrible writing for a clever man but he said, "All well". Isn't that good? She were that happy.'

'That's lovely,' said Daisy, but decided to say nothing else. If Mr Fischer had sent a card, bought probably in London, to his former landlady stating that all was well, then it did indeed look as if Adair's VIP passenger addressed as 'Doctor' was their Mr Fischer.

He'll tell us if he can when he can, she decided, and so she changed the conversation by asking Phil what he could tell her about his time in the Royal Navy.

A very gloomy-looking Bernie brought the post a few days later.

Daisy was tidying the refuge room but she came out when she heard the shop doorbell. 'Any letters for me, Bernie?'

'Happy New Year, Daisy,' said Bernie, handing over two letters. 'I hope they're happy letters – I've delivered too many of them damn brown ones this week.'

'These are happy letters, Bernie. One's from another WAAF and the other's from Grace – do you remember Grace?'

'Megan Paterson's sister. What a tragedy that was. Tell her good luck from me, Daisy.'

'I will.' Daisy waited until the postman had gone. Was it possible that people could change so much in a few weeks? Like Flora, Bernie seemed older and greyer somehow.

'Has Bernie a family, Dad?'

''Course he has. His old dad lives with him and then

he has a wife and two lads. Too young for the Forces,' he answered Daisy's next question before she had asked it.

'I'll sit on the stairs to read these. The refuge room's airless somehow.'

'Well, of course it is, pet. It's got no windows – open the door if you're working in there.'

Daisy lifted her hand as if in acceptance and took her letters outside. She opened Grace's first, and yes, there at the top was the address of a farm in a place called East Lothian. She had not received Daisy's letter but mentioned her sister's death.

I can't say I miss Megan – she never wanted me and I've no idea why she even took me in but I would never have wanted her to die. I've come to terms with it. Your mum and dad and Sally's have been more real family than whatever family I had. Don't worry about me. I really enjoy the WLA and have met nice people although I will never forget my first friends.

Keep in touch, Daisy, and if you hear from Sam, say hello from me.

Grace

The second letter, from Charlie, was an invitation for Daisy to join her and her father for the Tuesday and Wednesday of the following week. Her father had tickets for a play and

if there's isn't an air raid we should have a lovely time. Daddy always has supper at the Savoy after the theatre and the food is good.

> If you can relieve my boredom, dear Daisy, send me the arrival time of your train and I'll meet you.

'I can't accept,' she announced after she had told her parents of the invitation.

'Whyever not? It'll be ever so nice to go to a real theatre and then supper at the Savoy. Sounds like something out of a film, Daisy, and look at what you'll have to talk about when you see Sally.'

'But, Mum, theatre tickets and supper at the Savoy. That's a really posh place.'

'We know that. And if you're worrying about repaying your friend, she's welcome to have her tea here any time she's in Dartford. Come to think of it, Fred, with the boys never here no more, we could put the girls in there and use their little room for visitors.'

'Good idea, Flora. See, Daisy, your friend could spend the night too. Not a problem. Wish we'd thought about that when Phil was here. He could have helped move the beds.'

'Don't shift beds, Dad, there's no time left this leave. Maybe I could ask Charlie next time.'

Daisy was slightly ill at ease and she could feel her mother looking at her. Finally Flora spoke. 'If you was worried we're not good enough for your friend, Daisy, then I'd think careful about what kind of friends you want.'

'Charlie's not like that, Mum, she's really great. You'd like her. She's nice. I wish there was a better word than nice but that's all I can think of.'

'Well, your dad and me will look forward to meeting her. But Dad says you heard from Grace.'

215

The awkward moment was over but had left Daisy feeling thoroughly ashamed of herself. She was the problem, not Charlie.

Next morning Miss Partridge came into the shop. She carried a parcel, which she put down on the polished counter. 'Daisy, dear, I met your father going about his duties last night and he told me you are off to the theatre in London. An interesting play?'

'I hope so, Miss Partridge. My friend's father is a big fan of Miss Christie, but really I'm just excited to be going to London.'

'And the Savoy. Such a lovely hotel. Would you believe that a long time ago a young man proposed to me in the Savoy?'

Daisy and Rose had made up stories about Miss Partridge, and several of the other elderly single ladies who came into the shop, but supper at the Savoy had not been part of the story. 'I wouldn't doubt it at all, Miss Partridge. But—'

'Not a tragic story, Daisy, dear. He had also proposed to another young lady, keeping his options open, as it were, and when he came back from Europe, he chose her. Happened all over Europe, I suppose. Water under the bridge. When your dear father was telling me last night I had a thought.' She slid the parcel in Daisy's direction. 'I hope this isn't offensive, Daisy, but I thought perhaps you might want to buy or make a new frock and, as it happens, I kept a few of my special dresses. It would be lovely if they could be useful to a young woman in this war. Terribly old-fashioned but the materials are beautiful.'

'Oh, Miss Partridge, how very kind of you. Thank you.'

'I was going to give them to charity but I just couldn't bring myself to give anything to that rather awful Miss Paterson, nothing charitable about her – or me, I suppose. I'll leave them with you and if they're of no use, perhaps you'd give them to the new girl who's working there. I'll be back to do my hours this afternoon if Flora wants to go shopping.' She turned towards the door.

'Let me just open them . . .'

'I said goodbye to them last night, dear. Back at two.'

Daisy stood for a moment and then opened the parcel, carefully saving the paper. Inside lay a confection of silver material and shiny black beads. A narrow silver and black sash was folded up under it, and below that lay a peach-coloured froth of a material she had never seen before except in films. She held up the silver and black cocktail dress and gazed at it in awe.

A flapper. Imagine, little Miss Partridge a flapper. She must have looked fabulous.

Both dresses were exquisitely made and both very much out of fashion.

'Cuppa, Daisy? Oh, what's that, pet? Absolutely gorgeous.' Flora with a steaming mug of tea in each hand had pushed the door open with her bottom and was standing looking at the shimmering heap of fabric.

Daisy took the tea and explained as her mother examined the two dresses.

'My wedding dress weren't near as lovely as these, Daisy. They're a bit much for the theatre, don't you think, but the silver and black one with the beads would be lovely for dinner, maybe with a little jacket. Or wait, this sash would really dress up a plain black frock, turn it into one that could be worn all evening.'

'The top of the frock's too 1920s, Mum, all those beads. I'd look silly.'

They stood solemnly, drinking their tea and looking at the dresses.

'Mrs Roban,' said Flora suddenly.

'Who's Mrs Roban?'

'A refugee. Came to church last week and the Reverend says as she's looking for work. Seems she worked in Brussels with a . . . oh, what's the word, a person that makes expensive clothes? Begins with C.'

'No idea, Mum, but if she's a dressmaker, maybe she could do something with this. I never had a frock made for me before.'

When Miss Partridge arrived to do her twice-weekly two hours in the shop, Flora thanked her and told her of the plan. Miss Partridge was thrilled. 'Oh, now we are helping two people. Reverend Tiverton is sponsoring Mrs Roban and her family – her husband has disappeared, unfortunately – but I wish I'd thought of her, Daisy. She was trained by a well-known couturier. I would hurry over before she becomes too busy.'

Daisy and her mother left Miss Partridge quite happily in charge of the shop and walked along to Overy Street and across the bridge to the little house that had been found for the Roban family.

It was almost two hours later before they walked back again, both bursting with feminine delight at the frivolous afternoon they'd had, devoted entirely to talking about clothes.

* * *

This was much more exciting than the last time she had come up to London. The train was just as full but this time her only fear was that she would make a fool of herself in front of Charlie's father, and not that she would not be found good enough to join the WAAF. The platforms were crowded, lines of children tagged like Christmas parcels, distraught families, military personnel looking for their girls, girls looking for the only one in the crowds in uniform that they wanted to see. And there, sailing through them, and wearing – heavens, was it really a fur coat – came Charlotte Featherstone. The crowds, especially the men, parted for her as the Red Sea is said to have parted for Moses, and then she was at the window. 'Daisy, how wonderful. So lovely to see you. Come along, the car's just outside.'

Daisy stepped down, case in one hand, handbag in the other, and followed in her wake.

A car was waiting for them outside the station, a very large car with a man, a uniformed chauffeur, standing beside the rear doors. Daisy waited for Charlie to say, 'Home, James,' which is what ladies who had chauffeurs said in all the films she had ever seen, but Charlie said nothing except 'Thank you' when 'James' opened the door for her. She slid across the soft leather seat and Daisy, who had been relieved of her small suitcase by the chauffeur, slid in beside her.

'Poor old London's had a bit of a bashing, even since we went to Wilmslow, Daisy. Makes me sad and rather angry, but I suppose our boys are pounding chunks out of the enemy too.'

Daisy said nothing, and not because she was giving herself up to the unexpected luxury but because she could not seem to see 'the enemy'. Absolutely easy to hate Hitler, his acolytes, and his actions, but was not Germany inhabited by decent people – like Mr Fischer, for instance – who would rather be living a normal life?

'Don't think about it, Daisy,' Charlie said, just as she and Daisy were propelled forward onto the floor, where they stayed listening to the wild screeching and squealing of brakes and gears until the car stopped.

'You all right, miss? That hole weren't there when I come down here last night and I didn't see it for the smoke an' haze.'

'We're fine, Charlie,' said Charlie, after a nod from Daisy. They got out and looked at the great crack on the road's surface. Three roadmen had been working in and around the hole.

'God in Heaven. How awful if we'd hit them,' breathed Charlie. 'Are you men all right?'

'Fine, miss, we ducked. We're closing the road. It shoulda been done but we're going in too many directions at the same time.'

'Come on, Ebenezer,' said Charlie. 'You need a good strong cup of tea.'

'I thought you called him Charlie.' They were relaxing as the lovely motorcar moved more smoothly along.

'It's his name, but when I decided I wanted to be Charlie – and don't laugh, I was very small – Daddy said he never knew who was going to answer him when he shouted. I call him almost anything except Charlie – usually.'

A few minutes later they were at Charlie's London home, a very lovely white building on a wide street of similar buildings. Daisy was relieved when Charlie opened the door herself and ushered Daisy inside. The chauffeur had disappeared down some steps, taking Daisy's little case with him.

'Let's go in here and I'll ring for tea before I show you your room. That chair's comfy.'

Daisy was almost afraid to sit in the chair, which seemed to be made of a fine, almost golden wood, and was upholstered in a striped red and gold material. A beautiful dolphin was carved where each arm joined the legs.

'Sit down, Daisy. That takes my father and he's a lot heavier than you. Tea will be here immediately unless you'd like something stronger.' Charlie flopped down in a more modern armchair. 'Welcome to Belgravia.'

They chatted happily over tea and delicious scones, with cream and raspberry jam, and Daisy began to relax as Charlie chattered on. Voices, she felt, were so important. She could listen to Charlie all day, or to . . . No, she would not think of Adair Maxwell.

TWELVE

Charlie's father was involved in meetings and so the girls had dinner together in what Charlie called 'the breakfast room'.

'You look absolutely lovely, Daisy. That dress is a stunner. Could I be very rude and ask you where you got it? It has couturier written all over it.'

Over the delicious, if fairly simple meal, Daisy told her all about Miss Partridge and Mrs Roban. 'There was a sash of sorts, Charlie, possibly worn around the neck like a necklace instead of the long strings of pearls flappers wore, but clever Mrs Roban remade the top and turned it into shoulders and these little sleeves. Is it really up to date, Charlie?'

'Absolutely, and Mummy and I will want to have Mrs Roban's address. She'll do really well, Daisy.'

'She advertised for any kind of sewing the day after they arrived – put a notice in the post office window. She's so grateful to be safe in England and wants to earn her keep for herself and her children. Don't think there's much chance of finding her husband alive.'

Charlie jumped up. 'No gloom this evening. Go powder

your nose; we're meeting Daddy in less than twenty minutes . . .'

Six hours later an exhilarated Daisy slipped off her lovely frock in the bedroom that would be the first one that she had ever slept in all alone. The privacy was just another joyful experience. She prepared for bed in her own private bathroom and then climbed into the very feminine bed. She was sure she would never sleep as memories crowded in one after the other: the chauffeur-driven car, the beautiful house, meeting Charlie's father, who was not at all frightening but as much fun as his daughter, the London theatre, her first visit to a professional theatre and then, as if she had not experienced enough, supper in the elegant and crowded Savoy. What a tale she would have to tell her parents and write to her brothers.

Deciding to write to Sam and Phil was her last coherent thought. The next thing she knew was when an aproned maid brought in a pot of tea with soldiers of hot buttered toast.

That evening she arrived back in Dartford just as the air-raid sirens went and, like many others, was forced to take refuge in an overcrowed shelter. She stood pressed up against other people, one of whom smelled rather unpleasantly, and tried to think of nothing but the perfect time she had enjoyed. But her mind would not obey her. Where was her father, who had been coming to meet her? Surely he had found a shelter. Were her mother and sister safe in the refuge room?

The noise was deafening and it went on and on. Some soldiers tried to start a singsong. 'Come on, ladies and gents, a few choruses of 'Roll out the Barrel'.' After a half-hearted attempt at that old song, they tried 'Pack Up Your Troubles in Your Old Kit Bag' and Daisy sang along as lustily as she could. She was a WAAF; it was her duty and privilege to help, in any way, to win this war. That thought kept her going through the drone of the planes, the booms from bombs and whatever else exploding, and even the sound of their own ack-ack guns firing at the enemy.

The rather hoarse leader had just begun the fifth repeat of a rather tired 'The Lambeth Walk' when the all clear sounded, and the exhausted crowd, too tired and worried to do anything but creep, made their slow way out into the street to a disaster scene. Fires were blazing everywhere, especially on the other side of Mill Pond Road where many of the chemical and munitions factories were situated.

Daisy, aware that her father must be out there in that mayhem, had no clear idea what to do for the best. Should she stand still and wait, in the hope that he was safe and would come to the shelter nearest the station or should she begin to walk home? Flames lit up this part of town, but once she was beyond the fires, down Hythe Street and as far perhaps as Home Gardens and so well on her way to High Street, it was unlikely that there would be much visibility. Was the sky dark? She could not see because a huge mass of smoke and fire lay between her and any stars that might have dared to shine. Torches, with their lights dimmed, were allowed during blackouts but she had not thought beyond seeing her father at the barrier. She stood for a moment, getting her bearings.

'Come on, our Daisy.' Her father, covered in smoke and soot, almost hobbled towards her. 'Firemen need us. You remember how to use a stirrup pump?'

There was no time to hug, to express their joy that each was alive; that would come later. For now they were fire wardens who knew how to kill incendiaries, how to recognise an unexploded bomb, and how to put out smaller fires.

'The van's copped it, Daisy, love. We'll have to walk home,' said Fred some hours later, and that was when Daisy realised that she had lost her little suitcase, but, much more importantly, her beautiful dress.

Once in a lifetime, she thought. She said nothing. What was the point? She had no idea where to begin looking and it was almost morning.

'It's only a dress,' she mumbled, 'and not a life.'

'What's that, love?'

'Saying I'd kill for a cuppa, Dad.'

'Me an' all, love.'

Daisy had by now relaxed into her pre-WAAF self and so, towards the end of her leave, she was sitting in the kitchen enjoying a cup of tea with her mother when Mr Churchill broadcast on the radio. Daisy was thrilled. Usually she read reports of his stirring speeches or heard a recording weeks after the broadcast, but here the great man was speaking, as it were, directly to her. He spoke of his belief that Hitler assumed that Britain would cave in after the fall of France. Britain, of course, did not. He wanted the nation to realise that Hitler would certainly be preparing and planning even more horrific attacks on Great Britain but he emphasised his faith in the resilience of the British. Daisy felt herself grow stronger as she listened to the speech. He quoted from a letter sent to him by the President of the United States, Mr Roosevelt. The President had used a poem by Longfellow to tell Mr Churchill what the world thought of Britain. The world, he said, was 'hanging breathless' as it waited to learn Britain's fate. And then the genius that was the Prime Minister had answered the worries. If America supplies us with the tools we need, said Mr Churchill, 'we will finish the job.'

'And we will, Mum, we will.'

Flora looked down at her cold tea. 'That were so stirring, Daisy, I never touched my tea. Let's have a nice cup of Oxo instead.'

Dear Mum, thought Daisy. Trying so hard to bury her fears, to steer life back to the ordinary and everyday. But Daisy knew the veneer of cheerfulness was wafer thin.

Two weeks into her training at her new air base, Daisy was summoned to the squadron leader's office. She was terrified. She was, she knew, working very hard and learning a great deal. The skilled mechanic who was supervising her was pleased, or so he said, with her progress. So this summons could not be about work. It had to be her family. Who? Phil, Rose? Sam? Had something even more horrifying than prison camp happened to Sam?

Outside the door she straightened her cap, her tie and her shoulders, then knocked.

'Come in.'

Tentatively, Daisy opened the door. 'You sent for me, sir.'

But it was Wing Commander Anstruther who was in the office, not sitting at the desk but standing at the window staring out, as far as she could see, at nothing. He turned and walked over to the desk. 'Sit down, Miss Petrie.'

Oh God, it was bad news, but why him?

She sat down as correctly as she could on the wooden chair by the desk.

'I'm afraid I have some very bad news for you. A few weeks ago, you were staying with your friend Charlotte in London.' He waited.

'Yes, sir.'

'I regret very much having to tell you that the house received a direct hit – on the night you left – and the occupants were killed. Sir Charles Featherstone, his daughter, Charlotte, and two members of staff: the house-keeper and the chauffeur. The maid, Poppy Smith, was seriously injured and, I'm sorry, but when she recovered consciousness, she was quite sure that "Miss Charlotte's friend" was also in the house.'

Daisy started up. 'No, oh, no, please.' Seeing the understanding look on his face she sank back into the chair. He, too, was suffering. If he had not known Charlie well – and she knew she would never know whether or not that was the case – he was certainly a friend of her parents.

'I'm sorry, but she was so sure of it that Lady Featherstone insisted that they spend time looking for you. Needless to say we are all very happy that you had already left.' He stood up and lifted a small parcel from the desk. 'Lady Featherstone asked me to give you this. She says Charlie would have wanted you to have them.'

He handed her the parcel. 'Will you be all right?'

She looked up at him, into the kind eyes that had helped the terrified Charlie climb the wall. 'Yes, sir,' she said, and saluted, and the wing commander returned the salute.

As she left the room she wondered if she was imagining things for she could have sworn she heard him say softly, 'Do it for Charlie, Daisy.'

No, a wing commander would never address a mere aircraftswoman second class by her Christian name.

Back in her hut, she put the parcel in a drawer, changed into her overalls and went back to work where she struggled to keep her over-active mind from working. She saw beautiful, vital Charlie crushed and bleeding under fallen masonry, and then in the exquisite dress she had worn to the theatre and had sworn 'isn't a patch on yours, Daisy', and then white with terror as she climbed the gym wall.

'You're no' a bit o' use tae me the day, Daisy. Wis it bad news, hen?' the Scots mechanic asked.

She nodded.

'Then away and hae a hot shower followed by a nice cuppa tea, lotsa sugar. I'll see you the morn when you've turned back intae a mechanic.'

She stumbled towards the hut, hoping that none of the other girls was there. *Turned back into a mechanic.* He was said to be the best aircraft mechanic on the base and he had said she was doing well. *Do it for Charlie.*

She remembered the little boy and his innocent play on the Heath. I have two of them now, she told herself.

She burst into healing tears and lay sobbing on her bed until there was not a tear left in her body. How long had she known Charlie? Three months? And yet she felt almost unbearable pain. Nothing, surely, could feel worse than this. She obeyed Scottie's orders, took a hot shower and drank a pot of hot sweet tea.

She felt totally exhausted, wrung out like a limp sheet on washing day. She leaned over, took out the precious parcel and opened it. There was a small silver-framed picture of Charlie – in complete flying gear, in the pilot's seat of a Tiger Moth.

'Oh, modest, lovely Charlie.' Daisy smiled but could feel tears – where were they coming from – welling up again. The other little packet held a leather pouch that contained the silver belt.

'Too much, too much.' She pushed them under the pillow, lay down and sobbed pitifully until she fell asleep.

Daisy did turn back into a mechanic, so much so that Sergeant Gordon, the senior mechanic, worried about her.

'There's lads here would kill tae take you to the dancing, Daisy. You don't hiv tae marry one o' them if you hiv a lad elsewhere.'

Had her mother not said something like that a long time ago?

'There's a war on, Sarge.' The girls in her hut asked her constantly to join them on various excursions but somehow she had no appetite for entertainment. Even the suggestion of going dancing, or for a meal out, or to the theatre in nearby Salisbury held no appeal. This course, like the first one, was to last eight weeks. She had left school before she was fifteen years old. She needed to study.

'Very amusing. Daisy, trust me, a wee bit o' fun never hurt anybody.'

'I know, Sarge, but you're the best mechanic in the business, everybody says so, and I want to learn everything you can teach me.'

'There's nowt left for you tae learn but the Highland Fling, and that's no' on my list.' He looked at her questioningly as she sat astride the nose of the plane on which they were working. 'You went up with that Spitfire pilot?'

'Yes.'

'Why? How?'

'I met him before the war. My brothers had taught me a lot about engines and I helped him with his aircraft engine, pretty basic one. He took me up as a thank you.'

'Simple as that.'

'Yes, Sergeant Gordon.'

'Well, Daisy, the exam's next Saturday. You'll easy be top. I'll see if I can gie you a wee push to a base that has flyers on it. You'll get a bittie leave. Have you a home tae go to?'

'Yes, in Dartford.'

'Dartford, never been there, but it's no' half getting a belting, right on Bombers' Alley.'

At the end of the eight-week course, Daisy did attain top marks in the mechanics course, and was promoted. The promotion brought her an extra shilling a day in her wage packet, which delighted her. While other girls thought of silk stockings, shampoo – if it could be found – and lipstick, she thought, stamps! Since Christmas she had been writing weekly letters to her brothers, one in his prison camp, the other 'somewhere at sea'. She was also making an effort to keep up a correspondence with her old school friends, Sally and Grace, and, of course, she wrote more regularly to her parents, always remembering to ask how their protégés, George and Jake, were managing.

It was unfair that Rose alone had to shoulder the burden of worry over their mother, and if even the skimpiest of letters cheered her, then letters she would receive. Daisy had no idea whether or not Sam or Phil ever received any of her letters – but Charlie had suggested bombarding the over-worked Red Cross in the hope that at least one would reach Sam. In the eight weeks she had been on the base, she had received one letter from Phil, one from Grace, a short note from Sally talking about a part in a play, and two from her parents. Adair Maxwell wrote twice. The second one, she had decided, she would answer on the train to Dartford.

That was the same day that a badly shot-up Spitfire piloted by Adair Maxwell limped home from a raid and made a forced landing in a field in Kent.

Daisy had thought long and hard about Adair and his letters. She had meant to answer the first one, which arrived shortly after their flight over the airfield had been observed by so many of the base personnel.

Do I love him? Is loving him, which I think I do, the same as being in love with him? I have no idea. What do I know about love? She had lain awake night after night trying to resurrect her feelings when in Adair's company. To say she felt *comfortable* did not seem romantic. Surely if one was in love one did not feel comfortable. After all, she was perfectly comfortable in her mother's kitchen. And comfortable was certainly not what she had felt after the second kiss on New Year's morning.

How she missed Charlie. She would have had something sensible or even funny to say that would have put all Daisy's worries into some kind of perspective.

On the second night of her leave, Daisy was settling down to listen to the wireless when once again their peace was blasted by the desperate wailing of the air-raid warnings. A few minutes later the threatening drone of the bombers could be heard below the shriek, as, once more, they prepared to rain death and destruction on that little corner of England.

'We should live in this blooming refuge room,' groaned Flora, as she hurried downstairs with her daughters. 'Wonder where your dad'll be.'

Daisy and Rose said nothing. Their father, like the other wardens, would be doing his job, patrolling his area, looking for fires, watching for bombs, trying to get help to the wounded, and dousing as many fires as they could. At the same time, they would still be looking for any households showing even the smallest chink of light.

Had Flora been expecting an answer? She answered herself as she tried to make herself comfortable in the small, airless room. 'He'll be doing his duty like the others. Up and down the High Street he'll go.' She closed her eyes as if that might also shut out the frightening muffled thumps of impact.

'That was close.' Rose, who had been putting curling rags on her long hair prior to meeting her boyfriend when he came off duty, carried on doing the simple task. 'Stan's working late tonight so I hope this is over before ten. We were going down the Swan for a drink, Daisy. You're welcome to come too.'

'Sit drinking warm beer watching you and Stan gazing at each other. I don't think so, thanks.'

'You wouldn't be a gooseberry. There's other lads come too.'

But Daisy, her thoughts already busy elsewhere, did not answer.

After a time, Flora opened the box that held food supplies and took out the Thermos flask of hot cocoa, which she had made earlier in the evening – just in case. She made a hot drink every day and could count on her fingers the number of times the drink had not been needed.

She enjoyed her comforting drink and then took out her knitting. She was determined to look forward positively and so was knitting Fred a new pullover in his Bowling Club colours.

'We have any more air raids I'll have this finished long before the season starts,' she said cheerfully. 'Then I'll knit summer cardigans for you two; pale yellow would be lovely on you, Daisy. What do you . . .?' She dropped her knitting. 'No, my Sam'll need new clothes when he gets home and he'll get home soon now, won't he, girls?'

Daisy and Rose looked at each other. They had talked for hours in their bedroom and knew that each of them worried about their mother. Sometimes she was very quiet and introverted and at other times she seemed too animated, jumping from one subject or topic to another, like the young cat next door jumped from one leaf to another in autumn. So much grief had rained down on her in the past two years. The wounding and then capturing of her eldest son and the death of her youngest were surely enough tragedy for anyone, but her three other children were all in one way or another fighting for freedom. Rose had told Daisy that her mother still worried over her, although her injury had been slight, and that she watched fretfully for Bernie the postman and could barely conceal her disappointment on the many days when no mail was received.

'Dad tries teasing her, Daisy,' Rose had said. 'He says things like, "They can't be winning the war if they're spending every minute writing notes to you." She does try to cheer up but sometimes this house is just so gloomy. Makes me miserable. I'd like to join up; thinking of the Auxiliary Territorial Service. Stan told me about it. There's lots of jobs I could do in the ATS, mechanics, driving, all sorts.'

'Won't you miss Stan?'

''Course, but he might get called up himself if it doesn't stop soon.'

What would sensible, practical Rose think of her relationship with Adair? Would she say there was no relationship? Daisy figuratively straightened her backbone and decided that if she had to wonder whether or not she loved Adair, then, obviously she did not.

Now she looked at her twin sister and shrugged. At the moment it seemed that they could only help their mother cope with life by supporting her as much as possible. That meant any spare time would be spent writing letters.

She was dozing on the floor when the all clear sounded.

'You won't be meeting Stan as late as this, pet?'

'No, he said if it were after ten, he'd be as well to go home.'

They began to gather up the cups and the Thermos,

Flora's knitting and anything else that was not usually left in the little room.

'I'll wash these before I go to bed,' offered Daisy, as she was the only one who did not need to jump out of bed early, and that was when they heard knocking on the door of the shop.

'Who's knocking at this time of night? Don't tell me your dad's lost his keys.'

'Happens, Mum,' said Rose as she hurried through the shop to open up.

An unidentifiable heavy-set figure could be seen through the glass in the top half of the door.

As Rose wrestled with the lock they heard a voice. 'It's only me, Alf Humble.'

Flora pulled the door open. 'Alf, oh, no, something's happened to Fred. I knew it; I just knew it.'

'Mum,' said the girls together as Alf closed the door behind him.

'There, there, Flora. As far as I know Fred's fine; he's doing fire and injury reports. No, I'm afraid it's you I've come to see, Daisy. I'm sorry it's so late, pet, but I got caught up in the raid and had to sit it out in a shelter. Quite an experience.'

'Me?'

'Yes, lass.' He turned to Flora. 'Could we go upstairs, Flora, or into your refuge room? The world can see us through the shop window.'

He turned to look at Daisy, who was staring at him, her eyes wide in her pale face. Charlie was dead. Now someone else was dead. Who?

'Upstairs, Daisy love, and Rose'll make us all a nice hot cup of tea.' Flora, once more in control, ushered her daughter and her unexpected guest upstairs, talking all the way. 'Does Nancy know where you are, Alf?'

'I phoned her from a call box. She'll be sound asleep by now. Lovely and quiet in the country.'

'Alf, tell me.' Was it Adair? It had to be.

'I got a call from the County Hospital earlier this evening, Daisy. Adair's got me down as next of kin and he's there, lass; had to crash-land in a field yesterday.'

No. 'No, it's not possible.'

But Alf Humble did not make jokes; he did not tell lies. Alf was one of the most honest people she had ever met, would ever meet.

'He's here, Daisy, in the hospital.' He saw the fear in her eyes, reached forward and took her cold hand. 'He's been shot up a bit and one leg's broken from the crash, but he's going to be fine.'

'He can't be here, Alf. It's a mistake. This is Dartford and he's from. . . . Oh, Alf, I don't know where he's from.'

'Don't really matter where he's from, pet, his plane came down in Kent, outside Dartford, and this is the nearest hospital. He carries a card with the name of next of kin. I think the lad's only living relative is the fellow that owns The Old Manor but he's away with the army somewhere. That left me. And then, didn't they find a wee note from a Daisy who lives on Dartford High Street in his shirt pocket.'

Daisy felt herself blushing. 'I was only thanking him for a flying lesson.'

Alf laughed. 'So you won't walk up West Hill tomorrow to see the wounded airman?'

Rose was there with a tray of tea and some slices of

Flora's latest attempt at an eggless cake, and no one seemed to notice that Daisy had not answered.

'Quite tasty for a cake without eggs, Alf. What do you think?'

Before he had time to answer they heard a noise downstairs and then Fred's cheery voice as he climbed the staircase.

'What a night,' he began, and then when he saw Alf, a look of concern crossed his face. 'What brings you to see us this late, Alf? Any problems?'

And so Alf had to tell his story all over again. 'Hope there's enough hot water to get half the grime off you, Fred. Just as well you're not a vain man.' Everyone laughed and Alf started again. 'High time I was off, though. I checked my lorry when I phoned Nancy – a few dents in the doors from flying shrapnel but there were dents already and I'll hand the shrapnel over to the scrap collectors. I'd not be quite so happy if any of it had gone through the doors, though.'

Daisy, who had expected to fall fast asleep as soon as she got into bed, did not sleep at all that night. She closed her eyes when her sister woke and pretended to be asleep until Rose and both her parents had gone to work. Alf had said that she would not be allowed to see Adair until the afternoon but she knew that she could not wait a moment longer. Sitting in the hospital or walking aimlessly around its grounds was far better than having to deal with her parents' gentleness. The night before she had wanted to scream, 'It's Adair who's hurt, not me,' but she had managed to keep quiet.

Now she washed and dressed, discarding her first choice of civilian clothes for her WAAF uniform. Hospitals had rules but was it possible that a sympathetic nurse might let a WAAF in for a minute or two if the ward was not too busy? She had no particular desire to parade through Dartford in uniform – that came under what Fred and Flora had always discouraged: 'calling attention to yourself'. But since it was too pleasant a spring day for her to wear her raincoat, she had no choice.

Without so much as a cup of tea, she crept downstairs, shoes in hand, and slipped out of the back door.

Within a few minutes she was regretting her decision as she ran the gauntlet of old school-mates or their mothers, as well as customers of the family shop. She was forced to stop each time and answer questions and, of course, to ask questions of those she had not seen for some time. At last she was out of the busy centre of the town and able to cover ground more quickly. She reflected on how kind people were. Even girls with whom she had not been particularly friendly at school wanted to stop, to praise her for being in the Forces, to tell her of other friends who were now overseas or casualties of war. Daisy tried to cheer herself up by remembering her conversation with one girl who had been on the running team. Not yet twenty years old, and already the mother of one lovely little girl.

One toddler and another baby before winter. Would I want that life? Daisy answered herself with an emphatic no, but then she thought of Adair and she seemed to feel, for a moment, the demanding pressure of his lips on hers at the New Year's Eve dance.

What would it be like to be loved by Adair, to . . . Shocked by where her thoughts were going, Daisy doubled her speed and forced her mind to focus only on the burned-out or damaged buildings, and therefore damaged or destroyed lives, that she was passing.

She reached the hospital and realised that she now had a blinding headache, a direct result of eating nothing that morning. If she didn't have something soon she knew from experience that she would be sick.

Down the hill, in the town, she had passed a WVS van. They would have offered her a cup of tea.

'Problem?' A man she thought might be an orderly had appeared and was smiling at her. 'You look as if you need to sit down.'

'No, it's nothing. I was hoping to see a friend and – sorry, I've got a stupid headache.' At the same time, to her deep embarrassment, her empty stomach argued its case with a loud rumbling.

'C'mon, you'll be no use to your lad if you're sick all over him. It is a lad you're here to see?'

Unable to speak, Daisy nodded and allowed him to lead her into a little room where she was encouraged to sink into a chair. 'I'll get you a cuppa and a bun or something. We've barely enough time to look after the real casualties without their beautiful girlfriends collapsing on us. Don't look so ashamed, love, you're more than welcome to a cuppa if it helps you cheer up one of our lads.'

He was back in a few minutes, a mug of hot, sweet tea in one hand and a plate with a small bun on it in the other. 'Told the cook you're a WAAF and she's given you a scraping of real butter. Now get that down you and don't move till I come back.'

'Yessir,' she said automatically and he laughed from the door. 'Nurse, Mr Wishaw, or just Frank will do, love. Now don't let that butter go to waste.'

Twenty minutes or so later, Frank returned to see how she was doing. The tea and the bun were gone. 'You rushed out without a bite this morning, didn't you? Now depending on who you want to see, your promising never to start the day without breakfast, and what's going on in his ward, I might be able to spirit you in.'

She stood up. 'Thank you, Frank, for the tea and the food. His name's Maxwell.'

'Well, well, Squadron Leader Maxwell? It has to be him, only male military of that name. Doctor's done his round so I can let you hide behind a curtain for five minutes. Sister shouldn't be there for a while but, like most sisters, she's a law, as they say. C'mon, you look better so smile. I want him feeling better when you leave, not worse.'

Daisy followed Frank's tall, broad form along corridors and through doors until he stopped at the ward where Adair was a patient. 'Wait a minute,' he said, and went in alone.

'Coast's clear. In you go.'

'Frank, is he . . .?' She stopped and tried to begin again. 'Is he very ill?'

'There's no damage to his pretty face, if that's what you mean.' Frank's voice had completely lost its friendliness.

'Is he very ill?' she asked again, and her voice was almost as angry as the nurse's.

He smiled down at her. 'Nothing vital's been hit, love, but he'll be with us for a few weeks. I'll tell you more when you come out.'

Daisy pushed open the door and looked at a long surgical ward with at least twelve beds on each side. The room was full of a strong smell of some kind of antiseptic. Daisy wrinkled her nose in distaste.

'Second from the end on the left,' came a disembodied voice, 'and you only have to worry if they're near the door.'

Daisy did not even want to begin to think what that cryptic remark might mean. She walked firmly down the ward, not looking at any of the men lying down or propped up in any of the beds. She stopped at the bed second from the end.

Adair was lying down, his eyes closed. His left leg was in some kind of sling and his right arm was heavily bandaged. What was obviously a new bandage was round his head. His face was bruised and scratched and he had the most colourful black eye. She was surprised by the sight of glorious yellow daffodils brightening the whole ward from what looked like a milk jug on the side table. She looked around. None of the other tables held flowers. 'Wonder who brought these?' she murmured.

'Alf,' came a whisper. 'Poor chap was fearfully embarrassed. Chap in the next bed asked him when the baby was due.'

Daisy blushed to the roots of her hair.

'Sorry,' he said, 'guard down.'

'Adair.'

'Daisy.' He held out his left hand and she held it. She felt that she never wanted to let go. 'Daisy,' he said again, 'how wonderful. I watched you come down the ward but convinced myself I was hallucinating.'

'If that means you thought you were seeing things that weren't there, I am here.'

'Afraid I can't get up. Mangled my leg a bit.'

'And your arm.'

'Arm? Oh, yes, forgot. Bullets, I think. Can't feel a thing, Daisy, floating.'

Was he losing his mind – or worse? Floating? What did he mean? She squeezed his hand but had no awareness that she did so.

'You are here, Daisy. You're real.'

'Of course I am. A nurse let me in; I shouldn't be here.'

Apart from a visit to Rose she had never visited a patient in hospital and had never dreamed that she would ever visit an injured pilot who had been forced to crash-land. What should she say? Damn. The WAAF had guidebooks for everything but not this.

'Are you still floating, Adair?'

'Floating? Learned in the swimming baths at school. Knew a chap who could lie there and read. Never managed that but learned to drift. Lovely. Drifting on top of the water.'

'Your head?'

'Hurts. Heading for some farm workers, Daisy.' He seemed agitated and tried to rise but fell back down.

'You missed them.' *Please God let me be right. Alf would have said something.*

'Tried to pull her up over them. Remember stones, lots of stones.'

'Time for you to leave, miss. Has he been reliving the crash?' The nurse, Frank, was beside the bed.

She nodded.

'You hit a dry-stone dyke, lad. The farm workers would have been softer but they're grateful to you.'

'Thank God,' said Daisy.

'Thank the pilot, love. The farmer said he can't

understand where he got the strength – pulled his bird out of a nosedive, up, and bang, destroyed his dyke. Cheap at the price. Now off you go and don't come back till visiting hours. Go on, give him a kiss and scarper.'

Daisy looked up at Frank and down at Adair, whose eyes were closed. She bent, and very gently kissed his lips, almost the only part of his face not bruised and battered.

She had just left the room when a nursing sister sailed down the corridor towards the ward.

'I am pretending that I do not see you, young woman. Now run before I step on you.'

Daisy ran.

THIRTEEN

Daisy visited Adair every day – at the proper visiting hours, until the end of her leave.

The first few days had been difficult as he was heavily sedated. She was glad to find out that his 'floating' was nothing serious, merely his way of trying to explain how he felt as the medications took effect.

Daisy saw Frank Wishaw almost every day too, and took him a plate of her mother's apple turnovers for the nurses' tea break. He was devoted to his work and to his patients, having been a very young volunteer during the Great War.

'That's where I learned to look after people, Daisy. It was a mess out there – still have nightmares about the trenches – but at least I got a career out of it.'

As a seventeen-year-old, Frank, big enough to be taken for a man much older, had been pressed into service by an overworked doctor. At first he carried injured or even dead soldiers, and the doctor had been impressed by the respectful way in which the big lad had treated the patients. 'I got on-the-field first-hand training from one of the best in the business and managed to get into nurses' training in the early thirties. Shocked people, a man wanting to be a nurse, not a doctor, but things are changing.'

'Would you have liked to train as a doctor, Frank?'

'A lad from Billingsgate, grateful to get a job hefting crates of fish? Lord love you, lass, I left school at twelve and wasn't there much when I was there. Got most of my education right there on the battlefield from a saint.' He stared into his cup, and his face was sad.

'Where is he now?'

'Blown to bits in 1918, two days before the war ended. Now, you best get off and say goodbye to your squadron leader. Any idea where you're going to next?'

'Not yet. Hope it's somewhere where there's real planes to work on.'

'Watch out for them propellers. You wouldn't believe the number of . . . cut arms there are on airfields.'

'I'll be careful, Frank,' said Daisy, who knew that he had substituted 'cut arms' for the truer 'severed arms'. 'And remember, my mum's expecting you to drop in for a cuppa on your day off.'

They said goodbye rather sadly as Daisy had come to like and admire the nurse. Adair too spoke highly of him. They knew that, like Adair, he had no real family and so Daisy had taken him home with her one day. Flora, mother of five, had immediately decided that Frank needed to be looked after, and was she not the very person to do it?

'Between your little crooks and Frank, she'll have something concrete to do for the war effort, instead of worrying and moping over us,' the twins had agreed happily.

But now in the hospital for the last time, Daisy wondered

245

how she would cope in the coming weeks when she could not see Adair or ask Frank, splendid Frank, how he was. Adair's wounds were healing. His broken leg had been set, and other damage to the leg repaired, the three bullets that had lodged in his shoulder and arm had been removed and the areas were healing nicely, as were the bruises, bumps and cuts on his head. He had stopped 'floating' but sometimes, or so it seemed to Daisy, he was ill at ease, their conversation stilted.

She walked along the now so familiar corridor, acknowledging, as she walked, the various members of staff whom she had met, and admitting for the first time that it was the kiss, nothing more than a soft pressure of her lips on his, that was the problem.

She had visited him every day since and, depending on his condition, had either gently kissed his bruised face as she left or not kissed him at all. Adair had never referred to the kiss. He had been unconscious, surely, when she had kissed his lips. Or had he merely been 'floating' and found her forward?

Oh, how she wished that she were more experienced. She should have tagged along with Rose to those dances. Had Rose not told her, just last night, that in the few years since they had left school she had kissed, she thought, at least nine lads?

And she can't even remember for sure, worried the despairing Daisy. Most of the men she herself had met in the past five years were either delightful old men like Mr Fischer or totally unsuitable men, military personnel like Tomas Sapenak – or Adair Maxwell.

She managed to smile as she walked down the length of the busy ward. Some men were sitting up chatting to visitors, but these were in the minority. Most relatives and friends lived too far away to visit on a regular basis. One or two of the beds were curtained off because the patient was desperately ill. Daisy caught a glimpse of a middle-aged woman, sitting by the bed of a man who probably did not even know she was there. She had been there the last two times Daisy had visited. Has she even left his bedside? Daisy wondered. She looks exactly the same each time, hat, coat, gloves, her Sunday best. His mother, perhaps?

Daisy felt oppressed by grief and was glad to reach Adair's bed. He was sitting up watching her. She took his hand. 'Hello.'

'Hello, Daisy Petrie.'

She was lost for words. Where was she to start? What could she or should she say?

She started with his nurse. 'Mum's going to look after Nurse Wishaw. He loves her apple turnovers; that was all it took.'

'I'm glad. He's a wonderful man but too lonely.'

Both were silent for a moment, neither seeming able to say what was uppermost in the mind.

'Your leave is over, Daisy.'

She felt her eyes brighten with tears. 'Yes.'

'Any idea where you're going?'

'Haven't received anything so far.'

'I was awake, Daisy, and absolutely *compos mentis*.'

She bowed her head.

'You wouldn't have kissed me had you known?'

'I don't know.'

He held out his free hand, now released from the sling. 'Please come over here, Daisy Petrie.'

She moved forward so that she was standing at the head of the bed, near his head. She was still holding his left hand.

'There's a chair. Please sit down.'

She obeyed.

'I like seeing you sitting there, Daisy. I like seeing you.'

Love scenes in the cinema didn't go like this – if this is a love scene. What could she say; what should she say?

The truth. 'I like seeing you, Adair.'

'Enough to lean over and kiss me?'

'Oh, Adair, of course I do.' She leaned over and he whispered, 'Not my bruises this time,' and she obliged by kissing his lips.

She had released his hands and he reached up and pulled her towards him and returned the kiss. No gentle kiss now but a kiss that sent rivers of fire coursing through her body.

'Allow your visitor to come up for air, Squadron Leader.'

Frank was there. 'Surgeon wants to have a look at his leg, Daisy. Can you wait outside for a few minutes?'

Daisy stood up, ready to go.

'You could give him a little more medicine, pet; seems to be doing him a world of good.'

Daisy blushed but was quite happy to lean forward again but this time the kiss was a chaste pressure on his forehead.

'See, Nurse,' said Adair. 'Doesn't my bruise look better?'

Daisy laughed and went off to wait in the hospital canteen until the surgeon's visit was over.

When she returned she heard that the surgeon had

expressed his delight that each of Adair's wounds was healing beautifully, so much so that he would be allowed to go to a convalescent facility where he would receive physiotherapy for his injured leg. There would be, he assured Adair, no lasting difficulty. Squadron Leader Maxwell could well be in action within weeks, not months.

Adair was delighted. Daisy was not. Her time in Wiltshire was over and, as yet, she had no knowledge of where she would be sent next. Several bases had training facilities for mechanics, engineers and such. She could be sent to any one of them, and some were a long way from the London area. She had been so grateful to Sergeant Gordon for his offer to recommend her that asking for any more help would never occur to her.

She had had one more poignant meeting with Adair.

'You will write, Daisy?'

She nodded.

'I have no idea when we'll see each other again, possibly not for months.'

She held back the tears that she could feel forming. 'There's a war on, Officer.'

He laughed and looked eloquently at his bandages. 'Sorry, ma'am, I forgot.'

Daisy stood up. She knew that if she sat there by the bed, holding his hand a second longer, she would begin to weep and a letter in a magazine she had read on the train from Wiltshire had advised Forces Sweethearts never to cry in the presence of a loved one: 'Be brave and show him only a smiling face. Weep when you are alone.'

'I'd best go.'

He gripped her hand. 'There's a lot I want to say to you,

Daisy Petrie, but it's too soon. There's an entire lovely summer to enjoy and let's try to meet, but if I have leave at Christmas, I'll ask Alf and Nancy to have me.'

'I'll try to be at home for Christmas.'

'We could meet.'

She nodded.

'In the meantime, we'll write. Not stiff little letters, Daisy, but letters from you, telling me about all your work and the new base. Tell me about the happy things too, Daisy. I want you to join in and to have fun. There are all sorts of good things on a large base: sports facilities, a swimming pool, a cinema, even theatre groups.'

'Gosh, no. My friend Sally is the actress. She's going to be very famous, and an actor manager has asked her to join an ENSA troop.'

'Good for Sally. ENSA is a great morale booster.'

A sharp spear of envy entered her. Adair was impressed by Sally. Immediately she was ashamed of herself. 'She's very good and really beautiful.'

'Kiss me goodbye, beautiful, special Daisy.'

The tears waited until she was on her way home.

It was a perfect early summer evening. Lilacs were in bloom on trees in almost every garden on King Edward Avenue. Late tulips marched along garden paths, covering the ground in a lovely carpet of gold and red. The colours and the scents of the lilacs should have cheered her but she felt pressed down by a weight of unhappiness. Just when she was beginning to really know Adair, to openly welcome whatever was growing between them, they were to part. No walking out for Daisy Petrie. No sitting in the cinema, hot hand clutching hot hand, no stopping some evening at a dance in a

250

social hall, no walking home, arm in arm along lilac-
scented avenues. The scent of the lilacs was now
completely obliterated by the residual smell of burning
– so much beauty and ugliness, side by side. In the
gutter at her feet were three shell casings and she bent
down to pick them up. Metal. Think positively. Collect
it for the war effort.

Daisy dropped the casings into her handbag and,
before starting off again, looked for a moment at a
beautiful sky.

This will end, she decided, and I will see him again
– some day soon.

Petrie's Groceries and Fine Teas was full of people when
Daisy arrived back from the hospital. The shop was often
very busy, especially on Fridays, when pay packets or
allowances were received, and on Saturday mornings for
the same reasons, but this was just another day. Perhaps
a special consignment was in of some foodstuff that had
been in short supply?

'Daisy, my dear, have you heard the news?' Miss
Partridge doing her utmost to answer all the questions
was battling nobly behind the counter. 'Your mother is
upstairs making yet another pot of tea – perhaps you
could help her.'

'What's happened? Where's Dad?'

'I want your dear mother to tell you, and your father
has gone to the wholesaler's.'

Daisy muscled her way through the women who were
talking loudly and vociferously. She caught snatches of
conversation.

'Wonderful . . .'

251

'High time poor Mrs P had something to cheer her up . . .'

'I heard there was some Cheddar. Anybody see the Cheddar . . .?'

She fled past the crowd and ran upstairs and into the kitchen. Her mother, trying to wipe away the tears streaming down her face, was loading a tray with cups and the kettle was singing on the hotplate. 'Mum, what on earth's going on?'

On hearing her Flora turned round. 'Oh, Daisy, pet, you'll never believe it,' she said before once more bursting into tears.

Daisy took the milk bottle her mother was holding and set it down on the table. 'Now, forget this tea party you're giving, and tell me what's going on.'

Flora took her handkerchief from her apron pocket and blew her nose. 'Read it yourself, pet. Isn't it a miracle?'

For a fleeting moment Daisy thought she was going to hear that Ron was not dead after all, but she read the name 'Sam' on the flimsy paper that her mother had handed to her.

'Bernie's told the whole street, and the people we've had in today . . . two ounces of this, a packet of that, but really they wanted to hear the news.'

Daisy read the short letter from the Red Cross offices in Geneva and burst into tears, and for a few minutes mother and daughter cried happily together. Daisy recovered first and read the letter aloud.

Dear Mr Petrie,

A message has been received from the German authorities that your son Sergeant Sam Petrie escaped from a working party on 4 April of this year and is still at large. We will send further news as we receive it.

'Sam's escaped? Where is he? Where was he? Is he alone?'

'We don't know, but he's free, Daisy, free, and he'll be on his way home, and I won't let him leave again.'

Daisy was thrilled but she was also very afraid. They had never been able to ascertain where Sam was being held or if he had been moved. Was he in Germany or Poland or somewhere else entirely? And how would a man from Dartford manage in a country where he did not speak the language?

A hundred questions rushed without answers into her mind. Was he in uniform? Had they worn prison uniform? Either one would identify him. Did he have any foreign money? Had he learned any of the language in the prison camp? Again she wondered if he was alone. Alone and frightened? No, Sam Petrie feared nothing and could handle anything.

She smiled brightly at her mother. 'You'd better get that new jumper started,' she said. She would keep her fears and worries to herself. 'Now away downstairs to all those people and I'll take care of the tea party.'

Much later, after the shop had finally closed, and all the teacups, even the best ones from the display cupboard in the front room, were washed and put away, Fred, Flora and their daughters sat round the table in the kitchen and caught up with one another.

'Great to have a night off,' said Fred, 'and I'll be a happy man if I can sleep in my own bed tonight.' He tried to suppress a groan as he looked at the evening meal Flora had prepared.

Food rationing and shortages were really pinching the country now. Even though they owned a grocery shop the Petries were adamant that they would have only the rations or allocations to which they were entitled. Everything was in short supply, and tonight, after Flora's generosity of the afternoon, the family were eating fish cakes made without fish. There was not even a fresh egg to bind the mashed potatoes and beans together.

His hunger and his dislike of fish cakes without even a bit of tinned fish – surely Flora could have found some sardines – reminded Fred of an exciting possibility. 'You'll never guess what I heard at the ARP station this afternoon – popped in to make sure they didn't need me.'

'What did you hear, Dad?' Rose asked as she pushed her 'fish cake' round and round her plate.

'Everyone's keeping pigs. Great idea—' he began but was interrupted.

'Where are we supposed to keep a pig, Fred Petrie, and who's going to kill it?'

Fred reached out his hand and patted Flora's as she placed her fork on the table. 'Gently, love, Tom Stafford at the fire station is who. Well, I don't know if Tom hisself is planning to kill it, but he's willing to put up a pen and shelter and start a pig club. There's a bit of land at the back and there'll be a big notice right on the front window asking for scraps but, more importantly, Tom's looking for folk who'll take a share of the pig. He thinks maybe five shillings a share or four shillings and sixpence – seemingly that sounds better. We bring our scraps, like

254

that plateful you're playing with, our Rose, and then come Christmas we get a lovely share. Just think, fresh pork or a nice bit of bacon or, better still, ham for Christmas dinner. What do you say now, Flora, love?'

There was a reminiscent look in Flora's eyes. When had she last cooked a real ham? 'Real ham, Fred?'

'It's a real pig.'

'What if we buy two shares?'

'We get two shares of the pig.'

'How big's a share?' Rose was more practical. 'There's plenty on this street would buy a share and then what? We pay fifteen shillings and get three sausages.'

'No, lass. More people wants a share, more porkers Tom'll buy. Seems he's got a cousin not too far away has a sow expecting a litter. These damn U-boats scuttling all our ships, even farmers are having trouble fattening their animals and so they're selling. Seems everybody in London's doing it. Some posh bloke's even got one in what used to be 'is swimming pool; no water in it, o'course, since they got bombed.'

'And all we have to do is pay our five bob and take scraps to the fire station?'

'That's it. Good job for George an' Jake; they'll love it and makes them feel useful.'

'My Sam'll be home for Christmas. He loves a nice bit of ham, or what about roast pork with apple sauce? Perfect.'

Fred and Rose said nothing but they looked at Daisy, who had remained quiet. 'What about you, Daisy, love?'

'I'm a WAAF, Dad. Who knows where I'll be at Christmas?'

Flora, who for a moment had been lost in thoughts of cooking a wonderful Christmas dinner for her eldest son, turned to Daisy. 'That reminds me, pet, what's happening with your pilot friend?'

'He's going to be fine, Mum.'

'That's nice. So you won't be visiting him any more?'

Daisy did not answer immediately. She looked around the little kitchen where the family had had so many happy meals: Christmases, Easters, and birthdays. She looked at her father's prized wireless. Just recently he had listened to a new programme. 'Getting my education in my old age, love,' he had told her as they listened one day during her leave to *The Brains Trust*. This question-and-answer programme was already well on its way to becoming a national favourite. When would she be back again to enjoy all these simple family joys?

Flora was looking at her, surprise in her eyes.

'Sorry, Mum, I was just remembering that this kitchen is my favourite place. And no, I will not be visiting Adair in the hospital. Soon he'll be going to a convalescent hospital and I'll be at a new air base.'

'We're glad the lad's better, but really it wouldn't be a good idea for you to get too . . . too what did you say, Fred?'

Fred was flustered. He would have preferred that Daisy not know that she was being discussed. 'Can't remember but it is better that, natural like, you're separated, Daisy.'

They were right, of course they were right. She and Adair had nothing in common apart perhaps from a love of planes. But every time they had met, it was as if a small breeze blew on a spark that had been lit the moment he had popped up out of the cockpit of the *Daisy*, his face and hands covered in dirt and oil. The spark had not been extinguished by separation, but grew ever stronger.

'He's hoping to spend Christmas at the Humbles'. If I get leave we'll meet.'

'That's nice, pet,' said Fred.

'It's ages till Christmas,' Fred reminded Flora later when they were preparing to go to bed and she had been, once again, saying how much she worried about Daisy. 'Just let nature take its course. She'll meet a nice lad at this new base. Probably lots o' lads more like us.'

Her posting had to come today. The ringing of Rose's alarm clock woke Daisy but she stayed, curled up in bed, to allow her sister to have the family's bathroom to herself. Her parents, as always, were up and had already washed before them. Her mind was busy. Had the WAAF forgotten all about her? She had passed the tests and been promoted. Had they thought they'd told her then when and where she was supposed to go? No, she would not panic. The letter would come today. Rose was still busy in the bathroom and so Daisy jumped up, put on her dressing gown and went into the kitchen to help her mother.

'Stir the porridge while I get dressed, pet, and make some toast. Alf brought some butter when he was in . . .' she hesitated.

'Visiting Adair, Mum. He's Adair's next of kin. How nice of Nancy to send us some of her fresh butter. You could give her some of your share of the pig come Christmas. And no, they never did get round to keeping pigs,' she added quickly as she could see the question forming in her mother's mind. 'Too many other things to look after.'

'And will you look out the old atlas, pet? Your dad and me was trying to figure out where our Sam would be going. Nice if we can see him in our minds. If he's walking to Switzerland he'd be in lovely mountains.'

Again she looked absolutely desolate and Daisy quickly agreed with her that to look at maps of Europe would be a good idea. At least it would give her something to do. She would have to see Frank Wishaw before she left, to encourage him to visit her parents. A big lad wanting feeding up was just what her mother needed. But worry followed worry. Rose was also determined to join the Forces.

'I've never been further than Brighton, Daisy. I want some excitement,' she had said the night before as they'd talked before falling asleep

'Being hurt in an air raid isn't excitement enough for you?'

'Some might say I'd already done my bit, but Stan and me's talked. We like each other a lot but we're not even twenty yet. Plenty of time.'

Daisy remembered those sweet moments by Adair's bed when his eyes had said, even promised, so much. 'Couldn't agree more, Rose.'

It was a lovely morning and so Daisy decided to walk over to the cinema where her friend Sally Brewer had fallen in love with not only the silver screen but several of the actors appearing on it. It was so long since she'd seen Sally, who had written just before Christmas about a new part in a play. Sally would not be there but Daisy felt guilty about not visiting the parents who had often slipped Sally's three particular friends into the cinema.

258

Mrs Brewer was thrilled to see her. It was almost a year since Daisy had seen Sally's mum and she looked different, much thinner than before, although, like her daughter, she had always been thin.

Now she enveloped Daisy in a warm hug. 'Daisy Petrie, we knew you were at home and if we hadn't seen you I'd have been that sad.'

'Sorry, Mrs Brewer. A friend crash-landed near here and is in the County Hospital, and visiting took up some time, and then, well, you know about things at home.'

'I do, indeed, Daisy. Now come on into the office. I'll make a cuppa and then you can take one up to Ernie in his booth. He'll be that delighted to see you.'

Soon they were sitting in the ticket booth chattering away. Mrs Brewer showed Daisy several professional photographs of Sally and talked about all the struggles that beset aspiring actresses.

'And it's not just auditioning for parts, Daisy, love, but – maybe I shouldn't say but there's some men in the business who are . . . who are . . . let's just say who are far from being gentlemen. But I dare say a pretty girl like you has trouble too.'

Daisy was sure her eyebrows had disappeared into her hairline as she listened to Sally's mother talk. 'Gosh, no, Mrs Brewer. I work with other women mostly and we're studying all the time. Not much time to meet men, bad or good.'

'But you're in the air force. There's thousands of men there.'

'The WAAF isn't the RAF. We're auxiliaries, helpers, and we're all women. All the men from the RAF that I've met have been . . .' she thought for a moment: Adair,

Sergeant Gordon. Wing Commander Anstruther, Wing Commander Sapenak, '. . . they've been just super.'

'Oh, I'm glad. Not had time to find someone to walk out with then?'

How to answer truthfully? 'I'll be off on a course any minute now, Mrs Brewer, and I'll be burning the midnight oil studying.'

'That's my Sally too. Now why don't you take a cuppa up to Ernie? Would you believe that he gets lonely – night after night, even Sundays now, packed cinema, and he's lonely. Seems a lifetime ago that you four just couldn't be prised apart and now . . . Here, give him a bit of chocolate too.'

'We're still friends, Mrs B. It's only distance that separates us.'

'I hope so, love. Now give us a kiss and don't spill Ernie's tea.'

Quite difficult not to spill tea when being ferociously hugged but Daisy managed to extricate herself without accident and walked off across the pseudo-marble floor and up the wide red-carpeted stairs until she found the little booth where Sally's father spent most of his time.

His welcome was not quite so exuberant as his wife's but he was obviously delighted to see Daisy.

'Saw wee Grace at Christmas,' he said as he drank his tea. He shook his head and was silent for a moment before carrying on. 'What a mess that was, but at least she knows she's got a home with Brewers and Petries. Grace hoped there might be some family information among Megan's papers but couldn't find a thing, not a photograph, a Christmas card, nothing.'

'Which probably proves that Megan didn't like her family or they didn't like her.'

'I think that's it. But we couldn't find anything about Grace. Where did she come from? She can't remember. Who put her on the train? She thinks it was a nun. Where did the train come from? No idea, but there was talk at the time about Scotland – or was it Ireland? We hear from her now and again. Not much time for writing but she's happy.'

Again there was a silence for a moment as each thought.

'Have you told her about Sam's escape?'

Startled, Daisy looked at him. 'I never even thought, Mr Brewer. I'll write to her this afternoon. Some friend, me.'

'Don't worry, Daisy, love. Grace had a thing about your Sam, big handsome lad who was always kind to her. It was the same as my Sally and all those film stars. Means nothing.'

'Happen you're right,' said Daisy as they hugged goodbye. But I don't think you are, she said to herself as she walked briskly home.

'Had a nice chat?' her father asked as she came into the shop.

'Lovely, but Sally's mum's lost weight.'

'I hope you told her you noticed. She's right proud of it because she's taking a class at the YWCA.'

'There never was anything of her before.'

'Thin lot, all her family.' He took his chamois leather cloth from under the counter and moved over to wipe a squashed fly off the display window. 'There's a brown envelope for you, Daisy. Mum's got it.'

'Oh, great. Fantastic.' She started for the stairs.

'You're so keen to leave us, love?'

Daisy stopped and turned to him. 'Never. I was scared I'd been told and lost the information. Talk later.' She turned again and fled upstairs.

The message was more or less the same as the initial one. Aircraftswoman Petrie was to travel by train – a travel warrant was included – to RAF Halton in Buckinghamshire, where she was to take up her new duties.

The much-used atlas was pressed into service by an excited Daisy. She knew that RAF Halton was a major technical training school that had, in fact, been established during the Great War. But where exactly was Buckinghamshire, and where was the town of Wendover or indeed the little village of Halton?

She was delighted to find that her new base was only thirty-five miles or so from London. That meant visits home during her eighteen weeks of training might not be impossible. That would please her parents.

FOURTEEN

Two days later Daisy arrived at RAF Halton but, this
time, she was not with one other slightly nervous recruit.
The railway station was wall-to-wall blue uniforms, both
men and women. She looked round hopefully but there
was not a single face that she even remotely recognised.
Her grief at Charlie's loss welled up more powerfully
than ever and she fought desperately to control herself.
Had Charlie been there she would have been making
friends all over the place, but Daisy was not Charlie.

Daisy picked up her bags and followed the heaving
mass of humanity out of the station. She travelled to the
base on a bus that, like the station, was crowded, and
the noise level reminded her of her one and only school
trip to London. How her teenage friends had shouted
and sung. Enough to give anyone a headache.

'Bella White.' The WAAF in the window seat introduced herself. 'You look like a rabbit caught in headlights.
Relax. They're nervous.' She held out her hand and Daisy
shook it.

'Daisy Petrie,' she said.

They chatted all the way to the camp, as Bella was

not slow to ask questions or to tell part of her personal history if the conversation lagged. She was twenty years old, lived with her mother and grandmother in Derby and had worked as the receptionist in an office. She could type, did not take shorthand, could file, and was used to making and receiving telephone calls.

'My boyfriend told me he preferred my cousin, Sheila. He had to, since I found them . . . let's say in a fairly compromising situation when I visited my aunt Flo's flat. Two years I walked out with him and didn't allow no funny stuff, not without a ring on my finger. Seems Sheila's allergic to base metals. So I joined up, left them high and dry. You have a lad?'

Daisy, who was not quite sure what the unknown Sheila's allergy had to do with anything, said, 'I'm not walking out with anyone.'

'Well, there's plenty of spare men around Halton; you'll soon find one.'

Daisy wondered if Bella had enlisted simply because of the abundance of unmarried men. She would not ask but was quite sure Bella would have told her had she dared – or cared.

'I was a shop assistant before I enlisted,' she said, 'but I always wanted to do something more exciting. Being a receptionist in an office must have been quite interesting.'

'Bored me silly. I joined the WAAF because I thought it would be more fun – really thought they'd plonk me behind a typewriter. Just think, maybe I could have typed a letter to Mr Churchill, but they said I showed aptitude for engineering. Don't know that I believe them; my mum read in the paper as how they just can't get enough technicians to keep our planes in the air. Well, I'm not stupid and I don't mind working hard. This war's giving a lot of us a chance to better ourselves. What kind of shop did you work in – department store, I should think by looking at you.'

'Me in a department store? No, Bella. I worked in a small grocery shop; dried peas, porridge oats, eggs, tea, just the things families need every day.'

'You've got a look of class, not class like that frozen pea over there – ' she pointed to a young woman in a really beautiful two-piece costume – 'but still class.'

Daisy had no idea whether or not to say thank you but by then they had arrived at the camp.

If she had thought Wilmslow large, RAF Halton was endless, and she laughed a little as she thought of herself and Charlie hobbling up the main road at Wilmslow in their best shoes. They wouldn't catch her this time. She was a seasoned WAAF, in good sturdy military-issue shoes.

Hours later she lay exhausted in her bed in a large hut with twenty or so other women. Bella was not among them and she hardly knew whether to be pleased or sorry. Snores and the lighter noises made by sleepers whistled around the long bare room, and Daisy lay waiting for sleep, missing her family, thinking of Adair and too aware of her resurrected grief at Charlie's death.

Do it for Charlie. The voice echoed in her head together with her own promise to an unknown little child on Dartford Heath. Excitement grew in her. She had passed one hurdle and was now even closer to her dream. In eighteen weeks, a mere four and a half months, she would be fully qualified to work on aircraft engines.

But was that all she wanted? Was it even remotely possible that one day she might fly, not a Spitfire or a

Lancaster but a small plane like the *Daisy*? But how? There were no pilots in the WAAF, and the Air Transport Auxiliary was staffed by civilians. Had she enlisted too quickly?

She lay for some time looking at positives and negatives. There were so many positives. In the WAAF she had learned skills and she had found and lost a friend. *Do you like me enough to kiss me, Daisy?* The voice echoed in her head and she smiled at the very sound. Surely being a WAAF had brought her closer to Adair, and made it easier for her to have another flying lesson. Halton looked as if it was stacked with aircraft. Perhaps here, there would be more opportunities. Excitement at that blissful thought was making sleep impossible, but with her first full day on the course ahead of her she needed to sleep.

She turned over onto her right side, her favourite sleeping position, but the last thought she had before finally falling into a disturbed sleep was, once again: the ATA is a civilian organisation. How could that be overcome?

The next three days were soon a blur in her memory, so full were they of activity and change. She began to recognise some of the other women and girls in her hut and in her unit. Mainly they were known by their surnames, as that is how the instructors addressed them. It seemed that she never sat beside the same WAAF twice in a row at a class or even in the mess hall, and had totally forgotten Bella until they found themselves in the same line for dinner.

'Great camp, Daisy, don't you think? A swimming pool and a cinema, for starters, and have you seen the

Officers' Club – it's a stately home, for goodness' sake – I'd love to get in there. I'm going into Aylesbury on Saturday to buy a swimming costume. Come with me and we can come back in time for the "Welcome New Recruits" dance.'

Daisy had no wish to hurt Bella; she had been very kind and friendly on the bus, but she wanted to really know her way around before she made decisions about friendships or anything else. 'I haven't got my bearings yet, Bella; I was planning to have a good look around and to write letters at the weekend, but thanks.'

'Suit yourself.'

'How are you enjoying the course?'

Bella smiled. 'Haven't a clue, but one of the mechanics is giving me a bit of extra help. He might come in with me on Saturday. I could ask him to bring a mate.'

'Not this Saturday, Bella, maybe another week.'

'So you are as stuck up as Miss Frozen Pea. Your loss,' said Bella, and turned away to start picking up her meal.

Feeling rather miserable, Daisy had no choice but to follow her and when she had her selection she walked around the hut looking for a seat.

'Seat here, Petrie,' called a WAAF, waving madly.

Thankfully Daisy sat down at a table where several WAAFs were seated and, thankfully, recognised two from her billet. It was the most enjoyable meal she had had since she arrived. The food was . . . nourishing, she decided was the best word to describe it, but with the two girls, Joan and Maggie, introducing themselves – and all the others calling out their names and smiling a welcome – she began to feel part of the camp.

In one of their first lectures the recruits had been told

much of the history of the base. It had been a private estate owned by the de Rothschild family. Before the Great War, the then owner had offered the estate to the army for summer manoeuvres. His initial generous offer had expanded as the war had gone on, and in 1917 a technical school had been established on the estate. By the end of the war, thousands of well-trained technicians had passed though its doors. In 1919 the estate was bought by the War Office to be the training base for officer cadets in the newly formed Royal Air Force.

Daisy could hardly believe that her own Prime Minister, Winston Churchill, had been a key figure in the forming of the air force.

Dad'll be fascinated by that, she thought, him being a big fan of Mr Churchill, and just think, because of something our Prime Minister said before I was even born, I'm here learning a life-changing trade and so are thousands of other people, men and women.

She was more excited and inspired than ever. Even if she never flew she would help keep planes flying, and all those pilots would be thinking of people like the boy on the Heath, his mum, Charlie and her dad.

I'm here to learn, she told herself, and that comes before any old swimming pool.

It was her training instructor who talked to her about mixing business and pleasure.

'You're doing well, Daisy, you're a natural, but I never see you around the base or going into Wendover or even Halton; nice little village. All work and no play. Not good. I am ordering you to go to the cinema on Friday night. Errol Flynn's on. You women like him.'

'Not as much as he likes himself, Corporal. James Stewart, now . . .'

'I don't care who it is, girl. Go to the cinema.'

Daisy looked at him. Corporal Singer was not all that much older than she was, ten, fifteen years maybe. He was not much taller either, which some of the girls said spoiled his chances. Daisy did not think height or age would concern her too much if she really liked someone, and Corporal Singer was likeable. He was terrific at his job; there was nothing about aircraft engines that he did not know and, possibly more importantly, he was very patient. Once or twice one of her fellow WAAFs had burst into tears of frustration – but the trainer merely continued calmly and allowed the girl to recover without making a show of her. Not all the trainers were patient. Many, in fact, made it clear right from the start that they had no tolerance for women in the services, except as cooks and cleaners. That attitude often led to hostility.

Desperate as she was to finish the course successfully, Daisy decided that she would accept the corporal's suggestion and take some time off from her studying. She liked swimming but had no costume with her and so, for the moment, swimming was out. Thanks to Mr Brewer she had seen all the films advertised in the base cinema but she looked at the Recruits' Notice Board to see what else might be on offer.

A visit to a local Jacobean mansion, named Hartwell, was advertised. It sounded just the type of activity that she thought she would enjoy. She loved Dartford's historic past and here, on the very edge of the camp, was a building where an exiled French king had lived and where his wife had died.

'Imagine that,' she said out loud as she read the notice, and almost jumped out of her skin when a voice behind her said, 'Imagine what?'

Two girls from her hut, Joan and Maggie, had come up behind her quietly.

'Wow, you two frightened the life out of me.'

'Do you always stand talking to yourself, Daisy? Reprehensible conduct unbefitting a WAAF.' Maggie, whose vocabulary was right up there with Charlie's, was laughing to show that she was joking.

'Look at that, girls,' Daisy said, pointing to the notice. 'There's a tour of this house, Hartwell mansion. It says it's Jacobean; that's got to do with kings, isn't it, not architecture.'

'Probably both, but I didn't do much history at school. I remember bits about the Romans and lots about Cavaliers and Roundheads. *And When Did You Last See Your Father?*'

Since the looks on the faces of Daisy and Joan clearly asked, 'What are you talking about?' Maggie finished off, 'It's the architecture that was in fashion during the reign of the first King James.'

'It's got lovely gardens too,' said Daisy.

'Then let's rent bicycles and go over on Saturday.'

Daisy was pleased to have something planned for her free time – that should please the corporal – but she still wanted to get her letters written. As yet, she had not told Sally of her visit to her parents, and she really must write to her mother. She would love to hear about the proposed visit to the historic house. Hartwell, such a lovely name. She wondered if it had originally been spelled Heartwell, perhaps something to do with how living in or even seeing such a lovely place would make hearts feel well.

Probably totally wrong, Daisy Petrie, she told herself and looked forward to finding out for sure on the following Saturday.

At the end of classes next day she told Corporal Singer of her plans.

'Great idea. You're not going by yourself, are you?'

'No, Corporal, two girls from the same hut are going with me.'

'Good, company's more fun,' he said, but for a moment she felt that her answer had disappointed him.

Was he going to say he'd come too? No, don't be conceited, Daisy. What would I have said if he had asked to come?

But that was something she definitely did not want to think about.

She recognised the writing on one of the letters that were handed to her that evening but not on the other. One was from her mother – and could wait a moment. She looked at the other letter, tried to decipher the postmark, even smelled it, but it told her nothing.

'Are you going to read it or eat it, Daisy?' asked Joan, who had managed to push herself into the supper line beside Daisy. 'Maggie's saving us seats.'

'I don't know who it's from.'

'A secret admirer. Looks very masculine writing to me. C'mon, by the time we get to what's left of the pork, you can have read it and answered it.'

Daisy laughed and slit open the envelope.

Inside was one sheet of very thin writing paper. The

address of another air base was printed on the top right-hand corner.

Dear Daisy,

Adair is now at the rehabilitation unit – address and telephone number at the end of the letter. He can't write as he still hasn't the use of his right hand, but he would be very happy if you would write to him from time to time, or if you would ring him any evening or send him the telephone number of your nearest telephone booth and he will ring you.

He is, he says, almost back to full strength – he is not, it will take a little more time – and is hoping to be flying soon. He would like to hear about your courses.

Be well, Daisy

It was signed 'Tomas'.

She waited to share it until they were seated. 'It's from a friend of a friend who was injured recently.' She could never tell her two new friends that the friends were both senior air force officers. 'I'd better write to cheer him up.'

'Him? How exciting. Tell us everything. Is he in the army? Where is he stationed? Is he in hospital? Is he handsome? Is he rich? How old is he? Can we be your bridesmaids? Will they let you stay in the WAAF now that you're getting married?'

The silly but good-natured questions were fired at her like bullets out of a gun. She chose to answer the one she thought the silliest. 'No, you may not be my bridesmaids.'

As she had expected, her answer resulted in loud, mainly

incomprehensible protestations, in which the words 'utter selfishness' featured heavily.

'The other letter is from my mother and a postal order for five shillings is enclosed. We can have a fabulous tea at this Hartwell place.'

Daisy applied herself to her supper and thought about her letters while the talk swelled and sank around her. Her mother had also said that Alf had come in to tell her that Adair Maxwell had been moved. Flora had been unable to resist adding, 'It's for the best, pet.'

What did her parents fear from Adair? Daisy could count on her fingers the number of times they had met. Surely her parents did not expect a lifetime of commitment to be built on a few meetings. She, Daisy, admitted to her private self that Adair was very important to her, but surely her parents could see that he was moving cautiously too. As always, the memories of their kisses filled her with hope and longing, but she had been raised in a hard school and did not expect to have something very special handed to her on a silver plate.

'Hello, calling Aircraftswoman Petrie. We've asked you twice if you want Spotted Dick for pudding.'

'Sorry, thinking about my mum's letter. She still hasn't heard from the Red Cross about my brother. He was captured at Dunkirk but has escaped and we don't know where he is.' Flora had mentioned her concern over Sam in the letter. 'You two would be mad for Sam. Tall, handsome, fair hair.'

'Lead us to him, but first Spotted Dick?'

'No, thanks, really hate raisins and sultanas.'

The three of them walked around the camp after supper. It was so vast that they were still unsure of directions, but once more it was a lovely evening and it was a joy just to stroll. So far there had been no air raids although they had had practice sessions that had mainly meant diving into great trenches. To someone from the Bomb Run of Kent it seemed very peaceful.

Daisy sat on her bed waiting for her turn in the shower and thought about a letter to Adair. Would a telephone call be easier? But Tomas had not said how late recuperating patients were allowed to stay up. She would telephone him the next evening, just before dinner. In the meantime she would study her notes on bombers.

The next evening Daisy made sure that she had plenty of pennies, although Maggie had assured her that three pence would probably be enough, and went off to make her telephone call. In her life Daisy had made very few telephone calls and was nervous, not only of speaking to Adair – although every fibre of her being longed to hear his voice – but also of the very practical aspect of putting in the correct number of pennies and of pressing the correct button. She read the instructions on the telephone very carefully, fed in her pennies and pressed button A.

Hurrah. She heard the telephone ringing and, after a few seconds, a voice said, 'No 2 Rehabilitation Centre, Staff Nurse Hawkins speaking,' and Daisy had time to calm down.

'May I speak to Adair, I mean Squadron Leader Maxwell, please?'

'And who is calling, please?'

Should she give her rank? No, best not. 'Daisy,' she said, 'Daisy Petrie.'

'Hold on and I'll see if he's available.'

She heard brisk footsteps going away from the telephone and across a tiled floor, and she listened to silence while she tried to hear the hum of the wires that carried the messages. Then there came a shuffling sound and at last . . .

'Maxwell here.'

'It's Daisy.'

No one could have mistaken the joy in his voice as he repeated, 'Daisy.'

'Are you feeling better?'

'Hearing your voice has . . .' He stopped for a long moment and Daisy stayed listening to disembodied footsteps. 'Hearing your voice has made me feel . . . wonderful. Are you well, Daisy? Are the courses going well?'

She told him about Corporal Singer's teaching. 'He's ever so patient but firm too, Adair, and he knows his engines.'

She stopped as she heard him laugh.

'Does he know his engines, my precious Daisy?'

'You're laughing at me. Some of them don't know them as well as they should – to be teaching it, I mean.'

'I'm not laughing at you, Daisy Petrie, never. I'm laughing with joy, joy that you're part of my life. Oh God, here comes the dragon. I have to go. Be safe, Daisy Petrie.'

She stood, the cold black receiver pressed against her ear. 'The dragon'? Who was the dragon? The sister who had brought him to the telephone? Daisy smiled with happiness. She had had Frau Führer, and he had his dragon. Frau Führer had cared deeply for her charges and, no doubt, his dragon was just as caring.

*   *   *

It rained all day on Saturday. Cycling and walking though gardens full of dripping trees did not fill any of the girls with enthusiasm. They agreed to leave the visit until a better day.

'Someone's teaching the rumba in the recreation hall,' Joan informed them. 'Either of you know how to rumba?'

Two blank faces looked up at her.

'Thought not. Right, let's get our raincoats and go over. Come on, Daisy, put that manual down. In fact, put it under your mattress till Monday morning. Auntie has spoken.'

'There is a test next Friday and we have to pass.'

'Can you read and write?'

'Of course.'

'Then you'll pass.'

Learning to do a proper rumba might be fun, Daisy decided, and she had danced with her sister and other female friends before. Happened all the time at church socials.

'Sounds good.'

She left the manual on top of her locker and followed Joan and Maggie out into the rain-swept road.

A few minutes later, they shrugged off wet coats in the recce hall and, to their surprise, saw that it was full of personnel, and many of them were men.

'Hey, hey, fabulous,' said Maggie. 'Let's find one with a sense of rhythm.'

Daisy had no chance to look for a partner, for she heard her name called. Hurrying across the width of the hall came Corporal Singer.

'Hello, girls, nice to see you. Will you be my partner, Daisy?'

'Devil you know,' whispered Maggie as Daisy walked into the middle of the hall with her partner.

Maggie and Joan were preparing to dance together but were delighted to be approached by several men.

'Decisions, decisions,' laughed Maggie. 'OK, lads, step forward any lad who doesn't have two left feet.'

FIFTEEN

The rumba class was a great success.

Corporal Singer, whose name was Matt, was actually an extremely good dancer, and Daisy, who was quite inexperienced, soon discovered that a good partner made dancing fun. They danced to records, learning each step individually and then putting them together. She could see that her friends were also having a good time although, she decided judiciously, the airmen they were partnered with were not nearly as good as Matt. Both girls had worried less about dancing ability and more about the height of prospective partners as Maggie assured Daisy that dancing partners usually came up to her neck and Joan seemed always to be chosen by men who towered above her. On that first dancing class they smiled happily, partnered by airmen of exactly the right height.

'Made to measure,' they said happily as all six sat out together during a break in the dancing and drank warm beer.

At the puzzled looks from the men, the girls just laughed. 'Don't worry, boys. All under control.'

Matt joined in the conversation and, during the remainder of the afternoon, danced with both Joan and Maggie. Daisy was never allowed to be a wallflower, and once or twice while she was dancing she saw Matt looking over at her. The look made her somewhat uneasy. It was almost as if he disapproved of her dancing with someone else.

Couldn't possibly be what he's thinking, she tried to reassure herself.

Matt himself made his feelings clear when he partnered her in a later dance. 'You're one of my trainees, Daisy, and you're doing well. I like you very much and you make a really good partner – great balance – but it wouldn't be good for us to dance together too often. I hope you understand.'

'Understand, Matt? Understand what?'

He held her uncomfortably close as he danced her round the hall. 'Don't want anyone thinking you got good marks because we're stepping out.'

Daisy was so surprised that she stopped dead, smack in the middle of the floor. 'But we're not.'

'Dance, Daisy, people are looking. I know we're not, and we won't while you're doing my course, but I thought week after next when the course is over, well, maybe you'd let me take you out.'

Daisy was not completely taken by surprise but she still had trouble answering immediately. To her relief, and Corporal Singer's annoyance, she was whirled out of his arms by another burly dancer.

'Smashin' dancer, pet. I bin watching you all afternoon. Want to sit out and have a beer?'

'No, thanks. I've had one and actually I have to go

back to my hut . . .' she tried to find an acceptable reason for leaving in the middle of the class, '. . . because my mother's going to telephone.'

He took no offence. 'OK, pet, too bad, I'll see you another time.'

'Right.'

Daisy was grateful that her partner stopped trampling his way around the floor and led her over to the watching dancers. Joan was there, waiting for Maggie, who was dancing.

'Great fun, Daisy, but my feet can take no more. Are you ready to go back?'

'Maggie won't mind?'

'Of course not. Wave to her and let's get out of here.'

Daisy, with or without Matt's help, passed the initial course and progressed to the second one. She learned nothing there that she had not learned either by trial and error or from working with Adair, and passed again. She had managed to avoid meetings with Matt, and Joan and Maggie were very good at looking out for him.

'Intruder spotted,' they would whisper, and guide Daisy in the opposite direction.

'He's a nice chap, Daisy, and he's a corporal. What's the harm in going to the cinema with him or dancing? You dance really well together,' said Joan when the three young women were making the most of some free time to enjoy the glorious summer weather.

'He's too intense.'

'Lucky you. You afraid you won't be able to fight him off?'

Daisy rolled over onto her stomach on the grass. 'I

have . . . I had . . . three older brothers; fighting off is not a problem. I just don't want to be . . .'

'Stuck with him,' volunteered Joan.

'No, attached to anyone. I'm here to become a fully qualified mechanic. Right now that is the only thing that is important to me. I absolutely love working on an engine with the mechanics. Some of them are terrific.'

Maggie stopped making a daisy chain, leaned forward and set it on Daisy's head. 'There, lovely. Anyone take you up yet?'

'Who, what do you mean, take me up? In a plane you mean?' They could not know about Adair. Surely not.

'Of course in a plane. There's a very tasty pilot, in fact there are several very tasty pilots, who are so grateful for the hard work we WAAFs put into keeping their birds airworthy that, occasionally, just occasionally, they have been known to check the engine out with a passenger on board.'

'Is that legal?'

'Legal or allowed? Have absolutely no idea, but the first time one of them asks me . . .' she waited, watching their faces, started to laugh and finished, '. . . I'll say no.'

'You're insane. A flight with an air force pilot? I'd say yes and jump in before he could change his mind. What about you, Daisy, would you go up, if one of the pilots asked?'

This was her time to be honest, to tell them that not only had she already had a flight but also several flying lessons. She said nothing but her mind was working ferociously. What if they didn't believe her? What if they believed her but thought she was boasting?

'If it takes you that long to decide, Daisy, then I rather

281

think you're not up for it. Someone in our village once flew to France on holiday. Can you believe it? There wasn't another topic of conversation for weeks. Holidays by air. Close your eyes and picture yourself flying to, say, the Bahamas, and standing at the top of the stairs in the smartest little white costume – because of the glorious weather – and then walking down the steps like—'

'"The man who broke the bank at Monte Carlo,"' sang Joan, and they all laughed.

The summer went on and the crops in the Buckinghamshire fields ripened steadily. All the time Daisy and her friends worked and studied and moved, step by step, nearer to the great day when they would become accredited aircraft engineers.

Daisy was known to be one of the best mechanics and several of the pilots were very pleased when she was working on their planes. She went up with two of them but neither offered to let her handle the controls. Yet she felt that each time she went up in a plane, watching the manoeuvres of a competent pilot, was worthwhile.

Tomas flew in once or twice and was able to take her up once.

'My passenger will be here for two hours, Daisy, and I have permission to practise a manoeuvre – and to take a trainee mechanic up to listen to my engine.'

'And I'm the mechanic?' She could scarcely believe it.

'I can't hand over to you but if you listen well, you will be learning. Besides that, though, certain people of importance know about you, Daisy. You are being watched. Not all are convinced that a woman can make or even should make a good pilot. Walk very carefully. We are, what is the phrase, sticking the neck out?'

She certainly wanted no one, especially not Adair or Tomas, to be in any trouble over her ambition.

Daisy was so busy that she had no time to check Wednesday's post until she was on her way to bed. Her heart seemed to flip right over as she saw that there was a note from Adair. She knew his writing and even the type of envelopes he used and, although she longed to open it up and read, she held it to her heart for a long moment.

This is silly, Daisy Petrie. You're like one of them foolish girls in the films, always mooning around after some fella. Read the letter.

At first the letter disappointed her as there were only three lines.

Daisy
   Be at the call box at nine thirty on Thursday evening. Please.
   Adair

On Thursday she could scarcely keep her mind on her work. Adair was going to ring her. She would hear his voice. The thought filled her with delight. But then she wondered at the urgency of the note. Why was he calling and why had he not said why in the note? No time to add more? He was going away, that was it. He had been posted to . . . she had no idea where but somewhere far away, Scotland, perhaps. Would she miss him? Of course she would.

But, as it is, you don't see him very often, not once since he returned to active duty, she argued with herself. Why would you miss someone you never see anyway?

Because you . . . she stopped. What had she been about to say? But that too was silly, because you cannot love someone – there she had said the word – if you never see him.

'Petrie,' yelled a voice in her ear, startling her so that she almost fell off her perch on the Spitfire. 'The Spitfire engine is not a delicate, fragile machine and can, take my word for it, tolerate a great deal more elbow grease than you're giving it. Be good enough to start all over again.'

'Yes, Sergeant, sorry, Sergeant.'

It was not her finest hour.

She resolved to keep her mind engaged on the aircraft engine without bringing any more ire down on her head and so she ruthlessly banished any thoughts of Adair Maxwell until suppertime. With Joan and Maggie she walked up to the canteen.

'Nearly ran screaming out of the hangar today,' confessed Joan, and her friends looked at her in some surprise.

'Why?'

'The noise. I thought, if one more WAAF starts scraping away with a file, I'll run them through with the damned thing.'

'Joan Boyd!' The others pretended shock.

'How many damn planes with damn trainees filing away important bits can they get in a hangar? Scrape, scrape, scrape; every scrape rattled my teeth.'

By the time they had calmed Joan and eaten supper it was time for Daisy to walk up to the telephone booth. She managed to appear nonchalant as she tried not to run in her anxiety to reach it. And then she stopped in despair. Someone was already chatting happily and feeding pennies into the machine. She looked at her watch. No one could speak for seven minutes, could they?

Daisy stood and then, thinking that it might be taken as rude to stare at someone making a telephone call, she walked a little away, turned and came back. The booth was still occupied. She looked at her watch. One minute to . . .

The glass door opened just as the telephone rang. The WAAF turned back to answer it but Daisy called, 'It's for me.'

'Let's see, shall we?'

Daisy stood, her stomach in a knot, as the girl spoke into the receiver.

'Daisy?'

'Yes, thank you.' She took the rather warm receiver. 'Hello.'

'Daisy, my sweet little Daisy, how are you?'

'I'm fine, but how are you? Is your leg really well?'

'Fit as a fiddle. We have been . . . stretched, is perhaps the best word, but I'm coming down to Halton this weekend . . .' He stopped as he heard her gasp of joy. 'Work, I'm afraid, bringing down important cargo, but I will have a few hours on Sunday before I ship it to London. I'm going to try to wangle a lesson for you. Are you available?'

Whatever she had been doing she knew that she would have found some way out of it. Oh, wicked Daisy. 'I'm free.'

'Good, got to go, but I'll get a message to you somehow. We boys in blue look after one another.'

The telephone went dead. She replaced the receiver and waited for a few minutes in case he was able to reconnect but then she went out and the door swung closed behind her. Her ears stayed tuned but the telephone did not ring.

Friday was the longest day in her entire life so far and she filled it with endless study. She would not think that soon she would see him, but would focus on her dream. So Daisy worked. Although all the course leaders knew her as an exemplary student, some were surprised by how dissatisfied she was with her own work, checking and rechecking everything she did.

After each meal she hurried to the airfield to see what planes were in, looking for a visitor, but had no luck. She reneged on plans to see a film with Joan and Maggie, and instead read or wrote letters and in between took little walks in the summer evening air.

Several of the office blocks were occupied, but then they usually were and so that told her nothing. The curtains were drawn on the base commander's office windows and that unusual fact caused her heart to beat rapidly.

Enough, she told herself as she stood in the scalding shower on Saturday morning. You are cycling to Wendover today.

And she did. In spite of her mind and heart being elsewhere, she did enjoy herself, and Joan and Maggie were as patient as only good friends can be.

Sunday came and, to her surprise, the chaplain handed her a note as he shook hands as his 'parishioners' left the small building.

'No time for lunch. Airfield now.'

She laughed with joy. How cryptic. Surely he did not have to be so secretive. He reminded her of Sam. She gave Maggie her leather shoulder bag, said, 'Thanks,' and hurried off.

Adair, in a flying suit, was at the door of a hangar. He moved back inside, she followed him and to her great surprise, he pulled her into his arms and kissed her, an embrace full of pent-up emotion that took all strength from her legs.

He laughed when they came up for air. 'I should apologise, madam, and you in uniform, but I have wanted to do that for such a long time. I love you, Daisy Petrie.'

She looked up at him, her feelings for him evident to see in her eyes. He kissed her again and this time she responded.

'Daisy, do you . . .?'

'Yes.'

He pulled back first. 'I can think of nothing better than to stand here all afternoon kissing Daisy Petrie but . . . wouldn't you rather have a flying lesson?' He took her answer for granted and led her into the little office. 'Pull that on over your clothes,' he said, pointing to a flying suit that lay across a chair. 'I've been loaned a little bird and you have permission to take a flying lesson.'

Daisy had so many questions. Who owned the 'bird'? Who had given permission for her lesson? She was so excited that her fingers fumbled with cords and fasteners but at last she was ready.

'On with the helmet. Everyone should be at lunch, but just in case.'

A minute later two normal-looking flyers walked nonchalantly out of the hangar and across the field to where a twin-engined Oxford stood waiting. This was the RAF's favourite training plane and there were several on the base. Many times since her arrival Daisy had been filled with almost painful envy as she saw them flying against the blue sky above her.

Once they were both aboard, Adair became very serious. 'You can see that there is room for three, Daisy, pilot, trainer – I'll have to be both of them today – and pupil; that's you. We also use Oxfords for other training, and can find room for a navigator, a bomb-aimer, a camera operator and a radio operator. This little genius is used to train each member of a bomber crew but I'll tell you all that later. I'll take her up and then I'll hand her over to you. All right?'

She nodded, too happy and excited to find her tongue. First an Aeronca, then a Tiger Moth and now – an Oxford. Was this really happening? Could anything be more wonderful than being here, flying like a bird with Adair?

Beside her, Adair laughed. 'Open your eyes, little Daisy; you are supposed to be watching my every move.'

'I can't seem to take it in.'

'It's real, Daisy. You, me and a plane. How I'd love to fly you to Paris for your missed lunch. One day, my darling Daisy, when this war is over.'

What a perfect Sunday. She would, she knew, remember every moment, every word spoken, for the rest of her life. Too soon they were descending. Adair reminded Daisy of the propeller pitch lever, a slightly different adjustment to landing as she had known it. This lever had to be moved from 'course' to 'fine' for landing or otherwise the landing, even for an experienced pilot, could be tricky as the Oxford had a tendency to drift off the straight line.

'Gently, gently, pull back; that's it.'

The Oxford landed smoothly and ran along the airstrip until it came to a complete halt.

'Time to go, little aviator. I'll try to get back soon.' He looked at his watch. 'I've cut it rather fine. My cargo may already be in the hangar.'

'But you did have permission, Adair?'

'The Oxford belongs to the base commander, Daisy, darling. Does that answer your question?'

'He gave me permission?' She could scarcely believe the commander even knew her name.

'Yes. His daughter flies with the ATA. He's one of the new brilliant forward-looking minds. Just don't talk about it yet; there wasn't a base Oxford available.'

'How do I thank him?'

'You don't, not yet.'

It was rather frightening knowing that such a senior officer knew about the existence of Daisy Petrie. She was doubly determined to be the perfect aircraftswoman, and to make sure he did not regret his generosity. Dear heavens, what if she'd scratched it? Daisy jumped out and ran around to make sure the plane was as perfect as when they had taken her up and, relieved, hurried into the office to take off the flying suit.

A tall, thin man was sitting on the chair where the flying suit had been lying and he stood up as Daisy and Adair entered. 'Here I am, Squadron Leader; it is good of you to take me to London.'

Daisy gasped. She knew that voice. It was, no, it could not possibly be . . . She pulled off the helmet but he spoke first.

'I came early to see if your pupil was really my old friend from Dartford. So, Daisy, my dear, you did find something more exciting than lentils and tea leaves.'

'Mr Fischer. It is you. Oh, I'm so happy that you're safe.

We were all so worried and no one would tell us anything, and poor Mrs Porter was really upset. I tried to get her to take in Belgian refugees but actually I think she's keeping the house for you.' She stopped, cringing with embarrassment at having, as she thought, let her tongue run away with her.

'Say cheerio, Daisy, darling.' Adair kissed her forehead gently and turned to his passenger. 'Like you, sir, Daisy is a secret weapon.'

Daisy returned to her billet nursing three wonderful secrets. One, Mr Fischer – that is, Dr Fischer – was an eminent scientist, engaged in secret work for the Government; two, the base commander himself knew of her dreams of flying and was actively encouraging her; and three, Adair Maxwell loved her. Four. The number was four not three, for Daisy now knew that she loved Adair Maxwell as deeply as it was possible for a woman to love a man. The thought of one day being his wife almost took the breath from her body. She felt so light that she wondered why she did not float over the airbase.

The smell of roast chicken drifted to her from open doors and she remembered that she had had no lunch but she felt that she did not care if she ever ate again.

How long could one live on joy alone?

Next morning, as usual, she was ravenously hungry and laughed at her fancies as she ate an enormous breakfast. Her score in her last written test had been slightly lower than the ones that had preceded it and so she went to class with an even deeper ambition.

She wrote to Adair twice but had no reply. This lack of news did not worry her unduly as his days and nights were filled with dramas she could not begin to understand. No more little notes were handed to her by smiling clergymen. No need now for secrecy or fear. She had admitted her love for Adair and knew that he loved her. Life could never get better.

Daisy did, however, receive a letter from Flora.

You'll never believe, Daisy, but we've been bombed again. High-explosive bombs hit Kent Road the other night. Families wiped out, of course. The Scala was hit too but no one was there, thank the lord. All in all fifteen houses just wiped off the face of the earth. You wouldn't believe the noise. I'll hear it in my head till my dying day and the world looked like it was on fire. Flames shooting up ever so high and your dad out in it. Came home looking like one of them zombie things from the pictures.

Frank's popped in a few times. He's quite happy with a cuppa and a Spam fritter, likes family company, I think. Nice fella. Gets on well with the lads. Letter from Phil, he's OK, thank heaven, and we are glad you are so far away. Never thought I'd hear myself say that.

Love,
Mum

My mum and dad are fighting in a way too, decided Daisy. The unusually long letter had made her eyes sparkle with tears. Sometimes it felt as if they had to be living in a nightmare, the worst bad dream ever, but waking up each morning only showed, more cruelly than ever, that Britain, including dear old Dartford, was fighting a war.

She became aware of a plane flying overhead and looked up. She could hear the drone of large engines, a sound that could be either frightening or comforting, depending on the plane's nationality, but there was no sight of any aircraft. Already it was far away, although the rumble carried on. All that flew lazily around and around in the blue sky was a large gull.

Now did Adair say that was an effect of the speed of sound or the speed of flight? She made a note to ask him next time they met and went back to her study.

Every one of her classmates seemed, these days, to be fully focused on working hard and passing the examinations. The dancing class was cancelled because fewer and fewer devotees turned up. Only permanent staff filled the cinema.

'Wonder where we'll be posted?'

'If we pass,' mumbled Joan, who worked hard and worried even harder.

'We could be sent anywhere,' said Maggie. 'Northern Ireland or – horrible thought – Scotland.'

'What's so awful about Scotland?' Daisy thought she would actually like to go to another country.

'It's not Merrie England,' answered Maggie. 'We'd be stuck in the wilderness for ever. Too far for a forty-eight-hour pass and where could we go for a twenty-four-hour one? The cinema and fish and chips in the nearest town.'

'Sounds lovely, doesn't it, Joan? I can smell the chips already.' Daisy was determined to be cheery.

Soon, very soon, this long gruelling course would be over and she and her friends would be fully trained mechanics. 'Just think, girl, as mechanics we're set up for after the war. An airport, the nearest garage, won't matter, we're qualified,' said Joan.

'After the war, if there is an after the war, I intend to marry a man . . .' Maggie stopped and thought, '. . . a man who makes me laugh.'

'And who's rich and handsome and kind; he'd have to be kind, wouldn't he, Daisy?'

'He'd have to be kind, yes.'

'Like your pilot?' Both Joan and Maggie knew that she had had some lessons and, while happy for her, were quite content to watch from the ground.

'He's kind, or he wouldn't be teaching me to fly.'

Maggie asked a serious question. 'Could you go up alone with the training you've had, Daisy?'

Daisy found herself blushing. She had no desire to boast, but Joan and Maggie were her friends and deserved the truth. 'I have been up alone. Honestly, it's no harder than driving a van; just have to get it into the air and back down again.'

Joan shuddered. 'Couldn't do it, couldn't. I think pilots are absolutely amazing but these little feet will stay firmly on the ground.'

'Now, Joan, what if I were to say that I know a lovely, slightly older pilot, and if he were to offer to give you a flying lesson . . .'

Joan and Maggie looked at each other and then at Daisy. 'We are willing to be swept off our feet, physically as well as metaphorically speaking.' Maggie spoke for both.

'This is silly. Come on, time for bed. We'll be useless in the morning and there's a practical test; need to be alert.'

SIXTEEN

Daisy had slept badly – perhaps the hut was too warm – and she woke early. Her eyelids felt as if they had been glued together. Once she had managed to open them, she decided to shower, dress, and go for a brisk walk before breakfast.

No matter the hour, the camp was busy. Civilian and military personnel were walking around, some, like Daisy, barely awake, and others obviously coming off night duty and heading back to their billets.

'Daisy.'

The voice surprised her. She knew it – calm, gentle, authoritative – but what a surprise to hear it here at Halton. She smiled brightly while having a quick look around to see if anyone on her course was present to see her chatting amiably with a wing commander. And how incredibly strange that she had actually, just the evening before, been about to tell her two friends about him. What could he be doing here?

'Tomas, how lovely to see you. Did you fly down?'

'No, Daisy, I drove. I came especially to see you.' He held out his hand. 'Walk with me, please.'

From having been too hot and uncomfortable she was now ice cold. Something had happened, something so appalling that only Tomas could talk to her about it. 'Tomas, what is it? Is anything wrong?'

'Please, my dear friend, I meant to be here before you rose.'

He took her arm and she was forced almost to run as she hurried along beside him. It was Adair. It had to be. His leg had not set properly – had she not said that he had not given it enough time? Yes, that was it. His broken leg had not set and was causing problems. Goodness, every pilot and flight mechanic knew how difficult it was to climb into some of those bombers with two good legs. How much more difficult with only one.

She looked ahead. The Methodist chapel. What on earth was Tomas doing? She started to laugh, a laugh that he recognised as hysterical.

'Come, Daisy, we can talk here.'

She pulled away. 'No Tomas. I'm not Methodist. I'm C of E.' She had nothing against Methodists, and probably Tomas, being Czechoslovakian, did not quite understand, but he did have a firm grasp of her arm.

'We can talk in private here, Daisy. Come, my dear.'

She could fight no longer and collapsed against him, every atom of energy used.

They were inside the small building and he led her into a tiny office that contained little besides two chairs and a small table, obviously used as a desk. For a moment or two there was absolute silence. Neither seemed willing to break it, but Tomas was the bearer of the news and knew what he had to say. He knew too that there was no way to make it easier or kinder.

'Daisy, Adair was shot down over the Channel last night. There was no warning; the enemy appeared from out of a cloud. He was the leader, Daisy, in the front, and there was nothing anyone could do, no time for evasive action, although they say he stood his plane on its head. Who could stand a plane on its head, little Daisy, but our friend?'

'They'll pick him up.' She jumped up. 'Oh, Tomas, you mustn't let the Germans pick him up.'

'We picked him up.'

Hope surged and then sank without a trace as she saw the pain and sorrow on the Czech airman's face.

'No hope?'

He shook his head.

She stood up, holding herself together as best she could. 'Oh God, he gave me his lucky scarf. I had his scarf. Oh, Tomas . . .'

'Stop it, stop this nonsense. I thought better of you and so did Adair.'

She looked at him, tears trembling on the ends of her eyelashes. 'I'm sorry. What happens now?'

'The air force will contact his next of kin.'

'Alf?'

He swallowed a laugh with a tear. 'Wouldn't that be wonderful? No, he has a cousin whose lawyers will arrange an interment. I'm sorry, Daisy, but even this noble cousin is not within what they term degrees of kinship to be given leave. Besides, the War Office doesn't seem to be very sure where he is; somewhere in North Africa, I think. Adair will be buried in the crypt of the chapel in his cousin's home.'

'The Old Manor,' she said, and burst into tears.

Tomas held her and she lay against him and cried until she could cry no more. Then, slightly embarrassed, she straightened up. 'Oh, Tomas, what are we going to do?'

He stood up and pulled her up with him. Holding her by the arms he looked down into her eyes. 'You and I, dear Daisy, are going to be glad that he was in our lives, and we are going to work as hard as we can to win this war. Every time I fly, I say, "This is for Czechoslovakia," but now I will fly and fight for my country, and this lovely green place which has given me a life and a chance to fight back, and I will add: "This is for Adair, a very young Englishman, a *perfect gentle knight*." Is that not what your Chaucer says?'

Charlie would have known what he was talking about. 'I don't know, Tomas, but thank you for coming to tell me. Silly, but we hoped there would be ham for Christmas this year. I wanted to give Alf my share and he would share . . .' She could not continue.

'I must go back. You have a friend . . .?'

'Breakfast time, Wing Commander, and then I have a class.'

They walked quietly together towards the area where they had first met. A staff car with a uniformed driver was there.

Tomas stopped. He stood looking towards the car. 'We are friends, Daisy, yes?'

'We are friends, Tomas, yes.' She saluted and then watched him walk across to the car. She did not watch it drive away.

Her face in the mirror was not a pretty sight. Her eyes were so swollen she looked as if she could have been in a fight, and her skin was blotched. What could she do before she went to class? She groaned as she remembered that it was to be a practical class and her eyes certainly did not give the impression of being alert. Charlie would have known what to do. Her make-up bag had always seemed to contain whatever it was that anyone needed. Daisy heard a sob and realised that she had made the sound.

Don't think, Daisy. You've cried all you're going to, thanks to Tomas. But try as she would, she could not forget the beautiful picture of Adair, running towards her across the grass, waving his lucky yellow scarf.

She ran the cold tap until it was ice cold and then splashed water over her face. She took some toilet paper from a stall and soaked that and held it against her eyes until she heard someone enter the toilet.

'Hay fever? Poor thing. My gran swears by honey. Bit late for you this summer but next posting, make sure to use local honey and don't let them sell you anything but.'

The voice stopped and Daisy threw her sodden paper in the wastebasket and hurried out.

'Hay fever,' she muttered when anyone looked at her oddly. 'Thanks, it's nothing,' when they commiserated with her and by dinnertime she was almost ready to believe it herself.

She said nothing to Joan and Maggie. Words made the appalling nightmare real. If they thought she was not quite herself they said nothing. Everyone was allowed a few days a month to be difficult, and besides, they were all tense as the course drew to its end.

Daisy did not write home. She could not. Alf would tell them.

Adair's station commander was rather surprised to be told that Alf Humble, a farmer from Dartford, was listed as Adair's next of kin. The War Office had no record of Alf although one of the secretaries pointed out that the address of one next of kin and the address of the other were remarkably similar. The Old Manor for the first, and Old Manor Farm for the second.

'Some mistake. Obviously this Humble fellow tenants the farm and since the house has been requisitioned he's got the spare set of keys.'

Therefore it was only when a large car drove up to the farmhouse one sunny summer afternoon, and a uniformed officer asked that the crypt be opened that Alf and Nancy found out about Adair's tragic death.

'You can't bury the lad without 'is friends around him. There's Wing Commander Sapenak, and what about 'is lordship, he'll want to be here even if just for form's sake. They hardly ever saw each other but they was cousins, and there's Daisy. Daisy Petrie. You can find her. She's a WAAF. Lad was teaching her to fly.'

In the end, only Tomas and Alf attended the interment. Alf was angry but Tomas calmed him.

'I told Daisy, Alf, and it's impossible for her to come, or Adair's cousin – he's in North Africa. Had we buried him in a military cemetery he would have had a guard of honour, but it is right that he should lie here; his mother is here. The entire squadron mourns, old friend.'

'How was the lass?'

'She loved him very much, I think, but she is strong and will find a way to deal. You too.'

'He were like a son to us. I think my Nancy pretended he were hers when she was making him a pie. Don't really know how us'll cope.'

'I knew him for so little time, Alf. But he was a special person. And now I must return.' Tomas shook hands with Alf and turned to leave.

Alf watched him walk down the driveway to a waiting car. 'You know where we are, lad, when you need a cuppa or a bed for the night.'

Tomas did not look back but he lifted his hand in acknowledgement.

'You have done extremely well, Aircraftswoman Petrie.' The commander shook Daisy's hand. 'Any air base will be delighted to have you. Good luck.'

'Thank you, sir.' Daisy saluted Group Captain Lamb and stepped back smartly.

She was a fully trained aircraft mechanic and had papers that proved it. For the first time in weeks her spirits lifted as she thought how proud her parents would be. Her case was packed, her gifts from Charlie, which she would take with her to every posting, wrapped carefully in her pyjamas in case they were thrown around on the train. She waved to Joan and Maggie, who were waiting for her, and hurried to meet them. Both had passed well and had already been given their postings. Now, like Daisy, they were heading home for ten days' leave. By now they knew of Adair's death but, after the first shocked expressions of grief, they had agreed with Daisy that no one talk about it.

'Did his nibs say anything about your posting, Daisy?'

'No, just that any base would be happy to have me. Sounds like it, doesn't it?'

'They're fighting over you, that's what's happening.'

To Daisy's surprise, her friends suddenly pulled themselves up and saluted.

'At ease, ladies.'

'Tomas, what are you doing here? Sorry, sir, I mean Wing Commander Sapenak.'

'Just friends today, Daisy.' He shook hands with each of the girls, introducing himself as he did so. 'Daisy and I are old friends,' he explained, and then he turned back to Daisy. 'I tried to get here in time for the parade but last night was busy. Now, if you don't have plans with these other friends . . .'

'We're just off, sir, rushing for a train. 'Bye, Daisy, don't forget to write.'

There was a moment of silence once Joan and Maggie had hurried off.

'It is good to have friends, Daisy. I had hoped, as I said, to be here earlier, but I would like to take you to lunch, perhaps on the way to London.'

'London?'

'You go first to London, yes?'

She nodded.

'And I have business in London and hoped to drive you to the Dartford train on my way. Unfortunately I cannot take you home.'

Thank God for that, thought Daisy. She could not begin to think what the neighbours would say if they saw her arriving home with an officer in RAF uniform.

301

And as for her parents . . . 'You're very kind, Tomas, but I can easily catch a train.'

'I assure you I did not arrange the London meeting, Daisy. I am only a small cog in a very big wheel.'

She looked up into his face and saw new marks of sadness there. She knew nothing about this man, except that he had come to Britain from Czechoslovakia to fly fighter missions against their mutual enemy, that the governments of both countries had decorated him – and that Adair Maxwell had called him friend.

With eyes sparkling with tears, she smiled at him. 'Lunch and a lift to London would be lovely.'

They stopped at a country pub where the landlord apologised profusely for the poor selection he was able to offer them. 'In a month or two we'll have some game birds, sir, delicious.' He sighed. 'And later, venison, but today all I have is chicken, mutton or rabbit. Hoped I might have a nice trout but, afraid not.'

Tomas was tired of rabbit and so they ordered mutton stew, which was served with beautifully prepared vegetables. Tomas looked at them in some awe.

'No boiled cabbage, and in fact nothing is boiled to death. We must remember this Buckinghamshire pub, Daisy.'

They drank cider with the meal and laughed as Daisy told Tomas that the chicken would probably have been an old hen.

'They can say mutton without shame. What is wrong to say old hen?'

'In English, mutton sounds better than old hen.'

The chatter was light and the smell of freshly mown grass from an open window competed with the odours of beautifully cooked food. Daisy felt relaxed and, if not happy, at least she had found some sort of peace. The months ahead would not be easy but she knew that she was trained and capable. She would so much have liked to tell Adair how well she had done.

She had to stop thinking of Adair. Tonight she would be at home and soon the letter would come telling her where she was to be stationed.

Tomas dropped her off at her London station and she was delighted to find that a train that stopped at Dartford was leaving in a few minutes.

She had not told her parents the time of her arrival and so she knew there would be no one to meet her, but she was quite happy to walk from the station. Ten days at home, plenty of time to catch up with friends. The train was crowded but she was content to stand outside a carriage in the corridor, gazing out of the window. There was evidence of intense bombing everywhere, reinforcing her awareness of just how dangerous and difficult life had been in this pleasant corner of England.

I'm a mechanic now, she told the gaping holes and empty buildings. We'll help keep our pilots flying to protect us. Just you wait and see.

At Dartford she was passing the waiting room when a railway employee came out of it, glanced at her, walked a few steps and then stopped and came back. 'Sorry to startle you, miss, but is you the WAAF as was here in March when we 'ad the air raid?'

There must have been scores of girls in uniform passing through the station, Daisy thought, but she told him that yes, she had come home on leave in March.

'Just that there's a little suitcase in Lost and Found, miss, and the gentleman as 'anded it in said as how a pretty little WAAF with shiny brown hair had dropped it in the fuss but he couldn't see her anywhere to give it to her.'

Her suitcase. Miss Partridge's dress. Oh, surely not after all this time.

'I did lose a suitcase, has the most beautiful dress in it.'

'You won't want to lose a pretty frock, not with clothing coupons as scarce as they are.'

It was a very happy girl who walked home that evening, a suitcase in each hand.

Fred was in the act of cleaning the shop window when he looked up and saw his daughter coming slowly along the street. He dropped the duster and ran out, regardless of who saw him. 'Daisy, love, you should have told us and I'd have fetched you. Oh, your mum will be that glad to see you, and our Rose an' all.'

He took both suitcases and hurried her along, firing questions as they went. 'Two suitcases. Why didn't you take a taxi? Why didn't you tell me? I'd have been at the station.'

'I know, but I didn't have two suitcases when I got on the train; this one's been in Dartford Lost and Found all this time. And I wouldn't waste money on a taxi, if I could have found one, petrol being scarce as it is, because I've got lovely comfy leather shoes.' She laughed and tucked one hand into his arm. 'How's everything?'

Since they had already arrived at the shop Fred didn't answer. He closed the door behind them and locked it. Then he walked to the foot of the staircase and called up, 'I've somebody here wanting a cuppa, Flora, anything doing?'

A few minutes later a slightly flustered Flora was at the top of the stairs seeing one of her children walking upstairs.

'Hello, Mum, ten days' leave. Today was passing out parade.'

Naturally she had to explain what 'passing out' meant and then had to take off her handbag from where she'd strung it across her body, having no free hand because of finding the lost suitcase. In her handbag were her papers that showed that Aircraftswoman Petrie Daisy was now a mechanic, first class.

'Oh, we're that proud of you, and just wait till Rose hears, and our Phil.'

Fred explained that letters from Phil were few and far between. 'We hadn't heard a peep since he left after Christmas and then your mum gets four all at once just two weeks ago. Very confusing since we didn't know which one to open first. First letter says the new ship is the last word and the next one says he hoped they'd soon transfer to their new ship. He's been in Malta, would you believe, but they couldn't go ashore. They was just delivering supplies and I think something happened to the ship there and that's why they needed a new one. Malta's had a battering, and no supplies getting through. But you can read them later. Now have a nice cuppa while we wait for Rose. Tell us all about where you go next and then we'll let Rose tell her news.'

'She's not marrying Stan?' asked Daisy as she accepted a cup from her mother. To her horror, Flora burst into tears.

Fred and his daughter tried to soothe and comfort her but Flora was too upset. They held her and let her cry until she hiccuped to a halt.

'Drink your tea, Mum. You'll feel better.'

Flora found her handkerchief in her apron pocket, wiped her wet cheeks, and then blew her nose somewhat ferociously. 'Why would I be worried about Stan? It's you I'm worried about.'

Daisy had not the slightest idea what her mother meant. She could not know about Adair, could she?

'Great, here's Rose,' she said in excitement, and began to run downstairs.

'No, Daisy, don't hug me,' said Rose. I'm filthy. We had a bit of a fire; I'm covered in smoke and stink to high heaven. Mum, Dad, see you in a minute.' She disappeared into the bathroom and Daisy returned to the kitchen.

'A fire? In a munitions factory? Who'd credit it?'

'She's OK?' asked Flora, getting to her feet.

'Just needs a bath, Mum. Know what's the best thing about the WAAF? Showers. Next base might not even have hot water; some have—' She stopped as a look of distress had crossed Flora's face. 'What is it, Mum? Rose's fine.'

'Oh, Daisy, love, Alf told us. He said you was upset.'

So that was what had made her cry. Not Rose and whatever her news was, but Adair. She closed her eyes for a second. She should have known she would have to talk about . . . about Adair's death. But how could she without losing control herself?'

She took a deep breath. 'Right, let's talk about this once and then it's over, Mum, over.' Could she tell them the absolute truth, tell of the wonder of falling in love and the greater wonder of having that love returned? If they discovered the real tragedy, they would weep more. She tried to smile. 'Adair, my friend, a very special friend, was shot down and killed. He's buried in the crypt at The Old Manor because the house belongs to his family. But Alf hasn't seen me, I wasn't there, and so he shouldn't have said anything to you about me. I lost another friend. Now I'm going to change out of my uniform and we won't talk about it any more.'

She did not wait for an answer from either parent but as she walked away she heard Flora say, 'She's bottling it all up inside, Fred, and that's not good.'

In the small bedroom that she had shared with Rose for eighteen years, Daisy took off her blue uniform and hung it up in the wardrobe. Then she found her old dressing gown, put it on and lay down on her bed with her eyes closed. Sam missing, Ron dead, Charlie dead, Adair dead. What good would crying do? It could not bring the dead to life again.

'Daisy.' Rose had come back in. 'Super to see you. Heavens, it's months. Sorry about your friend.'

She could not talk, even to Rose, the sister who had shared every secret of her life, her other half. She had a feeling that once started, talking or weeping, she would never stop. She sat up and watched Rose brush her lovely hair and smiled as she remembered how she had envied her sister's golden curls. 'Mum says you have news. I thought she meant that you were getting married.'

'Married? What an awful thought. No, I've finally applied to the ATS. We're army really, and there's lots of jobs, everything from cooking and cleaning, which I will not do, all the way up to driving lorries and even staff cars, you know, for senior officers and the like. Just think, Daisy, what if I was to drive Mr Churchill? Would Dad ever come off the ceiling?'

'He'd be the proudest man in England, Rose. It does sound fantastic.' Daisy remembered the driver who had driven Tomas – a man, and in air force uniform, but she said nothing. After all, maybe each service had its own rules.

'I had to get permission, and Mum didn't want Dad to sign, but I said if he didn't I'd run off to London or somewhere and get a job in a garage till I was older.' She saw the expression on Daisy's face and laughed. 'I could get a job in a garage, Daisy, because I'm good and I'm not exactly what you'd call a delicate little flower, am I? And Daze, it's easier now. Two years ago, there was lots of men. There aren't so many available now, so . . .' She stopped as tears of unbearable grief began to run silently down Daisy's face. Rose got onto the bed beside her, held her sister in her arms and they stayed there until much later, when Flora tentatively called them for supper.

SEVENTEEN

A letter from Grace was sent on from Halton and Daisy answered it, explaining that she had no idea where she was to be posted now that she had finished her training. To Grace's request for news of Sam, she was able to say nothing but did pass on the Red Cross address in Geneva and, of course, told her friend that if any news was received, Grace would be informed. Apart from her concern over Sam's wellbeing, Grace had written of little except the pleasure she felt at being outdoors in lovely weather watching much-needed food grow.

It was quite a happy letter and Daisy was pleased.

Her father told her that he had met Alf Humble at the farmers' market.

'He hopes you'll cycle out to see them, pet. Nancy needs a bit of bolstering too. She loved that lad like he were her own.'

'I can't Dad, not yet.' She did not add that she felt that if she were to go out to Old Manor Farm a ghost would accompany her. It would walk with her up the driveway, sit with her under the shade of a great tree, laugh with her . . . No, she sent her love and added, 'Next time.' She knew the ghost would be there because he was with her now. Sitting wrapped in her sister's loving arms she had felt the most amazing peace, had looked up and there looking at her were Charlie and Adair, both smiling. That was when she learned that the people we love do not die. They stay alive in the heart for ever. There were no memories of Adair in the flat above the shop, but at the farm . . . she could not bear them, not yet.

Each day of her leave she helped her mother with housework or with cooking, and she waited until Bernie had brought the mail. But she could not speak even to Bernie, and waited, heart in mouth, at the top of the stair until he carried on with his round. She did force herself to go down to talk to Miss Partridge and to show her the beautiful recovered frock.

It was surprisingly easy to talk to Miss Partridge; Daisy had never appreciated her more.

'How lovely, Daisy, dear, and how wonderful that there is still honesty in this sad little world of ours. You shall wear it again, won't you, at some lovely occasion at your next base? How terribly exciting.' She sighed. 'I should so love to see you wear it, my dear.'

And so Daisy had hurried back to the flat with the dress and had made a splendid entrance wearing it and, oh, something she had quite forgotten, a pair of silver dancing shoes that Charlie had sworn hurt her feet.

That was when she had taken the silver-framed picture of Charlie out of the drawer and put it proudly on the little mantelpiece in her bedroom. She saw Charlie with her heart; let others see her with their eyes.

Each day life grew brighter. If only the letter about her posting would come.

Flora and Miss Partridge were in the shop a few mornings later when they were surprised to see a Roman Catholic priest walking down the street, obviously looking for a particular number.

'I've never seen this priest before, Flora,' said Miss Partridge. 'I thought I knew most of the clergymen in the area. Wonder who he's looking for. Let's hope George hasn't been up to something.'

George and Jake Preston, Daisy had been delighted to see, were doing extremely well at Petrie's Groceries and Fine Teas where, each day, Flora looked forward to cooking their next meal.

The priest saw them watching his progress and tipped his hat to them as he stopped outside on the pavement. To their surprise he then walked to the shop door and came in.

Flora had no idea how to address a priest and since, in her opinion, High Church Miss Partridge knew all there was to know about religious matters, she urged her forward.

'Good morning, Father, may we help you?'

'Good morning,' said the priest. 'I am looking for Mrs Petrie, Mrs Flora Petrie.'

'I'm Mrs Petrie,' said Flora, 'but what can I do for you?' She tried but found that she could not bring herself to address a man young enough to be her son as 'Father'. This one, too, had a foreign accent, a familiar one, but she could not place it.

The priest took a very creased and crushed envelope

out of his pocket and with a smile handed it to Flora. 'This has taken some time to reach you, Mrs Petrie, and for that I do apologise. Please do read it and then we can talk, yes?'

'Perhaps you could take Father . . .?' Miss Partridge looked questioningly at the priest.

'Petrungero. Alessandro Petrungero.'

'Flora, why don't you go upstairs where you can sit down? I'll take care of the shop, don't worry.'

'Would you like to come up to the flat . . .? I'll make tea.'

Flora led the way upstairs and into their rarely used front room.

'Don't concern yourself with me, Mrs Petrie. I will sit here and you can read your letter and then ask me whatever you want.'

Father Petrungero sat down in one of the two armchairs and Flora seated herself on the sofa. She looked at the envelope but it told her nothing and again she looked at the priest as if she could not bring herself to hope for happiness.

'Read your letter, Mrs Petrie. It reached me from a good friend in Switzerland.'

Flora opened the envelope, carefully so as not to damage either the envelope or the paper inside. Her heart leaped with joy as she recognised the handwriting.

Dear Mum, Dad and family,

It's me, Sam, and I'm safe. I can't tell you where I'm staying except that I'm in Italy. The people are very kind and took care of me when I got here and never asked for nothing. I will still be fighting and I

312

will work for my keep – this is a poor country and I can't just take. Trust who brings this to you. There are good people everywhere.

I love you all,
Sam

By the time she had finished reading, tears were streaming down her cheeks. She lifted the letter to her face to try to reread but the words swam before her eyes.

'Let me make a pot of tea, Mrs Petrie.'

Flora had recovered her composure by the time Father Petrungero had made tea. He found cups and milk, and brought the filled cups into the front room.

'Very pleasant room, Mrs Petrie. I imagine the family has had some lovely times in here.'

He chatted on about the flat, the street, Dartford and his own home, Rome, and by the time he had finished describing several of Rome's historic sites, Flora was prepared to ask questions.

'My Sam's well?'

'He says he is.'

'But you haven't heard or – ' she started up from her chair – 'you haven't seen him?'

'No. I am but one of many cogs in a wheel, Mrs Petrie, useful only because I speak English and Italian. The letter came, as I said, from a friend in Switzerland. He received it from his brother in Rome, who received it from someone in the place where your son is hiding.'

'And where's that? Oh, please tell me, and tell me how he got to where he is.'

He leaned forward and looked at Flora out of eyes that were too old for his face, eyes that had seen things no one should be made to see. 'Mrs Petrie, very brave people are caring for your son and for others like him. They have little, but what they have they share. One of them has risked a great deal by starting this letter on its journey across Europe. It is like a chain, one end is here in Dartford, and the other end is wherever Sam is.'

'It's dangerous, isn't it?'

'Yes,' he answered simply.

'Can you tell them we thank them more than we can say?'

He smiled and stood up. 'They know that. Goodbye for now, Mrs Petrie.'

'Will I . . . can he . . .?' She stopped, fearful of asking too much.

'God bless you, and if a letter comes, someone will get it to you.'

She walked with him to the top of the stairs. 'Don't come down,' he said, 'I know the way.'

'Thank you, Father.' She was surprised at how easily the word slipped out now.

Daisy and the priest passed each other in the doorway. He raised his hat to her and, at the same time, she stepped aside to let the clergyman go first. She was taken completely by surprise when she entered the family shop only to see her mother and the very proper Miss Partridge dancing around, narrowly avoiding the barrels of rice and lentils.

'Well, well,' laughed Daisy. 'Lovely footwork, Miss Partridge. Don't ask me to return your frocks.'

Two middle-aged ladies, feeling decidedly silly, stopped their mad waltz and Flora handed Daisy the letter. 'Look at that, Daisy Petrie, and tell me if it doesn't deserve a dance.'

Daisy, who had been walking in the lovely Central Park, took the thin scrap of paper and read it. 'Oh, Mum, oh, Mum . . .' She could say no more.

'I'm going off to the ARP depot to let your dad see this. Can't bear for him not to read it until tonight. Will you two look after the shop?'

She took their assent for granted and without even putting on a cardigan, hurried out of the shop. Daisy looked in dismay at Miss Partridge. She had not planned to help in the shop.

'George will be here soon, Daisy, dear, and, in the meantime, you must face old customers sometime; most of them will be quite in awe of you, you know. Everyone knows you're a WAAF and everyone knows that you have had flying lessons. You're quite the celebrity.'

'I don't want—' began Daisy.

'We very rarely do get what we want out of life, my dear. Now off you go upstairs and make us a nice cup of tea. Father Alessandro made it for Flora but she was too excited to remember me. I'll hold off the starving masses till you come back down.'

Daisy was laughing as she went upstairs. When had she last laughed? Miss Partridge was funny. How could she possibly have terrorised them, even Sam, as they were growing up? How had they not been able to see her, the real Miss Partridge? 'I see you now, dear Miss Partridge,' she whispered, as she put another half-spoon of tea leaves in the pot.

The hour she spent in the shop with Miss Partridge was not a busy one. The vicar came in for his allocation

315

of eggs and assured her that he was there if, at any time, she needed to talk or seek counsel. 'Did you really have flying lessons, Daisy?'

'Yes, Vicar, and we flew over the church and I waved to you but, of course, it was daylight and you weren't guarding the tower.'

'How exciting, Daisy, dear. I should like to see what this little world of ours looks like from the sky.'

'You will, Vicar,' said Miss Partridge, and Daisy held her breath until the vicar laughed and then she joined in.

'I do hope so, my dear Miss Partridge, I do hope so.'

'Such a holy man,' said Miss Partridge when the vicar had left with his two eggs. 'And surprisingly practical. My own dear father was functioning on a different level from the rest of the family. So impossible to communicate with and, of course, his church would have burned to the ground before he could work out how to use a stirrup pump. That word always makes me smell horses. Don't know why.'

Daisy, wisely, said nothing and turned round to serve Mrs Roberts, who had come in to see if Daisy was actually working in the shop.

'You're looking well, Daisy. And different somehow.'

'I'm older, Mrs Roberts.'

'Grown up too fast, lass, like all our young people. I hear you're in the WAAF and passed your examinations.'

'Yes, I did,' said Daisy as she weighed tea leaves on the beautiful brass scales.

'Never thought I'd say good can sometimes come out of bad, but it's true. The world will be a different place for women when this war is over. They told me you flew a plane, well, I know that's not true – men would never allow it – but life's opening up, isn't it, lass?'

'Yes, Mrs Roberts.'

'Hope you weighed this proper.' She held up her packet of tea leaves as if testing the weight.

'Yes, Mrs Roberts.' Through the wide shop window Daisy was delighted to see her parents walking home, arm in arm. Their son had contacted them. They were happy.

She took Mrs Roberts's money, gave her the correct change and was ready to whisk back upstairs unless her parents wanted her to stay.

'I think we'll take a break when George comes, Miss Partridge,' said Fred. 'Our Sam out of Germany, our Daisy home for a holiday. I think a small toast is required.'

Miss Partridge was pleased to help him put up the blackout curtains as young George was not tall enough to handle them.

The letter arrived in the next day's post.

Fred shouted from the foot of the stairs – it was a busy time and he could not leave the shop – and Daisy almost fell in her haste to get downstairs.

'Back in a minute, Dad.'

It was from the War Office, and Daisy found that she was almost afraid to open it. Why did it somehow loom larger than other letters she had received?

She sat cross-legged on her white cotton bedspread and opened the envelope. She read the letter and then reread it.

Why?

She read it again. But, no, there was no mistake. She had not been given a new posting. Instead she had been asked to attend an interview, the following week, in London.

Gazing at the neatly typed letter with the cramped, indecipherable handwritten signature told her nothing. Neither did the small, framed picture of Lake Windermere on the wall above her bed help. She looked across at the picture of amazing red autumn leaves on trees in a place called Vermont. She had cut both those pictures out of a *National Geographic Magazine* while she was at school, and usually gazing at their beauty soothed her. She planned to visit both to see for herself if such beauty really existed.

'Daisy?'

On hearing her father's voice, she jumped off the bed and hurried downstairs. If she was lucky her mother would be back from the market and she would not have to discuss the letter twice.

There was no sign of Flora.

'What do you think it means, Dad? Bit cryptic, I think the word is. I'm in the WAAF, I've passed all the courses and they're supposed to say something like Aircraftswoman Petrie is to report at dadada on dadada. A travel warrant is enclosed.'

Fred too examined the letter for hidden meanings. 'There's two Daisy Petries in England, common enough name. They've sent hers to you and yours to her.'

Daisy wanted to believe that. 'The letter's not quite the same as the other one; all that's the same is the bit about the travel warrant.'

'Don't fret, lass. Why don't you take advantage of your time off and this sunshine and go off on your bike?'

A cycle run would clear her head. She was being stupid. But what if the WAAF was angry with her, if somehow she'd got something wrong when she was at Halton, or, oh God, the top brass has heard about the flying and they're furious? Too much time this week to think, that was the problem.

'Good idea, Dad.'

A few minutes later she was cycling through Dartford with no particular destination in mind. Some flowers on the pavement, tall bronze irises, caught her eye as she passed a flower shop and then she knew where she was going.

Nancy Humble was surprised but delighted to see her. 'Daisy, love, I'm that pleased you've come by, and it's good timing – there's an apple pie in the oven. How are you, pet?'

'I can't stop for pie, Nancy, or I'll never do what I came for. She lifted the glorious flowers out of her basket. 'Alf around?'

'He's tidying up the path outside the chapel, Daisy. Two lads were here yesterday, Simon and Toby, saying as how others'll drop in as and when. We want it all nice for them, and for him.' She took out her handkerchief and blew her nose, but if that was supposed to halt the flow of tears, it did not, and once again Daisy found herself the comforter.

'Don't mind me, sorry, I'm like a watering can – can't seem to stop.' She sniffed loudly. 'Least his mother'll be glad to have him with her, never knew 'im at all, from what we hear. Off you go, pet, over to the big house and round the back. It's all there.'

Daisy walked sadly back towards The Old Manor, thinking of Simon and Toby. And others would come too. One day maybe I'll be happy just to remember that I knew you, Adair, she thought.

Alf saw her coming long before she saw him. He

straightened up from weeding between the paving stones and waited for her. 'Hello, lass.' He looked down at the irises. 'That were his mother's name, Iris. I only knew that because it's on her headstone. He'll like them.' He took the large ring of over-sized keys from his tool bag and took her through the lovely old chapel to the darker and sadder crypt. 'There you are, pet. Them irises'll brighten the place up. You take as long as you want. I've plenty of work needs doing.'

Daisy stood by the huge marble resting place of several members of Adair's family. How cold she was. Would she ever feel warm again? The reality, the finality of death hit her. The tears ran unchecked down her face and into the neck of her cotton blouse. *Adair is dead. Oh my God, it's true. I will never see him, hear his voice* . . .

Whispering promise . . . his beautiful voice had whispered promise, hope.

Some seed had been sown and had begun to grow. Such a tiny pearl, she thought now, a beautiful little pearl. Had it been given time, one day it would have grown into a pearl of such perfection that those who saw it would have wondered.

Daisy put her head down and wept till she could weep no more. The irises had dropped out of her nerveless hands and spilled their glorious bronze and purple spikes across the ground at her feet. She bent to pick them up and then arranged them on the monument. She closed her eyes. *Is he here? Will something tell me he is not gone for ever?* Nothing happened. Nothing. She was alone in the crypt . . . Daisy smiled. She was not alone. She would never be alone. Those we love stay alive in our hearts.

'Adair, I have to go up to London next week. It's a bit scary because they haven't sent me a notification of my next posting. But it's fine, I did well. I got top marks. You'd have been so proud. I have to go or my mum'll worry but I'll come back. Maybe Christmas.' She held back a sob. 'I miss you in the world. Be well, Adair Maxwell.'

She walked towards the open door and stopped to look back. No, she could not possibly have heard, 'Be well, Daisy Petrie.'

EIGHTEEN

Flora made a fish-paste sandwich for Daisy to eat on the train, together with a slice of her now perfected eggless cake and an apple. When had they last seen bananas or oranges? They had had cherries a few weeks ago, large and luscious, but there had been no way to keep them fresh for Daisy coming home. Maybe, she thought, the WAAF was able to get cherries and Daisy had had some. She certainly had eaten strawberries – possibly they grew in Buckinghamshire, well as Kent. She had been clever like Nancy this summer and put up some fruits. And, her big, special surprise. She had made some chutney, bottled it and had it hidden under their bed for a Christmas surprise. Wouldn't that be ever so special on Christmas Day with the share of ham they was to get? She'd ask the Humbles for Christmas dinner. Ever so kind and generous with the children, the Humbles had been over the years, and now Nancy was not coping well with that boy dead. Funny how worrying about a pal's misery helps you deal with your own. She'd make a point about telling the Humbles about George and Jake Preston helping out around the shop. 'You'll see George soon; Fred's going to take him on rounds,' she would say. But mainly she would let Nancy read the letter from Sam. That would cheer them up – all his life they'd known Sam.

Daisy interrupted her thoughts. 'Mum, I'll miss the train.'

Gawd, she'd be much too early if she left now. 'You've time, love. Here, I made you a nice picnic lunch and you can get a really good cuppa in the canteen at the station. Eat your sandwich with it; nobody'll mind.'

'I have to go, Mum. Thank you. Picnic looks super and I'll have a cup if I'm early. See you tonight.'

'You look so . . . so just right, Daisy, like that uniform was made special for you. Dad's on tonight but Rose and me'll meet every train from London. No, don't fuss, what else would we be doing with the evening?'

'Not every train; I've no idea how long this interview will take.' She smiled. Of course her mother would meet her train; nothing she could say would dissuade her. 'If I'm there before you I'll start to walk home.' Daisy picked up her packed lunch and put it in her bag, kissed her mother and left.

Her mind was still in turmoil and the idea of a picnic lunch was unappealing. All she wanted was for the day to be over.

Four hours later the meeting that she had feared so much was finished and she was walking out of the office, still reeling from the effect of everything she had heard.

She had arrived early; not a good idea as she had had more time to worry. But at last she was called in. Several men, most in uniform, a few in civilian clothes, were seated round a table. She was pleased to see that Tomas was there.

'Do sit down, Aircraftswoman Petrie.' A man in civilian clothes directed her to an empty seat between two other empty seats, so that she was, at the same time, part and not part of the group.

'Miss Petrie, would you mind telling the Board just why you joined the WAAF.'

She recognised Group Captain Lamb, the base commander at Halton. When she did not answer immediately he smiled at her. 'Several of us see a remarkable young woman, Miss Petrie. Is the answer a simple one?'

'I don't know, sir. I wanted to work with planes.'

'Why?' asked a vaguely aggressive voice. 'Why planes, not boats or lorries or, perhaps even better, ambulances.'

Daisy had never really asked herself the simple question but now the answer came. 'I had some experience of planes, sir.'

'Explain.'

'I helped . . .' She looked across and her gaze met Tomas's kind eyes and an almost imperceptible nod. 'I helped a pilot strip and repair the engine of his Aeronca.'

A different voice came from one of the blue uniforms. 'By Jove, an Aeronca, lovely little plane; haven't seen one in ten years.'

'And he took me up with him, sir, by way of saying thank you for my help.'

'And so you joined the WAAF and asked to train as a mechanic.'

'No, sir. I promised the little boy . . .' she blushed furiously. Silly, unsophisticated Daisy Petrie.

'The little boy?' Wing Commander Anstruther was beside Tomas. 'What little boy, Miss Petrie?'

'My sister and me, I mean my sister and I saw a

324

Messerschmitt deliberately strafe a little boy flying a kite on Dartford Heath.' She stopped for a second as the horror of that day enveloped her but she recovered and continued. 'I couldn't help him but I promised him I'd do something to stop them, the enemy. I'm good with engines, been driving them and working on them with my brothers since I was about eight.'

'Why not the ATS?' Another voice she did not recognise.

'A friend . . . was teaching me to fly.' She could not say another word. If she did, she would break down and cry.

'Our distinguished Czechoslovakian friend has also given Aircraftswoman Petrie a flying lesson, have you not, Wing Commander?'

Tomas looked at Daisy and she saw a question in his eyes that she did not understand. He smiled and said, 'Indeed, sir, a most capable pupil, and if I may add what Miss Petrie seems too modest to say, her original flying instructor was Squadron Leader Adair Maxwell.'

Looks were exchanged among the interviewing board and then Group Captain Lamb stood up. 'Miss Petrie, was there time for you to fly solo?'

For a moment she could not speak. She closed her eyes and said quietly, 'Yes, sir.'

The civilian stood up. 'Lieutenant Travers, would you take Miss Petrie to my office? There should be coffee for her there. See to it, if it isn't. The rest of us will have coffee here and talk. Thank you, Miss Petrie. You have been most helpful.'

She was dismissed. The young air force officer indicated that she should follow him and she saluted, hoping that she was facing the right person, and followed him.

'No one prepared you for all that brass, did they? Scary lot, one or two dinosaurs who think women should stay in the home cooking tasty treats, but some you'd follow anywhere, men like Anstruther and Lamb. I don't know the Czech officer.' He looked at her enquiringly.

'Wing Commander Sapenak? I've met him a few times; occasionally he flew in and out of Halton.'

He laughed. 'How much of that grilling did you take in, Miss Petrie? He told the Board, and I quote, "a most able pupil".'

He opened the door to a rather imposing office just as a WAAF came hurrying along the corridor from another direction. She was carrying a heavily laden tray.

Daisy may have been too nervous to fully assimilate what had happened in the interview but she did notice that Lieutenant Travers did not take the tray. Adair would have . . . any of the men she knew well would have taken it.

'I'll come back for you when they want to see you again, Miss Petrie.'

She thanked him. He left and Daisy sat down thankfully and looked round. Her attention was drawn to a large signed photograph of the Prime Minister and, awed, she got up to examine the signature. What would Dad say? There were other photographs she did not recognise, including one of the civilian who was part of the Board. One day, perhaps she might be brave enough to ask Tomas who the man was.

She poured coffee into a beautiful little cup that had the Royal Air Force insignia printed on it, sat down in a very comfortable armchair and sipped her coffee. She had no idea of the purpose of this meeting and was quite sure that whatever it was, she had failed but, oh, to be able to share this experience with someone. Two beloved faces appeared in her mind's eye and she struggled to hold back a tear.

She had begun to count the number of aircraft in the spectacular pictures spread across two walls and had reached twenty-nine when Lieutenant Travers returned.

'Enjoy your coffee?'

'Yes, thank you.'

'Good.'

He led Daisy back along the corridor to the boardroom, held open the door and Daisy entered. A picture from a book from her Sunday school days flashed before her – Daniel in the Lion's Den.

'Do sit down, Miss Petrie . . .' The voice was kind.

Two hours later she was on her way home, happy in the knowledge that her mother and her sister would be at Dartford Station. She saw them anxiously scanning the windows as the train pulled in.

Daisy opened her window and waved. 'Got a seat for once,' she called to them, and then she was out of the train and hugging her mother till poor Flora protested.

'Are you all right, Daisy? They haven't thrown you out? You're going to another base, right?'

'Yes, I'm all right. No, they haven't thrown me out. Yes, I'm going to another base, a place called White Waltham, which is a spit from here, near Maidenhead. I could have been posted to Northern Ireland or Scotland but there I'll be a train journey from home. Isn't that wonderful?'

Daisy enjoyed tantalising them as she deliberately held back the beautiful, beautiful words. And then she said, quite calmly, 'Guess what? I'm going to be a pilot.'

Flora immediately burst in to tears, but these tears were happy ones.

They walked home, all three talking at once, until Daisy said, 'Dad's going to want to hear the whole story. Let's go home, make some tea, Mum; lost my sandwich somewhere and all I've had is two cups of coffee.'

'Oh, you poor thing. Well, let's hope somebody as needed it found it. Didn't you get nothing at the office place, pet?'

'Coffee on a tray out of a china cup, Mum – couldn't touch the biscuits – and guess what, a signed picture of Mr Churchill watched me drink it.'

'Well, I never did,' said Flora in awe.

Daisy would have had time to tell most of her story long before Fred returned, for there was an air raid that sent them tumbling downstairs and into the refuge room.

'Try to sleep, Mum,' suggested Daisy at some point during the long night, but any attempt at anything other than sitting together in terror listening to the devastation going on all around them was futile.

'I wish I'd signed up for fire-watching,' said Rose. 'It's not being able to see as gets to me. There's people being killed and injured out there and we can't do nothing.'

'Our soldiers and airmen are doing it for us, Rose, love,' said Daisy, putting her arm around her twin sister. 'Listen, some of the guns are our guns, firing back at them.' She thought desperately. 'I had a walk round after the interview, walked up Oxford Street. I tell you, we have got to go up there just to look in the shops. There was a large picture, a bit difficult to see with the paper on the windows, but it was of an American actress, Lucille Ball. Ever heard of her?'

Her listeners shook their heads.

'She's ever so pretty, the reddest curly hair you ever saw, really short, not natural, though. She was wearing a dress that was lovely. A pale gold material, very simple, long-sleeved but the sleeves were really unusual. I don't know how they did it, but they were sort of loose to the elbow and then they got really tight to the wrist and there wasn't a join at the shoulders. It was all one-piece, lovely. And she had such elegant shoes with it, heels, of course, but they had a fairly wide strap around the ankles.'

'Fastenings,' said Flora suddenly, and her daughters looked at her.

'Fastenings?'

'The sleeves, o'course. Fastenings on the inside of the arm, all the way up to the elbow.'

'Clever you, Mum. I couldn't work it out, but the dress, or dresses copied from it, I suppose, are on sale. Latest look for autumn, it says.'

They went quiet as they all realised they had been so involved with the description of the dress that they had not noticed that the noise in the world outside had changed. They could hear the clanging of the volunteer fire brigade, but it grew fainter and fainter as the trucks moved away from the centre of the town.

No one spoke as they tidied up the refuge room, gathered up their things and walked wearily back upstairs. Only then did Flora speak. 'Don't turn on any lights, girls. I'm going to risk a peek.'

The peek revealed nothing. There was both moonlight and starlight, but without going outside, they could see nothing. 'Can't see if the sky's gone red. Can't see any flames.'

'I'm going down,' said Daisy suddenly. 'I'm a WAAF; surely I can do something.'

Before they could respond she had run back downstairs and soon they heard the back door being opened.

Daisy edged her way out and, keeping close to the untouched buildings of the street, walked further into town. Far, far beyond the centre, flames shot dramatically into the air and sparks rained down and were immediately extinguished. A haze of smoke and ash was moving slowly, shutting out the stars. Daisy stood quietly for a moment and then stepped out of the shadows.

'Dash it, woman, wear summat white when you're out during blackout. What if I'd been a car?' He stopped, stared, 'Daisy?' Fred grasped his daughter. 'What in the name of God are you doing? Have you been home?'

'Hours ago, Dad. We're all fine. I thought there might be something I could do.'

'Yes, there is. Stay safe and well during an air raid so you can go back and do your job in the morning.'

He kept a tight hold of her hand as they hurried back home. 'Does your mum know you're out?'

'Yes, but Rose's with her. She's fine. We were in the refuge room together. What's it been like, Dad?' Even in darkness she could see that he was amazingly dirty and he smelled of smoke.

'Not near as bad as we've had. Too confusing, Daisy; we'll find out in the morning. I'm that tired I can scarce put one foot afore the other.'

They had reached the back door to the flat and Fred took out his key to open it but as soon as he touched the door, it opened a crack and Rose's anxious face peered out.

'Thank heaven, Dad. Mum's upstairs boiling kettles for cocoa and washing; she knew you'd be black.'

'And too tired to do anything but wash my face and fall into bed.' He started upstairs and then remembered Daisy's interview and turned. 'Daisy, love—' he began.

'It's fine, Dad. I got a new job, tell you in the morning.'

'Later in the morning,' Rose pointed out. 'Now, sorry, Daisy, but since I'll be at the factory when you start talking tomorrow, you'll have to tell me now.'

Both girls were sound asleep before Daisy had got past the first part of her story.

They were all awake at breakfast time and ready to hear all about it. Flora decided to grill the week's ration of bacon and served it with old bread she had fried in the bacon fat and a little dripping.

'A substantial breakfast needed after you nearly being starved yesterday, Daisy,' said Flora happily as she put the plates on the table. 'Now better start, so our Rose can get off to work.'

Daisy went over the entire day from the minute she had stepped on the train at Dartford Station. She told them all about the important people and the senior officers who had asked her questions. 'And Group Captain Lamb, who's head of the base, actually said as how several senior officers were pleased with me, or words like that, Mum, but that was the gist. I thought I was hearing things and then they sent me away to this lovely office with paintings and nice furniture and the photograph of Mr Churchill, oh, and there was one of the King too, and I had coffee. And would you believe, when they sent for me to come back, they said that – ' and here she choked up with emotion – 'they said that

Wing Commander Anstruther told the base commander that Charlie's mother wanted the Board to know that her husband had intended to recommend me for pilot training. That nearly did for me. I never met her and I never wrote when . . . it happened.'

Everyone was quiet as they tried to take in all that they were hearing.

'But here's what's been arranged,' continued Daisy, who was determined to tell the exciting, almost unbelievable story once and for all, 'I'm in the WAAF, which is military, and the ATA is civilian and so I'm not eligible, but there is a "mitigating circumstance", they said. Some bigwigs are discussing using WAAFs to fly with the ATA or joining the two units, but right now they're separate. So, at a "higher level" I am being transferred from the WAAF to the ATA, and meantime I'm posted to White Waltham. I told you that already, Mum, but it's the main ATA base and I'm very lucky. At first I'll continue to work as a mechanic. But, listen to this, time and schedules permitting, I'll be given serious flying lessons.'

Flora, who had been holding on to the teapot as if her life depended on it, put it down on the floral tablecloth and looked at Fred and then at Daisy. 'Flying lessons. But you won't go in one of them planes by yourself?'

'No, Mum, not when I'm having lessons,' said Daisy, adding under her breath, 'not yet.'

At that moment there came thunderous knocking at the side door. The noise was somehow full of despair and Daisy flew downstairs, three at a time.

'Careful, Daisy, careful,' called Fred, hurrying along behind her, but Daisy threw open the door. George

Preston, as black as a chimney sweep, almost fell into her arms.

During the air raid, while his mother and younger brother crouched, in fear and trembling, in the tiny space under the scullery sink, George slipped out, hoping that he would find hot chips – a tasty treat for his mother. There was a café on the High Street where he could sometimes buy chips at the back door. In his pocket he had a whole shilling, not nicked but given to him by Mr Petrie for giving the van a good clean-out. His mum did her best, but she wasn't a great cook and never, never did chips, lovely hot slices of potato fried to a nice crisp in boiling hot, spluttery oil.

He hurried along, his hands over his ears to drown out that roar as the great death-dealing monsters flew overhead, freezing every now and again against a wall as he heard that most terrifying sound, the crump that told him a deadly bomb had fallen quite close to where he sheltered. Caught up in the raid, pushed into an air raid shelter, he spent several hours, protecting his chips from grasping hands, feeling them growing colder and less mouth-watering by the second. He would not eat them, no matter how hungry he became – they were for his mum. And no one else would take them from him.

Eventually George slept.

'They're dead, miss, dead, both of them. I only went to get Mum some chips.' He clutched Daisy and wept.

Rose, who had followed her father, picked up George and, helped by the shorter Fred, carried him sobbing and protesting up to the kitchen where Flora was waiting.

'There, there, Georgie, get your breath and drink some

tea. Then you can tell us everything. We've all the time in the world, lambie.' She took the cup that Daisy held out and lifted it to his lips.

'They're gone,' he said, horror in his eyes, 'Mam, wee Jake, the house, nothin's left, nothin'. There's a pile of bricks and smoke and a terrible smell, and bits keep falling, bits of glass and a pot came from nowhere – landed at my feet; it's hellish.'

The Petries looked at one another over his bowed head and Flora held him tighter as Fred reached for his coat, nodded to his wife and daughters, and left quietly. He would find out exactly what had happened.

'There's porridge on the cooker, George, and a lovely sausage. Daisy'll fetch you some and then you should have a rest.'

'The bed's gone,' he whispered.

'There's three beds in that room just waiting for boys,' said Flora, pointing to the door of her sons' room.

George was too traumatised to eat, but he followed Flora into the large bedroom and sat down on a bed while she looked for pyjamas that might do. When she returned the boy was sound asleep on the bed. Flora eased off his ill-fitting boots, covered him with a blanket and went back to the kitchen to wait for Fred.

Since Rose had to get to work, Daisy pulled an apron over her striped cotton shirt-waist dress and went down to open the shop while Rose tidied away the mainly uneaten breakfast. Then she returned to the bedroom where she sat waiting and remembering other boys who had slept in these beds.

It was not long before Fred returned with his horrifying story.

'Direct hit,' he told them. 'No chance for wee Jake or his mother. Had George been there . . .' He shook his head and said no more.

'He'll stay with us, Fred. He can stay off the school too; near time for him leaving and he's too upset now to do anything but try to recover.'

No one argued with Flora when her mind was made up, and besides, the twins agreed with her. George would be good for her and she would be good for George. Daisy was happy to leave home with the knowledge that young George, for whom she would always feel responsible, was being cared for properly.

She spent her first exhausting week at her new station working in an enormous hangar where the planes awaiting inspection were lined up. Planes came in on a fairly regular basis, depending on how many miles they had flown. The sergeant to whom she had been assigned set her to work on the engines of a Lancaster bomber. It was a challenge since she had never seen the type of plane, never mind its workings, before. At the end of her first nail-biting shift the sergeant seemed pleased.

'You seem to know one end of a spanner from the other, girl, which is quite an achievement, considering some of the trained – it's the adjective they gave me so it's the one I'll use – flight mechanics that have turned up here.' He shook his grizzled head. 'Why are you girls not content to be where you're supposed to be? Dunno what the world is coming to, I really don't. But it's in for a penny, in for a pound, girl. The workload is unbelievable and, in the end, you're responsible for your work, nobody else, so get used to it. Lads' lives depend on you.'

Daisy had no need of his lecture but wisely kept her opinions to herself.

Two weeks after she started she was transferred to official pilot training.

The sergeant tried hard to congratulate her. 'I hope you make as good a pilot as you are a mechanic, Petrie, but what a loss to the team. You don't like it up there, come back. We'll find a place for you.'

Daisy was touched by his brusque kindness but she could not hide the glow of happiness; she was officially a member of the Air Transport Auxiliary. The fulfilment of her dream was within her grasp.

The course would consist of hours of classroom training followed by equal or even more hours of practical training. She embraced this new regime wholeheartedly, working hard without complaint. Images of the child on the Heath, of Ron, Charlie and now Adair, seemed to smile encouragingly at her. 'It's also for the living,' she told them and herself, too. More and more planes were being rushed out of the aircraft factories, the trainees were told, and more and more pilots were needed to fly them.

The more she had to learn, the more aware she became of how much she had missed by leaving school so young. Beside some of the other girls and women who were coming into the ATA from professional lives, she felt inferior, but most of them were very friendly and welcoming.

'We're all in this together, Daisy,' one of the trainers assured her, 'and what is important in the ATA is not who you are but how well you fly.'

That was encouraging, and she remembered Adair and

Tomas. They had said she would make a good pilot and they were experienced professionals. For the first time she began to look forward, with more excitement than fear, to her first flight as a qualified ATA pilot. That, however, was still a long way off.

She had classes in meteorology, about which she knew nothing, map reading, which was easy as she had been reading road maps since she was eight or ten, 'technical data', which was a nightmare because there was just so much of it, and other subjects. Since she was a fully qualified flight mechanic she sailed through the course on engines.

'You will be flying below the clouds, and so we won't waste time we don't have on teaching you to navigate. Planes are equipped with a compass, possibly a gyro, and you will have a map.'

'Radios, surely?' asked a sophisticated older woman.

'Not in the new aircraft you'll be flying, madame.'

Tomas contacted her from time to time, and twice he was there to give her a few more flying hours. She asked him questions. 'How will I know where I'm going when I'm up there by myself?'

'If we had all the time in the world, Daisy, we would train you to use navigational instruments but there just is not time enough. You will have a compass. The inexperienced ferry pilots will have to rely on maps of the ground beneath them, and the ground itself. You plan a route on your map, you look for features such as rivers, lakes, railway lines, church towers, bridges, anything that will help you, and then you memorise it. You listen to the weather reports; bad weather is as much a danger to you as the might of the German air force. You must be aware of barrage balloons – fly near their huge cables and you are unlikely to survive – watch out for what we call friendly fire from anti-aircraft batteries, but you cannot mark anything on your map—'

'Why not?' she interrupted. 'I know there's a huge defence gun on Dartford Heath and so I don't need to put that on my map, but if someone else tells me to watch out for—'

He interrupted her in turn. 'You commit to memory, Daisy. There must be nothing on your map that would prove useful to the enemy.'

'But airfields are marked.'

'Of course, and the enemy has always known where each one is, as we know the location of theirs. An airfield isn't built overnight, Daisy; no point in trying to hide them. Easier to hide the planes.'

'How?'

'We do not put them in the hangars, one maybe, or two, especially if they need work. But you will see planes sitting on runways in full view.'

Daisy was incensed. 'That's crazy.'

'Not at all. If there are twenty planes, for example, in a hangar, a direct hit destroys probably all, but if there are twenty here and there all over a large area, the enemy bomber will be shot down before he can inflict too much damage.'

'A squadron?'

'Could wipe out an entire force but we have to rely on our fighter pilots keeping them away. You still want to fly?'

'You know I do.'

'That's my girl. Now let's go flying.'

338

She looked at him. He was still as tall and as slender as he had been when they first met, but his sad grey eyes showed evidence of even more pain. His dark hair, which had been speckled with grey almost as if the silver had been shaken onto the black, was now streaked with silver and the lines of sorrow were even more deeply etched. She wanted to cheer him. 'Where did you learn to fly, Tomas?'

'In the Czechoslovakian air force, Daisy, in the thirties; a good life before this insanity.'

She wanted to know more about him, about his family, if he had one, but there was something about him that said, 'Do not intrude.' But there was no barrier when she asked about flight.

Usually he took her up in an Oxford – she did not ask if it belonged to Group Captain Lamb. The heady day came when Tomas said that her official trainer would agree that she was more than ready for the arduous life of a ferry pilot. 'But we, you and me, will concentrate on confidence. I want you to plan a flight from here to Old Manor Farm, Daisy, and to memorise it.'

Her heart was pounding. Did he really mean to fly there some lovely afternoon, to put down, perhaps to visit Adair's grave? 'And when I have memorised it?'

'Then you will fly there; I will follow you, and we will see how you do.'

She consulted the maps, made her own and committed it to memory. But Tomas did not appear.

She was determined not to worry. Tomas was a pilot and as well as giving up his free time to teach her to fly, he flew operations. She would wait, and while she was waiting she would work, but she had to admit she was rather hurt that he had not found a way of letting her know. She found herself thinking of him often. She saw how he had set aside his grief for his first and closest British friend in his efforts to help her come to terms with Adair's death; she remembered his patience as he taught her not only to fly but to keep herself alive while she was doing so. Dear Tomas, so like Adair in many ways but so different in others. With increasing clarity she saw how much she needed him in her life.

She decided to find out the relevant take-off, landing, and cruising speeds of all the aircraft she might possibly fly and to learn them off by heart. Next she mastered the drill of vital actions for the same planes; H was hydraulics, T was trimmers, and so on. She flew several dual flights in the training Magister, a Class One aircraft and one of the many light aeroplanes that, as a ferry pilot, she would be expected to fly often. It would be so nice to share these experiences with Tomas – after all, Tomas would understand – but still he did not come.

Her first solo flight as an ATA trainee was both a terrifying and an exciting experience. After that, like the other trainees, she had to make several cross-country flights. These flights were particularly important as the pilots had to learn where there were dangers, such as barrage balloons with their frightening, often invisible, cables, and even defensive gun placements. Best to avoid those, if possible. They learned too, the positions of the stations to which they would deliver planes or pilots or supplies, even all three. Daisy loved every minute, but there was also a sadness that there was no one here with whom she could really share her joy.

She wrote to her parents, and to her friends. Her mother and Grace replied. Sally, according to Flora, was auditioning for a part in a propaganda film and everyone in the area was terribly excited. Flora received the news of Daisy's momentous solo flight with the rather dispiriting,

> Your dad and me are pleased for you and hope you are being very careful. There was a Spitfire came down in a back garden just a few streets away. We wouldn't like anything like that to happen to you. George was awful frightened and couldn't go outside all day but he says hello. He's always asking about you.

Grace, however, was suitably impressed.

> Absolutely fantastic news, Daisy. I shall look up in the sky over Bedfordshire and wave to all the light aircraft and I'll tell all the girls I work with – two Poles, a Scot and three English girls – that one of them is bound to be my friend Daisy. I don't suppose you can dip, if that's the word, yet!! If you can, then do. We shall all wave like mad.

Daisy was delighted with Grace's reaction and pleased that she had added details of what she had been doing. She thought she was to be transferred to a farm in Devon before Christmas and had already written to the Brewers about plans for any Christmas leave.

Christmas. How quickly the seasons were coming around. This would be the third Christmas of this war. It's supposed to have been over long before this, Daisy sighed. Would it ever be over? And where was Tomas? He had not been lost. She would certainly have been told if he had disappeared.

NINETEEN

October gave way to November. Daisy and her fellow trainees graduated and received their beautiful little golden wings with the letters 'ATA' inside a circle between them. They would wear this insignia proudly on their uniforms. Daisy Petrie was now officially an ATA ferry pilot.

Her first task was not an arduous one, merely to take an Oxford to a station near Carlisle.

She planned her route, which included a refuelling stop, and memorised it. The forecast was, unfortunately, for typical November weather, but Daisy was too stimulated by the realisation that this flight was what made the long arduous months of trial and tribulation worthwhile to worry about weather. She would manage. All she had to do was fly low enough to see the railway line she intended to follow and so, she crossed her fingers that flying through November weather would not be too much of an ordeal.

'Remember it's damned cold up there, Daisy,' said one of the very experienced pilots in her group, 'Wear your warmest undies and at least two pairs of socks, and good luck.'

And Adair's scarf, thought Daisy as she thanked her.

'See you back in the mess in a few days.'

That was when Daisy realised that she had no idea how she was supposed to get back. After all, she was leaving the Oxford in Carlisle. 'Excuse me, sorry, but one more question? How do I get back?'

The older woman laughed. 'Oh, poor darling; we're not looking after our chicks very well, are we? Before every trip, unless you know you're flying a crate back, pick up a rail warrant in the office. Trains are bloody in winter. Good idea always to ask around at the base – if a plane's coming this way, you might just hitch a lift. All right?'

'Thank you so much.' Daisy felt that she was being a nuisance and was sure the first officer was trying hard not to glance at her watch.

'Glad to help. Good luck,' and with a wave she was off down the corridor.

Later, complete with railway warrant, Third Officer Petrie was off on her first ferry flight. She wanted everything to go smoothly and instructed herself as she taxied along, now pull up and away we go.

She was airborne, a perfect take-off. *Oh, Adair, I'm beginning to do my bit, see my wings.*

That first flight, even with some fog, mist and unfriendly winds, was uneventful. She stopped, wishing that there had been some way of letting the station know that she was coming, and refuelled.

'Don't fret; you're our third today. You've time for a cuppa or, better still, hot soup.'

Daisy was delighted to have the bowl of thick, wonderful-smelling, tasty soup. She could not isolate the main flavour and asked one of the canteen staff.

'No idea. Cook throws in all the left-over bits of cheese from the officers' mess; sometimes it's great, sometimes it's . . .' He tried to think of an acceptable adjective, 'not' was the best he could do.

Flying Officer Petrie was delighted to have landed on a good day.

She took off again and found herself flying, for the first time, through sleet that landed on her windscreens, covering them up as quickly as she wiped it off. She was debating whether or not to descend to a lower altitude in an effort to get away from it when the Oxford pushed its lovely nose through a patch of sleet and rain and they were in the clear.

The further north one goes in a British winter, the earlier it begins to get dark. Daisy sang tunelessly to keep her spirits up, and looked down to see, if possible, where she was. Her heart lurched. The railway line had gone – it just was not there. For a moment she panicked and then, was she imagining things, but in her head she heard a voice. 'Listen to me, Daisy. I am here with you and you must listen and remember everything I say. Then, when I am not with you, concentrate and you will hear me.'

'Adair?'

How silly. For a moment . . . In her head she could hear his voice, and she listened. She reset her compass and slowly changed her course until there, below her, was the railway line.

Thirty-five minutes later she was approaching the runway and following the calm voice that told her, step by step, how to land, to taxi and to stop.

When she had completed the instructions for leaving a plane, she picked up her overnight bag and her maps, and climbed out. On legs that seemed somehow to have turned to unmanageable rubber she found her way to the office where she was to have her chit signed to prove that she had handed over one Oxford.

Later she was welcomed to dinner in the officers' mess, and wondered if she would ever be able to behave as if she felt she actually belonged to this group. It had never occurred to her that pilots were officers, even female pilots who had moved from the mechanics pool.

One of the men at the table told her that unfortunately no plane was going in her direction for a few days. 'But we're jolly glad to have the Oxford. Least we can do is take you to the station.'

They did and her home station ATA officer had been absolutely correct. Trains were bloody, if by that she meant they were absolutely freezing. Daisy had been cold while flying but her suit had kept her from freezing. As the train inched its way south, she felt that she would be better off if she were to pull her flying suit out of her suitcase and put it on over her uniform, greatcoat and all. Wind whistled through the train and her ankles and legs were so cold that she felt she might cry. The thought of her mother's face were she to see her 'delicate' daughter now made her smile and she forced herself to paint pretty pictures in her head until the nightmare journey finally rattled to a halt. But her one overwhelming thought as she – and six rather happy airmen – finally reached the base in a taxi with a broken window was: I'm an ATA pilot and have successfully ferried my first plane.

The airmen insisted that she not pay a part of the taxi fare. 'Honour and privilege to travel with you, ma'am.'

*   *   *

Daisy was given Christmas week off and she looked forward to going home, especially as she had not been at home the Christmas before. She had promised to attend the base New Year's Eve dance with several ATA pilots, both men and women, and for her first dance at the base she wanted her lovely dress, her Mrs Roban dress, which was, of course, now safely at home.

It would be lovely to have good news of Tomas's whereabouts before her leave started and so she took her courage in both hands and asked several of the working pilots if they knew him, or of him.

'Sapenak?' A pilot who had worked for a civil airline before joining the ATA thought hard. 'It'd be easier if he flew in and out of here, Miss Petrie, then we would certainly be up to date with news. But, one thing I can tell you, if Sapenak had bought it, we'd know.'

Daisy felt incredible relief. 'You're quite sure?'

'Very respected flyer, Sapenak. We would know.'

'Thank you.'

'Thank me by saving me a dance at the New Year's Eve shindig.'

She smiled at him. 'Delighted, sir. But may I ask you one more question.'

'Of course. If I know the answer I'll tell you, if I don't know, I'll tell you that too.'

Daisy blushed. Here she was asking questions about Tomas and all because he had not contacted her in several weeks. Why should he? He owed her nothing. It was the other way round . . . except that he had asked her to memorise a route and had promised to fly it with her. He had broken a promise and somehow Daisy knew that Tomas Sapenak was not the kind of person who broke promises.

'Wing Commander Sapenak is a fighter pilot and if he had been on a mission and been shot down, you would know but . . . could he have been doing something else?'

'Of course he could. It's war, Miss Petrie; there's a dozen things a multilingual experienced pilot like Sapenak could be doing. He could have flown into enemy territory to pick up something or someone. Even we humble ferry pilots do other things besides take plane X from A to B, you know.'

'I'm a bit silly to worry then.'

He shrugged. 'No idea, depends on how close you two are.'

Daisy blushed again. 'We had a mutual friend, that's all. I didn't know he was multilingual, if that means more than speaking English and whatever they speak in Czechoslovakia.'

'It does. I'll hold you to that dance . . . and I hope you've heard from him before Christmas.'

Daisy thanked him and went off to her billet where she made a pot of tea and sat down to drink it and to brood.

Tomas, Adair's friend, was, no, not that. Tomas had not kept a promise. Unusual. Neither had he been in touch to explain why. Therefore he was either in a place from where it was impossible to contact her or he was in trouble.

She almost spilled her tea as the hut seemed to shake from the force of a thunderous knocking at the door. Daisy replaced her cup and ran to the door.

A figure stood outside, fist raised to bang again. 'Petrie? Good. Phone for you, Ops office.' The messenger, whoever he was, turned and ran, and Daisy followed.

A telephone call? When had she last had a . . . oh, please don't let it be bad news.

She was breathless when she reached the office that was the heart of the station. Two uniformed airmen were busy at desks but the black telephone on the table in front of the window had its receiver firmly in place. Daisy's face must have expressed her feelings, for one of the airmen looked and smiled. 'He's ringing back, ma'am, about . . .' and at that moment the telephone rang.

The airmen gestured for Daisy to answer it.

She did. 'Hello,' she said tentatively.

'Hello, Daisy, how are you? Tomas here.'

Oh, such relief to hear her friend's voice. 'Tomas? Where are you?'

'Home,' he said, which told her exactly nothing. 'Daisy, I'm sorry I didn't keep my promise. I have been a little busy.'

What could she say? It was impossible to ask questions with two airmen hearing every word she said. 'It's all right.'

'Are you going home for Christmas?'

'Yes.'

'Then let me take you out to dinner on Christmas Eve.'

Christmas Eve. Family tradition meant that the Petries went to the Midnight Service on Christmas Eve. 'I go to church on Christmas Eve – in Dartford.'

'We could have dinner first, Daisy, and I will explain everything. Please say yes.'

'Yes.'

'I will be in touch. Good night, Daisy.'

'Good night.'

The sound of silence hummed along the wires and Daisy quietly replaced the receiver, thanked the room's occupants, and went back to her billet.

How she wished that there had been more time to talk. She realised that she had agreed to have dinner with Tomas on Christmas Eve. Would he want her to meet him somewhere in the centre of the town? What if he wanted to meet her at the flat? She was not ashamed of her home – her parents had furnished it very nicely and it was scrupulously clean – but she worried about her mother's reaction when she told her, as she would have to do, that she would not be at home for tea on Christmas Eve but would be dining out with a Czechoslovakian pilot. At least he was not an aristocrat; at least she thought he was not. Daisy, however, knew that a gentleman like Tomas would expect to meet a girl at her home, to introduce himself to her parents. Oh, please don't let this be a nightmare. Let Mum be so involved with George that she forgets to worry about Czechoslovaks. And why didn't Tomas come here to the station to have dinner with me? Where would he be staying on Christmas Eve? In Dartford? That was it. It was obvious, was it not, that Tomas was planning to spend Christmas with the Humbles?

During the next few weeks she flew several missions, twice ferrying planes and three times ferrying RAF pilots. Like every other ATA pilot she treasured her small ring-binder with its sheaf of notes on the idiosyncrasies of the different types of planes in the various classes. She wondered if she would ever get used to finding herself expected to safely fly a plane that she not only had never flown before but also had never actually seen before. In a perfect world there would have been hours of instruction in every type of aircraft but this was not a perfect world.

To her great surprise, for he was not the usual family writer, Fred wrote of how proud he was of his 'little girl'.

A girl, and one half the size of a pint at that, flying a blooming great plane. As your dad I would have wished for a easy life for you, pet, but, again as your dad, I have to say as how my heart beats loud with such pride in you, and Rose too, working hard as a man in that factory. We saw changes after the Great War, women doing work side by side with lads, but we never thought anything like this would come. If I was to see you flying a plane my heart would jump into my mouth with fear and it'd never get back in place but I am the proudest dad in Dartford and always will be. Young George is pulling more than his weight. He's good company for your mam and is begging me to teach him to drive. No word of his father – good riddance, I say – and George doesn't ask. I never thought my Flora could part with our Ron's things but she's making over everything that's suitable for young George, and his coupons have gone for new shoes and winter boots. He's drawing a picture of you in a plane. Don't know nothing about art but I can see it's a plane and you're in it so that's good, right?

She folded the letter carefully and put it away with her other treasures.

A few days later Tomas telephoned again. 'Daisy, do you know Hythe Street in Dartford?'

'Yes.'

'Good, there is a restaurant there, Frederick Comber's restaurant, number eighty-seven. You know this?'

'I have never eaten there, Tomas, but yes, I know where it is.'

'Good, but you have not eat the food.'

'No, but I'm sure it will be as good as any other restaurant – there are shortages everywhere.'

'I know, but I want something nice for you. There is also a hotel named The Bull Hotel, and this is on the High Street. You know this place?'

'Not really, although I must have passed it a thousand times.'

'In Prague or even London I would know, but Dartford I do not know.'

Daisy smiled. As if she cared about the restaurant, but it was rather nice that Tomas wanted it to be special. 'Tomas, it is going to be very nice sitting down and having a chat without hurrying or running out of pennies.'

'You arc kind, Daisy, and so we say then the first one. I will find it but the time is very scarce and so will you meet me there? This is rude, I know, but—'

She was relieved and interrupted him. 'That will be very nice, Tomas.'

'Nice? I can scarcely believe I ask such a thing and what my father would have said I shudder to think. But please believe it is not bad manners that make this necessary. Of course, I will deliver you home safely or to your church, whichever is more convenient.'

'It's quite all right, Tomas. It will be lovely to see you.

351

Comber's should be easy for you to find as the buildings opposite, really an engineering works, have been camouflaged to look like a row of terraced houses.' She thought for a moment, 'Well, from the air, that is.'

'But I do not fly, Daisy,' he said, and she liked the sound of his laughter. 'I will find.'

Daisy wondered whether or not she could ask her next question and then decided to go ahead; much depended on his answer. 'Tomas, will you be staying with Alf and Nancy?'

'Yes. That is a problem?'

'No. It's just that, this year, I think I told you, we're having real English ham for our Christmas dinner, and I thought, if you had air force business in Dartford, perhaps you would like to have a meal with my family.'

'Oh, dear Daisy, how you are thoughtful but no, I must refuse your very generous offer. Alf has asked me to stay for the few days of my leave. They are very kind; I think that maybe for them I am a connection with . . .'

'Adair.' Daisy was amazed by how calm she sounded. 'Alf told me Nancy thought of him as the son she never had.'

'Yes, it is so very sad. But I must not talk more and return to work. I look forward so much to Christmas Eve.'

Daisy hurried away from the call box through the sleet and the biting wind. Christmas Eve, almost a year since . . . She stopped and two other women ran past her, yelling out, 'Come on, Petrie, you'll catch your death out here.'

That brought her to her senses and she waved even though they could not see and hurried after them, desperately hoping that there was nothing on the pavement for her to fall over.

The billet was warm, the blindingly hot pipe that carried the smoke from the fire out through the roof sending comforting warmth into every corner of the rather basic room.

'Going home for Christmas, Daisy?' asked one of the girls, handing her a mug of hot cocoa. 'Lucky duck. I'm on this year but if I'm up on Christmas Eve, I fully expect to encounter jolly Old Saint Nick.'

The girls spent the next few hours talking nonsense but having relaxing fun, and Daisy, after a few minutes of worrying, joined in and found that her colleagues laughed with her just as they did with one another.

How wonderful it was to be a small part of this wonderful group.

A few weeks later, she walked home through the streets of Dartford, carrying her case and her carrier with its carefully chosen Christmas presents, which she had wrapped as artistically as she could in old newspapers. As she walked she looked out for a stand selling sprigs of holly. Holly, if she was lucky, complete with red berries, would make the parcels beautiful.

She had alerted no one to her arrival and so there was no one at the station to meet her. It was more difficult than ever to judge accurately when trains would be leaving or arriving these days, or even whether there would be a train at all. Daisy was determined not to think of events or realities that made her unhappy. Tomorrow, Wednesday, was Christmas Eve, and she was going out to dinner with someone she liked very much. She would think of that.

Everything was perfect. It was cold and bracing, but

not raining and there was no horrid fog. She was lucky enough to find a stall that sold not only holly with berries, but also some mistletoe, and Daisy bought a few bunches of each. She bumped into old school friends, and customers of her parents' shop but, seeing how burdened she was, everyone seemed content merely to exchange happy seasonal greetings.

Her parents, Miss Partridge and George were busy in the shop. She watched them for a few minutes, remembering, for the first time, Dr Fischer's comment about how one day she might be glad to have simple pleasures to enjoy.

How right you are, dear Dr Fischer. She wondered where the elderly man was and hoped his Christmas was happy.

And then her father looked up from his work and saw her. 'It's our Daisy,' he sang out as, George beside him, they ran to the door, 'home for Christmas.'

The evening was perfect. A letter, would Daisy believe, had been received from Phil. It had been written weeks, even months, before, but it was wonderful to be able to read it. He was, he said, as brown as a nut, and much discussion had obviously gone on already about where his ship might be or have been. And then, just after Rose had arrived home, tired, hungry and rather dirty, an envelope was almost reverently taken down from behind the clock. Inside was a Christmas card from Sam. The same Italian priest who had kindly translated the Italian greeting had delivered the card. Of course it said 'Happy Christmas', but written under it in Sam's handwriting was, 'See you soon.'

It was well into Christmas Eve before they went off to bed, still wondering about exactly what Sam had meant.

*   *   *

354

'Where's Daisy?' Fred looked at his wife's face and saw signs of recent tears. 'What is it, love? Where's our Daisy?'

'Don't you remember? She told us last night, but I were that thrilled with hearing from my lads, I didn't really take it in. She's gone out to dinner – dinner, mark you – with that Czechoslovakia pilot, Thomas something.'

'Well, well, well. Isn't that nice, love? Sounds posh, off to dinner.'

Flora got up out of her chair where she had been sewing pretty glass buttons on the cardigan she had knitted as Daisy's Christmas present. 'Sorry, Fred, your tea's keeping warm in the oven.'

'Nice buttons,' said Fred approvingly as he walked into the kitchen and took his usual seat.

Flora held up the cardigan. 'Come off a blouse I found in the sale at the church last month. Quite pleased with them, I am, and the wool's almost the same colour as that boy's scarf she wears with everything.'

Flora had folded the cardigan up neatly and moved it away from any danger from her shepherd's pie. She put a plate down, saying as always, 'Watch it, it's hot,' and sat down across the table from him. 'That's why I weren't happy this fellow turning up tonight, Fred. It were the holidays last year when she really got herself involved with the boy from the Old Manor family, and won't seeing this friend bring it all back?'

Fred sniffed his pie appreciatively, 'What you got in here today, love, fillet steak?'

As he had hoped, his wife laughed. 'O'course, but it came disguised in a Spam tin.' She waited while he finished one forkful and took another. 'Rose told me he were here looking for her last Christmas. The other lad were still alive then, the English lad . . .'

Fred was rapidly losing his appetite. 'Flora, there weren't nothing underhand in that; he were here on military business and thought he'd say hello to a friend. Maybe this year he come special, maybe he were at the crypt. Alf says lads come regular, those that Adair whatshisname taught or flew with, just paying their respects.' He returned his attention to his plate.

For a time the only sound was the occasional clink of Fred's fork or the soft ticking of the clock. Flora looked up at it. 'I were planning to go to the Midnight Service if there isn't an air raid. Miss Partridge took George shopping – he carries her errands – and she'll feed him and take him to church with her. Wouldn't it be lovely if our girls came too?'

'They will if they get home in time, always have, love. Why should this year be any different?'

'Because it is different, Fred, because of him, the pilot.'

Fred stood up abruptly. He took his plate to the sink and washed it hurriedly and certainly not as well as Flora would have done. 'Lordy, near half-nine already. I'll make a cuppa?'

When Flora said nothing he carried on with his self-appointed task, talking all the time. 'This is a good opportunity to wrap that cardy, love, afore she gets home and sees it. I saw you had that nice paper with the holly leaves. D'you know, I remember when we bought that? Red Cross Christmas sale, 1939. Paid two pence halfpenny for the two large sheets, quite a bargain.'

Flora had picked up the cardigan but whatever she intended to do was interrupted by the sound of the back

356

door opening, followed by the noise of several female voices.

'They've both come home, love, and brought their friends.'

In a moment the kitchen was full. Daisy and Rose, Sally and Grace. It was a picture from the past but it was very real. Everyone hugged and talked at the same time.

Fred looked to the top of the stairs in the expectation of seeing others. 'Stan's gone home to walk his mum and his gran to church but Tomas had other plans, that right, Daisy?'

'Yes. I asked him to come to Christmas dinner with us, Mum. I knew you wouldn't mind, seeing as how we've got all that lovely ham.' She did not see the look almost of horror on her mother's face as she spoke and added, 'But Nancy and Alf had asked him to spend his leave with them. Wasn't that nice of them?'

'Good,' said Flora. 'I mean it's nice foreigners have somewhere to go.'

'Look who we found at Sally's,' said Rose swiftly, pushing Grace forward.

The rest of the evening was spent drinking cocoa and catching up on one another's news, much of it already gone over at the Brewers'. Just before half-past eleven they put on outdoor clothes again and headed for the church for the Midnight Service.

'Seems like yesterday we were walking along here together,' said Sally, 'but it's years.'

They argued happily as, arm in arm, the four girls walked along with Flora and Fred walking along behind. It was not until late next morning when the available members of the Petrie family – and George – were together in the kitchen continuing the preparations for what was going to be an absolutely superb Christmas meal that Daisy decided to question her mother about her attitude to Tomas.

'Mum, you wouldn't have minded if my friend had been able to come for a meal today, would you?'

''Course she wouldn't, would you, love?' Fred answered for his wife.

'I'd give anybody as needs it a meal, Daisy, you know that. It's just I'm not good with foreigners.'

Rather more fiercely than necessary, Daisy chopped the ends of some Brussels sprouts that Flora had bought from the local greengrocer. Grace's little garden was no longer available to them. 'Dr Fischer was in the shop three times a week for years, Mum, and then Dad says you did really well with the Italian priest who brought the messages from Sam. Tomas is a foreigner, yes, but he's in our air force and risking his life every day for us.'

Fred had noted the promotion of their Mr Fischer to Dr Fischer and, afraid that tension might spoil Christmas Day, he was happy to change the subject by asking Daisy about Mr Fischer's sudden status.

Her father's question did not take her concern over her mother's attitude to Tomas out of her mind, but Daisy realised at once what her father was trying to do. 'I'll have to ask you all to keep this under your hats because it's very hush-hush, not even to tell Stan, Rose. Georgie,' and she looked at him almost fiercely, 'this really is where "talk costs lives".'

With all four nodding vigorously she told her family all about her meetings with their former customer.

'Well, I never,' said Fred. 'Always knew he were a very clever man. What do you think, love?'

'I always liked him; he sat in the refuge room with us once, didn't he, Daisy?'

Daisy carried on preparing her sprouts but she smiled at her mother. 'Yes, he did, Mum, and told us a really big word for creepy-crawlies.'

'And what's that?' asked Rose, but neither her mother nor her sister had the slightest idea.

The rest of the day went very well. The ham they had all saved up for each week was, they agreed, the most delicious ham ever tasted.

'And more on the cool shelf in the larder,' said Flora, adding, 'Christmas, never know when someone might drop in.'

'Don't tell anyone, pet. We'll be mobbed if word got round that Petries has got spare baked ham.'

All tension seemed to have drained away and the family were able to talk and laugh together. In the early evening they each wrote a long letter to Phil, wondering when they would reach him, wherever he was, and a short note, signed by all of them, to Sam. That note, Daisy thought, might well take longer to deliver across Europe than the letters to Phil who was 'somewhere at sea'.

'We've got our girls, Fred, and Sam's alive and, please God, our Phil.'

'Navy would get word to us, love, don't fret, and let's make sure the few days we have with our Daisy are . . .' He could not finish since he knew what he wanted to say would upset Flora.

Flora reached out and touched his hand. 'I know fine

well what you mean to say, Fred Petrie, and I been thinking. I don't want my Daisy marrying a foreign person; sorry, but that's me and I can't change. She's a lovely English girl and I don't want her away in some foreign place. I want her here with me. Why can't she find a nice local boy like Stan?'

'Because she hasn't, and since she don't live at home, she won't. This new ATA station is mixed. I thought as how all the pilots was women but happens there's more men than women in the ATA. Seems it's not long since they had only eight women, and all of them classy women who could fly planes anyway. The air force won't take a pilot as is over twenty-five, which is plain daft, if you ask me.' He looked sad for a moment and then laughed, 'But nobody ever does. The ATA pilots is well-qualified; some of them flew commercial flights, like for holidays or carrying cargo. Maybe, if we don't keep on at her, Daisy'll pal up with some of them.'

Daisy, however, was totally focused on fulfilling her promise to a little boy on Dartford Heath.

TWENTY

Christmas was over. Daisy travelled back to White Waltham in time to bring in the New Year, but, unfortunately, not in time for the dance. Not that anyone in her billet felt like dancing the old year away. Daisy had heard during her holiday that her friend who had laughed about encountering Father Christmas on Christmas Eve had, instead, met a swarm of enemy aircraft and had been shot down. It was not a happy start to this New Year.

Daisy found it difficult to believe that it was, in fact, 1942. So much had happened in a few years. She had enjoyed Christmas, being with her family, and seeing all her friends again. And, yes, it had been very . . . nice, she decided, having dinner with Tomas. No, it had been better than that. She had felt light and feathery, like the bubbles in champagne, especially when he had taken her hand. For a moment she had thought, hoped, which . . .? Now she looked out at bleak winter landscapes she realised that she had no memory at all of what they had eaten. Her memory was full of all they said. Soon he would write or telephone to tell her how his time had gone with the Humbles. He had not, he told her, looked forward to visiting Adair's grave with them, preferring always to grieve alone. 'But it will please Nancy, who was more mother to him than any of his family.'

Although he had spoken readily of his friendship with Adair and his feelings about the kind farmer and his wife, he had told her nothing at all about his disappearance. And he never will, she thought, until the war is over. That was when she knew that she hoped very much that they would still be friends when the war ended, no matter how many years that would be.

Her thoughts were interrupted by the train's arrival at the station and she was delighted to find that she was not the only ferry pilot arriving and so would not be alone on arrival at the base.

She had scarcely settled in when work started in earnest: flying lessons in Class One planes such as the Magister, in which she had trained already, and the Swordfish and the Gladiator, which were quite new. Ferry trips began too. She prayed that she was ready. In the early days of 1942 these flights could be miserable. Winter weather made flying difficult, and long, cold and complicated train journeys back were exhausting. Daisy tried hard to keep up her spirits; she wanted the early euphoria to stay with her.

Occasionally she was able to fly back as a passenger. In this way, she met many more RAF pilots. Some talked and she learned a great deal from them; others preferred to concentrate on the flight and she learned by observing them. Each and every one of these return journeys was so much better than a train in winter. The most exciting one, from a purely personal perspective, was when she discovered that the pilot in the cockpit was actually one of the eight original women ATA pilots, each already a legend. Daisy said nothing during that trip; in fact she hardly dared breathe until she heard the pilot laugh and say, 'There is enough oxygen for both of us, Daisy.'

She knows my name, she actually knows my name. Could life be any more exciting?

Letters from home reached her easily and those from friends followed her from her last station. As soon as she could she replied, giving the address of the new station. Twice she returned from a trip to find that Tomas had telephoned but he merely left a message that he would try again.

Why did he not leave a number where she could reach him?

Because he's never in the same place twice, she answered herself.

In March she was given a real task: to fly to an RAF station, pick up a Spitfire pilot and take him and the plane to a station near Dover. Daisy was excited by the challenge and wrote to tell her parents all about it.

At first it was a flight like any other flight. Flying Officer Dorward waited to be picked up at his station near Bath. After refuelling, if necessary, she was to deliver her passenger, 'preferably in one piece', to his destination and then carry on with the plane to Luton, an ATA station, where she was to leave it. She was then to find her way back to White Waltham as quickly as she could.

She studied her maps carefully, as always looking for significant pointers and hazards.

Early in the morning of the flight, the weather forecast was good. Daisy breathed a relieved sigh, as cloudy, misty weather was as much an enemy of pilots – especially female pilots who relied on visibility rather than instruments – as the human enemy.

She pulled on a flying suit, taking care to wrap Adair's cashmere scarf around her neck, folding the ends across her chest for extra warmth before doing up the fastening.

She looked at her maps – although she had spent the evening before studying them – and her little book of 'flying instructions', checked the plane thoroughly, and only when she was satisfied did she climb aboard. The voice in her head kept time with her own voice as she worked through take-off instructions and she smiled with satisfaction when she was airborne.

She sang to herself. 'Oh, Johnny, Oh, Johnny', followed by 'The Last Time I Saw Paris' and, because she was near the south coast, 'The White Cliffs of Dover'. She knew none of them well, but hummed along in the spaces. It was, she decided, a very pleasant way to spend a Sunday morning.

And then everything changed. A wind off the English Channel brought mist and rain with it. Soon it became more and more difficult to see ahead of her, or below, for that matter. She looked at her compass, prayed it was behaving itself and carried on. Singing did not help. She put up her left hand and touched the soft cashmere of Adair's scarf.

That was when she heard the roar of an approaching plane. Please let it be one of ours, she muttered as she peered through her windscreen. Coming straight for her was a German fighter plane; she was amazed to find herself trying to recognise it. A Heinkel, she thought, although she had only ever seen a line drawing of one.

What should she do? What would the Heinkel pilot

expect her to do? In that split second between hearing the plane approach and seeing it, Daisy was amazed to find that she was unbelievably calm.

'Adair, Charlie, be with me now,' she said – and put the Magister into a dive.

Why had she not tried to go up to hide in the clouds? She would never know, but some force, something other than her brain, had guided her. The enemy plane, guns firing, went right over her head as Daisy fought to control her dive. He had turned. He was behind her. Diving, diving.

With all her strength Daisy pulled up the light plane. The enemy plane, perhaps surprised by her instinctive tactic, went straight as an arrow, past her. She was both frightened and horrified to hear a loud roar as it crashed and burst into flames.

She was down out of the cloud and mist and filled with relief as she saw that the plane had narrowly avoided a centuries-old church and had carried on into the hillside. The flames, surely, would be visible for miles.

Now Daisy's brain was refusing to work. Was there something in their little rule book covering what to do in the event of causing an enemy plane to crash? She had no idea but her task was to pick up a pilot and get him to his Spitfire and she had lost time. She decided to carry on to the airfield.

She began to tremble and struggled to control herself. She was also beginning to feel decidedly sick. Thoughts of how humiliating it would be to be horribly sick in the cockpit of one of His Majesty's aircraft helped her gain some strength.

Instead of singing she kept saying, 'I will not be sick, I will not be sick,' until she saw the runway below her.

'Five minutes more, Daisy, that's all. Come on, let's have a perfect landing.'

It was not the best landing ever but the plane and its rather seedy pilot were unscathed. Religiously, Daisy went through all the instructions for taxiing and stopping.

An engineer ran along beside her as she taxied. 'Take her straight to the fuel pumps. You're late.'

Daisy did as she was told but the smell of fuel was just too much for her stomach and she jumped out of the cockpit and vomited all over the ground. She was ready to burst into tears of mingled fright and frustration when she heard an irate voice.

'Damn it all,' it yelled. 'Did I not say women were totally useless?' and there stood her passenger. He looked at her as she stood there shaking and controlling her tears. 'Go on woman, get yourself cleaned up and I'll fly the damned thing to base for you. Be quick.'

Daisy fled, first to clean up and throw ice-cold water, of which there was plenty, over her face, and then, reasonably clean but not at all sweet-smelling, she returned to her now refuelled plane.

'In you go, Flying Officer,' said the engineer who had met her on her arrival. 'He's not a bad bloke – we heard as how a plane had come down and he was sure it was 'is taxi. Glad it wasn't.'

'Me too,' said Daisy, managing a weak smile.

Twenty minutes later she was beginning to recover and was even well enough to appreciate how professionally Flying Officer Dorward handled her plane. He looked round quickly and saw her watching. 'Sorry you were sick. You look ghastly, by the way, but there's a Thermos flask

– of tea, unfortunately – rolling around there somewhere. Do help yourself.'

Hot sweet tea. Nectar from the gods.

No one seemed to mind that the passenger was piloting the plane while the pilot drank tea in the back. Thanks to the tea and the rest Daisy felt able to continue, but the station commander decided that it was now rather late and the weather had definitely taken a turn for the worse.

'I'll ring ahead and tell them you'll fly in tomorrow a.m. You're welcome to the mess for dinner and we'll find a bed for you somewhere.'

But now that she was safely on the ground, the realisation of what had actually happened during the first flight hit Daisy. *I'm responsible for the death of a man. He was the enemy and he wanted to kill me but he was a human being, a pilot like Tomas.* Even distressed as she was, Daisy knew that for the first time in a year, she had not thought of Adair first.

The commander must not see her trembling. She managed to convince him that she would be perfectly happy to be allowed to clean up her flying suit and to retire early.

She was shown to a billet where several bedsteads were obviously not in use and chose one near the door. Since the trip was an extended one, she had brought her little bag of overnight things and her wash bag. She wanted badly to clean her teeth. Life always seemed better when her teeth were clean. A nice hot bath would have been delightful too. She remembered the luxurious bathroom at Charlie's father's flat. Funny that she had not thought of it until this day. That bathroom, with its soft pink towels, its heated rails and its jars of lovely scented lotions was no more. But, much more importantly, Charlie was no more.

Daisy hurried to wash and to get in between the rather cold sheets, but the billet was warm and she was soon comfortable. Although she was exhausted, more from tension than from actual work, she took a long time to fall asleep. Thoughts chased one another round and round in her head. She had promised to avenge her loved ones, and the little boy whom she did not know, but actually to contemplate an act of revenge or to feel happy over the death of any human being was quite a different matter.

I didn't shoot down that plane but I feel responsible. He must have known he couldn't control his dive but he missed the ancient church. Chance? I think he swerved.

Oh, how she wished there was someone to talk to. Tomas? Surely Tomas, with his years of experience, could help her make sense of the day.

She fell asleep.

Next morning she was up early, ate a good breakfast in the mess, and let all the proper officials know that she was leaving.

'We'll let Luton know you're on your way. Should be there in time for morning coffee.'

Daisy laughed, agreed, and went to her plane.

On the pilot's seat was a small bouquet of exquisite hothouse flowers. Their glorious perfume filled the area. A small white card was attached to the flowers.

Please forgive my appalling crassness. The spotter who saw the Heinkel come down also observed your brilliant manoeuvre. Well done. I'm honoured to have been your ferry pilot.

Sebastian Dorward

Daisy was thrilled. They were the first flowers she had ever received.

They'll never keep till I'm back in Dartford, she told herself, but I'll keep a few petals to show Mum and Rose. Wonder where on earth he got flowers like that in the middle of the night.

The journey to Luton was uneventful although an area of sky was crisscrossed by the elaborate smoke trails caused by a dogfight. Once again Daisy was struck by the thin dividing lines between beauty and ugliness, life and death.

She set the plane down at the airfield and was glad to have the chit signed. She had delivered the plane and she supposed she had delivered the pilot, but perhaps he had delivered himself.

Had a plane been going to White Waltham she could have been a passenger but she was out of luck. A refuelling lorry was heading for London and the driver had no objection to taking a passenger along. Daisy picked up her bag and her flowers and climbed in. Compared to some of the journeys she had made recently, this was easy and pleasant. The lorry driver, who told her his name was Eddie, drove her right to the airfield.

'Thanks, Eddie, I shall look out for you. Definitely preferable to train travel.'

To Daisy's surprise, she was told to report to the base commander's office immediately. For a moment, she could not think why he might want to see her. On the way to his office, still carrying her little overnight bag and her bouquet, she realised that he must have been told of her narrow escape. She worried. Had she done the right thing? She was right to try to avoid being shot down; it did not take a genius to work that out, but had she forgotten some protocol? Surely she was correct to fly on rather than setting down as close to the accident as possible.

The office seemed to be full of people, among them some of the legends of the ATA. She had done something wrong and was to be ceremoniously drummed out.

Suddenly everyone was clapping, the noise echoing in every corner of the building. And then the singing started – 'For She's a Jolly Good Fellow' – and Daisy realised that they, the men and women whom she revered and hoped to emulate, were singing to her. The base photographer took several photographs: of Daisy alone, holding her flowers; of Daisy and the base commander; of Daisy and the ATA's most senior woman pilot; and of Daisy in front of the entire group.

'One day, Flying Officer, we will wine and dine you in style but in the meantime, we salute your courage, your quick thinking, and your professionalism. We are proud to have you with us.'

Daisy's muttered, 'Thank you,' was lost in the cheers.

Thirty minutes later she was checking out another plane.

Daisy was pleased to have so much work to do. She knew that she was not a heroine and felt rather silly at being fêted. After all, what had she done? Simply taken evasive action. The unfortunate German pilot had been unable to pull out of his dive and had crashed on a hill. She did not want to think about it, or about him. He had been a pilot, just as Adair had been. They had been on opposite sides but now they were both dead. She touched the scarf, Adair's scarf, which she wore constantly. He had given it, his lucky scarf, to her and she had survived. She would continue to wear it and she would work.

She wrote telling her parents that she was now studying the Class Two planes. She did not say that Class Two consisted of fighter planes, but she named two types, the Defiant and the Mustang, names she was positive would mean nothing to her parents. Very carefully she omitted two others, the Hurricane and the Spitfire. Was there anyone in Britain who did not know those planes? She knew her mother would lie awake at night worrying if her daughter were to say that she might soon be allowed to fly a Spitfire.

Neither did she tell her parents how close she had come to crashing. On the day that they received her letter, however, they were much too excited to actually concern themselves with something so mundane as the types of planes their daughter was flying.

Early one morning, Fred had been opening the blackout curtains when he glanced out into the street as he always did. As usual, even so early, the street was busy. At the far end of the street and moving briskly towards him was a figure that caught his eyes; there was something so very familiar about the tall thin form. It was the way the man walked, more than anything else, but Fred felt his heart begin to beat more quickly and the blood to run around his body as if it was suddenly so glad to be alive.

He wiped his eyes, which seemed to have misted over, looked again and then Fred Petrie, known throughout Dartford for imperturbability, threw down the duster he was holding and ran out of the shop and into the street.

Flora, who had just reached the foot of the stairs, saw her husband – in his slippers – race out of the shop and, terrified at what she might be about to see, raced after him.

She ran a few paces, stopped and burst into tears. 'Sam, my Sam,' she sobbed, and attempted again to catch up with her husband.

'There, there, Flora, it is your Sam.' Miss Partridge, coming in a little early, for today was fresh egg day, put her arms around her friend and employer. 'You're not seeing things, Flora dear. See, Sam is hugging his father, and he'll be here with you in no time at all.'

And so it was. Sam Petrie, thinner than when he had left England, but bronzed and weather-beaten, caught his mother in his arms and, as if roles had been reversed, became the consoling parent to the sobbing child. 'There, there, Mum, don't cry. It's me and I'm fine. I'm home again and all the way across Europe I were dreaming of your apple fritters.'

They reached the shop and there, at the door, stood a young lad whom Sam did not know. The boy looked at him, smiled shyly and made to slip past him but Sam reached out a very strong hand and held the boy. 'Who's this then, Mum? A new help?' He looked down at George. 'No need to leave, lad. By looks of that crowd gathering there, seems to me you'll be needed more than ever.'

Petrie's Groceries and Fine Teas had never been as patronised by non-customers as it was that day. Even the editor of the local newspaper sent a reporter and a photographer. At last a piece of local news that everyone could share. Sergeant Sam Petrie, injured at Dunkirk, captured by the Germans, from whom he eventually escaped, had returned safe and sound to the bosom of his family. In the few minutes before 'customers' started filling the shop, Fred had time to explain George's presence.

'He sleeps in your room, Sam, but we'll find somewhere else for him.'

'D'you snore, lad?' asked Sam, looking down at the boy.

George nodded. 'Somethin' terrible, sir.'

'Good,' said Sam, ruffling his hair. 'It'll be like old times, an' I'm Sam.'

Miss Partridge tentatively suggested that the shop close for the day but Fred said no, it was unfair to their customers.

'Customers looks forward to their fresh eggs of a Tuesday, Miss Partridge. We'll take it in turns to be behind the counter.'

Flora wanted nothing more than to take her son upstairs and to look at him. He had been gone for two years. She felt that she never wanted to let him out of her sight again.

After the initial rush of visitors, Sam asked to be left alone in the flat above the shop with his family – and he included George. In a day or two, he added, he would be happy to see old friends.

Rose, overwhelmed by the return of her brother, had refused to go into the munitions factory. 'They can sack me,' she said, 'but today I'm staying at home.'

The vicar, Mr Tiverton, went to make Rose's apologies to the management and returned with good wishes to the whole family.

Miss Partridge stayed in the shop for the whole day, and even though Fred and Rose and George took turns helping, she was exhausted when they closed the doors at five thirty.

'Come upstairs and eat a bite of supper with us,' Rose tried to persuade her, but she was adamant. The family needed to be alone with their son and brother.

'I'll take George, Rose.'

Rose smiled. She had seen Sam look at George the way he had once looked at Grace, and at any other child who needed help. 'Sam'll care for him, Miss Partridge, and just you wait, wee George will care for Sam.'

Miss Partridge agreed, but was surprised when Fred came down to walk with her to her home. 'I'm on duty tonight, Miss Partridge. Not much of an example to my son, as brave as he's been, if I use him as an excuse not to do my duty. I know he's home and will sleep sound in his own bed tonight. That thought will keep me company on my rounds. Now we'll need to get a letter off to our Daisy.'

But here Miss Partridge had a better idea.

A few days later, Daisy was thrilled to hear that she was to expect a telephone call at two o'clock in the afternoon.

'Just as well you got back last night, Daisy. He rang up but said he'd ring again today.'

He? Tomas. It had to be Tomas. How she longed to talk with him, to tell him of the frightening experience, to hear his measured view on how she had handled herself.

She lunched with other pilots, who found her distracted. It was, however, quite common for overworked pilots to be a little distracted and so no one made any remarks. Each pilot knew exactly what the others went through and accepted occasional lapses.

At five minutes before two, Daisy was walking up and

down outside the officers' mess waiting, waiting, and waiting. And then came that distinctive ring and she pulled open the door. 'Hello, Daisy Petrie speaking.'

'Hello, Daisy.'

It was not the voice she expected but, in some ways, it was even better. She was so stunned that she leaned back against the glass for support. 'Sam? No, it can't be. Sam, is that you, really you?'

'It's me, Daisy. Mr Tiverton let me use The Rectory telephone. He and Miss Partridge arranged it. How are you, Daisy? A flyer? I can't believe it. I'm that proud I could burst with it.'

They talked for a few minutes and Daisy discovered that, yes, he had heard of Ron's death and knew that Phil was somewhere on a ship. She asked about his escape.

'Too much to tell on the telephone, Daisy; it's the vicar's money. I got to the south of France and a British flyer picked us up, me and some others that I met along the way; scariest thing ever, getting in that crate. How can you do it? I'll tell you the whole story when you come home. Got to go.'

The line went dead and Daisy, trembling with emotion, replaced the receiver and walked out into a snowstorm. She had been so enthralled at hearing her brother's voice that she had not even been aware of the clouds that had come in.

No flying today, she thought as she ran for shelter.

For the next two weeks, Daisy and the other ATA pilots, weather permitting, were ferrying not once each day but two or three times. The aircraft factories were turning out new planes to reinforce the air force and, sadly, to replace those that had been shot down. The ATA pilots spent days picking up new planes as they came off the factory floor and delivering them to stations anywhere in Great Britain and Northern Ireland where they were needed. Daisy found that she preferred short flights, as she began to learn the shortest, safest ways to get from one station to another. Two nights out of three she was happy to sleep in what she now called 'my own bed'. For a girl who had lived in the same comfortable but rather crowded flat all her life, becoming used to living in different billets and feeling 'at home' was quite a surprise. She felt older, more mature, ready to go anywhere at any time.

Every pilot had looked forward to spring. It had been such a long cold and dark winter. Spring brought colour, and Daisy looked with delight on the early green shoots of daffodils and other spring flowers. She remembered the arduous work of digging in the hard soil of her friend Grace's little garden, scarcely more than a patch. It had been tough but they had enjoyed the challenge, and Daisy felt that she, like Grace, would never forget the joy of picking and eating the few vegetables that they had planted – and cared for – themselves.

Each station she visited had plantings of some kind and Daisy enjoyed them all.

One day, when this war was over, somehow she would find a way to have a garden, an English cottage garden like one she had seen in a magazine. In the meantime, life went on.

She had applied for a pass; even twelve hours would allow her to get home and hear her brother's truly amazing story. She'd learned only the bare bones: that he'd been shot and almost drowned at Dunkirk, rescued and taken to a hospital run by Roman Catholic sisters. Next, a prison camp and later an escape. Somehow he had escaped from his prison and made his way to Italy. Why? How? Who had helped, for he must have had help from somewhere? It was like a story in a book except that it was not a story. What had actually happened to her big brother? He had lived and worked in Italy, had left the wonderful people who had hidden him and had made his way to France and from there, home. Twelve hours was not long enough to do more than skim the surface of his story.

Two weeks after she had applied for leave, there was still no hint that she might be granted a few hours to go home. She had not heard from Tomas or Grace; in fact no one had been in touch with her for weeks. She blamed the war. Everyone blamed everything on the war.

And one evening when she returned, hungry and tired, from a flight to East Fortune Airport, a station in Scotland, there Tomas was, in uniform, beside the runway watching her fly in.

Her heart, which had been heavy, began to dance with joy.

'Almost perfect, Flying Officer,' he said with a smile as he helped her leave the little plane.

She held his arm as she took off her heavy flying boots and then released him to shrug herself out of the flying suit. They stood, for a moment, simply looking at each other. Slightly embarrassed, Daisy broke the silence. 'Tomas, it's lovely to see you. Are you well?'

She could hardly believe that she had actually asked such an inane question.

He took it seriously, and with her flying clothes over his arm said, 'I am very well, Daisy, and I am so happy to see that you are also.'

They walked together towards the officers' mess. 'I am told that you have now flown, can I say, internationally?'

Quickly she looked up to see if he was laughing but his face was quite serious. 'All the way to Scotland, over the Lake District, which I have always wanted to see. Have you been there?'

'I have flown in and out of Prestwick but that is not seeing a country. Some of it is very beautiful, from the air.'

He was ill at ease and knowing that made Daisy feel in control. She had not seen nor heard from him since Christmas Eve and now it seemed that he wanted to chatter about scenery.

She stopped walking. 'Tomas, why are you here? Are you here to see me or are you here because you are delivering one of your special cargos, your valuable parcels?'

'I have tried to see you several times. Today I, what is it they say, called in the favours. I was going to Belfast but asked a friend to go in my place. Then I borrowed a plane and came . . . to see you, Daisy Petrie.'

She smiled. 'Thank you. Are you staying with us?'

'I have been offered a bed for the night and I have accepted. So now we can join our colleagues for a meal. This is good with you?'

'I'm only third class.'

He laughed and moved towards her as if he might . . . no, she could not allow herself to think what he might have wanted to do.

'You have always been of the first class, Daisy Petrie. Come, you can freshen up in the mess and while you do I will see what they can find for us to eat.'

As always, the mess was busy. Tomas knew many of

the pilots and they chatted together over some very watered-down alcoholic drink that Daisy was quite sure she had never sampled before – and would be quite happy never to have again. At last, however, the group split up naturally and she found herself at a small table with Tomas. Plates of some wonderful-smelling stew were put down in front of them.

'Rabbit, or is it chicken, which is in fact an old hen, or lamb stew, which is really mutton?' Tomas was remembering their pub meal.

'I don't care. I'm so hungry and it smells wonderful.'

'It does, but let's not spoil it with the boiled cabbage.'

They laughed like old friends, ate the stew that they never did truly recognise, and talked and talked.

'My brother came home, my oldest brother, Sam. A priest, a Roman Catholic one, brought Mum a letter – from Italy. Sam said he had escaped from the prison camp. Somehow he made his way to Italy but I've no idea where the camp was. He was working in Italy.' She stopped. 'I thought I must have told you on Christmas Eve but I didn't.'

'We were talking of other things. Now tell me, how did he come home from Italy?'

'He got to France somehow and a British plane picked him up. That's the sort of work you do, Tomas, isn't it?'

'We all pick up and deliver many kinds of parcels, Daisy. I'm glad your brother is safe. Is he well?'

She explained that she had not yet been given a pass to go to Dartford to see him.

'It will come. He writes?'

'Out of the habit of writing. He never was good. But he's alive and he's safe. Rose thinks he plans to rejoin his regiment.'

'That will depend on his physical and mental state, my dear.'

'I know, and I know Sam; he'll want to be back doing his bit.'

It was time to go. They said good night to the others and Tomas, who was sleeping in the mess, said that he would walk back with Daisy to her billet.

'Bed for you any time you need one, Wing Commander,' called one of the senior officers, and some of the others laughed. Daisy did not see Tomas blush.

It was a beautiful evening, piercingly cold, but the sky was bright with twinkling stars and a bright moon showed its face. Daisy thought she would not be able to bear it if there were to be an alert or a raid. There had been two recently; jumping into trenches had become a regular part of daily life.

How odd to find that Tomas was thinking the same. 'The night sky is a thing of great beauty. Obscene to think that any minute death and destruction could come screaming towards us.'

'Don't say that, Tomas; don't even think it. It happens too often without our dwelling on it.'

He stopped, turned towards her as if there was something really important that he must say.

Daisy looked up at his finely drawn face and waited but he said nothing. 'What is it?'

'Daisy, I am wondering about how to say what I want to say. You may have noticed, I lose control of the English language when I am . . .'

He could not continue and Daisy hid a smile. He could not possibly have been about to say 'nervous'. No, not a much-decorated flying ace.

'With nerves,' he finished, and once more she had to hide her smile.

'It's only me – Daisy Petrie. You can say whatever you want.'

He grasped her by the arms and, aware of what he was doing, let her go again. 'But I cannot; it is not right.'

Suddenly it was as clear and shiny to Daisy as the magnificent sky above. Did she want him to say it? She looked down at the ground, aware that she knew more about the heart of a plane than the heart of a man.

'Tomas, why did an experienced pilot like you come down to an old stable to help me learn to fly?'

'But that is easy. The first time, the first time only, I came because it was something I could do to repay Adair for his infinite kindness. I came to help teach you because Adair was my first friend in this new country. But, believe me, after that I came because I wanted to see you. One day, the day you flew solo, Adair told me – in so many words – that he was falling in love. What could I do? He was my friend; he had little, but everything he had, he shared with me. I was pleased for him that he had found a nice girl and when I understood that, I liked Daisy Petrie too. I said, Good, because it is good that you like the woman your friend will marry. Besides, I am so much older than you.' He bowed his head and she wondered if it was so that she could see the silver streaks in the thick, once-black hair, but he straightened up and looked directly at her. 'I have thirty-four years.'

'Thirty-four? Oh, Tomas.' Daisy started to laugh. 'I'm sorry; I thought you were older. Perhaps it's your eyes; they are so sad.'

He looked at her with those sad eyes, eyes that had

witnessed so much pain, and she understood that he had decided to leave. He would not stay in the mess. He was going. But he must not leave, not like this, not with misunderstanding. 'Tomas, don't go. I didn't care. Do you understand? I thought you were older but I didn't care, I don't care.'

He removed his cap and held it in both hands in front of him. Now his eyes, which had been so dull a few seconds before, were shining – surely not with tears. 'You don't mind that I am old enough to be your father?'

Daisy did a quick piece of mental arithmetic. 'My, oh my, but you mature early in Czechoslovakia.'

She smiled as a light blush warmed his pale cheeks. 'You are barely fourteen years older than me, Tomas.' She looked down at his cap. 'Put it back on before you ruin it.'

'Believe me, Daisy, I want nothing more than to stay here with you for ever but . . .'

'I know, Wing Commander, there's a war on.'

He stood for a moment and Daisy stood looking back at him.

'Are we still friends, Tomas?'

He took a brisk step towards her and then stepped back. 'If that is what you want, Daisy, I will always be your friend.'

What should she say? Did she want friendship or, could it possibly be that she wanted more? 'Can you tell me where you're going?'

'Of course, tomorrow early, I return to my squadron and where I go from there depends very much on the enemy.'

'No more flying into occupied territory to pick up "special cargo"?'

'Daisy, you, better than anyone, know that I will do whatever I am asked to do.'

'I know, and, Tomas . . .' Should she say it? Was it too soon? '. . . I love you for it.'

He threw his cap in the air and hugged her tightly against his chest. The night air was freezing cold but Daisy felt that she would never, could never, be cold again.

They were at the door of her billet and again stood silently, looking into each other's eyes, asking and answering questions without a word being spoken.

He bent and kissed her very gently on the lips. 'Good night, my little love. I will see you as often as I can.'

'Be well, Tomas Sapenak.'

Daisy wrote letters when she returned from her delivery the next evening. The first one was to Tomas. It was very simple.

My darling Tomas,

Guess what. Tomorrow they're going to let me fly a Spitfire. I wish you were here to see it but, of course, I remember that you said that I was in your heart as you are in mine. *Ergo*, as our dear Adair would say, you will see me.

Love,
Your Daisy

Read on for an exclusive extract from Grace's story, *Wave Me Goodbye*. The next compelling book to feature *Churchill's Angels* . . .

Late February 1940

She had been right to do it, to pack up her few personal belongings and go without a word to anyone, even to those who had been so kind to her for many years. She regretted that. Not the kindness, of course, but the manner of her leaving. How could she explain to them that she could no longer bear her present existence; the hostility of her own sister, the uncomfortable, unwelcoming damp little house that she and, she supposed, Megan, called home? Even her job in the office of the Munitions' factory was unfulfilling. The only thing brightening her life had been the friendship of the Brewer and Petrie families, the small garden that she and her friends had created, and daydreams of Sam Petrie. Winter frosts had killed the garden that had given her such pleasure but Sam, like too many others, had gone bravely to battle and had not returned. As far as she knew Sam was a prisoner of war somewhere in Europe. She tried to picture Europe; surely in school she must have seen a map, but all she could visualise was a huge land mass somewhere across the English Channel. Useless to dream of him, not because he was missing – Sam would return, he had to return – but because he loved Sally Brewer.

It was easy to picture Sally, with her long black hair and her glorious blue eyes. Sally, an aspiring actress, was almost as tall as any one of the three Petrie sons, and a perfect foil for Sam's Nordic blondness. How could she, plain Grace Paterson who did not even know who her parents were, be attractive to a man like Sam? Oh, he had been kind to her when she was a child but Sam, oldest of a large family, had been kind to everyone. What would he think of her when he heard some day that she had disappeared without a word?

Grace sobbed, burying her face in her pillow in case any of the other girls were to come in and hear her. Her conscience, however, kept pricking her and eventually she found that intolerable. 'You have to write, Grace, you owe them that much.'

She got up, straightened the grey woollen blanket and thumped her fat pillow into shape. 'Right, I'm not going to lie here whimpering. I will write to everyone and then, when it's off my mind, I'm going to try to be the best Land Girl in the whole of the Land Army.'

She picked up the notebook she had bought in nearby Sevenoaks, and moved down the room between the long rows of iron bedsteads, each with its warm grey blankets, and here and there an old, much-loved toy brought from home for comfort. She reached the desk where, for once, no other girl was sitting and examined the lined jotter pages. Immediately Grace worried that she ought to have spent a little of her hard-earned money on buying proper writing paper. She shook her head and promised herself that she would do just that when her four weeks of training were completed and she had moved on to a working farm.

'Mrs Petrie and Mrs Brewer won't mind,' she told herself.

When had she first met them? More than half a lifetime ago but, since she was not yet twenty, half a lifetime wasn't long. Grace sighed. Ten, eleven Christmases spent at her friend, Sally Brewer's home, ten birthdays either with the Brewers or with the Petries. But when she thought of the Petrie family, it was not kind, comfortable Mrs Petrie or even her school friends, the twins, Rose and Daisy, who immediately came to vivid life in her mind but Sam, the eldest son who, for all she knew, might be dead.

No, he could not be dead. God would not be so cruel. She closed her eyes and immediately saw him, tall, blond, blue-eyed Sam, chasing the bullies who had pushed her down in the playground. He had picked her up, dusted her down and handed her over to the twins.

So many kindnesses and she had repaid them by slinking away, like a cat in the night, without a word of explanation or thanks. Again Grace turned her attention to the notebook and began to write.

Dear Mrs Petrie,

I've joined the Women's Land Army and I'm learning all about cows.

That unpromising beginning was torn up. She started again.

Dear Mrs Petrie,

I am very sorry for not telling you that I applied to join The Women's Land Army. It was working in the garden, growing the sprouts and things. It's hard to explain but, although it was really hard work, I enjoyed it. I felt . . .

She could not explain the pleasure or the satisfaction

that growing things had given her and so that effort, too, ended in the wastebasket. She tried to write to Mrs Brewer and four attempts ended beside the others. Grace stared in despair at the wall in front of her.

'Still awake? Want some cocoa? We're making it in the kitchen and they've left us some scones – with butter. Amazing how we're able to squeeze more food in at bedtime just a few hours after a three-course tea.'

One of Grace's roommates, Olive Turner, was standing in the doorway and the appetising smell of a freshly baked, and therefore hot scone wafted across the room.

Grace rose in some relief. 'It's hard work and fresh air does it,' she said. 'That smells heavenly.'

'And it's mine.' Olive laughed, and together the girls ran down the three flights of uncarpeted stairs to the kitchen where several of the other girls were crowded round the long wooden table. A plate, piled high with scones and several little pots, were clustered together in the centre of the table. Each pot was marked with a land girl's name and they were filled either with her own rationed pat of butter or raspberry jam.

'Home sweet home,' said Olive as she and Grace found empty chairs.

'My home was never like this,' said another girl, Betty Goode, as she bit into her scone.

The others laughed and Grace smiled but said nothing and the trainee land girls drank their hot cocoa and ate scones filled with farm butter and jam until their supervisor came in to remind them that cows would be waiting to be milked at five o'clock next morning. Groaning, the girls finished their supper, washed up, and made their way back upstairs to bed.

SHARE <u>YOUR</u> WARTIME STORIES

If reading *Churchill's Angels* has made you reflect
on your own wartime memories or those of others,
then we'd love to hear from you.

From rationing to evacuation, everyone has different
recollections of the war that deserve to be remembered.

To preserve your stories, we will feature them in a bespoke
ebook and will also publish one story in the back of
the third *Churchill's Angels* novel, *A Wing and a Prayer*,
publishing in 2014.

To submit your real-life wartime story, simply email
churchillsangels@harpercollins.co.uk

Entries should be between 1000 – 2000 words.

Turn over for full Terms & Conditions...

TERMS AND CONDITIONS APPLY:

1. This competition is promoted by HarperCollins Publishers ("HarperCollins"), 77-85 Fulham Palace Road, London, W6 8JB.

2. This promotion is open to all UK residents aged 18 and over except employees of HarperCollins and their immediate families, who are not allowed to enter the competition.

3. To submit your wartime short story, simply email churchillsangels@harpercollins.co.uk by 1 November 2013. Entries should be your own original work (between 1000 – 2000 words). No entries received after this date will be accepted. One entry allowed per person.

4. No cash or prize alternatives are available.

5. The winners of the story competition will be selected by HarperCollins in its sole judgment and notified by email no later than 17 January 2014.

6. HarperCollins' decision as to which stories will feature in the ebook and which story will feature in the back of the third book shall be final.

7. All entrants retain copyright in their entry, but by entering you agree to grant HarperCollins a non-exclusive, irrevocable worldwide royalty-free licence to publish your entry.

8. Any application containing incorrect, false or unreadable information will be rejected. Any applications made on behalf of or for another person or multiple entries will not be included in the competition.

9. The entry instructions are part of the Terms and Conditions for this competition.

10. By entering the competition you are agreeing to accept these Terms and Conditions. Any breach of these Terms and Conditions by you will mean that your entry will not be valid, and you will not be allowed to enter this competition.

11. By entering this competition, you are agreeing that if you win your name and image may be used for the purpose of announcing the winner in any related publicity with HarperCollins, without additional payment or permission.

12. Any personal information you give us will be used solely for this competition and will not be passed on to any other parties without your agreement. HarperCollins' privacy policy can be found at:

    http://www.harpercollins.co.uk/legal/Pages/privacy-policy.aspx

13. Under no circumstances will HarperCollins be responsible for any loss, damages, costs or expenses arising from or in any way connected with any errors, defects, interruptions, malfunctions or delays in the promotion of the competition or prize.

14. HarperCollins will not be responsible unless required by law, for any loss, changes, costs or expenses, which may arise in connection with this competition and HarperCollins can cancel or alter the competition at any stage.

15. Any dispute relating to the competition shall be governed by the laws of England and Wales and will be subject to the exclusive jurisdiction of the English courts.